PRAISE FOR THE MYTH

"This whimsical and enchanting tale, filled with poisonous injustice and seductively forbidden romance, will sink its claws into you and have you falling for the monsters."

— NICOLE FIORINA, AUTHOR, HOLLOW HEATHENS

". . . a fast-paced adventure story about prejudice and its consequences, the beauty of trust, and forbidden love."

— NATALIE MURRAY, AUTHOR, THE HEARTS & CROWNS TRILOGY

"A dash of darkness, a seductive romance, and a quest that promises death. A Cursed Kiss is a one-of-a-kind adventure in a mystical world you won't want to come back from.

— KRISTEN KRUSE, REVIEWER, LADY OF BOOKSHIRE

Prince of Seduction

A Myths of Airren Novel

Jenny Hickman

Copyright © 2022 by Jennifer Fyfe

All rights reserved.

No part of this book may be reproduced in any form or by any electronic or mechanical means, including information storage and retrieval systems, without written permission from the author, except for the use of brief quotations in a book review.

Publisher's Note: This is a work of fiction. Names, characters, places, and incidents are a product of the author's imagination. Locales and public names are sometimes used for atmospheric purposes. Any resemblances to actual people, living or dead, or to businesses, companies, events, institutions, or locales is completely coincidental.

Published by Midnight Tide Publishing.

www.midnighttidepublishing.com

Book Title / Jenny Hickman- 1st ed.

Paperback ISBN: 978-1-953238-88-7

Hardcover ISBN: 978-1-953238-87-0

Cover design by Cover Dungeon

Character art by Lauren Richelieu

AUTHOR'S NOTE

This book has scenes depicting grief and loss, violence, sexual assault, and contains sexual content. I have done my best to handle these elements sensitively, but if these issues could be considered triggering for you, please take note.

Pronunciation Guide

Gancanagh-(*gan•cawn•ah*)

Padraig- (*pa•drec*)

Tadhg- (*tie•g*)

Rían- (*ree•un*)

Fiadh- (*fee•ah*)

Ruairi- (*ror•ee*)

Áine- (*awn•ya*)

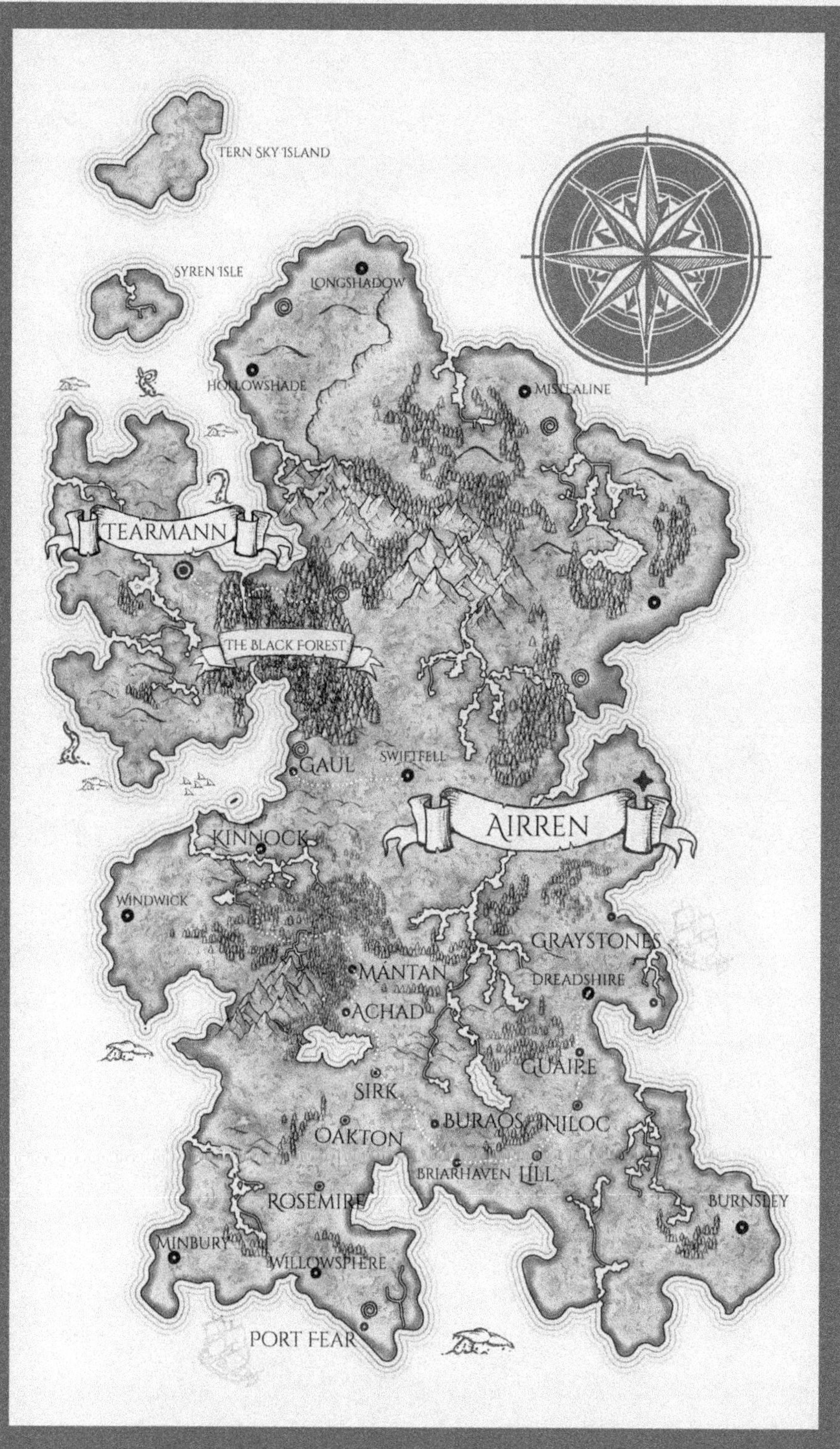

TERN SKY ISLAND
SYREN ISLE
LONGSHADOW
HOLLOWSHADE
MISTLALINE
TEARMANN
THE BLACK FOREST
GAUL
SWIFTFELL
AIRREN
KINNOCK
WINDWICK
GRAYSTONES
MANTAN
DREADSHIRE
ACHAD
GUAIRE
SIRK
BURAOS
NILOC
OAKTON
BRIARHAVEN
LILL
ROSEMIRE
BURNSLEY
MINBURY
WILLOWSPHERE
PORT FEAR

For everyone who fell
for a certain
fae prince

PROLOGUE

Women. I loved them.

Their softness, their curves, their sighs, and their scents.

I was young by immortal standards when my father, the last Danú ruler, was murdered and left everything to me. Not that "everything" consisted of much when he'd once ruled the entire island.

Still, the lure of power brought out the females in droves, all of them hoping to make a match with me or my brother. With nothing but eternity on the horizon, we did what any man in our position would do and made our way through them as quickly as possible.

To Rían, they were a distraction.

To me, they were an addiction.

Until Fiadh.

Never before had I seen such uncommon beauty. And the witch hadn't been affected by my false charm or flattery—at least, not at first. Making her an enticing conquest.

My father had warned me against consorting with witches. Like most of the shite he'd told me not to do, I'd done the exact opposite. After all, my mother had been a witch, and the hypocrite had married her. Then he'd gone off with her sister—who was also a witch—and countless others from covens across Airren.

One rule for Prince Midir and one rule for everyone else.

Now that Midir was dead, I made my own rules.

My bastard half-brother Rían had been so convinced I couldn't get Fiadh to sleep with me that he'd bet his favorite waistcoat. That waistcoat was currently balled up on the floor in Fiadh's bedroom, beneath the witch's red gown.

Adjusting the down pillow beneath my head, I smiled up at the thick red canopy above us. When he saw the stains and wrinkles, he would be furious. I couldn't wait.

"What are you thinking about, my love?" Fiadh asked, dragging a sharp nail down my chest, leaving a pink line. She enjoyed pain as much as she enjoyed pleasure—perhaps more. If it weren't for my immortal blood, I wouldn't have survived the first time we'd shared a bed. It had been six months and I still had the scars on my arms.

My mother's emerald ring glinted from my littlest finger as I reached for a strand of her raven hair. "Nothing of consequence." If she knew, she'd only get angry. And an angry Fiadh was a terrifying sight to behold.

Like most witches, Fiadh resided outside of Tearmann. They were solitary creatures, preferring to live by their own rules instead of following ours. Her house was located in the middle of a secluded forest, forty minutes' ride from the coast. Not that any of that mattered. I could evanesce and be there in a blink.

I hadn't been to the coast in ages. Perhaps I'd visit after I showed Rían his waistcoat.

She caught my hand, twisting the ring. My fingers closed reflexively until she peered at me from beneath the thick curtain of her lashes, her eyes the color of a honeydew melon. "Come now. You know I just want to try it on."

Why did she insist on doing this every time I came over? Still, I let her remove it, and she slipped the gold band onto her left ring finger. Had she always done that? She usually wore it on her right hand, I was almost sure of it. My heart began to race. She needed to take it off.

"What's wrong, my love?" The red silk sheet slipped down her slim waist to the swell of her hip, exposing a swath of soft, pale skin. "You look very serious. Is everything well at the castle?"

I'd come here to escape the problems at the castle, not deal with them.

For ages I'd been trying to meet with the Vellanian King in hopes of renegotiating the pittance my father had accepted from the humans before he'd been murdered. There was a rebellion brewing in the east and rumors of retaliation in Kinnock. The integrity of Gaul's portal had been compromised with the erection of a new cathedral on the city's edge. We needed to assign new gatekeepers to the portal on the other side of the Forest. Faerie trees were being burned to ash. An entire coven in Buraos had been executed as well.

Thinking of the mountain of work waiting back home gave me a pain in my feckin' head.

Before I could retrieve my ring, Fiadh's hand trailed down my stomach, slipping beneath the sheet. Cold fingers closed over me and . . . *Shit.* I'd get the ring back in a minute.

"You know the answer to that," I managed to say.

Fiadh clucked her tongue, stroking so slow it left my vision hazy. "*Humans.*" Her grip tightened to the point of pain. "They've forgotten we were here first."

It didn't matter who was here first, with treaties signed and new laws written—

Shit. Her hand was squeezing the life out of me.

A knowing smile lifted her red lips as she leaned forward to trace the column of my throat with her pointed tongue. Her grip loosened, and her hand started moving a little quicker. My magic writhed beneath my skin, begging to be unleashed.

I didn't have time for this. I was already late.

Feck it anyway. I'd make time.

I caught her by the hips, settling her on top of me. Losing

myself in a woman didn't fix anything but it did make the world fall away.

"If I were your queen," Fiadh said, her head falling back, thrusting her glorious chest forward. "I'd kill every last mortal on this island."

She looked like a queen, this beautiful, bloodthirsty woman. Black hair tumbling down alabaster skin like an onyx river, swaying in time with her breasts.

Even if we were to wed, she'd never be a queen.

There was only one queen on this island, and no one in their right mind would challenge the Phantom Queen for her title.

I'd never give Fiadh what she truly desired. To bind oneself to another for all of eternity was a particular sort of madness I wanted to part of. Marriage was for mortals with a life that spanned a few decades, not for those of us who lived forever.

The moment I finished, she rolled off me. This was the part I hated. The awkwardness of forced intimacy. Cuddling sounded about as appealing as marriage.

I pushed off the bed, crossing to the spelled bath steaming on the far side of the room, near a window overlooking the dark forest.

Golden mirrors tacked to the red walls reflected candles glowing on the armoire and Fiadh's overlarge dressing table, draped with the stay I'd removed hours earlier.

"Where are you going?" Fiadh whined from the mattress, legs still splayed and chest heaving.

"For a bath. I've important business to attend to when I get back." And the last thing I needed was to stroll into the great hall reeking of sex.

In my peripherals, I saw her stiffen. "Am I not important?"

I stepped into the hot water of the copper tub with a sigh, letting the warmth close over me and soothe my aching muscles. I'd overdone training with Ruairi earlier. Every time the big brute fought, he did so as if his life depended on it. Unlike me, he could actually die. So I supposed it did.

"You're the most important woman in my life," I told the scowling witch.

It wasn't a complete lie. I felt nothing for her beyond lust, but she was the most powerful witch currently sharing my bed, so she was important.

Just not in the sense she meant.

She swore as she got up, ripping her silk robe from the chaise and stuffing her arms into its long black sleeves. "You are the most selfish male I have ever met. You think just because you are a prince that you can take what you want."

"I only take what's freely given," I reminded her with a smirk.

Her face flushed from her chest all the way to her sharp cheekbones. "I'm leaving. Show yourself out." She didn't bother tying the robe before stalking into the hallway and slamming the door.

Her irritation would subside in a week or two. It always did. Who could I visit in the interim? Cloda was always a fun distraction. Or Maeve. No, Ailish. I hadn't been to visit the merrow in ages. And it would give me a chance to learn how many Vellanian ships they'd found lurking off Tearmann's coast. They never docked, just skulked off the cliffs like they were keeping an eye on my castle.

I took a deep breath and slipped beneath the surface. My plans drifted away in the blessed silence, leaving an emptiness in my chest that only subsided when I was buried deep inside a woman.

The situation in Airren was getting worse. The humans had executed Ruairi's cousin for threat of mischief. Threat of feckin' *mischief*.

Fiadh was right. We were here first, and yet we were the ones being persecuted.

The Danú had not lost the war because the human armies had been stronger. With one collective burst of power, every human on this island would've been decimated.

We'd lost the war because my father had shown mercy.

He'd said not all humans deserved to be exterminated,

believing that we would learn to live in peace. Now we were the ones being exterminated.

And it was my responsibility to fix it.

My lungs burned, starved of oxygen. When the emptiness in my chest began to ache, I broke through the water with a gasp. The fire in my lungs vanished. The pain in my chest remained.

Wiping the drops from my eyes, I found a woman with short blond hair curling around her cherub-like face smiling down at me.

"Hello," she giggled. Her skin had a faint luminescent glow, so I assumed she had faerie blood.

I'd seen this one flitting about the house, cooking and cleaning and stealing looks when she thought no one was watching. Had Fiadh called her Clare or Clara? It was something like that anyway.

I shoved my hair back from my forehead, returning her smile. "Hello."

She ran her fingers through the water, sending ripples toward my chest. "I was wonderin' if ye'd like some company?"

The ache in my chest began to loosen when her tongue darted from between full pink lips. Could I go for another round? My cock stirred. With a little help from my magic, I could probably find the energy. "It'd be a shame to waste this water on just me," I said with a playful splash.

Her giggle was like the chime of a bell. Definitely a faerie.

I lifted a dripping hand, touching the black satin laces across the bodice of her dress. "Shall I help you with these?"

She braced her hands on the side of the tub, allowing me to tug on the bow at the bottom. It would've been quicker to use magic, but this was the part I didn't want to speed up. The moment her glorious breasts fell free. The whisper of her sheer shift sliding down the ancient symbols covering her golden skin, landing in a pool of white at her toeless feet.

Damn, I loved women.

The water rose as she climbed in. When she sank on top of

me, her sea-blue eyes rolled back in her head. I caught her moan with my mouth.

The world and its troubles turned to shadows as her body slipped against mine over and over and over until—

"*How dare you*!"

Shit.

I shoved the faerie off of me. Fiadh stood at the foot of the bed, light green eyes wide and face contorted.

Shit.

Blackness leaked from beneath her skirt.

Her magic shouldn't be black. It should've been white.

"You come into my home," she seethed, her voice trembling, "tell me you love me, and then I catch you rutting with a feckin' *maid*?" The candle flames flared and shuddered.

My ring glowed from her left hand.

Shit.

She still had my feckin' ring. How had I been so careless? This was bad, but I could make it better. I always did. "Fiadh, please hear me out—"

"Enough! I won't hear any more of your lies." Her wrist twisted in a slow circle. She began murmuring in the ancient tongue.

My mouth clamped shut, and no matter how I tried, I couldn't open it. Evanescing was impossible. The wards around the house were too strong.

Shit.

The faerie sobbing at the other end of the tub clutched her arms around herself, trying unsuccessfully to conceal her nakedness. "P-please. D-don't hurt me."

"I don't blame you for being weak willed," Fiadh hissed, her eyes darkening to the same hellish hue as her magic. "But *you* . . ." She pointed a sharp black nail at me. "*You* know better. You *lied to me.*"

The invisible clamp over my mouth moved lower, to my

throat. She couldn't kill me—not unless she possessed an enchanted dagger. I'd only come back the way I always did.

"I gave you everything I had, everything I am, and you *used* me," she said slowly, as if the words were only beginning to sink in. "Just as you used *her*." She nodded toward the sobbing faerie.

My heart constricted in my chest when Fiadh's black eyes narrowed and she whispered, "*I'm going to make you pay*."

1

The last time I'd killed my brother, he'd reeked of burnt flesh for a week. But if Rían didn't stop smirking at me, I was going to throw him into the fire and hold him there until the flames robbed him of his last breath.

I laid across the settee, bored out of my feckin' mind, wishing there was something to do in this castle besides endure Rían's presence and Ruairi's relentless optimism.

I hated this room almost as much as I hated Rían. Thankfully, the darkness muted the lavish furnishings, gaudy floral curtains, rugs, and tapestries. It had been at least two hundred years since the parlor had been decorated. I couldn't remember who had been responsible for the travesty. Certainly not me. If it were up to me, I'd torch this room and everything in it. Including Rían.

"What's it going to be tonight, lads?" Ruairi asked from the drinks cart beneath the window. The bottles clinked together as he read the labels to find the ones he wanted. "Wine or puítin?"

I said "puítin" at the same time Rían said "wine."

I hadn't a head for either, so it didn't really matter. But puítin would make me pass out faster, and then I'd be back to daylight and another day of slogging through problems. Executions in Airren occurred every day now. No matter how many times we had advised our people to return to Tearmann, they always refused. With my jurisdiction ending at the Black Forest, there was nothing I could do to save them.

Ruairi returned with a tray of six glasses, two for each of us, half filled with clear puítin and half filled with green faerie wine.

My stomach roiled. Tonight wasn't going to end well, and tomorrow was Friday. The last thing I wanted was to sit and listen to my people squabble with a hangover.

He set the tray on the small table between my settee and their two chairs and took a seat. When I made no move to reach for either glass, Ruairi picked up the puítin and thrust it into my hand. "Stop moping about, Tadhg. Have a drink."

"I haven't had dinner yet." Which meant I'd be on my ass after a few sips.

Ruairi raised a black eyebrow. "Your point?"

Rían sniggered, swirling his crystal glass in his hand. "I have a brilliant idea."

"No." When Rían had an idea, it usually landed one of us—or someone else—in the underworld.

Ruairi kicked the settee's leg, spilling puítin down my shirt. "I want to hear what it is."

"I said, no." I didn't have the energy to die tonight. Plus, Eava, our kitchen witch, had made blackberry pie for dessert. Before Ruairi had shown up unannounced, my plan had been to eat enough of my dinner to appease Eava, then stuff my face with pie.

Rían sipped his wine slowly, as if savoring it. What was there to savor? It tasted like licking the bottom of a bowl of rotten fruit.

I gulped my puítin, loving the way it scorched my throat. The fire was better than feeling nothing at all.

"Ah, go on, Tadhg. It's a good one this time." Rían took another sip. Firelight played on the red tones in his short mahogany hair. He looked so much like our father in this light.

Which made me despise him all the more.

"Go on, then." It would take less time to hear him out than to argue.

From his waistcoat pocket, Rían withdrew three scraps of paper.

The Golden Falcon
The White Stag
The Green Serpent

"Each of us selects a pub and we see who lasts the longest inside. No glamours and no wards. Ruairi, you can stay shifted as a human to make it fair. Tadhg, you can shift into—oh, wait. Never mind."

The crystal glass shook in my hand. *Dammit,* I wanted to kill him.

"Winner takes all," Rían finished.

Rían's gambling had gotten worse since I'd killed Aveen. Idle hands and all that nonsense. He needed to find an occupation beyond irritating me since bedding his way across the island was off the table.

I took another drink of puítin.

Those three pubs were the most infamous in all of Airren, infested with mercenaries who murdered Danú for coin. And my younger brother wanted us to spend the night in them? Not a feckin' hope.

"I'm in." Ruairi withdrew a black medallion from his waistcoat pocket, threw it atop the scraps, and took a sip of faerie wine. How did he drink that shite without gagging?

I shot my best mate an incredulous glare. He was always the first to add to the pot even though he never had a hope of winning. The problem was that he had more money than sense and eternity on his hands.

"I'll pass." The blackberry pie called my name.

"Well, I'm in." There was a flash of gold as Rían withdrew something from his pocket and dropped it onto the pile.

The pair of gold triskelion cufflinks, gifted to Rían by our father, were his most prized possession. I had tried for a century to get him to bet them, and he'd always refused. His dark eyebrows lifted in silent challenge. The bastard *knew* I had no choice but to accept. It wasn't about the money. It was about beating Rían out of something he loved.

Ripping the button off of my own black waistcoat, I added it to the pot, knowing it'd give my brother a twitch. I'd sit in whatever pub I chose until morning if it meant winning his cufflinks.

Rían grinned as he folded the scraps. He shifted a bowl from the kitchen, dropped them in, and held it toward me, a mischievous glint in his blue gaze. "Let's choose where we're to die tonight, shall we?"

I inhaled a deep breath, closed my eyes, and stuck my hand into the bowl.

The Green Serpent

It would be my luck to pick the worst of the lot. And it was across the entire feckin' island from Tearmann, so I'd have to waste a considerable amount of magic getting there. Before I was cursed, I could've made the trip fifty times in a night, not a bother. Now? I'd be lucky to get home.

I lifted the glass of faerie wine and finished every last rancid drop. If I was to die tonight, I was going to die drunk.

The Green Serpent reeked of rot and sweat and stale drink. And I was fairly certain the mercenaries trading pooka claws at the table next to mine had bathed in shit.

I kept my head down, knowing what would happen if they caught me staring. Their whispers rattled through my head; they were as aware of my presence as I was of theirs. Wearing the enchanted kohl had been risky, but I refused to come into this hell hole without it.

For the moment, the situation seemed relatively safe. I was reading, after all. How threatening could I look with a book in my hands? The humans appeared more interested in drink than me. It wasn't until they got deeper in their cups that they'd begin plotting how to kill me and divvy up my parts.

Death was tedious, and finding the bits when I got back was always a feckin' nightmare. The last time it happened, it took me a fortnight to locate my thumbs.

"Like I was sayin', yer Lordship," the man beside me said, a spark of greed lighting his pinpoint eyes, "if ye just gave us half, we'd be able to buy enough port to turn a tidy profit." It looked as if Oran had put on a stone since I'd last seen him, and there was barely enough greasy gray hair to cover his head.

Every time we met, I had an overwhelming urge to force my magic into his oversized gullet and watch the life fade from those tiny eyes. It was nothing less than he deserved for trying to swindle me out of more gold, but there were more pressing matters at hand. Like not getting my head severed by the axe sitting next to the mercenary glancing at me from over his shoulder.

"I'm not giving you anything until you pay back what you owe." He'd already borrowed a small fortune for his smuggling venture. Unfortunately, he was one of only a handful of men willing to supply Tearmann with drink. I could've shifted all of it straight from the ships, but the damned treaty my father had signed forbade it.

Oran's grimy fingers wrapped around his flagon, and he raised it to his thin lips. "If I could pay what I owed ye, I wouldn't be askin' fer money."

The man was a leech.

I wouldn't put it past Rían to have told him I was here just to make me lose. After all, if I killed him, the other humans would take offense.

I glanced toward the broken clock on the shelf.

Four past eleven.

I'd already been here for two hours. Was Rían still out, or had he returned to the castle? Ruairi wasn't a contender. He couldn't return from the underworld, so he'd be back at the first hint of trouble.

On the other side of the room, the main door opened.

This was the type of place where ignoring that mundane detail could end in death. Everyone else seemed to know that too, as the boasting and swearing came to an abrupt halt.

A woman walked in, her face hidden within her cloak.

I'd known my fair share of female mercenaries, but the way she walked, all perfect posture and swaying hips, pointed more to her being an escort than a cold-blooded killer.

One of the mercenaries across the way nudged his friend. Nodded to the woman.

And grabbed a handful of her ass.

White hot rage clouded my vision.

I knew what it was like to be touched without consent. To have people take from you what you didn't want to give. Escort or not, this woman deserved the right to choose who touched her.

Brown hair. Leather vest. Crescent shaped tattoo on right forearm.

The vile bastard wouldn't leave this pub of his own volition.

The woman stumbled forward. Her skirts swirled when she twisted toward him.

"Ye've a fine arse 'neath all them skirts," the man slurred. "Five coppers fer a ride?"

Her hood lifted a fraction. Instead of responding, she threw back her shoulders and stomped toward the bar. The men around her grew rowdier. No one else had the bollocks to do anything but shout lewd suggestions and gesture to their cocks.

Orla emerged from her flat in between the two pubs. She was smart enough to keep her glamour in place on this side of the wall. If only there was something to be done about the scar her husband had left when he'd used a hot iron to brand the poor selkie.

And humans thought we were the monsters.

"I wonder if you might be able to help me," the mysterious

woman said, her voice surprisingly husky. The way she spoke was too refined for an escort. "You see, I'm looking for a man—"

"Pet, I've been lookin' fer a man in this pub fer forty years," Orla said, limping toward the bar, "and haven't found an honest one yet."

"A man to help me get to Tearmann," the woman finished.

Tearmann?

Orla's mouth flattened. "Why would someone like ye want to go there?"

Why, indeed? I flipped to the next page in my book, hoping to catch the woman's response. Humans knew better than to try and enter our territory. No one could hope to survive the Black Forest without an escort. And even then, it didn't guarantee they'd make it.

"I need to find the Gancanagh."

Shit.

The smile fell from Orla's weathered face. "These men will rob ye blind. Best be gone with ye and get the foolish notion of findin' the Gancanagh outta yer 'ead."

Orla's eyes flitted toward my table before shifting back to the woman.

Perhaps the stranger hadn't noticed.

Don't look at me. Look at Oran.

I squeezed the book in my hand, focusing on the weathered pages instead of the way the woman's shadowed eyes grazed over Oran and the drunkard passed out on the table to settle on me.

DON'T LOOK AT ME.

"Please," the woman said, turning back to the barmaid. "Surely you can recommend *someone*. It's a matter of life and death."

There were only two reasons human women came looking for me. And I wasn't interested in sex or death tonight. I wanted to beat Rían and celebrate my victory with pie.

Oran nudged me with his boot.

I kicked him in the shin and kept my eyes on the book. The

man who had assaulted the mysterious woman slipped from behind his table, adjusted himself, and started for the bar.

It took a flick of my wrist and a few whispered words to get his companion to tackle him. I kept the book in place with one hand and hid the other beneath the table.

One. Two. Three.

Three hits to leave his head lying in a puddle of his own blood.

If my magic had been at full strength, I would've turned him to ash.

Orla flung her hand toward the door. "Get outside and wait. I'll see what I can do."

"Thank you. Thank you so much." The woman gave Orla a coin and pivoted on the heel of her expensive boot only to find a bloodied body on the floor blocking her path. I held my breath, waiting for her reaction to tell me something about who she could be. Faint, scream, or—my personal favorite—fan herself with her impossibly pale hands.

The woman didn't do any of those things.

Those pale hands fisted at her sides. She lifted her boot.

And kicked him.

Twice.

I couldn't be imagining this. Couldn't be making this up.

Feck it all. I think I just fell in love.

The mercenaries' voices lifted in riotous cheers, none of them bothering to help the man dying on the floor. The woman sauntered toward the exit, threw open the door, and stepped into the night.

Oran jabbed me with his elbow. "That girl was lookin' fer ye."

My grip on the book tightened, but I didn't look up. "Was she?"

His bushy eyebrows came together. "Didn't ye hear her say it?"

Why was I destined to be surrounded by eejits?

Orla scowled at me from behind the bar. She obviously

thought whatever the woman wanted was my fault. But I'd never seen her before. Still, it would help no one if I didn't at least speak to her. If she wanted the same thing every other woman before her had wanted, I'd have no choice but to oblige.

That was a problem of my own making, and I wouldn't drag Orla into it. A matter of life and death, though? That seemed rather dramatic if all she wanted was a ride.

There was a second pub that catered to my people at the rear of the building, where it'd be safer to speak. According to the clock, it was a quarter past eleven. From the glassy-eyed stares being shot my way, I figured I'd worn out my welcome.

"Go and get her for me," I told Oran. "Bring her around back."

Oran's eyes widened, but he didn't budge. "Ye can't expect me to go fer free. Not all of us can pull coins out of our arse."

I should have made him shit a few coppers for his insolence. Instead, I collected a coin from my pocket and shoved it into his grubby palm. He clattered to his feet, then pushed past the mercenaries and out the door.

"What do you say, old man?" I kicked the drunkard beside me. His eyes didn't open. "How'd you like to be my puppet?"

The bloodied man on the floor let out a low groan, reminding me there was one last piece of business to attend to. I set my book aside and shifted the mercenary's axe into my hand. When I stood, my stool scraped against the floorboards. I could feel every eye on me as I stalked forward and stooped next to the man with pain-dulled eyes.

"It's time you learned to keep your hands to yourself," I whispered, adjusting my grip on the heavy axe. I wrapped a tendril of magic around his crooked arm, stretching it toward me. Fighting was useless, but he tried anyway. Stools clattered to the ground when the mercenaries shot to their feet. I aimed the blade at the man's wrist.

And let it fall.

2

The awful lighting in this room left me squinting at the words in my book. At least our side smelled better than the human side of the bar. Orla needed to put more candles out or something because the ones on the wall weren't doing shit. Despite the shite lighting, I could see the unmistakable black shadow of a curse living on the woman's lips. I'd have bet my castle that she'd been bargaining with a witch.

Was that why she wanted to see me? To bring charges against one of the witches? There was nothing I could do. Once a bargain was struck, it was illegal to interfere. If she was dumb enough to bargain, she deserved to suffer the consequences.

It took far too much magic to lift the drunkard's head and force my words through his dry, cracked lips. "*I hear yer lookin' fer the Gancanagh.*"

Damn, I hated that name. *Love talker.* That's what it meant. Love couldn't be further from my mind when the curse took over, forcing me to do things I didn't always want to do.

The woman's pointed chin thrust forward, bringing her black lips closer to the murky light. "That's right."

"*Dare I ask what business a girl like ye has with a faerie famous fer seducing young maids?*"

Her spine stiffened. "I need to—" The words cut off as if someone had stolen them from her throat.

I knew the pain on her face.

I knew her curse.

The same as mine. One of them, anyway.

A truth curse.

She'd been trying to lie to me. Her head would hurt something fierce if she kept it up.

At the door, Oran shifted his hulking weight, adjusting the thick belt buried beneath his stomach.

"I need to kill him," she breathed.

Well, that was unexpected.

Why would she want me dead? What had I done to her? I'd never seen the woman before in my life. There were plenty of people—humans and Danú alike—who wanted me dead.

But what possible reason could this high-born lady have?

Had I slept with her? No. I definitely would've remembered that voice. And those long legs hidden beneath her black skirts. She obviously didn't recognize me, so we hadn't slept together.

"*Afraid I'm not interested in murder today*," I said via the drunkard.

Dragging a purse from her belt, she tossed it onto the table. "I'll pay you. Half now. Half when we arrive at his castle."

Did she have a feckin' death wish? That was far too much money to be carrying around this side of the city.

A spark of greed lit Oran's dark eyes. If the bastard tried anything, I'd spill his guts on the floor before he could blink.

"*I need more silver like this island needs more rain*," the old man said after a little prompting. It felt as if I was forcing my magic through a feckin' block wall. The book in my hands began to shake. Keeping up this ruse was draining me too fast.

With the woman's cloak open, I could see a soft green glow coming from beneath the neck of her high-collared black dress. She must have been wearing an enchanted talisman.

A cursed human wearing a Danú talisman. Not something you saw every day.

"Fine." She yanked her cloak back over herself. "If you won't help, then I'll find someone else."

She had enough money to hire four mercenaries. Any one of those eejits from the other side of the wall would be more than happy to relieve her of the coins, even though not one would find me and live to tell the tale.

I should've left it. This human and her curse were none of my concern. If she was foolish enough to hire someone else, then she deserved to suffer the consequences.

One final question, and I would evanesce the hell out of here.

She reached for the purse. A burst of magic left the old man's age-spotted hand clutching the coins—and sweat pooling on my lower back. "*What makes ye think ye can get close enough to kill him?*"

Again, her chin lifted. "I have something he wants."

The confidence in her voice almost made me chuckle. "*Yer fair enough, but the Prince of Tearmann could have his pick of any woman.*"

"Not *me*," she ground out, her hands balling into fists.

What could she possibly have that would interest me? I found myself glancing toward that soft green glow. "*Go on then. Tell us what it is.*"

A heavy pause punctuated the air.

And then she said, "A ring."

I lost my grip on my magic, accidentally slamming the drunkard's head against the table. "An *emerald* ring?" I blurted, my heart pounding in my chest. It couldn't be. It couldn't.

The woman's pale hand flew to the green light. "How did you know?"

Shit shit shit. How had she gotten my feckin' ring?

I'd tried for centuries to retrieve it from the vindictive witch who'd cursed me. That ring was the answer to all my unspoken prayers. The only thing in this world that could set me free from the curses slithering beneath my skin.

I slammed the book closed, shifting it to the bar. "I've changed my mind. I'll do it." I'd get that ring back one way or another, even if I had to resort to torture. Although, I could think of a few more enjoyable ways to convince her. Like burying myself between her thighs and making her beg for release.

"*You're* Tadhg?" the woman choked.

"I am," I said with a strained smile. Feckin' brilliant. Oran had told her my feckin' name.

She stumbled back, eyes blown wide.

What the hell was her problem with me? Sure, my clothes were in an awful state, and I had on the enchanted kohl. The blood beneath my nails probably didn't give the best impression either. But that had been the mercenary's fault, not mine. The bastard bled like a stuck pig.

I was literally cursed to look like her feckin' fantasy. And yet she glared at me as if I'd turned myself into a feckin' serpent. "Is that going to be a problem?" I asked even though the answer was fairly feckin' obvious.

She pointed to the white-haired man. "Why can't he bring me?"

The woman preferred a man reeking of mead and vomit over *me*? The man wouldn't have been able to get her out of the pub in his state, let alone into Tearmann. I gave his boot a kick. The drunkard didn't so much as twitch. "He doesn't seem up to the task at present."

The woman's black lips pinched. "Then I'll ask someone else."

She'd rather brave a cross-country trip with a bloodthirsty mercenary?

"Suit yourself." She'd probably end up dead by the end of the week. And if she died, that ring would return to the person who gave it to her. To Fiadh. *Dammit.* This may be my one and only chance to get it back. "Although, no mercenary can get through the Black Forest alive, let alone into Tearmann. And the Gancanagh's castle?" I laughed. "Not a hope."

Crossing the Queen's Forest without permission meant paying the death tax. Hell, sometimes the Queen required the tax even if you did have permission. And in the extremely unlikely event that she made it to my castle, the wards around the gates would keep her out.

With narrowing eyes, the woman crossed her arms over her chest. "I suppose you know how to get me through the Black Forest."

I grinned, the shadow of my curse prowling beneath my skin. "I know how to get you through the Black Forest."

Her brow furrowed and hands twisted as she considered. With this feckin' curse, most women jumped at the chance to get me alone. Did I have something in my teeth? Had my cursed glamour stopped working?

"All right," she said with a resolute nod, as if she were the one doing me the favor. "You bring me to the Gancanagh, and I will pay you five hundred pieces of silver."

Oran swore under his breath.

"I'll meet you in the village square tomorrow, one hour before the market closes." I'd change her mind before the sun set, get my ring, and tell her to keep those coins.

Her daintily arched eyebrows rose slowly. "Before it closes? Why so late?"

Because if I was going to meet her again, I wanted to be at full strength. The little act with the drunkard had already cost me too much. And tomorrow was Friday, meaning I'd be spending most of my day with a plank of wood digging into my ass, listening to my people bicker.

Instead of telling her any of that, I said, "I have business to attend to. Oran?" The man straightened. "Show the lady out."

The miserable human's considerable girth jiggled when he shoved open the door. Grumbling under her breath, the woman tucked the purse into her pocket and stomped out. Her cloak billowed around her as she hurried up the narrow alley, away from the river.

She would be staying somewhere in town. Someplace nice, if the quality of her shiny boots and the heft of her purse were an accurate indication of her wealth.

"Follow her," I said, passing Oran another two coins. "Make sure she gets where she's going without incident. And when you find out where she's staying, come back and let Orla know."

He bobbed his head and reached for the handle. I caught his arm, digging my nails into his flabby flesh. "And Oran?" His beady eyes met mine. "If you touch her or tell her *anything*, I'll split you open and feed you your own entrails."

When I let him go, he stumbled into the door.

"N-no sir. Wouldn't dream of it s-sir." Oran drew the collar of his overcoat around his neck and disappeared into the night.

I collected my coat from the stool. The sound of rusty hinges whined from behind me. Orla leaned a shoulder against the door-frame to her flat located in the back of the pub, fiddling with the laces on the corset she wore outside her dress. The satin slipped through her thin fingers without making a sound. With the glamour removed, she looked like her old self: wavy black hair, straight nose. Full lips.

"Don't go," she said.

Those two words left me frozen in place, her wanton will taking over my own. I was so feckin' hungry I could eat an entire bakery's worth of desserts.

Her dark hair slipped over her breasts when she glanced back toward her home. "Come inside." With her heel, she pushed the door open a bit wider and took a retreating step into the candlelit room behind her. I could make out a crass wooden table, a worn woolen rug in front of the fireplace, the side of a settee—

That'll do.

A shudder ran through me as my curse broke free from its tether. By the time I reached her, the main door was locked and all our clothes were on the floor.

~

A surge of magic and a focused mind was all it took to get me back home. Evanescing was like using a portal without the portal.

Magic opened the door to where I wanted to go, and all I needed was to step through.

My body vibrated with exhaustion when I landed on the other side, my castle waiting like a shadowed fortress rising ominously against the blue-black sky. On wobbly legs, I breached the wards around the gates, hurrying through the empty courtyard to the heavy front door. Oscar, one of our only servants, wasn't around to open it, but it remained unlocked. Thank goodness for that. I wasn't sure I'd have the magic to evanesce inside. I briefly considered going upstairs and falling into bed.

But after the night I'd had, I needed a drink.

The parlor remained dark except for a blazing fire flickering off the worn stone floor. My brother sat on a wingback chair, his legs draped over one of the chair's arms while his head rested on the other. He didn't bother unpinning his gaze from the book in his hands. Snores echoed from the settee. Ruairi's mouth gaped open; an empty bottle of faerie wine was tucked beneath his arm.

I poured myself a glass of puítin from the decanter on the coffee table, then kicked the leg of Rían's chair. "Looks like I won."

Rían's nose wrinkled. "What time did you leave the pub to go off with whoever-she-was?"

"Quarter past eleven."

"You beat me by five feckin' minutes."

Before he'd met Aveen, my brother would've still been out, prowling the streets looking for trouble—or a bed to warm. Now he was my constant companion, which irritated me to no end.

Aveen had been mad to trust Rían, let alone fall in love with him. He didn't deserve any of it—and definitely not from a woman willing to sacrifice a year of her life to be with him.

I wouldn't even sacrifice this drink for Rían.

Still, she must have seen something in him worthy of redemption.

For the life of me, I couldn't figure out what it was.

He was handsome, I supposed. Blue eyes and suntanned skin

like our father, mahogany hair like his mother. And he had magic, which was always a perk with human women. He was powerful—one of the most powerful beings on this island since my magic had been bound. And he could glamour himself to look like anyone—I mean *anyone*.

All things I used to be able to do before I was cursed.

But he was also selfish, murderous, and deceitful. How someone like Rían had won over someone like Aveen still confounded me. It didn't make any feckin' sense.

The clear liquor numbed my throat when I took a drink. "It would've been longer, but someone came into the pub asking for an escort to Tearmann."

Rían licked his finger before turning the page. "And I care because . . . ?"

What was it about his voice that made me want to pick him up and throw him from the castle roof? I'd done it once.

Eava had given out because his body had crushed the pumpkins.

"It was a woman," I added, taking the seat across from him, pressing the back of my head into the plush velvet upholstery. One of the logs on the fire popped, sending orange sparks flying onto the stone hearth. "And she wants to kill me."

The book snapped closed and disappeared. Rían swung his legs to the ground, straightened, and looked at me. "I wasn't interested at first because your stories are usually shite and they always end the same way, but—" Frowning, he gestured at my waistcoat. "*Aaand* now I'm distracted. What the hell are you wearing?"

Rían and his damned clothes. Unlike him—in his black and silver waistcoat, crisp shirt spelled to never wrinkle, and impeccably pressed black breeches—I preferred to fade into the background as much as possible, especially when spending the evening with murderers.

"You know what? We'll circle back to this." Rían waved his hand at the missing buttons and stained sleeves shoved to my elbows. "Why does she want to kill you?"

"Not sure yet. She has my ring though."

Rían's blue eyes lit with excitement. He leaned forward, bracing his elbows on his knees. "Tell. Me. *Everything*."

My stomach rumbled, reminding me there were more pressing matters to attend to first. Plus, a chance to annoy my brother should never be wasted. "Later." I got up and started for the hall.

He appeared in front of me before I reached the door. "I want to know now."

I managed to evanesce to the kitchen.

Rían's echoing curse made me smile. He would check my room first. Then probably the study. He'd find me here eventually.

Pots and pans loomed overhead, mingling with the darkness. Lighting the candles on the high counter should've been child's play. I couldn't even summon a feckin' spark. Thankfully, Eava kept matches between her vials of wolfsbane and dandelion seeds. I struck one on the edge of the butcherblock counter. The smell of sulfur filled the air, twisting with the smoke as I held the lit flame to the candle's wick.

In the dim orange light, I began my search for pie.

There were boiled potatoes in a dish next to some slices of ham. Freshly baked loaves of bread beneath tea towels. A whole bushel of apples in the sink.

Dammit.

No feckin' pie.

I shuffled through the shelves and presses and checked inside the oven and—

"Looking for this?" My brother appeared, hip resting against the high counter, holding a crockery dish of half-eaten blackberry pie.

I tried to shift it to me, but his magic was too strong. "Give it to me."

Lifting the dish over his head, he clicked his tongue. "Now, Tadhg. That's not how this works. You give me what I want, then you get what you want."

"And you wonder why women fancy me over you," I shot back.

His eyes flashed. The sound of his teeth grinding together left me chuckling. "Tell me about the feckin' woman with the ring," he snarled, throwing the dish onto the high butcherblock table in the center of the room.

I set my glass beside the pie, grabbed a fork from the press, and sank onto one of the stools.

The pie was better than life itself. Eava had added extra sugar, making the top gritty and sweet. She was a feckin' saint.

Between bites, I told him about what had happened in The Green Serpent. He listened quietly until I finished, sipping every so often from a glass of shifted wine.

"And then she told me she needed to kill the Gancanagh." She didn't say she *wanted* to kill me but that she *needed* to. Her choice of words felt significant.

I took another bite of pie. Crunchy seeds stuck to my teeth; the crust on the bottom was soft and a bit undercooked. Just the way I liked it. "I said I'd help her."

His dark eyebrows lifted. "To get the ring."

"Of course to get the feckin' ring." What other reason would I have to "help" someone who wanted to kill me?

"And if she doesn't give it to you?"

"I'll convince her."

Rían snorted, saluting me with his drink. "Good luck with that."

"You don't think I can do it?"

He considered for a moment, head tilting as he sipped from his glass. "To have any hope of getting that ring, you'll both have to resist your curse." His lips lifted. "Which means you're shit out of luck."

His arrogance only made me more determined to succeed. Fate had put this woman and my ring within my reach for a reason.

"If you need help, I could always get the ring for you," Rían sneered.

There was no way in hell I was asking my little brother for help. No feckin' way.

"Mark my words. This time tomorrow night, I'll have that ring on my finger."

Rían's teeth flashed, and he flicked his wrist. "And if you don't," he said, setting two gold triskelion cufflinks on the table, "I get these back."

"You can have *one* back." I clinked my glass against his. The drink washed away the glorious taste of blackberries. I couldn't wait to pass out and put this day behind me. One more day with these curses.

One more day.

Speaking of curses . . . "I need you to collect a body."

Groaning, Rían's head dropped into his hands. "Who did you kill now?"

3

There was nothing particularly great about the castle's "great hall." Except perhaps the high ceilings. Although I'd been in plenty of buildings with high ceilings far more impressive than these. There weren't any adornments or ornate plaster coving or murals. Only whitewashed wood and dark, high beams.

The gathered crowd buzzed like a bunch of flies, shifting and groaning in the heat. Even with all the windows open, the place was like a feckin' furnace. I'd suggested Rían remove the wards on Fridays so we could get some air into this musty room. As usual, he refused. If the bulk of my magic hadn't been bound, I'd have done it myself.

No sense dwelling on it. There was nothing I could do until I retrieved my ring.

The line inched along, each complaint more tedious than the last. At this rate, I'd be lucky to make it back to Dreadshire by four. Rían sat next to me, fiddling with the silver buttons on his waistcoat, looking fresh as a feckin' daisy.

How was he not sweating?

The back of my shirt felt as if it'd been dropped in a puddle.

I looked back at Molls, a rare female clurichan whose dark dress bore the telltale stains of drink around the collar. Her wild red hair reminded me of a lion's mane. "As I was sayin', Prince Tadhg, those blasted children are stealin' my feckin' eggs."

Eggs sounded really good right about now. Perhaps I'd convince Eava to make me some before meeting my assassin. I was bound to be late anyway. What was another couple of minutes?

"Have you seen them stealing the eggs?" I asked. Molls was here every other week, blaming someone for something, and yet she'd never had a witness to confirm the accusations.

She propped her meaty fists onto her equally meaty hips. "No. But I know it's them."

"I'm afraid I cannot do anything unless you have proof. Have you thought about strengthening the wards around your coop?" Creating a ward was one of the first lessons we'd been taught as children, although not all Danú had the ability to do so. The magic of weaker factions, like clurichans and grogochs, tended to be tied to the earth. Meaning they could grow a fabulous garden but couldn't ward for shite.

Her thick jaw clenched. "I've made them as strong as I can."

I glanced over at Rían, too busy with his buttons to notice. "Rían?"

Blue eyes lifted to mine.

"Molls needs her wards strengthened so her eggs don't get stolen."

Although Rían made an indignant noise through his nose, he knew better than to defy me in front of an audience. "Fine. I'll strengthen your wards."

Molls bobbed her head. "Thank you, Prince Rían."

He waved his hand, dismissing the gratitude.

Her eyes narrowed on him, and he looked between the two of us like he was confused.

His hands dropped to the arms of his chair. "You want me to go *now*?"

"Sure, what else are you doing?"

A muscle in his jaw ticked, but he stood and stomped down

the dais, following Molls into the hallway. The moment I heard the front door slam, the tension in my shoulders eased, and I swore the temperature in the room cooled.

The next three people were there to pay taxes in silver, ripe red apples, and goats. It was a good thing Rían was gone. If he saw the two brown animals traipsing along the stones, he'd lose his feckin' mind. Not everyone had vaults of silver and gold.

Some people only had goats.

Aidan McManus, a leprechaun from up the coast, towed his daughter to the dais. She was a pretty thing, her white hair contrasting beautifully with her dark skin, and she stood twice as tall as her father. I couldn't quite recall, but I thought her mother was a selkie. The girl gave a half-hearted curtsy, her gaze never rising from her black boots.

Aidan's white whiskers twitched when he frowned. "Forgive me for havin' to waste yer time with this matter, my prince, but 'tis an urgent one."

I waited for him to explain what was so urgent, but all he did was dart a glare over his shoulder to the twenty or so people left in the hall. "I'm afraid it's of a"—his gaze flicked to his daughter's downcast face—"*sensitive* nature."

I stood from the uncomfortable wooden throne and waved for them to follow me into the study, ignoring the murmurs from the remaining crowd. It wasn't as if I was bringing the girl in here alone. She had a feckin' chaperone.

Shelves of books on Tearmann law towered on either side of the door and along the wall. Sunlight streamed through the high windows, baking the leather-and-ink-scented air.

"Now, then. What's the issue?" I asked, propping myself against my desk, bracing my hands on the edge.

Aidan and his daughter stopped an arm's length away.

"I caught old Ferdal's son defiling my poor Eilis in the middle of the feckin' night," Aidan ground out, the tips of his pointed ears going red.

The girl let out a whimper, her lower lip trembling.

Heat flared inside my chest. My fingers clenched the wood. No wonder he hadn't wanted to share the details outside. "And where is the boy now?"

"In my barn," Aidan said with a nod. "Have him clapped in iron chains like the criminal he is."

When the girl whimpered again, her father gave her arm a shake. Sniffling, she dragged her sleeve beneath her nose.

"Did he force himself on you?" I asked in a soft voice.

She glanced at her father before looking back down to her shoes.

"The prince asked ye a question, Eilis. Answer him."

Unease settled in my stomach next to the croissants I'd eaten for breakfast. There was something about the way her father kept answering for her that didn't sit right. I pushed away from my desk, sending them both back a step. "Eilis, would you feel comfortable speaking to me alone?" Aidan looked appalled by the suggestion. "I swear I will not touch you," I said, as much for her benefit as her father's.

She nodded but still did not meet my gaze.

"Aidan, step into the hallway and wait until I call for you." I gestured toward the door across the room.

He looked like he wanted to protest. In the end, he turned and stalked toward the door.

The soft click made the girl jump.

"Now, I'll ask you once more: did the boy force himself on you?"

Biting her lip, she shook her head, sending her white hair swaying over hunched shoulders.

"You're sure? You can tell me."

"I'm sure, yer highness. We fancy each other, Dillon and me. We didn't know my da was comin' home so early. And now he . . . he thinks we gotta get married."

"Do you *want* to marry this Dillon fellow?"

She shook her head, her dark eyes flaring as she raised her chin. "I don't want to marry anyone."

I almost smiled at the steel in her words. "Then it sounds to me like you need to go rescue your friend."

Her answering grin was like a balm to my soul.

"On your way out, send your father in."

Her smile faltered, but she threw her shoulders back and started for the door, the material of her skirts swaying with each step. "Da? The prince wants to see ye."

Aidan appeared, giving his daughter a curious look when she breezed past.

"Where's she goin'?" he threw over his shoulder at me.

I urged the door closed with a flick of my wrist. "To unlock her lover."

Aidan's body tensed; his hands fisted at his sides. "He *ruined* her."

Ruined. That word always confounded me. "Your daughter is not *ruined*. She has made a choice and does not deserve to be punished for it. If the boy had forced himself on her, that would be another matter entirely. But seeing as he did not, this issue does not concern me."

Aidan took a menacing step forward. "She needs to marry 'im."

All it took was a raise of my eyebrows to drain the redness from his face. If he forgot his place once more, I'd have to remind him. "I will not give my blessing for a marriage that is not consented to by all parties." That sort of idiocy belonged in the human world. Their traditions may have bled across our borders, but that did not mean I would abide by them.

And to marry in Tearmann, one needed my blessing. Or my brother's when I was . . . indisposed.

When he left, Aidan was the one hanging his head.

I checked the clock in the corner and groaned. How was it half two already?

Back in the hall, I found Rían slumped in his chair, looking bored as ever.

"You could've done something while I was gone, you know," I ground through my teeth.

"What would you call strengthening wards? Besides"—Rían waved toward the waiting crowd—"they haven't come to see me. They want to see you."

That was true. And Rían did more than his fair share considering my situation. Still, I could've used his help today. Not that I'd give him the satisfaction by admitting it.

Sinking onto the throne, I called the next person forward.

It took three more hours, but eventually, the final man left the hall. I almost fell out of the throne in relief.

Groaning, Rían stood and stretched his arms toward the ceiling. "Are you off?"

I did the same, my back popping with the movement. "Yes, but I shouldn't be long." If I put in some effort, I could convince her to invite me to her bed and be back within the hour. How hard could it be? A few smiles, some compliments, a suggestive comment or two, and she'd be lifting her own skirts. After the ride of her life, she'd surely be so besotted that she'd hand over the ring without batting an eye.

The alley behind The Green Serpent was deserted, as I knew it would be. No Danú in their right mind would come to this godforsaken place in broad daylight, and most humans were leery enough to avoid it altogether. The kohl stung my eyes when I smeared it on, but there was no telling what awaited me today.

A few people still milled about the market. When the first raindrops began to fall, they hurried for shelter. Refreshing mist cooled my overheated skin. I pretended the rain could wash away my many sins, leaving me clean and unburdened and free.

I kept walking until I saw a familiar figure in a gray cloak speaking to an elderly man next to a cramped black carriage. A man emitting the telltale green glow of a glamour.

He wore a black flat cap, long wool pants with muck on the hem, and a dark overcoat that reached his knees.

If the Airren authorities caught him using an illegal glamour, he'd be hanged. Considering his age and occupation, I figured he'd had plenty of experience keeping it up. His presence complicated things to no end. If the man knew who I was, he'd surely tell his mistress, and I could kiss my ring goodbye.

The old man's eyes skimmed over me without so much as a spark of recognition before he hobbled over to check the bindings on the horses.

The woman turned.

I nearly missed my next step.

The fading light of day highlighted her alabaster skin and sharp cheekbones. Thick lashes surrounded the most unusual pair of steel-gray eyes. The mist softened her long, dark brown hair into damp waves.

My fingers itched to unfasten that damned cloak to discover what she'd hidden beneath her high-neck black gown.

At least retrieving the ring wouldn't be a chore.

When she saw me, a deep wrinkle marred the space between her arched eyebrows. Her pinched mouth turned down in a disapproving frown. "What time do you call this?" she clipped.

The apology on my tongue died.

What time do you call this? What sort of greeting was that? I'd gotten here as soon as I could.

She lifted to her toes, scanning over my shoulder. "And where is your horse?"

Even if I didn't despise the beasts, I certainly wouldn't have been caught dead on one of them in this lawless country. And it was feckin' raining.

"I don't have a horse," I said, adjusting my clothes and bag to keep my hands busy.

The woman's brow furrowed.

The idea of being cooped up in a carriage with such a waspish human sounded as appealing as a day in the stocks.

Still, I wouldn't be able to get the ring if she didn't let me inside.

"You think I'm going to let you ride with me?"

"I can always stay here and let you find the Gancanagh on your own if you'd prefer."

The coachman shifted, pale blue eyes raking from my head to my old boots. I was nearly certain I'd never seen him before, but that didn't mean he hadn't seen me. The way he stared set me on edge. If he knew me, why did he remain silent?

The wasp let out a heavy sigh. "I suppose there's enough room for the both of us." Once again, her tone made it sound like she was doing me some sort of favor. As if I hadn't been the one to leave my castle and duties behind to waste my time with this.

I gave her a bow and a muttered, "You're too kind," then waited for her to climb the two steps into the carriage. The wide layers of her skirts rustled as she settled herself on the center of the tufted blue cushions, not leaving a bit of room for me.

I threw myself onto the trunk across the way and abandoned my bag on the floor next to my overcoat. I hated carriages almost as much as I despised horses. Fancy cages on wheels, too stuffy and close. I shoved my sleeves to my elbows, trying to get some air to my overheated skin. Why was it so feckin' warm in here? You'd swear it was the height of summer instead of the start of autumn.

These curtains were nice though. Blue with a swirly pattern woven into the heavy material. Something like this would be perfect for the parlor instead of those hideous flowery things.

"Where to, milady?" the coachman asked with a baleful glare in my direction.

Why was he asking her? She didn't know where we were headed. "We need to go to Guaire," I told him.

The coachman's gaze flicked to his mistress. "Milady?"

Her brittle smile reminded me of the painted porcelain dolls I'd seen in shops around the island. Easily shattered. "We need to head northwest," she said in the most condescending tone I'd ever heard. As if I were some simpleton.

We would need to go northwest if we were going to Tearmann. But we weren't. Not a hope. Being cursed to tell the truth had taught me a valuable lesson about wording bargains. I had promised to bring the wasp to the Gancanagh, not his castle. And since I *was* the Gancanagh, technically, I'd already fulfilled my end.

There was no sense traveling the treacherous northern paths when we could take the well-worn roads south. I could hardly convince her to give me that ring if we didn't travel anywhere.

"We travel to Guaire," I repeated in the same tone, returning the coachman's scowl. If he knew what was good for him, he'd go away with himself.

Although he didn't look pleased, he retreated.

"Is the Gancanagh *in* Guaire?" the wasp clipped.

I stretched my legs, trying to get comfortable on the blasted trunk. "Not at present. But I have some business to attend to before we travel to his castle." Business that involved the wasp and I in a scandalous situation, stripped bare of her stuffy, high-necked dress.

The half-truth slipped from my lips with only a blip of pain in my head.

Funny that living with a truth curse for so long had made me an even better liar.

Her nose wrinkled the way Rían's did when he saw stains on my clothes. "What sort of business could you possibly have that cannot wait?"

What business could I possibly have?

What *business*?

I'd show her what feckin' business. Beautiful or not, I'd need to be drunk to give such a condescending, holier-than-thou feckin' human a ride.

I yanked my bag from the floor, found my flask where I'd left it, and took a long drink. With the fiery liquid still coating my tongue, I smiled at the wasp and said, "The type of business that's none of yours."

Ohhh she did not like that. Not one bit.

Her teeth ground together, as if she were chewing glass. "Padraig? Will you take us to Guaire, please?"

A small victory, but a victory nonetheless.

The coachman, Padraig, latched the door. The carriage lurched forward when we took off. My spine scraped off the wall. The line of rivets beneath me would definitely leave a bruise.

This was a nice box, as far as boxes went, another sign of her obvious wealth. What else could I glean without actually having a conversation?

All-black dress. Interesting choice of attire. Rather dour, though, for one so young. Black was usually something you saw on elderly humans.

She wore no jewelry to speak of, save a simple gold band on her left ring finger.

Hold on.

She was married?

How had I missed that last night?

Feck it all. No wonder she showed no interest. If she was as rigid as her posture, there'd be no hope of me convincing her to let me warm her bed. I took another slug of faerie wine.

My brother would be unbearable when he found out he'd won back one of his cufflinks.

Feck it anyway.

Time to formulate a backup plan. The portal in Port Fear was five days' drive southwest. If I couldn't convince her to give me the ring by then, I'd bring her through, emerge next to the Black Forest, and scare the human out of her wits. Then, I'd agree to pay the Queen's Death tax with my own life in exchange for the ring. Simple.

"I'm not sure you realize this," I said, determined to turn this day around, "but you never gave me your name." Calling her "wasp" to her face probably wouldn't garner any goodwill.

"You may call me Lady Keelynn."

That feckin' *tone*.

She may be wearing a fine gown and shiny boots, but she wasn't better than me.

"Keelynn." A beautiful name, old as the hills rolling past the window. "Slender and fair." The woman may have been both, but she was also an awful uppity snob. If there was one thing I couldn't stand, it was a human with a chip on her shoulder. "I suppose it would suit you if you weren't planning on committing a heinous murder."

Color climbed from beneath her high collar, painting her jaw a dusky rose. "I suppose it's a good thing I'm not paying you for your opinion."

She didn't need to pay me for my opinion. I'd give it to her for free. "Maiden Death."

Her black lips pursed. "Excuse me?"

"I've decided I'm going to call you Maiden Death."

"You will not," she gasped, chest rising and falling in irritation.

"Mmmm . . . I think I will. Yes, Maiden Death is the perfect name for you." Perfect for an ignorant human who thought she could actually best me.

I'd been hunted for centuries.

Killed more times than years she'd been alive.

Even with my magic a pittance of what it once was, I could still boil the blood in her veins with a flick of my wrist.

I was a true immortal.

Maiden Death didn't stand a feckin' chance.

4

"SHE'S INSANE. ABSOLUTELY STARK RAVING MAD." MY WORDS echoed around the castle's wide entry hall. I threw my bag to the floor. The tin of enchanted kohl skidded across the stones, landing next to Rían's boot. He took one look at the thing before kicking it back. Mumbling my thanks, I tucked it into my overcoat pocket.

That woman.

That *feckin' woman.*

It hadn't helped that I'd been hungover and wrecked or that the rivets from the trunk dug into my ass every time we hit a blasted bump in the road. Still, I could've handled all those things if it weren't for *her*, looking at me like I would suddenly grow fangs and rip off her head.

Rían went back to arranging a bunch of blue flowers in a crystal vase on the hall table. He had probably made them that hideous shade because they were the color of his fiancée's eyes. He was forever doing things like that to make Eava pity him.

As if the old witch didn't pity him enough already.

"I take it today went well," the bastard said with a smile.

I inhaled through my nose and then exhaled through my mouth. *Once. Twice.* It didn't help cast the memories of that infernal woman out of my brain. "As well as can be expected for traveling with an aspiring murderer."

The wasp hadn't said one nice thing to me the entirety of the four-hour journey. Never bothered with a word of thanks for dropping everything to "assist" her.

Glancing at my fingers, Rían clicked his tongue. "No ring?" A sprig of baby's breath appeared in his hand; he forced it between the godawful blue roses.

"Not yet." Although enchanted objects couldn't be shifted, it hadn't stopped me from trying to call my ring to me. No matter what I did, the blasted thing remained concealed beneath Maiden Death's black shroud.

Rían stopped arranging the flowers. "And where's your little murderess now?"

"Staying the night in Guaire. We should be in Port Fear by the weekend."

"You're bringing her to a portal?" Wincing, Rían scratched the back of his neck. "You know the rules."

Rían and his feckin' rules. Always following them to the letter.

"What other choice do I have?" I would blindfold her so she didn't know where to find it again. Not that she could work the portal herself; the doors only opened with blood magic.

"You could ask me for help. I'd only require a minimal amount of begging."

"I'd rather die."

I didn't need Rían's help.

I could do this on my own.

I had never met anyone as repulsed by me. At first, I'd assumed it was because Keelynn was married. Then she'd told me her husband was dead. Had Fiadh's magic finally worn off? The damned witch had taken my ability to shapeshift, weaving it into my curse. My face and form changed from woman to woman. They were supposed to see what they wanted to see—the man of their "dreams."

It seemed like I was Keelynn's nightmare.

Rían went back to the flowers. "Have you thought about changing into something that's not covered in shite? You may look like a roguish pirate prince, but you smell like weeds and dirt. If you need some clean clothes—"

"I don't want your damn clothes." I escaped to the study to find the map of Airren spread on my desk. I'd love to make it to Lill tomorrow, but from the heaviness in my bones, I'd probably end up sleeping away most of the day.

Meaning it'd be another late start.

My eyes drifted toward Tearmann. Our world, banished to the far reaches of the northwest, felt more confined every day as more humans came to our shores.

The problem wasn't that humans were all bad but that they had been taught that we were evil monsters. Some of us were, but not the ones they were most scared of.

Pooka? Polite to a fault. Sure, Ruairi had killed me once or twice, but I'd deserved it. He certainly hadn't been trying to eat me. Pooka, like most Danú, were herbivores.

Banshees? They would rattle your eardrums, but that was about it. Cloda, the Queen of the Banshees, was my godmother. And out of all my aunts, she was the most pleasant.

Grogoch? Smelly, but their great sense of humor made up for it.

"What happens when you reach the Forest?" Rían asked from the doorway.

"I'll pay the tax for the ring." A trip to the underworld would be worth it.

"And if the Queen decides to kill her instead?"

I shrugged. "If the Queen kills the wasp, then it's no skin off my back as long as I have the ring first."

The ring was the only way to free myself of these curses and release the rest of my magic.

Well, not the *only* way.

But I'd given up on falling in love with someone—and having her love me in return—a long, long time ago.

If the price of my freedom was the life of one infuriating human, then so be it.

"By the way," Rían said, "they're holding executions in Mántan and Longshadow tomorrow."

Dammit. More of our citizens losing their lives over Airren's asinine laws. No magic. No glamours. No retaliating when attacked. No hope of any quality of life in that cursed country. "Can you make both?"

He shook his head. "They're both at noon."

"Have Ruairi oversee Mántan." It was closer, so he wouldn't waste too much magic getting there.

"I'm giving you five more days to sort this shite your way. Then I'm stepping in."

Either way, in five days, that ring would be mine.

The bastard shoved my shoulder hard enough to send me back a step. "Now, where the hell is my cufflink?"

The following day, I arrived to Keelynn's carriage with a plan formed in the wee hours of the morning. There may have been alcohol involved.

My head gave an answering thump.

A *lot* of alcohol.

Today, I would sleep—or at least feign sleep. I didn't have it in me to spend another day dodging the wasp's barbs. I'd lie down, close my eyes, waste a few hours in the box, then return to Tearmann.

I rounded the corner to find Keelynn and her coachman Padraig sitting in front of a bunch of yellow flowers outside the inn, playing cards.

I waved at the only bearable one, Padraig. "Good morning."

Keelynn fixed me with a hateful stare. "It's *not* morning."

"It is for me." I'd rolled out of bed an hour ago, dressed in the first clothes I'd found, then stuffed myself with Eava's crepes. *Eava*. Bless that old witch. She'd have me fat as a fool.

Before the wasp could say anything else rude, I smiled at the white-haired coachman. He seemed a decent enough fellow. In truth, I felt sorry for him, since he had such a miserable mistress. "We need to go to Niloc." We could hit Lill tomorrow and still be on schedule.

"It's not up to me," Padraig said in his raspy voice, straightening the deck of cards and stuffing them into his breast pocket.

"You wasted enough of my time yesterday," Keelynn insisted, standing and stomping her foot like it would make her seem more . . . I don't know. Imposing?

It didn't.

All it did was make me wince when the heel of her boot collided with the cobblestones.

Five more days. Not so bad. I'd been tortured for longer.

Only five more days.

"We cannot continue traveling southwest," she went on, "when we need to go *north*west to the castle."

I massaged my aching temples. Why had I let my brother talk me into opening that second bottle? "What do you say we compromise? I'll go to Niloc, and you go wherever the hell you want."

"How is that a compromise?"

Instead of answering, I started back the way I'd come, calling her bluff. Keelynn groaned and told Padraig to head southwest.

Once we were settled in the feckin' box, I found my flask and took a drink of ice cold water, keeping my eyes trained on the landscape speeding past.

Across from me, Keelynn shifted. I hadn't planned on glancing at her, but when I did, I found it hard to look away.

There was no denying that she was attractive, with thick, dark lashes framing those large, steely eyes. Straight nose with a slightly upturned tip. Dark hair pulled into a severe knot at the back of her head, held in place with pins. High black collar cutting off the smooth white column of her throat.

It looked dreadfully tight.

Anything around my neck reminded me of being hanged. The unrelenting pressure of a coarse rope biting into your throat. The slow agony of suffocation when the drop didn't snap your neck.

Chop off my head, impale me on a feckin' pike. Just don't send me to the gallows.

Keelynn bit her bottom lip with her perfect teeth as she stared down at the book in her lap. I had the overwhelming urge to run my tongue over the marks.

Not that I could.

If I went anywhere near her black mouth with mine, she'd keel over. Then I'd have two dead women in my castle, and my ring would return to Fiadh.

Wicked witch. Over two centuries had passed since she'd cursed me. She'd made a home on the east coast of Airren, as far from Tearmann as one could get without leaving the island. After all these years, I'd assumed she'd forgotten about me.

Apparently not.

Niloc was only a few hours south, but sitting on the damned trunk pretending to be passed out made it seem like an eternity. Especially with Keelynn smelling like lavender soap.

Soap used in the bath.

When she was naked.

Feckin' brilliant.

Now I was thinking about her naked.

Seven hundred and eighty-four. That was how many women I'd killed. Human or Danú, didn't matter, my magic could feel the tug of attraction like a fisherman reeling in his catch. Only I was the fish.

The first woman I killed had been a maid working in my own castle named Grainne Browne. I'd been in a sorry state, wallowing over my loss of magic. I'd been convinced a woman was what I'd needed to bring myself out of the depths of despair. She'd found me in my study, drunk as a clurichaun, and blushed so prettily when I smiled at her. She'd giggled as I'd kissed my way up her vanilla-scented neck.

The moment my mouth grazed her rosy, red lips, she'd seized.

The curse spread like wicked black fingers down her chin to her throat, and she'd collapsed into my arms.

After that, I'd tried staying in the castle, but being a recluse drove me mad. I'd tried making myself smell like dirt and shite and worn threadbare clothes, convincing my brother it was some sort of bet when it was actually an attempt to save my sanity.

No matter what I did, I couldn't escape.

The attraction was instantaneous.

Who wouldn't be attracted to a person who looked as though he'd stepped out of their wildest fantasy? The embodiment of their deepest, darkest desires.

The pull of attraction felt like invisible threads being tugged in different directions.

The one that yanked the hardest usually won.

My body would turn toward her. My feet would walk in her direction.

Then it was a matter of fate.

Until I'd figured out how to manipulate it, fighting the strings even as they drew tighter. I found the weakest of the lot, the most innocent, knowing she would be the least likely to whisper an offer by the end of the night.

And when none of them seemed naïve, I found the most attractive one, showed an interest, drank to the point of oblivion, and let my curse take the reins.

After number five hundred and two, I thought, *feck it.* If I was going to be used, I may as well enjoy it.

And I became the thing the legends warned people about.

I became the Gancanagh.

5

THE PLASTER WALL OF BRIARHAVEN'S FINEST BAWDY HOUSE BORE A fresh coat of poppy red paint. I'd been standing here for the last ten minutes, watching the respectable folks cross the cobbled street to pass by, like the perfumed air and raucous laughter would somehow taint them if they got too close. If someone didn't come along soon, I'd have to go in on my own.

Two young men, still pockmarked and gangly, burst from the pub next door, exchanging good-natured insults. When they saw me, they stopped dead in their tracks.

"Evening, lads." I nodded. "Good night?"

Their wide eyes bulged even as they mumbled a convoluted response.

I knocked my knuckle against the doorframe. "Are you going in?"

This time, they nodded.

I shifted a handful of silver, holding it toward them. "I'll give you each five pieces of silver to give Clara McNulty a message."

The taller of the two, with wispy black hair, glanced at his mate. "What's the message?"

"Tell her a prince is waiting for her outside."

When neither of them made to take the coins, I flicked my

wrist, forcing their hands forward, and dropped the money into their palms. "There. In you go." I nudged them toward the door, hoping they'd be terrified enough to come through.

I could have gone in on my own, but then I wouldn't get a lick of sleep and the owner would expect me to pay for something I didn't want. Briarhaven's inns didn't cater to the Danú. Going home tonight wasn't an option either. Not with my magic running low after spending last night acting a fool and all day refilling my flask.

If I wanted to get any rest tonight, Clara was my best bet.

I only hoped the messengers didn't get distracted once they got inside.

Minutes later, the door opened and a small blond burst onto the street. Large turquoise eyes landed on me. She rushed forward, throwing herself into my arms. A tinkling giggle tickled my neck. "You're here! I can't believe you're here," she squealed.

Her happiness at seeing me brought with it a wave of guilt for leaving it so long between visits. "I've been busy."

She felt thinner, lighter than she'd been a few years ago. Her smile was the same though, all teeth and ruby red lips. The dress she wore, if one could even call it a dress, had been made to accentuate her impossibly tiny waist and lift her breasts nearly to her chin.

After so many years indoors, her faerie markings were nearly invisible.

A soldier in red livery patrolling the street stopped beneath a lamp post, his hand falling to the pommel of his sword. "Take it inside, whore."

Clara squeezed my face between her palms. "You are mine tonight. Only mine. Promise me."

I grinned. "I promise."

The inside of the bawdy house had been painted the same shade as the exterior walls. Candles flickered in low black chandeliers, their orange light reflecting off the black crystals dripping toward the tables below.

Naked women draped themselves across laps of men staring through glazed eyes at the cards in their hands. Four others waited on a balcony, their silk robes untied, revealing shoulders and the tops of breasts.

A woman pushed through a black beaded curtain beside the staircase, the clicking sound delicate in comparison to the muffled moans coming from beyond the landing. She sauntered into the room in an opulent red dress, the bodice cinched tight and neckline obscenely low. Clara's hold on my hand tightened as the madame scanned the room, no doubt tallying her take from the crowd.

When she caught sight of me, her lips curled into a knowing smile. Time had been kind to the madame. She wasn't the stunning young woman she once was, but she was still beautiful, with dark hair curled and piled atop her head and tendrils falling to frame delicate features.

I felt the threads tugging from every direction, but the tightest pull belonged to the blond faerie at my side.

"Tadhg O'Cleirigh," the madame crooned, skirts swishing as she made her way between two gaming tables to wrap her fingers around my arm. The red paint on her nails looked like blood. "To what do I owe this delightful visit? Are you in search of a companion—or two?" She glared down her nose at Clara until the faerie released me.

"I'd like to book Clara for the night."

The woman pulled me toward the crystal curtain, parting the strands herself. "Clara's my best girl. I'm not sure it'll be possible to have her *all* night."

Negotiating. A game I knew all too well. Lucky for me, money wasn't an object. Not that the madame needed to know.

The office behind a locked door had white marble floors and a desk made of the same material. Shelves on either side of a small fireplace held row after row of wigs displayed on white marble "heads."

"If it doesn't suit, then I'll take my business elsewhere." I touched a pink wig styled to resemble a beehive. Bejeweled pins that looked like tiny flowers sparkled among the soft strands.

In this light, the thick layer of paint around the madame's eyes cracked like porcelain when she smiled. "It'll cost a small fortune."

Rhythmic pounding of a headboard against the wall sounded through the ceiling. I shifted enough coins to pay for the next twelve hours. "This should cover it."

With a delighted smirk, the madame dragged a key from her skirts and pressed it into my palm. "Enjoy."

I found Clara waiting for me at the door. "Come on," she said. "Let's go have some fun." She put her tiny hand in mine, leading me up the stairs, past the stalls with curtains for doors, to a bedroom at the far end. The sickly-sweet smell of too much perfume left my stomach roiling. The first thing I did was lock the door. The second was open the grimy back window overlooking the alley below.

I kicked off my boots while she removed the heeled shoes that added another two inches to her height. When I offered her a hand onto the bed, she gave me another dazzling smile. I climbed in next to her . . .

And we both started jumping.

The wooden headboard slammed in time with our bodies, up and down and up and down. Clara held both of her hands over her mouth to stifle her giggles.

"How dare you laugh," I whispered, giving her shoulder a smack. "You should be moaning in ecstasy."

Bouncing higher, Clara gave a high-pitched whimper. "Better?" she mouthed.

I had to bite my lip to keep from chuckling. "Much."

"What about you?" She gave me a dig in the ribs. "Am I not giving you the best ride of your life?"

I grunted and thumped a fist against the wall, sending Clara into another fit of giggles.

Her curls bounced like tiny springs in time with her chest. Toeless feet peeked from the holes at the ends of her stockings.

The madame would keep the bulk of the purse I'd handed over, and I knew Clara would refuse if I offered her more.

"How much longer?" she asked, face flushed. "My legs are getting tired."

I shook away my darkening thoughts. They'd do no one any good. "At least another hour."

She slapped my shoulder. "Get off it, you eejit. No one lasts that long."

"That's what you think."

"That's what I *know*. I've been a whore for over two hundred years."

I laughed. "So have I."

She took both of my hands, looking me in the eye, our jumping and the headboard picking up pace. "Will we give them a big finish?"

"Sure, why not? I've a reputation to uphold."

We both collapsed onto the bed with moans and groans and whimpers and giggles.

"Best ride I've had in years," she laughed, splaying her hands on the mattress, skirts bunched around her thin knees.

I didn't want to think about whether or not these sheets were clean. It felt so damn good to be out of that box.

Clara poked my arm. "I want steak tonight. And apple crumble."

I could barely keep my eyes open. "Let me sleep and you can have whatever you desire."

Clara pulled a pillow over her head, and we both drifted off.

I awoke with a start to a cacophony of banging headboards, low moans, and heavy grunts. Clara snored quietly beside me, the corner of the coverlet pulled over her shoulder. *Dammit.* I'd forgotten to close the feckin' window. I tried not to wake her when I rolled off the mattress, but the blasted thing dipped the moment I stood.

She jerked upright, her short hair slapping her cheeks as she searched the darkness. When her glowing eyes landed on me, she pressed a hand to her heaving chest. "Feckin' hell, Tadhg. You scared the shite out of me."

"Sorry." I closed the window and locked the latch. "It's so feckin' loud in here, isn't it? I don't know how you get any sleep."

The headboard knocked against the wall the moment she leaned against it. "This place isn't meant for sleep."

The slivered moon hanging outside the window sent silver waves across the uneven planked floor. I wasn't sure how long I'd slept, but I felt good. Good enough to make it back to Tearmann. "Steak and apple crumble, right? Anything else?"

She grinned at me from the bed, knees drawn beneath her chin. "Wine. Loads and loads of wine."

Eava was just arriving when I reached the castle kitchens, the old witch wearing the same gray dress she wore every other day. And just like every other day, she wrapped her arms around my ribs and gave me a big squeeze. "There's my boy." Her sugar-dusted hugs had been the best medicine when I was a young lad. Now they felt like coming home.

When she let me go, she propped her fists on her hips and gave me a stern frown. "Ye look like a man on a mission. What'll ye be needing?"

I placed Clara's order and added a tray of shortbread biscuits for later. Between magic and four centuries' worth of practice, Eava had the food ready in no time at all.

"That poor girl," she muttered, adding a final sprinkle of sugar over the top of the pie dish. "Are ye sure there's nothing to be done about her situation?"

I'd tried to help Clara so many times before but always hit the same barriers. After what had happened the day I was cursed, Fiadh had sold the faerie to a human living in Gaul, making her subject to Airren law. And according to Airren law, Clara was no longer a person but an object. An object that could be owned and bought and sold like a pair of feckin' boots. It didn't matter how much money I'd offered; her owners knew the woman was more valuable than coin.

When Clara found out, she'd laid into me like a cat-o-nine tails, giving me some shite about penance and guilt and deserving this fate.

I deserved this fate.

She didn't.

I shook my head, collecting the basket Eava had prepared before adding another bottle of wine. "Unfortunately, not."

Her lips tugged down in a heavy frown. "Best be off with ye, then. Send her my regards, won't ye?"

"I will of course."

When I arrived to the inn later that morning, I found the wasp standing next to the carriage, arms crossed over her chest, gray eyes narrowed at me.

It was amazing what a sober night's sleep could do to restore one's soul. Only two more days of this shite before we reached the portal. I'd given up hope of seducing her. If she didn't hand over the ring when we reached the Forest, Rían could take care of it.

I smiled at the wasp, determined to make today pleasant.

"I see you've been very busy with your *important business*," she said, pointing at my neck where Clara had left a few marks with her rouge this morning.

So much for being feckin' pleasant.

"You think I like—" The question died on my cursed tongue.

I knew what she thought of me. I knew what everyone thought of me. If she thought I liked living this way, then far be it from me to waste my breath on setting her straight. Her opinion of what I was couldn't be any lower than my own.

And I was in too good a mood to deal with her shite today.

Nope.

Not a hope.

I wasn't doing this.

"You know what? This isn't worth it." I turned on my heel and went straight back to the bawdy house. Since it was so early, I braved the entrance on my own, finding the place empty except for a couple rutting in the corner. Technically, I still had another hour with Clara, although if the madame caught me, she'd likely try to extort more money.

When I reached the door, I gave a quick rap with my knuckle.

"H-hello?" a weak voice chimed.

"It's me. I'm back for round seven."

"Tadhg? G-give me a moment to—" A choked sob cut off the explanation.

I threw the door aside, finding my friend curled into a ball in the corner next to a shattered lamp, right eye bruised and swollen, her lips fat and bloody.

"What the hell happened?" I'd only been gone twenty feckin' minutes.

Wincing, Clara scrubbed at the tears staining her cheeks black with kohl. "Th-there was another request. I th-thought it was you b-but it wasn't."

Heat enveloped my chest as I hurried forward, collecting her onto my lap. "What was his name?"

"I don't know."

"What did he look like?"

"He . . . he was a . . . a soldier."

The Airren soldiers infesting this land carried on like they owned the feckin' island and everyone in it. They were untouchable, above the law. "If you saw him again, could you identify him?" I'd comb this town for every single one of them if I had to.

"At this stage, they all look alike."

Feck it anyway. Rían would help. And Ruairi would as well once I told him what had happened. Keelynn and her pointless "quest" could wait.

"I'll be back. I'll get Rían and let him handle it."

Clara stared out the window toward the white and black magpies lining the next building's drainpipes. "What's the point? Even if you kill him, another one will take his place."

She was right. I couldn't be here all the time to fight these battles for her. What could I do? How could I help? In Tearmann, I had power. In Airren, I was only good for two things.

"You could kiss me." I'd offered so many times before, I assumed she'd refuse the way she always did.

Instead, her eyes flew to mine before dropping to my lips. No one could see the hideous thing lurking there, waiting to steal the next life. Not unless they had some sort of enchanted ocular device like my kohl. If they could, no one would dare come within reach.

She dropped the quilt from around her shoulder, turning fully to face me. "Will it hurt?"

"Only for a moment."

More tears welled in her glistening turquoise eyes. "Will ye think me a coward if I do? Yer as cursed as me and ye haven't given up yet."

I'd given up more times than I could count. I'd locked myself away, thrown myself from cliffs, drunk myself into oblivion for centuries.

"Look at me." I held her soft cheeks, cleaning her tears with my thumbs. "You are not a coward. You are the bravest person I know." My position as a prince had given me a reprieve from this curse. I had a home where I could hide. I had Ruairi and Owen and Eava and even Rían. Clara had no one. "Let me help you escape."

Sniffling, she nodded and pressed her lips to mine.

The black curse spread quickly to her heart. Her body seized, and the final sound to leave her blackened lips was a soft sigh. I sat there for far too long, holding my friend. I was the reason she'd been cursed with this fate, and now I was the reason she no longer drew breath. Even knowing it was temporary, that I had set her free, did nothing to dull the stabbing guilt wreaking havoc in my chest.

I called for the madame, telling the woman her "best girl" was dead. She railed at me, threatening to call the authorities.

I shifted a trunk of gold coins from the treasury, then evanesced back to the castle gates with Clara's body.

Pity clouded the eyes of those who'd gathered to trade and collect rations in the courtyard, making the shameful walk from the gates to the room where we kept the bodies feel twice as long. Once I'd settled Clara next to Orla, I drifted to the study to write her name in the ledger I kept of every life I'd taken.

Seven hundred and eighty-five.

Footsteps from the hallway ended at the door. I didn't have to turn to know my brother was there. "You've wasted enough time, Tadgh. You're needed here."

Needed.

Was I needed? It certainly didn't feel like it at the moment. "You're more than capable of ruling in my stead." It wasn't as if he had anything else to do.

I had to get my ring.

I had to rid myself of these curses once and for all.

"It's not my feckin' job."

Not his job? Not his *feckin' job*?

I whirled, finding him scowling next to the books on tax law. "This is *my* castle and *my* kingdom. Unless you wish to live in the Forest or relocate to Airren, I suggest you shut your gob and take care of things until I return."

6

WHEN I REACHED THE CARRIAGE, I DIDN'T HAVE IT IN ME TO return the tight smile Keelynn offered. "Padraig? Bring us to Oakton," I told the driver before climbing into the box and folding my coat beneath me to add a bit of extra padding.

Flask in hand, I didn't feel like pretending to sleep today. I didn't feel like pretending at all. So instead of drinking, I glared across the gap at the hateful woman who'd hired me. "Let me know when you're ready to apologize."

The moment she did, I was going to flat out ask for the ring. What's the worst that could happen? She'd spew hateful words at me? Been there. She'd tell me no? I'd evanesce straight to the castle and tell Rían to do whatever it took to get her to hand it over. I was finished pretending this journey was anything but a colossal waste of time.

Keelynn's mouth dropped open. "Why on earth should I apologize to you?"

Was she serious? "You have been nothing but rude and condescending since the moment we met. I'm helping you, remember?" And I used the term "helping" in the loosest sense of the word.

"Helping me?" Keelynn's pale cheeks looked like they'd been painted with Clara's rouge. Her hands clenched her black skirts.

"You haven't been *helping*. You've been hijacking my carriage and using threats to keep us traveling in the wrong direction!"

I knocked the flask against my knee, anger and rage and hate simmering close to the surface, a volcano about to erupt. "Did it ever occur to you that I have a reason for heading south? *Feckin' hell*," I muttered, praying for patience. "That I know more about my world than an ignorant human?"

"I am not ignorant!"

"You are if you believe that you can best an immortal who has been on this earth for centuries." I launched my flask into my bag and dug my nails into my legs to keep from strangling her. "I try to keep an open mind when it comes to humans, but you're making it exceedingly difficult. First you want to murder an innocent man and then—"

"The Gancanagh is *not* innocent. He's a murderer who seduces maidens and kills them with his poisoned lips."

Wait. Was she *serious*?

I couldn't help but laugh at the ridiculousness. Poisoned lips? What was this? A feckin' storybook?

"Where did you hear that load of bollocks? From your nursemaid? A crier?" I threw a hand toward the novel she'd been reading all week. "One of your *fairy tales*?"

"It's the truth," she insisted, lifting that haughty chin. "Otherwise, I wouldn't be able to say it."

How could anyone with a modicum of intelligence be so incredibly naïve? "Let me explain how a truth curse works. You won't be able to tell an outright lie or break your promises, but if you are *ignorant* and truly believe the myths and lies spouted by bigots, then you can say it without feeling like your skull is being crushed. If Fiadh didn't use dark magic, this, like most curses, will last a year and a day." And if she *had* used dark magic, then Keelynn would be cursed until the day she died or fell in love.

Keelynn's eyes narrowed. I wouldn't put it past her to fly across the carriage to pummel me with her small fists.

While I was at it, I may as well set her straight about myself.

"Now, let me give you a second lesson. The Gancanagh is a shapeshifter. You know what that means, yeah?"

She folded her arms over her heaving chest.

She was angry.

Good.

I was angrier.

"I'll take that as a 'no.' Don't worry. We can circle back."

The lies people spread about me used to be harmless. But these . . . these had obviously been bad enough to spark Keelynn's inner vigilante.

"As I said, the Gancanagh is a shapeshifter who determines his lover's deepest desires and seeks to fulfill them." The quickest way to escape a woman's bed was to give her what she wanted. So I did what so many men seemed unable—or unwilling—to do. I *listened.* To every soft sigh, every whimper, every cry, every word spoken and unspoken to learn exactly what would send her over the edge.

The subtle change in Keelynn's demeanor left my stomach tightening.

The slight hitch in her breathing.

The faint tremble of her lips as her tongue darted between them.

The involuntary shiver.

The darkness inside me began to stir, ready to answer the invitation.

"His lips are *cursed*, not *poisoned*," I explained, "and he doesn't go around kissing women unless they understand the consequences."

And, even knowing it would kill them, women had begged. For escape. For release. For a chance to break my curse. But lust and love didn't live in the same place.

And despite my centuries' worth of experience with women, I'd failed to learn how to move beyond the first to find the second. Fiadh hadn't needed to curse my lips to keep me from finding the one thing that could truly set me free.

That part of me, the part that knew how to love someone more than myself, had always been broken.

"You think you know everything, don't you?" Keelynn ground out, drawing me back to the present.

"I know more than you." So much more about pain and loss and hate than she could ever imagine.

Her steely eyes narrowed as she leaned forward, bracing her hands against her knees. "I *watched* your *innocent* Gancanagh murder my sister."

What? Wait. *What*? Her sister? Which one of my victims had a sister? She must be mistaken. Orla? No, no. Couldn't be her. I'd killed Orla the night I'd met Keelynn. She'd already been set on this foolish quest. There hadn't been anyone else in over a year.

No one else except—

Shit.

I caught her shoulders, needing to see her eyes when she spoke. To feel the vibrations from her words as she told me why the hell she thought I had killed her sister. "Tell me exactly what you saw."

She shoved me away, pressing herself into the cushion at her back. "I'm not telling you a thing."

"If you don't, then I will get out of this carriage and leave you to fend for yourself."

The glow from my ring around her neck flared at my words.

Her eyes widened. Her throat bobbed when she swallowed. It wasn't hate I saw on her pale face. It was fear.

She was terrified of me.

The realization felt like jumping into a cold sea.

She actually believed I would harm her. And why wouldn't she? I'd just grabbed her, hadn't I? And technically, I had planned to lead her to certain death.

"A-at my sister's betrothal ball, I caught Aveen in the garden with a man in a hooded cloak. I-I didn't get a look at his face, but I *saw* him kiss her. And the moment his lips touched hers, she died. Then he just . . . vanished. Leaving her there. I tried," she whispered, scraping at her chest, "I tried to wake her, b-but she was already . . ."

Shit.

Shit.

Aveen.

Her sister was Aveen.

Why the hell hadn't Rían told me his feckin' fiancée had a feckin' sister?

Get off it, you eejit. Of course he wouldn't have told me. I was the Gancanagh. He'd been trying to protect her. Who could blame him? I would've set my sights on Keelynn just to make him miserable.

There was no way he'd be willing to torture his fiancée's sister or let her anywhere near the Black Forest. And from the fear and disgust on her face, there was no hope I'd convince her to share my bed.

The ring—the *feckin' ring*—was right there, within my grasp, and I couldn't do a feckin' thing about it. Having tasted hope, seen it with my own eyes, only to have it ripped away was the worst torture I'd ever endured.

I took out my frustration on the trunk, wrestling with the urge to close my eyes and send myself straight to Rían so I could end him.

Dammit.

I had to keep myself under control because the more I let the darkness take over, the harder it was to get it back under wraps, and if I didn't kill someone—

I glanced at Keelynn.

—then I was going to do something I definitely shouldn't do.

Inhale-Exhale-Inhale-Exhale.

This was Rían's mess. He could clean it up. He could meet with Keelynn and explain that it had been his idea for Aveen to kiss me. Then she'd get this ridiculous notion of wanting to murder me out of her head and be so relieved that she'd hand the thing over.

"I'm sorry." None of this was her fault. She wasn't a mad vigilante, she was an innocent woman trying to avenge her sister. "When I get angry, it's hard for me to—"

A white porcelain sign up ahead stole my attention.

Three miles to Buraos? We weren't going to Buraos. We were going to Oakton.

My hand smacked against the cold pane of glass as I leaned forward to read the names again. "This isn't the right road."

"There's been a change of plans," Keelynn said, voice steady and chin high. "We're traveling to Buraos."

I distinctly remembered telling Padraig to go to Oakton. "We cannot stay in Buraos."

"We *will* stay in Bruaos."

Shit.

I needed a feckin' drink. I jerked open the lid to my flask, shifted something a helluva lot stronger than water, and drank until my eyes watered and stomach lurched. The last time I had been to Buraos, I'd ended up at the wrong end of a hangman's noose along with five other Danú. My neck hadn't snapped. I'd dangled there, slowly suffocating, watching the humans in the crowd laugh and jeer until death's unforgiving grip dragged me into darkness.

Never again.

My fingers twitched, and I could feel my magic growing stronger, forcing its way to the surface. "We're not staying in Buraos."

Keelynn smirked. "You. Don't. Have. A. Choice."

No choice?

No feckin' choice?

I may not have control over what I looked like. I may not have control over who I slept with. But as long as I remained free of iron chains, I had control over where I went.

And if this hateful woman thought I was going to set foot in a town bursting with mercenaries and soldiers, then she was about to be *very* disappointed.

I focused on the noise of the wheels bumping over the muddy terrain. All it took was a surge of magic and a flick of my wrist to send the left front wheel to my stables back home.

The lurching carriage slammed me into the wall.

Sent Keelynn flying onto my lap.

And set my body alight with inexplicable heat.

Criers and fanatics sometimes bathed in witch hazel to ward off the effects of a witch's magic. It didn't work, but if one of them touched you, it'd burn like hell. If Keelynn had bathed in witch hazel, I would've smelled it.

The woman only smelled of lavender and loathing.

The surge of desire when I felt her supple body squirmed against me was nothing compared to the tugging cord—

No. Not a cord.

A wrenching iron chain squeezing my chest until I couldn't breathe.

"Let go!" she squealed.

And she was gone. Pushing back to the bench and giving me a look so full of heated confusion, I was certain it mirrored my own.

How could I want *her* of all people? A human who despised everything about me. A woman so full of fear and hate that it oozed from her pores. It was my curse. It must be. There was no other explanation.

"*You're* the one who climbed on top of *me*."

With her cloak askew, I could see her chest rising and falling.

Breathless. Cheeks flushed. Tongue darting out to wet her lips. Even black from the curse, her lips were feckin' perfection. How had I not noticed? I'd been with her for days and never realized how full and plump they were when not pressed tightly in disapproval.

"Like I would ever want to be near something like you on purpose," she hissed, shoving her fallen hair from her forehead and ripping her book from where it had dropped.

Not someone.

Some*thing*.

That's what I was to her. A monster. A creature. A *thing* to be feared and despised.

The acid from her hatred left the air tasting bitter and cold.

"Lady Keelynn?" Padraig shouted from outside. "Could ye come out fer a moment? I need a word with ye in private."

Keelynn threw open the carriage door.

Padraig mumbled something about the wheel being gone. I could hear their footsteps sinking into the mud. This was a lost cause. Another way for Fiadh to torture me. Hope was nothing more than another feckin' curse.

I collected my things, jumped from the carriage, and started down the road.

Walking. Such a pleasure. Why did people insist on riding everywhere when most of them had two perfectly good legs?

Moisture thickened the air. Mud slipped beneath my boots. Birds chirped an evening song. The breeze ruffled through my hair.

"Where do you think you're going?" Keelynn called.

Surely she knew the answer to that already. "Away from you." Far and fast.

"But we need your help. We're missing a wheel."

The irritation in her clipped tone left me smiling. "I know."

The wasp caught up to me before I reached a bend in the road, digging her nails into my arm when she grabbed me. "You did this, didn't you?"

The way my skin burned beneath her death grip left a memory prickling in the dark recesses of my mind. A memory that vanished the moment Keelynn stumbled back, scrubbing her hand down her skirts.

"Careful, now. That's an awfully serious accusation." I tried not to smile, but she looked so irritated, and it had been such a shite day that I had to revel in her fury. "Well, Maiden Death, it appears I had a choice after all."

Walking away from the righteous indignation on her face had

to be one of the most satisfying experiences of my never-ending life.

"Stop! Don't leave us. Please don't go."

I wasn't a hero.

I wasn't going to stop.

I was going to keep walking.

Keelynn wasn't my problem anymore. She was Rían's.

Except . . .

She sounded genuinely frightened.

Of what? Trees and hedges and puddles? I was the most dangerous thing on this feckin' road.

For some reason, my steps slowed, and I found myself turning. Instead of stopping at Keelynn, I went straight for Padraig. The old man shrank back, nearly colliding with the horses. "Do you know who I am?" I asked, keeping my voice low so the wasp couldn't overhear.

A nod.

"And you haven't told your mistress. Why?"

Padraig's pale eyes flicked to where Keelynn waited, clutching her chest. "Ask yer brother."

I didn't need to ask my brother. Rían didn't leave loose ends. If Padraig had somehow learned he was involved with Aveen, Rían would've made it impossible to incriminate him—and me by association.

At least my secret was safe for now.

Too stubborn to bring back the wheel lest the wasp think I'd given in just because she'd given out, I flicked my wrist, shifting the dinner Eava had cooked for me.

"Listen carefully," I said, digging into my overcoat pocket, "I've left food and drink for you inside the carriage. Have as much as you want. And when you're finished, come out and reattach the wheel." I pressed Rían's cufflink into his palm in case any humans came by looking for trouble. Hopefully, the gold would be enough to keep them from harming the old man.

Padraig's jaw worked beneath the thin layer of white whiskers. "I want yer word that ye will see my lady safely to the village."

"You have it."

Tucking the cufflink into his pocket, he shouted down the road to his mistress, "Go ahead with master Tadhg. He promised the wheel will return soon."

I went back to where Keelynn waited beside a wide puddle, darkness closing in on her, and told her to keep up.

7

"There's an inn just there." I pointed to the sign for the Eanlann House Inn. The place was small but had been clean the last time I'd been here. Granted, that had been about twenty years ago. But it still looked the same, and as far as I knew, it was still owned by the Fyfe family.

Keelynn glanced at the inn, then back to me. "You must bring me to the door."

I reminded myself this was the last time I would be seeing her. I could smile past my irritation for a few more minutes. "*Must I*?"

"I would appreciate it if you accompanied me the rest of the way," she amended, her smile as false as her feigned manners.

"What's this?" I gasped, clutching my chest. "Are you asking me to be near you *on purpose*?"

Despite the dim light from the street lanterns, I could see a blush painting her cheeks.

Keelynn kicked a loose stone with the toe of her boot, probably wishing it were my head. "I shouldn't have said that to you. It was awful, and I'm sorry."

Hold on. She was *sorry*? Was that what she'd just said?

The apology seemed genuine enough. I supposed I owed it to

my brother's fiancée's sister to make sure she didn't get murdered on an empty street. Plus, I had promised Padraig.

"It's thirty bloody paces," I muttered. When we reached the red door, I bowed low and asked if she required any additional assistance, throwing in, "I'm remarkably good at unlacing stays," just to irritate her.

The indignant glare was to be expected. Then something in her expression changed as her gaze dropped to my hands. Her breathing caught. Her eyes fluttered closed.

The cord between us tightened. The shadow of my curse stirred to life, writhing beneath my skin, waiting for the invitation.

"*Stop*." Keelynn gasped, pressing a hand to her chest.

"Stop what?" I hadn't said a feckin' word.

"N-nothing." She backed toward the door and slipped inside.

The wasp must be off her nut.

I tried to evanesce back to the castle but couldn't dredge up enough magic. Right so. If I couldn't go home, I'd have to find someplace else to stay.

After I got a drink.

I meandered down the street to the first pub I came across. The place was empty except for two men sitting together at one of the low tables and a bartender reading behind the taps. The moment their eyes lifted to mine, their hands fell to their daggers.

The bartender told me to get the hell out.

Apparently, we weren't far enough west for me to drink alongside the humans.

Back outside, a black cat licked its paw beneath one of the wall lanterns. Instead of running away, it sauntered toward me, rubbing itself against my boot. *Must be a female then*, I thought with a laugh, giving her chin a scratch.

When I reached the green-door pub at the back, I nodded to two pooka drinking hot ale by the entrance as I made my way toward the bar. A barmaid with dark curls poured a pint of stout for a human leering at her chest. The low-cut dress she wore left little to the imagination.

A pity, really. I had a very vivid imagination.

When she saw me, her pouty pink lips lifted into a smile. She abandoned the tap to ask me what I was drinking—much to the chagrin of now-scowling human. It wasn't unheard of for humans to venture over to our side of the wall. Unlike them, we didn't care who came in as long as they didn't cause trouble.

And they were always good for a bit of amusement.

The stronger the drink the better. Anything to rid my mind of today's revelations. "Puítin, please."

With swaying hips, the woman retrieved a clay jug at the back of the bar. I paid her for the drink, fighting the tug in my core as I turned away. If I lingered, I knew how tonight would end. Wouldn't be the worst of fates. At least it'd rid my body of the week's worth of tension.

The leprechaun smoking next to the open fire gave me a wave. He looked vaguely familiar. Was his name John or Johnny or James or Jimmy? Something with a "J" anyway. I returned the wave, continuing to an empty table beside a man in a garish gold cloak clutching a crystal glass.

My sore arse ached the moment it landed on the wooden stool. When the puítin hit my throat, I forgot all about that pain and focused on the burn spreading to my chest. The second gulp left the room hazy and dull. The third turned the conversations and laughter around me into muffled murmurs, helping me focus on the only thing I wanted.

My ring.

It always came back to the ring. I could still beg Rían for help. He could try and reason with the wasp, explain as best he could what had happened that night. Would she believe him though? Doubtful. That woman had made her mind up about the Danú before we met. She hated us. Hated me.

I shouldn't have said that to you. It was awful, and I'm sorry.

She may hate me, but tonight she'd apologized. And appeared genuinely remorseful.

How long had we been traveling together? Three days? Four?

I couldn't rightly remember. She wouldn't have apologized to me on day one. Not a hope. Maybe I was starting to get to her. What if I gave it a little bit longer? Then I wouldn't have to get my brother involved.

I lifted my glass.

Fire, fire, drink it down . . .

I could try to work around my promise to keep the events of that night a secret and tell her the truth.

Right. The truth.

That woman wouldn't believe a word out of my cursed mouth. And with my promise complicating things, it'd be tricky to navigate. If I had on the ring, I could explain everything.

Maybe if she knew I couldn't lie either, she'd soften even more.

All I had to do was convince her to let me "borrow" it. And if that didn't work, I could bring her to my castle and show her Aveen. There'd be no denying it then.

I'd need permission from the Queen to cross the Black Forest twice, with assurance that she would forego the tax or accept my life in return. Once to arrive and once to leave. Couldn't hurt to ask. Rían wouldn't like it one bit though.

I should've known this mess was my brother's fault.

Why did he have to know? He hadn't told me about Keelynn, so I didn't feel obliged to tell him either.

Keelynn.

That woman just . . .

I guzzled what was left in my glass.

The barmaid watched from behind the taps, rubbing her fingers across her lips. She didn't look like a wasp. She looked soft and malleable. And the coy smile she aimed at me tugged those invisible threads.

What was left of my magic twisted across the floor, writhing shadows brushing against her ankles like the cat in the alley. Her brown eyes widened, searching around her legs. When she looked back at me with her delicately arched eyebrows raised, I spun my finger slowly, working the feeling beneath her skirts to her knees.

Then I stopped.

My father had been a lousy philandering cad, but he had taught me three valuable lessons that I had actually taken onboard before the whole Fiadh incident:

1. *Always ask permission.*
2. *If a woman tells you to stop, you stop.*
3. *If she tells you to keep going, then for the love of all that is holy, you had better keep going. Don't change a feckin' thing. Keep going.*

The barmaid bit her plump bottom lip, her teeth white against pink flesh. A blush crept along her neck, blooming on her cheeks. I saluted her with my empty glass.

A moment later, she sauntered around the bar, a full glass of puítin in her hand. Stopping between my knees, she bent low to set the drink down, giving me a grand view of what she hid beneath her dress. "Is there anything else ye want?" she purred.

A slow smile spread across my face. "Depends on what you're offering." Candlelight played with the red tones in her hair. Did Keelynn's hair have any red in it? I blinked away the unwelcome thought, focusing on the heavy rise and fall of this woman's chest.

The moment she plopped onto my lap, I had my answer.

"Are ye lost, milady?"

I couldn't be sure, but I thought the question came from one of the pooka. Not that it mattered. I was busy.

"No. I'm here for . . . I'm here for someone."

Hold on. I knew that husky voice. I lifted my head from the glorious expanse of Nuala's breasts to find the owner of the husky voice glaring at me . . . or maybe she was glaring at Nuala. Hard to tell in this light.

"*Keelynn*!" Damn she was pretty. Had she always been that pretty? Must be the drink. Everyone was prettier with drink. What was she doing here? This wasn't the right side of the wall. She didn't belong in a place like this. My hand waved at her. Wasn't sure why. Feckin' drunk hands doing things without my permission. We were supposed to swat wasps away, not call them toward us.

"It seems as if ye have a . . . little problem, milord," Nuala whispered in my ear, grinding her arse against my arousal.

"It's a little problem, is it?"

"I meant a *big* problem. A *very* big problem," she giggled.

A throat cleared behind me.

Nuala's nails dug into my shoulder. The response vanished off my tongue as I peered up at Keelynn's gray eyes.

"Have you come to join me for a drink?" I taunted the wasp, knowing full well the person she'd come to meet wasn't me. She was probably looking for Padraig.

The pooka who had greeted Keelynn waited at the bar, watching us through glowing yellow eyes. Nuala pushed to her feet, giving me a hard glare before going back to work.

What did I do? It wasn't my fault she had a job.

Speaking of jobs . . . my glass was almost as empty as the other . . . *three*? That couldn't be right. I'd only drank two. Hadn't I?

My assassin sat down and started fiddling with her black skirts. Which made me want to fiddle with her skirts. I had to adjust myself to keep from making my desire too feckin' obvious. It wasn't for her anyway. It was for the scowling barmaid.

"I've come to offer you a room," she said with a frown.

My curse stirred—the tug faint, easily severed. "Changed your mind about the laces then?"

Her eyes narrowed. "Don't be ridiculous. You're *not* unlacing my stay."

The tug grew stronger. Tighter. *Ohhhh*. The wasp was attracted to me and she *hated* it. Which only made me want to tease her more. "You just missed me then? Is that why you sought me out?"

"I sought you out to give you this." She reached into her cloak and slid whatever was in her hand across the drink-splattered table. Rían's cufflink. "You helped Padraig. In return, I would like to offer you proper lodgings."

"I'm perfectly capable of acquiring *proper lodgings* without your assistance." If I played my cards right, the barmaid would be helping me with my "problem" in her apartment upstairs as soon as she finished her shift. "Go back to your room before the *scary creatures* get you."

Nuala laughed.

Keelynn's eyes darkened. "Are you staying with her?"

"Does it matter?" As long as I showed tomorrow, she shouldn't care what I did with my free time.

"If you want to debase yourself, be my guest. But if you'd like a clean, comfortable room at the inn, it's yours."

Something behind me broke. A bottle? A window? Damn, I was drunk.

She couldn't be saying what I thought she was saying. I must be missing something.

I gulped from my glass, rolling her words around in my mind. "You want *me* . . . to come with *you* . . . to *your* inn?" That's what she'd said, right? Surely, she knew the implications of such an offer. With our ability to evanesce whenever we pleased—at least those of us who weren't cursed—the Danú didn't need inns. We stayed in them, sure.

But not to sleep.

Her head tilted slightly; her eyes roved from my hair to my waistcoat. For the first time since we had met, I was sorry I hadn't worn something a bit more respectable. Not that it would have made a difference.

"It's the least I can do after you helped Padraig."

"The least you can do . . ." I repeated.

Finally.

Finally.

Something was going my feckin' way. I wouldn't need to speak to the Queen and I wouldn't have to spend another day in that damned box. I'd convince her. I would. And I'd enjoy myself doing it.

"Well?" she snapped.

"How can I resist such a magnanimous offer from a generous human such as yourself?" Oh, I was going to enjoy this. What sort of stay kept her so rigid? What color would it be? Probably black, like her gowns. And she was probably the type of woman who liked everything to match. Black knickers. And black stockings as well. I'd take my time slipping her out of those. Or maybe she could leave them on. I shouldn't be as excited about this as I was. Definitely the drink.

Keelynn's nose wrinkled as she gestured toward my clothes. "Wash the kohl from your eyes and fix *this* so we can be on our way."

I flipped the cufflink, caught it in my waistcoat pocket, and told her to wait for me outside so I could pay and make myself appear respectable.

Ha. Me. Respectable. What a feckin' joke.

Nuala hurried from behind the bar, hips swaying in time with her wide skirts. "Come with me," she rushed, twisting toward a door at the back of the pub.

I didn't want to come with her anymore. I wanted to come with Keelynn.

Unfortunately, my cursed feet followed of their own volition.

The door closed, enveloping me in darkness. Hands tore at my belt. Unfastened my breeches. Slipped down to my groin. I groaned when Nuala's cold fingers clasped around me.

This was the hardest part. Reminding myself that this was a curse when it felt so feckin' good. When the moments stolen in darkness allowed me to forget what happened when daylight returned.

I caught her skirts, dragging them up to her waist.

Nuala's grip tightened as her warm, wet tongue traced the column of my throat. Her teeth grazed my jaw, but I turned my head away.

"Aren't ye going to kiss me?" she whispered.

My hand stilled on the waistband of her undergarments. "You don't want me to do that."

"I want to feel that pretty mouth of yers on mine."

"If you kiss me, you'll—"

Something brushed my lips. A choked whimper echoed in my ears, and the barmaid with the clever hands fell into a heap at my feet.

"*Die*," I snarled, slamming my fist into the feckin' wall.

I stuffed my aching flesh back into my breeches, fumbling with the buttons and belt. That woman hadn't deserved this. I should've been quicker to explain. Should've told her to turn around like I usually did so kissing me wasn't a feckin' option.

The moment I opened the closet door, the low conversations in the pub went silent. The two pooka slowly rose from their seats. The leprechaun set his pipe aside.

Pity filled their wide eyes. A look I'd come to know all too well.

"I . . . ah . . ." Raking a trembling hand through my hair, I glanced back toward the closet. "Would any of you be willing to bring her to the castle for me?" Shame heated my neck when all three men nodded. Whether they knew of my curse or not, I'd learned my people would stand by me no matter how many lives I took.

As long as those lives belonged to humans.

I shifted a purse of coins for each, waiting until all of them were gone before lifting my bag from the floor and withdrawing a clean shirt to exchange for the one that reeked of drink and perfume. Using the dirty garment, I scrubbed what remained of the kohl from my eyes. In my bag, I found a new cravat and tried to tie the damn thing, but it strangled me, so I loosened it and thought *to hell with it*. Good enough.

Collecting my coat from the stool, I made my way toward the door, hoping I didn't kill anyone else tonight.

8

The inn stunk of boiled cabbage and vinegar. Although the reception room had been painted a muted yellow instead of the green I remembered, it still had the same hideous set of dusty antlers mounted over the fireplace from two decades before.

"I'd like to purchase an additional room for the night," Keelynn told a woman filing her nails behind the desk. The mousy hair tied back from her face looked dry as straw.

"Fer yer friend 'ere?" The woman smiled at me, highlighting the wrinkles at the corners of her eyes and mouth.

I managed to smile back.

It could have been the drink, but I thought Keelynn stepped closer to me. "Yes, please."

"Sure, ye dinna have to stand on pretense with me, milady." The woman tapped her file against the desk. "I'll turn a blind eye fer three coppers."

"There is no pretense," Keelynn insisted. "I need a second room."

It seemed silly to waste her coin on a second room just to save face. Still, it wasn't my money, so I kept my mouth shut.

The woman looked between us, brow furrowed. "Yer really not stayin' together?"

"Absolutely not." Keelynn shuddered, as if the idea of spending the night with me repulsed her.

I'd leave her shuddering for an entirely different reason—

Hold on. With the truth curse she couldn't lie. Which meant she actually thought I needed a room. Which meant I wouldn't have the chance to convince her to let me have the ring.

"Then save yer coins. I've a cold bed he can warm if yer not usin' him." The woman dragged a nail along my forearm and raised her eyebrows. The tug around my midsection grew unbearable.

I didn't want to sleep in this smelly inn. And I sure as hell didn't want to sleep with that woman. Why hadn't I controlled my temper, conserved my magic, and evanesced home? If I told Keelynn not to bother with the room, whatever smidgeon of goodwill she may feel toward me would surely evaporate

"Don't touch him," Keelynn hissed. Her shaky hand flew to her mouth. Her eyes bulged.

Where the hell had that come from? She avoided looking at me, withdrawing her purse and telling the woman once again that I was to have my own room.

"Not a bit fun, is she?" the woman grumbled, accepting the coins.

"Not a bit," I said with a wink because apparently my curse thought I should flirt with the old bat.

The wasp brought me to a room with the number six painted on the door. I shouldn't have noticed how lovely her hair smelled, but I did. *Dammit.* She smelled lovely, and in the candlelight her dark waves looked so glossy and—

She started talking about my room, but all I could think about was wrapping that hair around my fist, drawing her head back, tasting the skin she hid beneath that high black collar.

Keelynn twisted, colliding with my chest.

Her heat. Her indignation. Her *scent.* Feck it anyway. I owed it to myself to at least try and convince her to stay with me, right?

"That's the second time you've tried to climb on top of me today."

She backed up a step, ramming into the wall. Her tongue nipped out, wetting her lips, even more perfect when I couldn't see the black.

My magic slipped free. Stalking. Waiting.

"Keelynn?"

Her gaze landed my mouth. The most dangerous part of me.

"Unless you need me to warm *your* cold bed . . ."

Say yes say yes say yes.

Her subtle lavender scent shouldn't be overwhelming, but it was and—She wasn't saying yes. *Dammit, wasp. Say yes.* She needed to forget she hated me for one feckin' night and give in.

She wasn't giving in. Sure, why would she? Hadn't she just watched me and Nuala go off together? I hadn't a hope of convincing her to stay with me tonight.

"I'm going to need . . . my key," I finished with a sigh.

She shoved the key at me and bolted for her own room, leaving me with a half-hard cock and a whole lot of disappointment.

The feckin' key didn't fit into the feckin' lock no matter how I jiggled it. I shoved it into my pocket and flicked my wrist. The door creaked open, and I had just reached the bed when I heard a faint knock. My heart clattered against my ribcage. I stumbled back to the door.

The woman from downstairs ducked beneath my arm and into the room. "Is yer bed cold?"

Shit. My brain wanted to tell her to get the hell out. My cursed mouth said, "I haven't checked."

Her shawl fell onto the footboard as she freed the leather strap holding her silver-streaked brown hair. "Will I check for ye?"

I didn't want to say yes. I was drunk and wrecked and not even moderately attracted to the woman.

My curse made it impossible to say no.

The ceiling above the bed had a crack in the plaster that I'd been staring at for the last hour. It ran from the corner all the way to the decorative medallion that marked the center of the room.

It didn't appear structural, so there was no fear of the ceiling collapsing. But it was unsightly and shouldn't have been there.

The woman next to me shifted in her sleep, mumbling something about payment. I hadn't asked her name, and she hadn't asked mine. When you couldn't choose what to do with your body, you stopped caring what anyone else did to you. And something inside you broke. It wasn't invisible. People could see it. But only if they looked in the right direction.

Like that damn crack in the ceiling.

The light coming through the gap in the heavy black drapes was still gray, so I figured I had a few hours before we had to leave.

I needed a feckin' bath.

When I went to roll off the bed, the mattress creaked. The woman shot upright, searching the murky darkness. Her eyes landed on me, and her thin lips quirked into a smile. "Where do ye think yer going?"

I collected my shirt and breeches from the dipped floorboards. "Away."

She caught my elbow, nails digging into my skin. "Don't leave. Not yet."

I glared down at those nails, short and stubby, set in hands with protruding veins. "Let me go." My head was feckin' throbbing.

Those nails sank deeper into my flesh. "I'll scream."

She thought I cared if she screamed? She could scream until her face turned blue, and I wouldn't give a shite.

Only if she screamed, and I couldn't evanesce, I'd probably end up getting myself killed. It'd take ages for me to return, and

I'd be late meeting Keelynn, erasing any headway I'd made yesterday.

"I'll tell you once more to stop touching me."

She sucked in a deep breath. Before the scream could break free, I pressed my mouth to hers.

Her body slumped onto the mattress, blackness spreading from her mouth to her bare chest. I'd have to get Rían to bring her to the castle. Although part of me wanted to leave her there, let her be buried in a pine box and wake up in a year and a day trapped until the air in the coffin ran out. It was only fair. That's what she'd tried to do to me.

Trap me.

I hated this feckin' country.

I managed to shift a bath, a bar of soap, and some water, but didn't have it in me to heat the feckin' thing. Sinking beneath the icy surface, I welcomed the blessed silence and tried to figure out how the hell I was supposed to convince a woman who hated me to help set me free.

I needed to get out of this shite mood. Pretend everything was all right. Try to build on the goodwill from yesterday.

Yesterday.

When Keelynn had apologized.

When she'd sought me out, braving a green-door pub.

When she'd bought me a room.

Maybe there was hope for me after all.

The moment I resurfaced, my eyes landed on the body.

Or maybe there wasn't.

9

THE REVELRY IN THE STREETS NEARLY BLEW THE HEAD OFF ME AS I crossed the stable to lean against one of the few walls without a shelf or tack or some other horsey shite dangling from it. The stable boys had run out the back door the moment I'd arrived, probably convinced I was going to eat their souls. Didn't people get tired of jumping to conclusions?

That was the problem with humans. By the time they could think for themselves, they were so entrenched in their views that changing their minds about us seemed like betraying their own kind.

Made no sense to me.

I changed my mind all the time.

Take Keelynn, for instance. A few days ago, I would've let her drown in the lake. And yet today, I hadn't hesitated to jump into the depths and drag her to shore.

Well, maybe I had hesitated a little. But the water had been feckin' freezing.

Seeing the wasp's soaked shift sticking to her like a second skin had almost been worth it. Until Padraig had threatened to stab me with the one feckin' weapon in this world that could actually kill me. All this time, I had assumed the woman was on a revenge mission. After seeing that dagger, I realized this wasn't about revenge. It was about resurrection.

I was lucky Padraig hadn't nicked me by accident with the feckin' thing.

The gray horse Padraig combed looked as though he'd rather eat me than the oats in front of him. Foul beast.

Padraig set the coarse brush aside. "What did ye say to him?" he asked reluctantly.

"I told him to check for himself if he didn't believe me."

Padraig's jaw dropped. "Ye didn't."

"Sure, why wouldn't I?"

Padraig gripped the edge of the horse trough, clutching his stomach, wheezing so hard, I thought he'd keel over there and then.

Something scraped from the entrance to the stables. I pretended not to see Keelynn passing by one of the empty horse stalls.

She'd changed. And put on a new black dress.

I shouldn't have noticed the way it nipped in, accentuating her waist or the way the lace at the front puckered over her breasts. Breasts I'd gotten a decent view of at the lake.

Breasts I wouldn't mind seeing again.

"What's so funny?" asked the wasp, pushing dark hair out of her eyes. Eyes that only a few hours ago had been red and panicked and searching.

"Nothing, milady," Padraig rushed. The only sign he'd been laughing was the strain in his voice.

Keelynn's eyes found mine.

And she smiled.

Not one of the pained winces or strained-lipped looks she'd given me on a daily basis. A full-blown, face-lighting smile that cast away the shadows and made a man believe in things like happiness and vows.

Behind her, Padraig shook his head, his eyes bulging.

What he didn't realize was that if the woman kept smiling at me like that, I'd tell her anything she wanted to know. "All I said was that the horse and I both have impressive—"

Padraig's hand shot out, catching her elbow. "I'm afraid master Tadhg's humor is not suited to a high-born lady's ears."

Still her smile remained.

And her eyebrows arched in a silent challenge.

A challenge I was more than happy to accept.

I pointed directly to the hulking black stallion's undercarriage, then held my hands in front of me.

Her face turned red and she—

Wait.

Did she glance at my breeches?

They got a little tighter as my body responded.

Time to issue a challenge of my own. "The stall at the end's empty if you'd like a closer look," I drawled.

With her cheeks so flushed, the last thing I expected her to say was, "Doesn't seem impressive enough to warrant my attention."

"*Milady*!" Padraig's flat cap slipped when he shook his head, his brow lined with disapproval.

I'd bend her over the haybales in the corner and show her something impressive. "You'd be surprised."

"Master Tadhg!" Padraig's limp miraculously disappeared when he stomped forward, catching me by the collar, forcing me to look at him. "Ye will remember to whom ye are speaking and stop this sort of talk immediately."

Keelynn watched me, a sparkle in those steely eyes and the slightest lift to her plump lips. I couldn't help but wink at her. That invisible thread around my middle drew taut. If she wanted to continue this conversation tonight, tomorrow, in the middle of the village square, I'd be more than willing to oblige. All she had to do was say the word.

Padraig, the old bastard, started yammering about lodgings and food, drawing her attention away from me and back to him. The warmth spreading in my chest went cold.

Don't look at him.

Look at me.

Finally, she did, and it was like watching the sun rise. All warmth and light and beauty. "Are you hungry, Tadhg?" she asked.

"Ravenous."

"What would you like to eat?"

Padraig shot me a glare that probably should've worried me since he could borrow that cursed blade any minute. "Funny you should ask—"

"Master Tadhg told me he wanted soup," Padraig blurted.

Keelynn's brows pulled together. My fingers itched to smooth the small crease between them. "Soup?"

I patted my stomach. "Warm and wet. What's not to love?"

I thought poor Padraig would have apoplexy.

Her slim shoulders lifted in a shrug. "All right . . . soup it is."

Each pub we tried was packed to the gills, overflowing with drunks and merrymakers, and one opportunistic pickpocket making the most of the festivities. I knew where we could go but wasn't sure Keelynn would approve. Thanks to my heroics this afternoon, she may have warmed to me, but that didn't mean she'd feel comfortable in one of the few Danú establishments in town.

After hearing Padraig grumbling about being turned away from yet another pub, I couldn't take it anymore. "I know a place that shouldn't be crowded at this hour." If Keelynn didn't want to go, then she could starve waiting in line with the rest of the humans.

Keelynn's hand fell to her stomach, her face and lips pale. "Is it far?"

"Not very. Come on." I didn't mean to brush against her when I passed. A simple accident caused by a puddle, a few loose stones, and a man stumbling from the pub next to us. The moment my arm grazed hers, it was like someone had splashed me with hot ash.

I skirted away as quickly as I could, but not before receiving another glare from Padraig. It had to be witch hazel, right? There was no other explanation for the way she made me burn.

Maeve's bar, located at the back of an alley behind the apothecary, hadn't changed in fifty years. Benches and trestle tables, three taps behind the bar, and a whitewashed fireplace with a fire that needed no fuel but never went out.

Padraig sat his glass aside to offer Maeve a crooked smile, leaving the owner blushing like a maiden. "Why don't ye give yer pegs a break and have a seat beside me?" he suggested, tapping the cards in his breast pocket. "We can play a game of quadrille."

A game of quadrille. Was that what they were calling it these days? I hid my smile in my pint.

"We close in an hour," she told him. "If yer still here, I'll play with ye." Maeve flicked her tea towel over her shoulder, then went about removing the empty glasses between us.

And the old man had given me shite about flirting with Keelynn.

"Did you know my first love was a faerie?" he said after a deep drink of his fresh pint, wiping white foam from his whiskers with his shirtsleeve.

Keelynn turned toward him and frowned.

I knew most of the faeries on this island, but the old man must have been at least four times my age. "What was her name?"

"She was called Binne." The tapping of Padraig's pipe punctuated his words.

Ah, Binne.

Beautiful.

Wicked sense of humor.

Helluva voice.

I hadn't seen her in almost a century. Last I heard, she'd given up her wings for some lad who lived up near Longshadow. "Melodious Binne."

"Voice of an angel." Padraig sighed. "Legs for days."

He had that right. Those legs were long enough to wrap around a man twice. I'd checked. On multiple occasions.

Keelynn slammed her glass onto the table, rattling my own. "Aren't faeries really small?"

"Not always." This was where the stories got things wrong. Faeries could become human-sized one day a season. Or, if they gave up their wings, they could stay human-sized forever. But that would mean giving up almost all of their power. There were a few who had done just that. Rían kept a record of them in one of his many ledgers. Most had given them up for silly things, like love. Some, like Clara, had their wings stolen from them. Thinking of Clara made me sad, so I squashed that right down, smiled at Keelynn, and added, "I'm half-fae and no one's ever called me small."

"I'm sure other faeries find you quite adequate."

I'd show her feckin' adequate.

Padraig lost his drink all over the table. "*Milady*!"

This night kept getting better and better. "Oh, I like drunk Keelynn." How many pints had she sipped? One? Two? Her eyes weren't glazed or glassy, yet the steely shield she usually held in place seemed to have slipped.

Padraig launched from his seat, grabbing my arm. "Whatever's in yer head, boy, get it out. She's had it hard enough since that wretch—"

The blush from Keelynn's cheeks evaporated when she clutched his hand. "Thank you, Padraig."

Wretch? What wretch? When I looked to Keelynn for an explanation, she started playing with the foam on top of her pint. It must've been bad to have stolen the smile from her lips.

"You'll hear no argument here," I said. "Any man with eyes in his head can see she's far too good for me." Almost every woman was far too good for someone like me. That didn't stop them from sinking to my level.

Padraig gave Keelynn a warm smile and a soft pat on the back of her hand. "If ye would excuse me, milady." Pushing away from the table, the old man stumbled toward the privy.

Finally.

Finally.

Alone.

Well, not alone, alone. The merrow and the pooka shot glances our way every so often. And Maeve was doing the washing up behind the taps. But at least Padraig had gone. Padraig with his interruptions and glares and judgement.

Some of Keelynn's hair had fallen from its pins. She brushed it behind her ear, sighing wistfully toward where her coachman had disappeared. Without my kohl, I could almost convince myself I was just a man and she was just a woman.

Sitting together in a pub.

Having a drink and a laugh.

If I were a human, would she be interested in me? She had been married, so she was no longer a maiden. Did she miss her husband warming her bed? Had she liked the way he had touched her? Had she liked—

"Why are you looking at me like that?" she asked.

So many reasons. None I should have said aloud. "You've confounded me." I shouldn't want to bed such a hateful wasp when there were plenty of women who would welcome me—including the merrow tugging on that invisible string.

Yet, here we sat.

"Don't do that with your mouth," she grumbled, snagging her pint and taking a deep sip. A drop of condensation from the glass fell onto her chest.

This ought to be good.

Leaning across the table, I asked what I shouldn't do with my mouth because at the moment, my mouth wanted to lick off the foam clinging to the bow of her upper lip.

"When you get annoyed, you do this," she explained.

Was she trying to frown or smirk or grimace? Whatever it was, I was fairly certain I had never made that face in my life. She started giggling. *Giggling.* And the sound was like a thousand chiming bells. Eventually, the giggling ceased, and she frowned again.

She reached across the table. "And it's a shame because you have a lovely mouth." Her fingertips may have been brushing my lips, but I felt the effects farther south.

"No, you have a lovely mouth," I whispered. The color of a blush rose. Plump and soft and made for kissing. "Whereas I have a wicked mouth that does terribly wicked things."

The cord between us dragged so tight, my ribs dug into the edge of the table.

Her tongue nipped out, catching my thumb for the briefest of seconds, lighting me ablaze. I'd been bedded by some of the most beautiful women on this island and yet with one miniscule swipe of this infuriating woman's tongue, I was full sure I'd melt.

Her pupils blew out. "Like what?"

Feck this.

We were leaving.

I shifted coins, slammed them on the table, and held out a hand. This woman was about to be mine.

And the ring. The ring was what really mattered.

"Come with me, and I'll show you." I'd show her everything she didn't know she was missing. I'd take my time. Have her trembling against my wicked mouth, tasting and savoring, and then I'd rid myself of these curses once and for all.

The moment her fingers laced with mine, my heart began to sing.

And then the feckin' guardian from hell evanesced behind her, taking Keelynn's hand and telling me to stay here.

I didn't want to stay in this pub that smelled of drink and old wood. I wanted to go with Keelynn. And she wanted me to. He knew that. He must've heard. I'd given her a choice, and she'd chosen me.

"I don't meant to overstep, milady," Padraig muttered, taking her arm, towing her away. "But believe me when I say that nothing good will come from . . . *associating* with someone like him."

Someone like me.

A monster.

A murderer.

A whore.

It was all true, but I didn't give a shit because she had chosen me. That was how this worked. She chose me. I get her. Grinding my teeth together, I fought the darkness welling in my chest. Keelynn would never forgive me if I painted these walls with her coachman's blood, but if he didn't let her go, that's what would happen.

Maeve evanesced to the door, halting their exit. "Leaving so soon? I was hoping ye'd stay a bit longer. We could have that *card* game."

Padraig's gaze flicked to me. "I need to see my lady safely to the inn."

I was disengaging his hand from Keelynn's before he realized. "Allow me to escort her." This time, I played the perfect gentleman and offered my arm.

"I don't think—" *Padraig.*

"Ye should stay—" *Maeve.*

"What are you—" *Padraig.*

"Enough!" Keelynn roared. "I am an adult." When she tried to prop her hands on her hips, they slipped. "I will make my own decisions." To Padraig, she said, "Stay with Maeve. Tadhg will escort me to the inn, won't you Tadhg?"

Feckin' right I would. "I will, of course."

Padraig caught me by the collar, light blue eyes starting to glow as his glamour slipped. "Lady Keelynn is drunk and doesn't know what she's after doin'. If ye try 'n bed her tonight, yer gonna meet the wrong end of that dagger in the morning."

She wasn't that drunk. Was she? Perhaps her eyes were a little more red around the edges than I'd originally thought. And she swayed a bit as she stood there watching us. A little tipsy was a far cry from sozzled. Still, I knew better than to bed a drunk woman if I could help it. "You have my word."

Padraig let me go with a stiff nod.

"What did he say to you?" Keelynn asked, taking my arm, allowing me to escort her into the fresh air.

"He made me swear not to bed you tonight."

Tomorrow was a new day.

Tomorrow I could do what I did best.

And prove to her that the Gancanagh would be worth more to her alive.

10

Music and dancing filled streets lit with blazing lanterns. More than a few couples snogged in dark corners. Scraps of lace and bits of ribbon hung from their cloak pockets.

Keelynn's side pressed against mine. The way her head leaned toward my shoulder made me want to draw her closer. She stopped to watch a squatty fiddler. Sweat rolled down his weathered brow, splashing onto the strings.

"What do you suppose they're celebrating?" she asked, bobbing on her toes to the reel.

"It's Lughnasa." My father's favorite holiday, and one of the few Rían had been allowed to join when he was younger. We used to collect wood for our own bonfires and light them down on the shore. Eava always baked blackberry tarts for Lughnasa.

Mmmm. Blackberries sounded really good. Once I saw Keelynn to the inn, I'd head home straight away and see if there were any left in the kitchens.

"Isn't that a pagan holiday?" Keelynn asked, still swaying to the music.

"It was centuries ago." Lughnasa was for drinking and dallying and the like, all under the guise of celebrating a bountiful harvest. "Now it's more of an excuse for a party than anything religious. I imagine there would've been some competitive games earlier in the week and from the looks of it, a handfasting or two as well."

"I think all marriages should start as handfastings," she muttered.

I found it hard to believe a woman like her approved of such casual relationships. "Really? And why is that?"

"Because sometimes people make mistakes," she said with a shrug. "And it's unfair for them to have to pay for those mistakes for the rest of their lives."

I'd made mistakes—too many to count.

And I'd been paying the price for centuries.

"You truly believe that?" If I told her the truth, would she still feel the same? Or did her forgiveness only extend to humans? Did she think the "monsters," as she'd called us, deserved our curses?

"I wouldn't have been able to say it if I didn't."

"Right. Yes. Of course."

Two people, cursed to tell the truth. What were the odds?

The dancers and musicians finished their heart-pounding reel, dispersing quickly, and yet all I wanted was to stand here and watch the lantern light play on the rich brown tones in Keelynn's falling hair.

What was wrong with me? I was turning into a feckin' simpleton.

"It's late. We should go." Before I did something incredibly stupid and ended up confessing the truth of who I was in search of some semblance of forgiveness. As long as she had that dagger, the truth needed to stay locked inside. Once I got her to the castle, she'd see for herself.

Inside the inn, a man sat on a creaky rocking chair, nursing what looked like a bad case of gout. His jawless face twisted into a derisive sneer, making it clear I was in for trouble. Before I had a chance to open my mouth, he started spouting some nonsense about denying *that thing* a room.

"Lucky for me, we've already organized rooms," I told the hateful toad. "Give us the keys so we can be on our way."

The bastard indicated one of the signs above him about credit.

"I'm not asking for credit." To prove it, I shifted a purse, pretending to drag it from my coat.

The man's eyes widened even as he snorted and shoved a stack of fliers aside.

No Dogs. No Creatures.

Even feckin' dogs had been given preference over the Danú.

"Ye can stay, milady, but *that*"—again, he jerked his chin toward me—"can stay in the stable with the other filthy animals."

I ought to rip his head from his stumpy neck to show him how much of a filthy animal I could be. Unfortunately, that wouldn't earn me any points with the woman watching me through wide, worried eyes.

"I will meet you back here at noon tomorrow," I told her, knowing a lost cause when I saw one. That should give me enough time to sleep off the hangover I planned on having after drinking in the castle.

Her pointed chin lifted. She turned back toward the toad. "Nonsense."

I told her to leave it. And what did the woman do? She ignored me. Hadn't she learned anything at the feckin' lake? When I gave her an order, I expected her to listen.

"I want my keys," she demanded.

"Did ye pay for the rooms?" the toad ground out.

"Not yet, but—"

"Then I'm afraid yer outta luck. I have no tolerance for monsters—or their whores. Get the hell out of here—*both* of you."

If she'd kept her damned mouth shut, she would've had a damned room. But no. She had to choose tonight of all feckin' nights to stand up for me, and now she'd be the one sleeping in the damned stables.

"How dare you! I am a lady. You will not treat me as though I am some common—"

I caught Keelynn's arm, hauling the scowling wasp back outside before she could make things worse. She scowled at me too, as if I was the one in the wrong. "What were you thinking?" I snarled. "You could've had a feckin' room."

"*Me*? I was defending myself! Defending *you*."

I was perfectly capable of defending myself. I didn't need some human to do it for me. "And I told you to let it be."

Like a candle in the wind, the fire in her eyes snuffed out. Her head turned this way and that, eyes scanning the empty street. The tendrils of dark curls framing her face trembled in the breeze. "Where am I going to sleep?" She rubbed her chest with the heel of her hand, gasping the way she'd done after almost drowning in that lake.

Rían used to suffer from awful panic attacks when he first moved into the castle. He never told me the cause, but I knew the signs.

I offered Keelynn my hand. She stared at it as if she didn't know what to do with the thing. "Come with me," I coaxed.

"Come with you where?"

Where indeed? The lights in the inn were all off. No surprise there. It was late. Still, if that toad had planned on renting Keelynn a room, there must be something available inside. "I'm going to get you a room." I couldn't leave her here on the street. There was no telling who could be stumbling out of the pubs at this hour. As afraid as she was of the Danú, I knew monsters lived on both sides of the border.

I brought her to the side of the building, tucking her next to the chimney. "Wait here."

"You're *leaving*?" Her hand flew to her chest the moment I let her go.

"Look at me." The fear I'd come to expect in her gray eyes

had been replaced by something else. Something that left my chest aching.

Trust.

Keelynn trusted me.

Me.

And I . . .

I . . .

I didn't know what to do with it.

Strange warmth spread through my core. *Dammit.* Now I felt guilty for calling her a feckin' wasp all this time. She shouldn't trust me. The moment I got my hands on that ring, I would betray her.

"I will be right back," I promised, knowing it was one I could keep. This wouldn't take long.

Magic swelled within me. With one burst of darkness, I found myself inside the inn, standing in a long, narrow hallway shrouded in shadows.

Technically, evanescing into a locked building broke both Tearmann and Airren laws, and if my fecker of a brother found out, he'd hold me accountable. But *technically*, we had rooms rented. It wasn't my fault the toad at the door had been a prejudiced bastard. If they weren't welcoming to the Danú, they should've had a sign on the exterior door.

Now, the question: which room? All the doors down this hall were closed. They would've rented the nicest ones first. At the top I came across a shite room with a shite bed that smelled like mildew and dust. Better than the stables with those devil beasts.

I evanesced back to where Keelynn huddled. "There's one free room. It's on the third floor."

She blinked up at me as if I'd sprouted another arm. "You got inside?"

"Of course I did." Where'd she think I'd gone?

"Weren't the doors locked? Can you just go wherever you want? Like, nothing can stop you?"

The short answer was, yes. I could go wherever I wanted—as

long as the place wasn't warded. Not that I was going to tell her that when she looked on the verge of another panic attack. I gave her some shite about locked doors and the law that seemed to do the trick. Again, all true, just not the whole truth. When I finished, she wasn't smiling.

Instead, she glowered at me as if I had told her the *actual* truth. "Where have you been staying?" she ground out.

"What do you mean?"

"I mean, where have you been sleeping at night?"

Why did it matter? "Here and there."

"That's not an answer."

Why was she pushing this? "Most nights, I just go home."

"And where is home?"

"I live in Tearmann." If she asked where in Tearmann, I'd have to find a way to deflect. Saying I lived in a castle would surely give me away.

She looked cute when she was this angry, all clenched jaw and narrowed eyes. I would've told her if it wasn't for the damned dagger at her back.

"Well then," she forced through clenched teeth, "I would appreciate it if you would help me get inside my inn before you pop off home."

As cute as she was, I didn't want her going to bed angry. I needed her happy tomorrow. Happy enough to hand over that ring. "Ah, come now, Maiden Death. There's no need to go back to being so formal. I appreciate what you tried to do tonight, it just wasn't necessary."

"Well, I would've appreciated if you told me instead of letting me make a fool of myself."

Hold on. How was any of this my fault? "I thought . . . What I mean is . . . I assumed you knew what inviting someone like me to your inn meant." That she understood the implications and didn't care. "Although now that I think of it, you did the same thing last night and paid for a separate room." She looked genuinely horrified. Where was the woman who had touched my mouth and teased me about the size of my cock? I wanted her back. "Do you want to go inside or stay out here?"

The pinched look of disapproval returned. "Since I don't want to sleep in the stable and I can't go home, I don't have much of a choice, now do I?" she huffed.

That was the gist of it.

The other inns would be full of patrons. I didn't know anyone in town besides Maeve. And I wasn't about to interrupt her and Padraig.

"What do I need to do?" Keelynn asked, planting her hands on her hips.

When I told her she needed to climb, you'd swear I'd suggested she bend over the feckin' hedge.

"Are you mad?" Keelynn's jaw dropped. "You expect me to climb up there?"

Not on her own, obviously. "I'll help you."

"Can't you just make me disappear?"

"If only." That earned me another scowl. I explained the mechanics of evanescing, my smile faltering as I confessed how weak I truly was. Before my curse, I could've brought her to that attic space a thousand times over and barely broken a sweat. Now? After saving her from the kelpie, I was tapped out. "At this stage, the best I could do is get you to the first set of windows. But then I may not have anything left to get us inside."

When she asked about the innkeeper catching us, I told her I'd gladly kill him.

For once, she didn't object.

11

Horse hooves clopped as the carriage rocked and swayed. Thankfully, I'd parked my arse on a soft blue cushion instead of Keelynn's trunk across the way. I fiddled with my flask, trying to keep my hands busy. It didn't help that the woman next to me smelled good enough to have for dessert. I kept hoping she'd look up from the book in her hands and suggest we make up for last night.

"Are you enjoying the book?" I asked, peering down at the pages.

With flushed cheeks, Keelynn closed the tome, tucking it behind her and folding her hands in her lap. "I've read it before."

"That's not what I asked."

"It's one of my favorites."

A Knight's Way was the story of a hero with golden morals who spouted pretty words. "What's your favorite part?" Her cheeks flushed even more. *Interesting*. "Is it when the heroic knight saves her from the witch?" I said slowly, watching her lick her lips. "Or when he ravishes her in a field of wildflowers?"

"I'm not answering that."

"The blush on your cheeks is all the answer I need." Any man seeking insight into the complex innerworkings of a woman's mind need look no further than her favorite romance novel.

"You really shouldn't say such improper things," she murmured.

"They're not nearly as improper as the things I don't say." Like that the field outside would be the perfect place to live out chapter twenty of her book. I'd even shift some shiny armor to make the fantasy more realistic. Although armor left one with dreadfully decreased mobility, and would make some of the positions hard to maintain for any length of time. But I'd be willing to give it a go.

"Tadhg . . ."

I loved the way she said my name. The start a clipped "T," and everything else a sigh. "I can't help that I'm cursed to tell the truth."

A smile played on those lips. So close yet so far. "You could not say anything at all."

"On a journey this long? I'd go mad." We still had far too many days before we reached the portal in Gaul.

Speaking of Gaul, I needed to organize a meeting with the Queen to ensure Keelynn's safe passage. My brother would never let me live it down if anything happened to Aveen's sister.

The chain Keelynn wore around her neck glistened in a rare flash of sunlight. For a brief moment I'd forgotten all about my mission—and hers—and almost started enjoying myself.

She nudged my shoulder. "I think you're already mad."

"Only a little." And only because she was so near.

A yawn interrupted the laugh she stifled behind her hand.

"What's wrong? Did your dreams of me keep you up too late?" I hadn't slept a feckin' wink. First thing I did when I woke was shift a bath for her, then I escaped to my castle to give myself some breathing room.

Her chin lifted. "I slept like a babe."

"What was all the moaning about then?" Not a lie. She had

made a few sleepy noises that sounded a bit like moans. At least that's what I'd call them.

"I didn't—" Those eyes narrowed, and she thumped me on the thigh. "You . . . you . . . You cad."

Why did I find her glare so endearing? I clutched my heart. "Such a scathing retort. I'm not sure I'll ever recover."

"I'm tired, but it has nothing to do with y—" A wince.

I *had* kept her up last night. Good. She'd kept me up as well.

All I did was raise my eyebrows.

She threw the book at me.

I caught the thing, flipping until I located chapter twenty. When I handed it back, her cheeks turned red as a beet. "This one's my personal favorite," I said, tapping the page where the heroic knight abandons his helmet to explore his fair maiden's secrets with his tongue.

Keelynn slammed the book closed, nearly catching my finger. Teasing her was quickly becoming one of my favorite things to do. Her reactions never disappointed.

She yawned again. "Not a word."

"If you're that tired, you should go to sleep." Because I planned on keeping her up all night. Again.

"And have you watch me? No, thank you."

"It didn't bother you last night."

She looked mortified. "You jest."

"It was only fair. You've been staring at me all week."

"I haven't been—" The words died on her strained lips, and she let out the sweetest curse.

My chuckle earned me another jab. "I can't blame you. I'd stare at me too."

Laughing and shaking her head, she settled herself deeper into the cushions. If anyone had told me a week ago that I'd be sitting here, wanting nothing more than to make this wasp laugh, I'd have called them an eejit.

Keelynn's lashes fluttered. The moment she gave in, she sighed.

I could've stared at her for the day. Every twitch of her lips, flutter of her lashes. Each soft, sleepy smile.

My heart started to ache. I didn't want to like Keelynn, much less care about her. This had to be about the ring. I'd do what I had to do—betray her if I must. Then leave this carriage, this woman, these curses behind.

I unscrewed the lid on my flask, drinking deep.

Why was it so warm in here? If only these windows opened. The blue walls felt as if they were closing in on me.

Keelynn was all I could smell. Keelynn was all I could see. Keelynn was all I could hear. These feckin' windows. This feckin' box. This . . .

I evanesced to the bench at the front of the carriage. The fresh, crisp breeze stole my breath, swirling around, fluttering what remained of the leaves on the trees.

Padraig cursed, nearly losing his grip on the reins. "What're ye doin' up here?"

"She's asleep."

He side-eyed me, then turned back and gave the reins a flick. The horses' tack jingled with each clopping step forward. Why did people take these feckin' carriages? I could walk almost as fast.

"What game are ye playing?" the old man grumbled.

"I could ask you the same thing. You must know she will not succeed. Why did you agree to help her in the first place?"

The wrinkles around his mouth deepened with his frown. He remained quiet for so long, I was sure he'd decided not to answer. Then he sighed and said, "I refused to help Lady Aveen thinkin' it would keep her safe, and look what happened. Figured with me at milady's side, she'd be safer than if she tried any of this on her own."

An admirable plan, to be sure. But also incredibly silly. He'd answered my questions willingly enough, so I felt I owed him an answer as well. "I need the ring."

His stooped shoulders hunched forward as he steered the box around a fallen tree. He didn't have anything to say about that. If

Padraig wanted me gone, he could've offered to put in a good word for me. Did he? Of course not.

"I don't remember you from Tearmann," I confessed.

Padraig gave the reins another flick. "Don't suppose ye would seeing as I haven't lived there in ages. My wife was human. The Queen refused her entry into the Forest, so I was forced to live out here."

Most of the Danú who lived outside of Tearmann had a similar story. There seemed to be no rhyme or reason to those the Queen allowed through and those she refused. Part of me thought it was simply her way of exerting her power since she had nothing else.

Some of my friends had married humans. I'd never understood the allure. To find someone you loved only to know you would eventually lose them. What was the point? "Is your wife still living?"

He shook his head. "Passed on a decade ago."

"And yet you didn't return to Tearmann. Why?"

"I'll give ye one guess."

One guess was all I needed. "Keelynn."

"*Lady* Keelynn to ye."

At first, I couldn't imagine how such a waspish woman could garner loyalty or love from anyone, let alone one of the Danú she despised. But I was beginning to understand.

"My girl has had a hard time of it," he went on.

I snorted. A hard time for an entitled human. What'd that look like? Too many dresses? Too many suitors? Too many shoes?

"She was always such a wild little thing," he mused with a heavy sigh, "believing in fairy tales, dancing through meadows, brewing nonsensical potions, kissing fellas hoping one of them would turn into a handsome prince." A chuckle. "Ye know the silly books the humans read. When her mam passed, it stole some of her spirit. Her Da has no fondness fer the Danú, and he passed that onto his youngest. Then she met a man far too fond of drink and women"—his eyes flashed to me—"*ye* know the type."

Knew the type? I *was* the type.

"She fell in love with that wretched boy. When her foolish father paired Lady Aveen with the lad, milady went off with this Ambassador fella to make him jealous. They got caught and were forced to wed."

I'd known about Aveen and her betrothed. Their forced union was the reason we were in this mess. For some reason, she wanted to be with Rían. And damn it all if my heartless brother didn't seem to want to be with her as well.

Padraig drove the carriage through a large puddle in the middle of the muddy road, clipping the high hedges.

Could there be more to this story? If Keelynn truly loved this fellow, that must've played a part in Aveen's decision to sacrifice her life. It certainly made more sense than giving it up solely for Rían.

For some reason, the thought of Keelynn loving this faceless human left my insides in a knot.

"And the Ambassador, was he a good man?" The only thing I'd gleaned was that his name had been Edward. She hadn't seemed particularly upset when she'd spoken of his death, but that didn't mean she'd been unaffected.

"Any man interested in courtin' an unmarried lady in the shadows isn't worth much, if ye ask me. She changed that night—the night Lady Aveen died."

"Trust that there is more at play here than meets the eye."

"I know what's at play," he snapped, pale blue eyes flaring like twin flames. "I've tried to keep my nose out of it, but know that if ye pull any shite with this one, I'll kill ye myself."

The threat left me sitting back, studying the man anew. "How can you care so much?" *When the humans care so little?*

"My wife and I loved those girls as if they were our own. This place—these people—know no better. And hiding in the shadows isn't going to help 'em learn."

Maybe not. Still . . . "I'd rather hide in the shadows than die in the light."

As if she'd heard my confession, Keelynn called my name.

I evanesced back into the carriage to find the wasp still asleep. Meaning she'd called for me in her dreams. As much as I'd teased her about it earlier, I hadn't expected it to be true.

Or to have my chest clenching in response.

I sank onto the bench at her side. She leaned into me, resting her head on my shoulder, hair tickling my chin and smelling like heaven.

She fell in love with that wretched boy.

What would it be like to be loved by someone like Keelynn? A woman willing to bargain with a witch and cross an entire country for a chance to bring back someone she cared for. Desperately naïve. But also desperately brave. Desperately loyal.

I stared out the window, watching the hedges get shorter, replaced by low stone walls and fields dotted with grazing cattle. Eventually, the random cottages grew more prevalent and closer together. When we reached a cobbled path, I knew we must be getting close to town.

"Maiden Death?" I gave Keelynn's shoulder a poke. She swatted my hand and continued snoozing away. I poked her again. "Keelynn?"

Her lips lifted into a sleepy smile.

"Wake up, wasp. You're drooling on my shirt."

The way she blushed when she shot upright and saw that she had, in fact, marked my shirt, left me fighting a smile.

Someone had thought it would be a good idea to paint the three-story inn the color of pea soup. Moss grew in clumps on the slate roof tiles surrounding uneven chimneys. Padraig opened the carriage door for Keelynn, offering her a weathered hand down onto the damp cobblestones. I climbed out after her, settling my bag across my chest.

"We'll see you in the morning?" Keelynn said with a small

smile. I tried not to be offended that she hadn't asked me to stay as well. Now that she knew I could evanesce, there was no point.

"I'll see you in the morning." With a nod, I turned to leave. Only, I didn't want to say goodbye. Not really. So I twisted back around. "Will you join me for a drink tonight?"

She would say no. Still, I'd be a fool not to ask.

"What do you say, Padraig?" Keelynn offered her coachman a warm smile. No wonder the man loved her. Basking in her light must be like waking up to sunshine every morning.

His gaze landed on me, narrowed and assessing. I couldn't help shifting my weight.

"I'll leave the pints to the young, milady," he said with a bob of his head. "Enjoy yerselves."

I couldn't believe it. That was good as giving his approval. No man approved of me within arm's reach of a woman he cared for. I didn't know what to make of it.

His approval made me feel . . . responsible.

I wasn't sure I liked it. I could barely handle being responsible for myself half the time. How was I supposed to be responsible for her as well?

Keelynn gave my arm a nudge. "Where will we go?"

I shook away my rising panic, glancing up and down the narrow street. I'd been through this town plenty of times but never had a reason to stop. There wasn't much. A butcher's next to the baker's. And an apothecary. The only place to get a drink seemed to be the inn where she was staying. "I'll meet you here. Say, eight o'clock?"

She agreed with a smile.

With nothing better to do for the next couple of hours, I evanesced to the castle. The moment I reached my room, my brother burst through the door.

"Where have you been?" he demanded.

Where'd he get the energy to be so feckin' dramatic all the time? "Busy." I went to my wardrobe in the corner.

"You were 'busy,' were you? Did you forget that you were

meant to meet me at the feckin' portal? I waited in Tara's house all feckin' day." He stalked over, gripping my arm, turning me, and pulling one of my hands toward him, then the other. "Dammit, Tadhg. I thought at least you'd have the feckin' ring."

"Not yet."

His jaw ticked. "Why do you look so chuffed with yourself then?"

"That's none of your business, now is it?" I tore out of his grip to slide the hangers in my wardrobe from one side to the other. Wasn't there anything in here without holes?

"You bedded the assassin, didn't you?"

"Not yet."

"Then what the hell have you been doing for the last three days?" he snarled, throwing his hands in the air.

"I've been getting to know a woman."

He blinked at me, mouth gaping. "You've been getting to know a woman," he repeated, shaking his head, eyes wide. "You've been *getting to know a woman*? Does this *woman* happen to be the one who wants you dead?"

"She's been misinformed. And I am attempting to set her straight."

"You said you were after the ring. You said that was all you wanted."

It had been all I wanted. Now? I wasn't so sure. And why did I need to choose between the ring and the woman who wore it? Why couldn't I have both?

Shrugging, I pulled out a shirt that used to be white and a faded black waistcoat.

Rían gave the clothes the same squinty-eyed, wrinkled-nose look he always did. "Those belong in the fire."

They did belong in the fire—not that I'd admit it aloud. I shoved them both back into the armoire and pulled out the next two shirts.

"Those are worse." His hands drummed against his thighs,

watching me drag out another two that looked no better than the rest. "Where's the assassin now?"

"As if I'd tell you."

Rían smirked.

Dammit. I'd protested too quickly.

My brother had a particular talent for impersonating people. He could shift his features to make himself look like anyone he wished. Once, he'd turned himself into Ruairi, and I'd been so drunk that I hadn't noticed. I foolishly ended up confessing to fancying a girl down the coast. What'd my brother do? He'd slept with her.

"If I let you pick out my clothes, you must swear not to leave this castle tonight."

"Done." He shoved me aside, tearing waistcoats and shirts and breeches out one by one, leaving them in a pile on the floor. "Shocking. That's what this is. Utterly shock—" He dragged a navy waistcoat from the back. "Is this *mine*?" he growled, poking his finger through one of the burn marks at the front.

"Is it?"

"You know damn well it is. What the hell happened?"

"Looks burnt."

"I can feckin' see it's burned. How did you burn it?"

I shrugged. I couldn't remember taking the thing, let alone what had happened to it.

Cursing, Rían flicked his wrist. A pile of new clothes appeared on the edge of my bed. "You can wear these."

The shirt felt stiff as a board. The blue waistcoat, with its shiny buttons and silver thread, looked like something you'd wear to a ball, not a dingy pub. And the cravat? Not a hope. But the black breeches should do. I picked those up and shifted a bath.

Rían glowered at the remaining pile. "What about the rest of them?"

"I'll not wear blue." Rían wore blue.

"Didn't seem to bother you when you stole this." He held up the ruined waistcoat.

"I'm allowed to change my mind."

"At least take the shirt."

"No, thank you. I'd like to be able to move."

Grumbling, Rían collected his things and evanesced. I ended up in his breeches and the shirt with the fewest stains. The seams on the right sleeve were a bit loose, but in a dark pub, it'd be barely noticeable.

Just before eight, I evanesced back to the alley at the far side of the inn. For some reason, my stomach felt a bit queasy. Not sure why. Could've been the mash and veg Eava had made for dinner. Or the chocolate cake I'd demolished afterwards.

Making my way through the murky darkness, I opened the inn's double doors and went inside to wait beneath a half-lit chandelier in the foyer.

A few minutes later, the wasp swept down the stairs, all black skirts and stiff posture.

She'd left her hair down, the soft brown waves reaching nearly to her waist. I wanted it wrapped around me, falling in time with her body. A dark curtain shielding us from the world as we discovered each other.

Something in me stirred to life.

Not in the usual places.

Higher.

In my chest.

And I didn't like it one bit.

12

TWO COUPLES SHARED A TABLE NEAR THE FIREPLACE IN THE SNUG at the front of the guesthouse. They glanced at us when we walked in, and their eyes widened. Their derogatory whispers carried on peat-scented air. Keelynn didn't seem to notice as I steered her toward a table near the exit.

"Are you drinking stout?" I asked.

Grimacing, Keelynn clutched the material at her waist. "I can't stomach it tonight. I'll have a glass of red wine, please."

I nodded and went to the dented bar at the back where two old men sipped from flagons of ale. The closer I drew, the worse they smelled. Farmers, from the look of their muck-riddled boots and faces creased by weather and age.

Light from the candles glinted off the liquor bottles displayed on the far wall. After pouring a pint of amber, the bartender approached me with narrowed eyes.

"Before I serve you," he said, his hand falling to the pistol tucked into the top of his breeches, "I want you to know that if you're lookin' for trouble, you'd best be doin' it elsewhere."

"I'm only interested in two glasses of red wine," I said with a congenial smile that made the man harrumph.

He collected a bottle from the end of the shelf, returning to fill two small glasses. When he told me the price, I almost changed my mind about the trouble. "That's twice as expensive as anywhere else." And I didn't need to taste what he had poured to know it was the cheapest available.

Cocking an eyebrow, he crossed his arms over his broad chest. "Do you want the wine or not?"

Prejudiced bastard.

Did shooting him with his own pistol count as "looking for trouble"?

Cursing under my breath, I handed over the coins. The man didn't deserve a 'thank you' for extorting me, so I grabbed the wine and pasted on a smile for my female companion.

"One *ladylike* glass of wine," I said, setting a long-stemmed glass in front of her, "and a gentlemanly glass of the same for myself."

"You? A gentleman?" She snorted. "Hardly."

"I could be if I tried." My parents had done their best with me. Eava reminded me of that on a daily basis. I could pretend, but what was the point? It wasn't as if I was normally trying to impress anyone.

"Yeah, right."

"You don't believe me?"

She shook her head.

"All right, then. How about a wager? For two hours of your choosing, I will be a perfect gentleman. If I don't meet your standards, you keep your coins when we reach Tearmann." It wasn't as if I needed the money. The treasury overflowed with coin, and we had storehouses across the country with more. The upside of having very few options when it came to trade and imports was that we never wasted funds on frivolous things. A handful of ships came to the small bay near the castle once a quarter. And if we needed anything else, I sent Rían to Airren to purchase it.

"And if you manage to pull it off?" she asked.

If I managed to pull it off . . . "You let me unlace your

stay." No sense mincing words at this stage. Not after I'd confessed my intentions last night.

Her breathing hitched ever so slightly. The invisible cord between us grew taut.

"All right."

Part of me had expected her to balk. The other part assumed she'd force me to play the doting courtier right now.

Instead, she turned her attention to the couples in the corner asking each other if Keelynn had seen my ears. They were attached to my feckin' head. You'd have to be blind to miss them.

Her lips flattened. "They're very rude."

Not half as rude as the bartender.

"They're curious," I countered. "Most humans cannot see any reason for one of you to be associating with someone like me. Beyond the obvious." I took a sip of wine. Shite. Just as I thought. If the bartender hadn't been watching, I would've shifted a bottle from my own cellar back at the castle.

Keelynn's head tilted, sending those glorious waves rolling over her slender shoulders. Tonight's mourning dress's square neckline hinted at the swells of her breasts. I was not complaining.

"Which is?"

Surely she was having a laugh. "Do you really not know?"

"They believe you and I are engaging in romantic relations."

There wasn't anyone romantic about the relations I wanted to have with her. "Yes. 'romantic relations.'" I liked where this conversation was headed.

"Does it happen often?"

"I'm not sure I understand your question." Did what happen often?

Her eyes dropped to where she swirled her glass of wine. "Humans and Danú. Being intimate. Together."

Feckin' hell, she was serious. Most humans hated us, but that didn't mean they weren't tempted to dance with the darkness. "Only all the feckin' time." If only she knew. I'd had plenty of trysts with the Danú, but most of the offers over the years had been from humans who felt entitled to take from me what I didn't want to give.

"Why?" she whispered, her husky voice thick.

"What do you mean, 'why'? For the same reason it happens between humans. Lust. A desire to procreate. Feckin' boredom. I don't know." There were a million reasons to fall into bed with someone. Not all of them good, but reasons nonetheless.

"Not love?"

"Not in my experience, no." Love had nothing to do with it. Sex was about mechanics and attraction and power. "This may come as a huge shock to you, but you're not that different from us." We had the same desires, the same needs.

"Then why haven't I been taught the 'truth' about the Danú?"

The truth had two sides, and all too often, people didn't want to hear them both. "Because it is easier to fear the unknown than to try to understand it." To get so wrapped up in stories and myths and lies that you couldn't see through them to the miniscule truths they concealed.

We were here.

We were willing to talk. Willing to share our truths.

No one on the human side seemed willing to listen.

"And unfortunately, the loudest voices often belong to the most fearful."

Keelynn looked at me for the longest time, as if she could see the monster that lived inside. As if she could see my truth. "Do you truly believe the Gancanagh is innocent?"

Not what I wanted to talk about. We needed to take a few steps back to romantic relations.

"He's not innocent by any means," I said, thinking of the names in my book back home. And the nameless people I'd killed using other methods. "However, he and I are . . . well acquainted." Not a lie. A careful truth. "And as I told you in the carriage, I know for a fact that he would never kiss a woman unless she understood the consequences." There had been the odd woman, like the barmaid, who had kissed me before I could warn them. And the innkeeper. I hadn't exactly told her outright what would happen. But she'd come after me. I had been defending myself.

Keelynn sipped her wine slowly, then set it down next to my glass. "Killing him is the only way to bring back Aveen."

"Is that what Fiadh told you?" A load of bollocks spouted by a vengeful witch.

Keelynn nodded.

"Let me guess. She also said if you used an enchanted dagger, then you could transfer his life force to Aveen, yeah?"

Another nod.

"Did it ever cross your mind that perhaps she was lying?" Keelynn didn't trust me or any of my kin, yet for some reason, she chose to trust one of the worst beings on this cursed island.

Her shoulders fell. "You're saying it won't work?"

It'd feckin' work, all right. And then I'd be dust, and that witch would have succeeded in breaking me. "Oh, no. Immortal blood is powerful enough to raise the dead, so it'd work. But it's excessive. And entirely unnecessary."

"What would you suggest I do?"

Give me the ring and go home, probably wouldn't keep me in her good graces. So I said, "Nothing."

Not a feckin' thing.

Sit there, look pretty, and then let me into her bed so I could use my body to convince hers to give away her only bargaining chip.

"You think I should accept my sister's fate even when I know I could change it?"

Here goes nothing. Either this would work or it wouldn't. "The Gancanagh's lips are *cursed*. So, whoever he kisses is—"

The words. They were right there. Right feckin' there.

She reached for me. "Are you all right?"

"*Whoever he kisses is*—" *Dammit.* One more word. One more feckin' word. Cursed. Not dead. Whoever I kissed was CURSED. I wanted to scream it, but every time I opened my mouth, it felt like my head was being cleaved from my body and impaled on a pike.

"The ring," I gasped. If she gave me the ring, this curse would subside. I could explain. I could tell her what was actually happening. "Let me see the ring."

Her hand flew to the ring hidden beneath her gown. "Absolutely not."

Now wasn't the time to be stubborn. Not when I was so feckin' close. "I cannot say what I need to say unless you give me the ring."

"Try."

I was feckin' trying! "I. *Can't.*"

"And I'm *not* handing it over."

I'd saved her. I'd helped her last night. I hadn't squeezed the life out of that beautiful neck all feckin' week. She owed me this. She owed me that ring. "Keelynn, please–"

The door burst open. The *crack* of splintering wood rattled through the pub. Cloying magic spun on an icy breeze.

Two women entered, their faces concealed within the shadows of their hooded cloaks. The way they moved, perfectly in sync as they started for us, left my stomach filled with dread.

"*Shit.*" What the hell were they doing here?

When the twins reached our table, they lifted their hands to draw back their hoods. Caer and Cait. One as beautiful as the other, and both equally as wicked. Normally, I'd be up for whatever they had in store. But not here. Not tonight.

From the corner of my eye, I saw the bartender reach for his pistol. The witches paid him no heed. They could send him to the underworld before he pulled off a shot.

Caer's lips tilted upward when her gaze met mine. "We heard a rumor you were here."

I turned toward them, blocking their view of the human at my table too late. "You know better than to listen to rumors, Caer."

"Who is your friend?" Cait tilted her head like a hawk considering its prey. Her eyes narrowed as she zeroed in on the glasses of wine between Keelynn and I.

"No one you need to concern yourself with," I told them.

"What's your name, girl?" she asked Keelynn.

"I said not to concern yourself with her. She's just someone I met at a pub."

The darkest parts of me rejoiced when Caer staked her claim with a possessive hand on my thigh.

Caer's tongue darted over red lips. "If that's true, then she wouldn't mind us stealing away her handsome companion for a little . . . fun."

All Keelynn had to do was say she wanted me to stay here. To make me some sort of offer before either of these women could. The witch's nails dug into my arm. Keelynn wasn't looking at me anymore. She was looking at the wine.

Don't look at the wine.

LOOK AT ME.

"He's all yours," she muttered, her voice as rigid as the table between us.

I felt myself deflate even as my arms snaked around the twins' waists. Their supple bodies angled toward me, their legs brushing mine from beneath their skirts. Skirts I'd be beneath soon enough. The darkness in me rejoiced, and the giddiness I had felt earlier was replaced with a predator-like focus.

The door opened.

The door closed.

In. Off. Out.

I didn't even need to leave town for that.

"You should've called over the moment you arrived," Caer purred, toying with the collar on my shirt, undoing one of the buttons. Her nail left a red mark on my skin as she trailed the sharpened black tip from my throat to my sternum. Pleasure and pain. That was what these two represented.

"After the last time, I wasn't sure you'd be up for it." When I had seen them a decade ago, they had come to blows over who was first. I hoped they had decided already because time wasn't on my side.

"We're better at sharing now," Cait assured me, tucking her hand into my front pocket, making her way toward my groin.

FINALLY.

Not finally. No. I could resist this. I could distract them and then I could come back and—Caer did the same on the other side, and it took every ounce of self-control I had to extricate their hands from my breeches with the darkness roaring in my ears, begging to be set free.

"Ladies, would you excuse me for a moment?" I ignored their pouts and the way their green eyes flashed in the dim street.

Their protest was brief, cut off after I promised to join them in their cottage straight away. Inside the pub, I found Keelynn sipping her wine. A dark look crossed her face when she saw me.

"Wait for me," I rushed, feeling the invisible threads tightening, dragging me toward the door. Then I told her I would be right back, hoping it was the truth.

Caer lounged on a chaise in front of the fire. Cait draped herself across a thick sheepskin rug. The matching black silk robes they wore clung to their curves while flames danced on their pale bare legs.

"All right. Who's first?" I had the buckle on my belt undone before Caer responded with a chiding click of her tongue.

"Come now, Tadhg. Is such behavior truly fitting for the one they call the Prince of Seduction?"

It wasn't. Not at all. But I had left the only person I felt like seducing drinking wine alone at the inn. I had been too slow. Too hesitant. If only I had suggested we share a bottle of wine in Keelynn's room instead of the bar. I would be with Keelynn right now, slipping my hands beneath her skirts, kissing her inner thigh, touching and tasting her most secret places.

"It's been a long day," I sighed. A long, disappointing day if I didn't turn it around.

Cait's teeth flashed, startlingly white in the shadows. "Did the human wear you out?"

"I already said you needn't concern yourself with her." Keelynn had no place in this conversation.

"She's not your usual type. So severe. And the black dress?" Caer snorted, allowing the silk tie barely holding her robe closed to slip between black-tipped fingers. "Drab and downright depressing."

I didn't want to talk about Keelynn. I wanted to get this over with.

"Enough about the human," Cait said, stroking the creamy rug beneath her. "We brought you here to discuss the little misunderstanding we had a few years back."

Misunderstanding? They had been caught murdering innocent humans and selling their innards to other witches for potions.

I sank onto the free chair, stretching my legs toward the fire. "What's there to discuss?"

"You must've heard of the executions in Mántan. They burned Olive and Aurora."

Olive and Aurora. Two witches almost as old as the twins before me now. I knew of the executions but hadn't read the names of those killed.

"Surely, after all this time, we have paid our debt," Cait went on. "We would like to return to our home in Tearmann."

Olive and Aurora hadn't deserved their fates. The same could not be said for the two witches in front of me.

Cait trailed a finger between her breasts, drawing my gaze lower. And lower. "Would you be willing," she said slowly, untying her robe, "to ask Rían to consider letting us back in?"

There wasn't a hope of him agreeing to that. I'd been otherwise occupied on the day these two stood trial, leaving their fate to my brother. For as long as I had known the man, Rían never went back on a ruling. He followed Tearmann law to the letter. "I will certainly ask," I said, pushing away from the chair. "If that's all, I really must be going."

With any luck, Keelynn would have ordered another round of drinks.

Caer caught my arm in a vice-like grip. "Ah-ah. We didn't just bring you here to discuss our request." She untied her robe and let it slip down her shoulders. "It's my turn to go first."

13

Why would it be nice and sunny and warm when it could be pissing down rain and cold enough to freeze the bollocks off a brass monkey? My head ached from all the drink I'd swamped to get me through last night. My body ached from being used by two insatiable witches with a penchant for violence. My heart ached from . . .

Actually, I didn't want to think about what could be going on there. Better to focus on avoiding the tiny rivers and lakes quickly overtaking the cobblestones as I hurried to where Padraig waited by the stables.

The moment he saw the sorry state of me, his expression darkened. "Ye look like shite."

I hadn't bothered looking at myself in the mirror this morning when I rolled out of bed. "I feel worse."

Something about the way he tapped the whip against his leg made me think he was considering using the thing on me. "What happened?"

"Witches."

The tapping stopped. "Ye went off with a witch?"

"Two, actually."

"I thought . . ." He let the words die there. There was no sense continuing. Whatever he thought would happen hadn't. "Yer some fool." He gave my shoulder a shove. "Hasn't this gone on long enough? Shouldn't ye be telling the truth?"

He wanted to talk about the truth, did he? The truth was that I was better off dallying with those feckin' witches because that was where I belonged. In a world of shadows and pain. "You're awfully high and feckin' mighty talking about truth. How long have you been hiding behind that feckin' glamour?"

He adjusted his grip on the whip, eyes faintly glowing. "I wouldn't need the feckin' glamour if yer father hadn't given up."

My father had been nursing a broken heart, hadn't cared a whit about anything or anyone after the humans had killed my mother. It should've enraged him, should've stoked his internal fire. Instead, her death had snuffed it out, and he'd given in to the humans' unfair demands.

Keelynn emerged from the inn, bowed head hidden beneath the hood of her cloak.

Padraig's eyes flitted toward a wide puddle reaching nearly to the waiting carriage. Raindrops splattered my boots, cleaning the sludge from the long walk back this morning.

My father may have given up, but I wouldn't make the same mistake.

One way or another, I would get that ring.

By the time I climbed into the box, Keelynn was already on the bench, skirts spread wide, glaring out the far window. She didn't bother making room for me.

Right, so. Back on the trunk.

The moment my arse hit the rivets, tears pricked the backs of my eyes. I should've been healed by now, but Caer and Cait had kept me up until all hours, making me work twice as hard. My magic would take time to replenish.

As cold as I was, my arse hurt worse, so I stripped off my coat and stuffed it beneath me just in time for Padraig to crack his whip, sending me back against the feckin' wall.

Welts from scalding candle wax and cuts from ceremonial

daggers and sharp nails marred my skin. At this rate, they'd be there all feckin' day.

Keelynn still hadn't looked at me. I couldn't blame her, after I'd asked her to wait and left her hanging. Had she stayed at the pub long, or had she known I'd betray her and left as soon as she'd finished her wine?

"What's worse than one witch?" I asked, fed up with the silence.

Those steely eyes swung toward me, the movement sending her plait falling behind her shoulder. When I repeated my question, she answered with a clipped, "I don't know."

"*Two* witches."

She didn't laugh at my poor excuse for a joke. Of course, she didn't. It wasn't feckin' funny. "I'm sorry for what happened last night. I was gone a lot longer than anticipated."

That pointed chin lifted, and she looked through me as if she could see straight to the wall at my back. "What you do in your free time is no business of mine."

My free time?

For the last feckin' week, I'd spent all my free feckin' time with her. "That's all you have to say to me?" I wanted her to shout and rail and tell me I was an eejit. Give me something—anything besides steely indifference.

The ring and my freedom felt a million miles away.

"*Dammit,* I said I was sorry. What do you want me to do?" Did she want me to grovel? To beg? How the hell did I get back to where we were yesterday?

The carriage careened to a halt, slamming my head against the unforgiving wall.

"I want you to stop messing with my bloody carriage!" Keelynn screeched, eyes narrowed into slits.

"That wasn't me!" Outside the window, a maze of ruins disappeared into a dreary forest.

"You're so full of—" Her eyes widened, and she called for Padraig.

The back of my neck prickled. Something was wrong. A familiar coppery tang hit my nostrils. Keelynn climbed out of the carriage before I could stop her.

"He won't be much help to you now, missus," a man drawled. Not Padraig. Someone else.

Keelynn's despondent cry for answers was all the confirmation I needed.

Padraig must be dead.

Whoever was outside with her had killed him.

"Easiest way to make a man stop a carriage is to stop his heart," said the man, a smile in his tone.

I couldn't see a feckin' thing in this box without giving away my position. I evanesced to what remained of the stairs inside a crumbling abbey, across the ditch from the carriage.

Padraig slumped on his bench, the white shirt beneath his heavy overcoat now painted deep red. A man stood next to Keelynn. Tall. Strong. Silver hair. Dagger in his hand, aimed at my salvation.

The magic that had failed to heal me stirred, still bound by the curse but fighting against its stranglehold.

I barely glanced at the three mercenaries in leather armor waiting in front of the old wall. The human took a menacing step toward Keelynn and asked for the ring.

Keelynn, bless her, for all her fear, refused him.

The moment the vile bastard put his feckin' hands on her to pull the gold band from her fingers, he signed his death warrant. His whispered threat left her face pale as a sheet.

"You have what you came for," she breathed, voice trembling. "Let me go."

The bastard shoved her away. "I have what I came for," he drawled, climbing to the front of the carriage and knocking Padraig's body to the ground, "but my men still need to claim their prize."

I shifted my kohl and painted my eyes, knowing what I had to do.

Giving in to the darkness that prowled beneath my skin meant more magic but less control. And dire consequences if I used too much.

I couldn't lose her.

The ring. I meant I couldn't lose the ring.

Closing my eyes, I slipped into writhing shadows and let the cursed magic thrumming in my veins take control.

Evanescing to the top of the broken high cross felt like freedom. The curse remained on Keelynn's lips, black as my soul. "*Three against one isn't a fair fight, lads.*" Damn, it felt good to stop denying the monster I was. To let her see that the darkness living within me couldn't be contained forever.

The tallest of the lot sneered. "We didn't know our prize had a friend."

"Look at its eyes," said the short, hairy fella. "Never seen anything like it."

It.

I may have been half faerie and half witch, but I was as male as the fat bastard who thought his tiny dagger would do anything but ignite my rage. The lanky one went straight for Keelynn, altering the order of execution.

"There's no need to be frightened. We're gonna treat ye like the lady ye are." The black-haired man thought he had a right to smile at her. To close the distance. To put his feckin' hands around her throat.

I inhaled and threw my hand toward the bastard, sending a bolt of power through his torso. His body lifted from the ground and ended up ramming headfirst into a tree.

His skull or his neck or some other bone in his worthless body cracked. He didn't rise again.

I evanesced behind the other two, my hands flexing, magic boiling in my blood. "*I had a shitty night last night, so consider yourselves lucky that I'm giving you a chance to run.*"

The scarred one laughed, towering over me like one of the trees. "Ye think ye can best the two of us?"

What a stupid feckin' question. Hadn't he seen what I'd done to his mate?

"Ye think we 'aven't dealt with yer kind?" He showed me his trophy necklace. It wasn't the fullest one I'd seen, but he had killed more than a few pooka and witches from the looks of it. "We're gonna make ye watch us fuck yer one," he said with a leering look toward Keelynn, "then carve her up like the pretty bird she is. Then I'll cut out yer eyes and add 'em to this."

An ambitious plan to be sure. One that would undoubtedly fail the moment I sliced open his torso and ripped the heart from his chest.

Keelynn watched me, her eyes blown out as she clutched her chest.

"*Turn around, Keelynn.*"

She didn't need to witness the carnage I was about to unleash on these two swine. They thought they could come here and take what didn't belong to them? They thought they could best *me*? I'd lived for three hundred years, endured pain and torture, suffered and died. Compared to me, they were nothing. Skittering cockroaches beneath my boots, made for crushing.

The hairy lad attacked. I broke his feckin' nose, sending him howling and stumbling toward the abbey. I shifted the dagger he'd dropped and drew a bloody smile across his throat. The shock in a man's eyes as life left him always confounded me. He honestly believed he could win.

The big lad had the good sense to try and run. But he'd had his chance. And he'd decided to stay for the fun.

I evanesced, cutting off his escape. A dagger and a slow death just wouldn't do for someone who had killed my people and wore their parts around his neck.

I shifted one of the swords from our armory, its weight familiar in my grip. A few swings later, the bastard was two legs shorter and down two arms. I wasn't sure exactly when he'd died, but when the bloody stump of him landed on the grass, his sightless eyes stared into the fading day.

A choked sob sounded at my back, where Keelynn dragged at her chest, gasping for air.

I ran past the bodies to her side and demanded that she look at me. If she didn't get her breathing under control, she would pass out. And from the coldness settling in my bones, I wouldn't be able to help her much longer. I took her shoulders, thankful she was wearing black so she couldn't see the bloodstains I'd left. Some of the darkness subsided, leaving only the whisper of shadows in my mind. "Look at me."

Her lashes fluttered open, gaze bouncing from me to a point at my back. "At me." *Not at them. Look at me.* Her eyes locked onto mine. "Take a deep breath."

"I-I-I . . ."

"Deep."

My hand rose and fell as she inhaled a short, shaky breath.

"Deeper. Deeper. Good. Hold it there. And release. Again."

I didn't let her stop until her breathing became even and steady and deep. Her eyes had flecks of brown. How had I never noticed before? Somehow, her lavender scent broke through the stench of blood and death, leaving my tongue tingling.

Damn, she was beautiful.

Her eyes flicked over my shoulder. "*Tadhg*!"

Stabbing pain sliced my side. I glanced down to see the flash of a blade as the lanky man I thought I'd killed tore his dagger from my gut. The gushing wound burned like the fires of hell. "Feckin' hell . . ." An iron blade. Like the feckin' soldiers used.

The man glanced at the dagger in his hand, then back at me, regret flashing in his brown eyes. I held out a trembling hand, wrapping a noose of magic right above the man's bobbing Adam's apple, tightening the cord until his face matched the blood on my hands. Relishing the way he fought as I lifted him clean off the ground, dangling like a worm on a string.

The spells I'd learned from my mother came flooding back as I spoke to the earth, calling for it to open. The price I'd have to pay would be worth it. The ground quaked, a beast waking from its long slumber, before cleaving in two, consuming bodies and bloody limbs. The man who'd stabbed me opened his mouth, to cry for mercy, no doubt.

Where was Padraig's mercy? And Keelynn's?

My side burned like the fires of hell. Where was mine?

I opened my hand, dropping him into his shallow grave, reveling in the sound of the earth claiming his life and mending itself, until all that remained of the altercation was the bloody grass and a slight mound running from the trees to the road.

"Keelynn?" Where had she—*Dammit.* "Keelynn!"

She'd collapsed onto the stones, heaving and retching. My feet felt like leaden weights as I stumbled toward her. Death was coming for me. I had to be quick. But my feckin' feet refused to go any faster. Eventually, I fell next to where she trembled. The moment my hand connected with her shoulder, she flew back.

"It's only me. It's only me." What was I saying? *I* was the one she feared. In a final act of foolishness, I shifted a flask of water. "Here."

She took it from me with shaking hands, cleaning her mouth and spitting in the grass. "It's just water."

"Would you rather something stronger?" She'd have to wait until I came back because I couldn't feel my legs or my torso as death's icy hand stretched toward my heart.

Thankfully, she shook her head. "You killed them. *All* of them."

What'd she think I'd do? Leave them go after they'd killed Padraig and threatened us both? "I told you to look away."

"I-I couldn't."

The forest swam in my eyes, dark spots gathering at the edge of my vision. The last thing I heard was Keelynn calling my name.

14

No matter how many times I'd died, the searing pain of coming back never eased. This time had been the same as every other: the burning, the panic of knowing there was no escape, that I had no choice but to lie there and endure every excruciating second.

But the strange sensation of someone pulling and dragging at me. Lifting my shirt. Pressing a cold hand to my stomach. That was all new.

My eyes flew open.

Keelynn hovered over me, my head on her thighs as she studied my abdomen with a furrowed brow, poking and prodding with frigid fingers.

"Anything else you want to check while you're down there?" I croaked.

Her scream echoed in the falling darkness. She jerked back. My head slipped, slamming against the stones littering the ground.

"Why aren't you hurt?" she hissed.

"I *am* hurt." Really feckin' hurt. *Owww*. I rubbed my sore skull, certain a lump would appear at any moment.

"Not your *head,* you fool. That man stabbed you."

"Did he?" My pathetic attempt at levity earned me another scowl. "I should think the answer to your question would be obvious."

She thought about it for a moment, worrying her bottom lip with her teeth. "Your magic did this?"

Of course it did. What else would it be?

I nodded.

"Can it heal others as well?"

"Why? Did they hurt you?" Her face, though smeared with dirt and tears, didn't look cut or bruised. Her neck still bore the grime from that bastard's hands. Was she in pain? I didn't have it in me to heal her yet, but in a couple of hours, after some food, I'd give her everything I had.

She took my hand, pulling me to unsteady legs. "Not me. Padraig."

It took a moment for the words to register.

"Keelynn . . . Stop." I couldn't do anything for Padraig. My eyes flew to the dagger at Keelynn's back, visible now that her cloak had been removed.

That wasn't entirely true. I could give my life in exchange for his.

I wrenched my hand free, nearly stumbling into the high cross. A mound of dirt and loose rubble rose beneath it, a black flat cap laid at the top.

She'd buried him.

"Padraig didn't deserve this." Tears glistened as they fell from her eyes. "You have to heal him. You have to bring him back. I'm asking you to try. I'm *begging.*"

"No." I couldn't do it.

"But he's one of you!"

She knew?

What was I saying? Of course she knew. When Padraig died, the glamour would've been removed. She knew the truth and had buried him anyway. Mourned him anyway. "Keelynn . . ."

I reached for her, my own heart breaking. I'd lost countless friends to senseless violence. The pain would ease but never heal.

She jerked away, betrayal written all over her pinched features. "Don't *touch* me."

How did I make her see? Make her understand? "I don't care if he's a human or a leprechaun or a feckin' dog," I said. "Life left Padraig the moment that dagger pierced his heart. This isn't a matter of healing, it's a matter of resurrection." And I wasn't able to say that I couldn't bring him back without the unforgiving pain of my truth curse stabbing my skull. I could bring him back. All I had to do was let her stab me with that cursed dagger and trade my life for his.

If it came down to the two of us, I knew which one she would choose.

I couldn't do it. Padraig may have been a far better man than I, but his death affected one person. Mine would bring Tearmann to its knees. "I'm sorry, but he's gone."

Her shoulders drooped as she stared at her friend's final resting place.

"We need to get out of here in case the man who killed him returns." When I was back to full strength, I'd find him and make him pay for what he'd taken from her.

In my current state, I was no good to anyone.

Keelynn didn't balk when I took her hand. Although her fingers were cold, warmth spread from her body to mine, buzzing with that strange fire I'd felt every time she'd touched me.

"We need to find shelter for the night. And food if I can manage it." I collected her cloak from where she'd left it, settling the heavy wool around her slumped shoulders.

The simplest thing would've been to continue along the road to the next town. Except there was no telling who we'd meet. Having a human find me covered in blood and Keelynn in shock wouldn't end well. I needed at least a few days to recover before going back to the underworld.

Where would we go?

How long had we traveled today? A mile, maybe? Meaning if we headed north, we should run into the Síonon River. Perhaps we'd find an abandoned cottage or stable nearby to shield us from the damp night ahead.

I led Keelynn into the forest. Ferns grew at the base of the trees; fallen leaves and twigs overtook the rest of the ground.

Padraig. The poor man.

Living his life only to have it stolen away by a human.

Did Keelynn desire vengeance for her friend the same way she had for her sister? Or would she accept his death more readily because it had been delivered at the hands of a human?

After all Keelynn had seen, did she still think us monsters? If only I could read her mind.

Although her tears had stopped, her weak posture remained.

When she began to limp, I slowed my pace. Had she turned her ankle? Her boots had looked new at the beginning of this journey; perhaps they'd given her blisters. Not that I could do anything about either until I got some food.

My stomach let out a pitiful gurgle, the apple and hunk of bread I'd taken from the twins' house long gone.

Her footsteps faltered, as if she'd only just realized we were deep in the woods. "Where are we going?"

"It should be around this bend." Or the next one. I could hear the river now, a soft rush of waves sweeping past stones, eroding the shore.

"What should?" she asked.

She'd see soon enough. We passed a fallen tree devoured by moss, wound our way between rocks and ferns to a small clearing at the bank of the river. The water wasn't too deep here—up to my shins at most. And the thick cropping of trees would give some shelter from the rain waiting to burst from the black clouds above.

Barring any major setbacks, if we followed the river tomorrow, we should reach the faeries by early evening.

I threw my bag onto a dry patch of ground, giving my magic a nudge to see how much had returned. It stirred, only a spark instead of a flame. "Shelter or food?"

Keelynn looked at me as if I'd spoken in a different language. "Excuse me?"

"There was a time when I could manage both after a fight, but not anymore, so you're going to have to choose one."

Her gaze swept from the bank to the branches. "We're staying *here*?"

Here seemed as good a place as any. Close to fresh water, far away from humans and their iron blades. "We don't have much of a choice. We're too far from anyone I know, and the nearest village is hours away."

"Why did you bring me through the forest? Why didn't we follow the road?"

"And risk encountering the man who murdered Padraig? I don't fancy dying"—*again*—"today, do you?"

More of her hair came loose when she shook her head. Her tongue nipped out as she mulled over her response. "Shelter," she said with a resolute nod.

Feck it anyway. I'd known she'd choose the more draining of the two. "We'll need firewood. Do you think you can handle that?" If I wanted to shift anything more than a canvas sheet, I'd need to conserve my energy.

Bless the woman, she didn't whinge or complain. She straightened her shoulders and said she could handle it.

"Good. Leave your cloak here and keep sight of the river so you don't get lost." I didn't have it in me to go traipsing about in the dark trying to locate her if she wandered too far.

"My cloak? Why?"

Hadn't she seen the blackness invading the sky? It was a wonder we weren't already drowned. "Because the heavens are about to open, and you'll want something warm and dry to wear tonight."

The moment she was out of sight, I headed in the opposite

direction until I hit deeper water. Sliding down the bank, I shucked off my shirt and breeches to wash them in the freezing river. As much as I didn't want to, I waded in, every part of me shrinking away from the icy liquid sweeping past.

"What the hell is your problem?" a voice growled from shore.

I slipped on the algae covered stones, landing face-first in the river. I came up sputtering like an eejit. "Feckin' hell, Rían." I shoved my dripping hair back from my eyes to glare at my brother. "How'd you find me?"

"How do you think?" he shot back, hands braced on his hips. Clean and dry and scowling.

Dammit. Eava and her scrying. What had I told her about helping my brother spy on me? To be fair, she only did it when she was proper worried. Which happened far more often than I'd admit.

"Since you're here, you may as well be useful and shift me some clean clothes."

Did he listen? No. The bastard folded his arms. "Why can't you do it yourself?"

I hated asking him for help. I hated asking him for anything. "Because I spent the night with Caer and Cait, the morning murdering three humans, and the afternoon in the feckin' underworld."

"Busy, busy." He clicked his tongue. "I see you still haven't gotten the ring."

The ring was the last thing on my mind with this water freezing the bollocks off me. I dipped my head back, giving my hair a quick scrub. "Clothes. Now."

When I stood, I found a clean pair of breeches, a shirt, and a towel stretched on a flat rock next to him.

"Any chance you could shift me something from the kitchens as well?"

The bastard went back to folding his arms and looking down on me. "Eava's upset you haven't been home. She's on strike."

Of course she was.

I dipped below the water once more, keeping my feet planted on the slick stones. When I resurfaced, I wiped the water from my face and started for shore. "Tell Eava I'll stop by tomorrow."

"Stop by?" Rían tossed me the towel. "Tadhg, you need to come back. I've things to be doing."

"I just need a little more time."

With another flick of his wrist, Rían's ceremonial dagger appeared, curved blade sharp and gleaming. "Give me ten minutes with the human."

The towel may have taken away the dampness, but it'd be ages before I warmed up. "Not happening."

"You actually like her, don't you?" The way he squinted made me want to cut out his eyes. "The woman wants your head on a feckin' platter, and *you like her*. And I thought I was bad." A chuckle. "Why don't you set your sights on one of the countless females who actually fancy you instead of wasting your time on one who wants you dead?"

"I don't—" My head throbbed when I tried to deny liking Keelynn. "It's complicated," I amended.

"How is it complicated? Fuck her and be done with it."

I couldn't do that when she wanted nothing to do with me, now could I? And even if I did convince Keelynn to sleep with me, I had a sinking feeling I would never want to be "done with it." I snagged the breeches from the rock, stuffing my feet into the rough wool legs. "Right. Because that's what you did."

"My situation is different."

"Because you're in love? That's a load of bollocks, and we both know it. The only person you're capable of loving is yourself."

Rían flicked his wrist. The sounds of the river and the forest faded to nothing inside the tost.

"Aveen is my soulmate."

"That's a load of—"

He aimed the dagger at my chest. "When I touch her, there's a spark that burns brighter than the light of a thousand candles.

Every fiber of my being yearns for her. Every day I'm forced to live without her is a feckin' nightmare. You," he sneered, gesturing at me with the blade, "with your 'cursed glamour,' with women falling at your feet, you wouldn't know the first thing about it because you're more incapable of love than I am."

The fire burning in my hands.

The latent desire.

The overwhelming need to be near someone even when she hated me.

"*Shit.*" That was it. What I'd been missing.

I'd assumed these . . . *feelings* and my body's intense reaction to Keelynn's touch, her presence, were just side effects of my curse. Had I been so focused on getting that ring—and keeping the wasp alive—that I'd missed what should've been plainly obvious?

Because Rían's yammering about the way his body responded to Aveen sounded a helluva lot like the way mine responded to her sister.

Fate. What a cruel, twisted bastard.

"Keelynn's my soulmate." The words tasted bitter, but the truth usually did.

The hand holding Rían's dagger dropped. His eyes began to glow like sapphire flames. "What did you say?"

Bad. This was so feckin' bad. "All that shite you just said," I muttered, the tightness in my chest unbearable. I raked a hand through my damp hair. It couldn't be. It couldn't. "I feel it when I touch Keelynn."

Rían's face went white as my shirt. "Who is Keelynn?"

Shit.

Shit shit shit.

"Who is Keelynn?" Rían demanded.

"Aveen's sister."

"You're fucking with me, right? You must be fucking with me."

I shook my head, still reeling from the revelation. "She caught us in the garden that night. She's the one who has the ring. The one who wants to kill me with that cursed dagger."

"What dagger?" His own dagger clattered to the ground. He grabbed my arms, giving me a bone-rattling shake. "Tell me what feckin' dagger."

"Small. Silver. Emerald in the hilt. Kills immortals."

He let me go with a snap, twisting on his heel to pace to the edge of the water and back again, kicking sand onto the stone and my clean shirt. "This is over. You're going straight back to the castle and leaving Keelynn to me."

Leave Keelynn to him? I may have lost my mind, but I wasn't that far gone. "Not a feckin' hope."

"You don't understand—"

"No, *you* don't understand. I helped you with your '*soulmate*' even when I thought your plan made no feckin' sense. Now you get to help me with mine."

He stilled, hands flexing into white-knuckled fists.

"Shift us something to eat and somewhere to stay the night," I told him, ripping the shirt from the ground. "Once I have the ring, I will be back."

Rían's jaw worked, but he flicked his wrist. As much as he hated me, I had been born first. The throne was mine. His duty was to obey me. And as unpredictable as my brother could be, he always put duty above all else.

"You cannot bring her to the Forest," he ground out, eyes wide and wild. He shook his head, hair falling over his forehead. "You'll have to find another way to get the ring."

Did he think me a fool? I'd already planned on meeting with the feckin' Queen to ensure Keelynn's safe passage. "If you're finished poking your nose in my business, I need you to kill someone." I described the man who'd robbed Keelynn and killed Padraig while Rían took in the information with a maniacal gleam in his too-bright blue eyes. The moment I finished, he collected his dagger from the ground and evanesced.

With my sopping clothes in hand, I climbed the bank to find a tiny cottage in the clearing. He could've shifted something larger, but I didn't complain because the moment I stepped inside and found a fire blazing in the hearth, my body gave up.

And then I saw the fish lying on the floor beside a stack of wood. That bastard knew I hated fish. And they weren't even cleaned. Once I had the energy, I'd shift their guts into Rían's favorite pair of boots.

15

THE RAIN HAD STARTED, MAKING IT DIFFICULT TO HEAR IF anyone was approaching. With no utensils or plates, I collected a few flat pieces of slate by the river and gave them a quick rinse. After cleaning the fish, something Eava had taught me to do once upon a time as punishment for stabbing Rían over the last biscuit, I settled them on another stone to cook.

The hinges groaned when the door opened. Keelynn stood in the entrance, arms laden with wood, hair and gown plastered to her thin frame. I hurried to collect the wood, adding it to the pile Rían had shifted and the few larger logs I'd gathered while waiting. "What took so long? I was afraid you'd gotten lost."

"Don't worry, the ring and I are here safe and sound." Despite the chill in her tone, her husky voice left me feeling warm all over. Keelynn pulled something from her dress pocket with purple-stained fingers. "I brought you food."

"You brought me food," I repeated like a mindless fool.

Blackberries.

I loved blackberries.

"I'm hardly going to eat them all myself," she said, gaze falling on the fire. "Although you obviously didn't need my help."

"I'd take a bushel of blackberries over a trout any day." Sweetness burst on my tongue when I popped one into my mouth. She shivered, her lips tinged blue—from cold or berries, it was hard to tell. "Give them here and get out of those wet clothes before you freeze to death."

I prepared our meager dinner while Keelynn withdrew the emerald dagger and placed it next to her boots. I couldn't help looking over my shoulder to find her struggling with the buttons at the front of her dress. Was it any wonder she struggled? Her hands must be frozen solid. I stood and closed the distance between us. Somehow, even drowned, she smelled like a field of lavender.

"Allow me?" I expected a sharp retort. Instead, her hands fell to her sides. She let me unfasten each clasp and peel her out of her dress the way I'd fantasized so many times this past week.

An ivory stay cinched her waist, thrusting her breasts upward beneath her shift.

"Turn around."

I shouldn't have enjoyed unlacing the satin ribbons. Uncovering her shoulders, tasting her pale skin, yearning for more.

She'd lost so much. The last thing she needed was me taking advantage of her.

But if she offered . . .

Cursing myself for not asking Rían to shift something for her to wear, I collected my clean shirt so she'd have something warm and dry to sleep in. "Here. Put this on."

Fighting the constant tug in my core, I turned from her wide eyes back to the fire. The fish looked cooked to me. I used my dagger to transfer it from the hot stones to the two cooler ones next to the portions of berries. Keelynn shuffled softly behind me, but I didn't dare turn around for fear of my self-control vanishing.

"Are you finished?" I asked.

"Yes."

Feck it all. She had legs for days beneath that shirt. And the black stockings she still wore highlighted the fact that the shirt only reached to her thighs, pale as moonlight.

There was only a slight tug from her, and yet my blood rushed south. It had been a long time since I'd been the one to feel more desire for a woman than the other way around.

I handed her one of the stones.

"Thank you. And not just for this." She nodded toward the cottage walls. "For everything."

"I know it's not what you're used to." She would've been used to fine dinners and parties and silver platters. Not fish on rocks.

"It's wonderful," she insisted.

Right. Wonderful. I picked apart the meat, scalding my fingertips. How many feckin' bones were in these things? Damn, I hated fish. The berries were excellent though.

"It is," she insisted. "I didn't think I would get any food tonight, so this is a feast."

"A feast. Right." In comparison to nothing, I supposed it was. If I weren't cursed, I could've shifted an actual feast. I would've loved to see the look on her face when she walked into this tiny cottage and found a table laden with delicacies and desserts. I could almost see the smile. The same one she'd given me the other day in the stable.

"Really. I've always wanted to go camping. Aveen and I used to beg our mother and father to let us camp in the gardens. They never did. So we'd steal scraps from the kitchen and bring them to our bedroom and eat in a makeshift tent in front of the fire."

How differently we'd grown up.

Ruairi and I used to camp all the time when we were children. And Rían as well when he was visiting. Only in Tearmann though. Never across the border.

"Tell me about her."

Keelynn popped a berry between her teeth, chewing slowly. "Why?"

"I want to know about the woman who is worth all of this." The woman who had captured my brother's attention and spurred the naïve, sheltered woman in front of me to leave the comfort of her home in search of a monster.

Keelynn launched into a story about how her sister had cared for her in the wake of their mother's death.

I couldn't help thinking of my own Mam's murder and how I'd been all alone in my grief. My father had been too lost to comfort me, not that we'd ever had that type of relationship. Others had grieved her passing as well, of course, but it wasn't the same.

"She sounds selfless." The exact opposite of the man Aveen had died to be with.

Keelynn's lips lifted into a sad smile. "She was. Aveen was selfless so that I could be selfish. And I was. So, so selfish." She hugged her legs against her chest, the flickering orange flames reflecting in the tears welling in her eyes. "I told her everything. My hopes. My fears. My dreams. She bore it all—did her best to make them come true. I was so self-absorbed that I never asked about *her* life. What *she* wanted. The night she died . . ."

The night I killed her, I silently amended.

I couldn't feel sorry.

If I'd refused, I never would've met *her*.

For the second time in as many days, I wondered what it would be like to be loved by a woman like this. To have her on my side, fighting for me instead of against me.

Foolish thoughts.

Foolish desires.

And yet the broken parts of me . . . wondered.

"It was her betrothal ball," Keelynn went on, wiggling her toes closer to the hearth, "and I was so hateful and angry toward her for something that wasn't her fault. Our father had arranged for her to marry the man I loved."

Ice flooded my veins.

She loved someone else.

Belonged to someone else.

"His name was Robert."

Robert. I'd always hated the name. Who in their right mind would name a child Robert? He sounded like a total wanker.

Keelynn's mirthless chuckle lifted the loose hairs from her cheek. "Aveen despised him. So did Padraig."

My respect for the dead man doubled.

"He was one of you," she breathed, shoulders curling in on themselves, leaving the shirt she wore gaping at the neck.

I banked the fire, adding a few more pieces of wood to stave off the chill. "I know. I could see his glamour on the day we met."

She wiped her eyes with the heel of her hand, sniffling softly. "Why don't you do that?"

"Do what?"

"Use a glamour to hide your ears."

"I used to hide them when I was young." After the first time I'd been killed by a human. I'd been twelve years old. Ruairi and I had evanesced to Swiftfell during yule. I'd been caught outside a pub by a bunch of drunkards who happened to have a spare iron chain hanging about. In my panic, I'd forgotten I could evanesce. By the time I remembered, it was too late.

"I wish he would've confided in me," she whispered to the flames.

With the way she'd treated me when we met, how could he? "Living among humans is dangerous for us. The more people know, the higher the risk of discovery."

Her brows drew together. "Dangerous for *you*? But you have magic."

"Magic isn't always enough to save us." Iron chains neutralized magic. Iron-lined cells kept us from evanescing. Curses made us weak. The emerald dagger glistening from beside her boots could send us to the underworld forever.

"All it takes is one human to make a false accusation. Airren law always rules in a human's favor." *Always*. "If Padraig had been caught using a glamour to conceal his identity, he would've been hanged." And if he hadn't used a glamour, finding honest work outside of Tearmann would've been nearly impossible.

"If it was so dangerous, why did he stay?"

I told her what Padraig had told me. That he'd stayed for her.

She stared into the flames, tears streaming down sunken cheeks, looking impossibly young and so, so devastated. She dropped her head as if hiding her face from me, sobbing into her hands. "It hurts. It hurts too much."

I felt her pain. My parents had been slaughtered. I'd lost friends and family and citizens day in, day out for centuries. You could never get used to death. You could only come to terms with it.

I crawled forward, slipping a hand around her waist, drawing her close. Inhaling her rain-kissed scent. I wanted to help but didn't know how.

My gaze landed on the dagger.

I could let her stab me with it and bring back her sister. It's what one of her storybook heroes would do. Sacrifice himself for the greater good.

But I was no hero.

I was a villain sentenced to lifelong punishment for my sins. And I could think of only one thing that would take her mind off what had happened.

"I can make it go away," I whispered against her ear, relishing the way she shivered. "Say the word, and I'll make the whole world go away." Not forever. Just for tonight.

"Please," she cried. "I don't want to hurt anymore."

The column of her throat tasted like lavender; the pulse at her neck thrummed beneath my tongue. Her head fell to my shoulder, thrusting her chest forward. Her nipples strained against the white shirt. When I saw my emerald ring hanging from the chain around her neck, resting between her breasts, an idea sparked in my mind.

"Put on the ring," I said.

"What?"

"Put it on." I needed to taste her lips. To know what it would be like to feel her tongue tangling with mine. To swallow her moans without losing her.

She fumbled for the chain, unfastening the clasp with trembling hands. The moment it settled on her finger, I could feel the thrum of its magic where we touched. I needed to know for sure that her curse was neutralized. Needed to know for sure what I wanted to do wouldn't compromise her in any way.

I needed her to lie.

Losing my fingers in her luxurious waves, still damp at the roots from the rain, I whispered, "Tell me you love me."

Her body stiffened.

"But . . . I don't."

Feck's sake, woman. Rip my heart out while you're at it. "*Lie.*"

"I . . . I love you."

It wasn't true. I knew it wasn't. And yet her lips tasted that bit sweeter for the lie when my mouth met hers. I hadn't kissed a woman properly since Fiadh. I'd forgotten how intimate it felt, being connected like this. And there was no one on this island I'd rather be experiencing it with than this hateful, beautiful wasp.

"Say it again," I begged.

"I love you."

The lie seeped into the darkest parts of me, warming and filling and breathing life into my barren heart. The words weren't real, but the woman was. Her mouth. Her tongue. The shirt she wore. The shirt I lifted over her head. The stockings and flushed skin.

I didn't need to hear her whimpers to know what she liked; she told me in the way she clutched my head to her chest as I teased the sensitive tips of her breasts with my tongue. Swirling. Nipping. Drawing out those delicious sounds.

There was too much to see. Too much to touch. Too much to taste.

Her ragged breaths caught when my fingers slid between her glorious thighs. Her nails skimmed my back when I dipped inside, finding her drenched and so tight, my eyes rolled back in my head. I could watch the delicious rapture on her face forever as my thumb circled the bundle of nerves hidden between folds of dripping heat.

When I withdrew, she whimpered. When I caught her hips and dragged her toward me, she gasped.

"Do you want to know a secret?" I whispered against her trembling knee, kissing my way along her petal-soft skin to the top of her stocking. Inching higher.

Her eyes burned into mine. "Yes."

"I've fantasized about burying myself between your thighs since the night we met." The moment I saw her kick that mercenary, I should've known I was doomed.

"Tadhg—"

She tasted of life and light and sweet redemption. Her hands tangled in my hair, pulling and dragging at the roots. Her thighs squeezed and shook.

I finally told her the truth. Spelling each word I couldn't say with my cursed tongue against her center.

That I was the monster she needed to murder.

That I was sorry for everything.

That her soul had been made to meld with mine.

That I was undeniably and irrevocably hers.

And when she came apart with a pulsing whisper, I wished there was a way to make her undeniably and irrevocably mine.

16

I HAD A NEW PLAN.

One that involved more of what had happened last night and less death.

For centuries I'd lived with my curses. What were a few more years? All I had to do was convince Keelynn to stay with me. Sure, she'd be upset when she learned the truth of my betrayal, but after last night, I was fairly certain I could convince her to forgive me. My body stirred. I'd convince her over and over and over again. She could keep the ring, and I would lock myself in the castle and stay away from anyone in a skirt except for her.

The sun kissed my cheeks the way I'd kissed Keelynn last night, leaving me almost as warm. That ring had been my salvation but not in the way I'd thought. Even the weight of my curses didn't feel as heavy on this glorious morning, the river burbling at my back and my soulmate inside the cottage.

I'd shifted my ledger in an attempt to try and sober myself. But staring at the names of my victims didn't trouble me the way it usually did. For the first time in a long time, I felt genuine hope welling inside my chest.

The door creaked, and Keelynn squeezed through the gap. A blush painted her cheeks when our eyes connected.

"Good morning."

That smile. I could stare at it forever. "Good morning," she returned. "How did you sleep?" She carried her boots to the river, dropping onto the pebbled shore. I loved that she didn't seem to mind getting her skirts dirty. Her bare feet dipped beneath the surface of a glimmering eddy.

I sent my ledger away. It'd do no good to have her see her sister's name written inside.

"Quite well considering the woman beside me snored like a drunken pooka." When I passed out next to Ruairi and the man woke me with his thunderous snores, I felt like holding a pillow over his face. When Keelynn had woken me this morning, I'd wanted to kiss her senseless.

"Ladies don't snore," she insisted, wiggling her toes, refusing to meet my gaze. "And if they *did* snore, a gentleman wouldn't mention it."

"Ah, but I am not a gentleman." Not by far. "And after last night, I'm not entirely convinced you're a lady." She was a wild goddess, brimming with unbridled passion. A creature to be worshipped every night and every day.

"Last night was a moment of weakness. It won't happen again."

That was her good sense talking. Fortunately for me, good sense tended to wane as darkness approached. And I had a lot of darkness. "Right. Of course. Out of curiosity, though, *why* can't it happen again?" *And again. And again. And again.*

"For one, we don't even like each other. And we're from two different worlds."

I liked her just fine when she wasn't being a hateful wasp. And our worlds weren't *that* different. Even as the thought crossed my mind, I almost laughed. What was I saying?

I was a murderous monster with a black soul, and she was an aspiring vigilante. Polar opposites if I'd ever seen them.

But after so many years, didn't I deserve something good? Didn't I deserve some light in my life? Why not with her?

Water splashed as she scrubbed at her hands. "Besides, you just want the ring so you can break your curse," she muttered.

That may have been true at first.

Now . . . I wasn't so sure.

After all, my ring was on her finger, not mine.

"The ring doesn't break curses, it neutralizes them." The only way to properly break a curse was with true love's kiss. Since no one could kiss me without losing her life, I didn't have a hope.

No one in their right mind would love someone like me.

She shook her hands, then wiped them against her black skirt. "If you want it so badly, why haven't you tried to steal it?"

I had. Multiple times. "Enchanted objects cannot be shifted or stolen. They must be freely gifted."

For some reason, my response made her frown. "I wish you would have told me about the ring."

"I didn't want you to lie to me."

"Unless it's to tell you that I love you." She laughed.

At my weakness.

At my pathetic request.

Was it so bad to want sex to feel like something more than a transaction? To want to feel loved? "Yes. Well . . . not all of us have the luxury of love. Sometimes we monsters like to pretend we're wanted for more than an escape or a distraction."

That's all I was. Something to numb the pain.

Now that she wore my ring, she could lie to me every single day, claiming to love me, but it would never be anything but a feckin' lie. I shoved to my feet, needing space to breathe without her pitying looks. So much for my new plan. Best get back to the old one.

Get to the castle. Show her the truth. Get the ring. Send her on her merry way back to her own feckin' world where she could find someone she *actually* liked.

"Tadhg, wait." The wasp got up too, kicking stones as she hurried after me. "I didn't mean that the way it came out. I genuinely—"

"Genuinely what? *Care*?" What a load of bollocks. She didn't care about me. She was just like every woman I'd been with for the last two hundred and fifty feckin' years. Only interested in what I could do. How I could make her feel. "You're such a shit liar, it's a wonder Fiadh bothered cursing you at all."

"Tadhg—"

"Let's not pretend this is more than it is. Like you said, we don't even like each other. You needed a distraction, and I was more than happy to oblige. That's it. End of discussion." And if she needed another one, I wouldn't have a choice in the matter. "Get your boots on. We need to be on our way."

How could I have thought for one second that this woman could be my soulmate?

I didn't have a feckin' soul.

~

Two feckin' hours. That was how long we stomped through the forest. Another feckin' hour. That was how long we traipsed through fields. I'd managed to go all day with only a minimal amount of talking. And the wasp hadn't seemed to mind. For a woman with such long legs, you'd think she'd walk a lot faster than she did. It took us ages to reach the faeries.

It felt good to be back among my own, like coming home. Keelynn, with her pinched look of disapproval, didn't seem to agree. Not that I cared what she thought. After all, she was only here to murder me.

I organized safe haven with a skeptical Áine, promising the wasp wouldn't harm them. Once the ancient tower house hidden in the forest came into view, I gestured toward the gray stone building and told Keelynn she could sleep there tonight. It looked ominous in the light flickering from the bonfire, but the space was clean and dry. At least there were beds. After spending last night on the floor, I was sure she'd appreciate that.

Not that I wanted to think about last night.

Áine shifted where she perched on my shoulder.

Keelynn's eyes narrowed at the white-haired faerie. "Where are you sleeping?" she asked.

Why did she care? It wasn't as if we'd be staying together. She'd made that perfectly clear this morning. Before I could answer, Áine flew to the ground, shifting into her human form with a burst of blinding white light.

The dress the faerie wore sparkled in what little light filtered through the branches. Unfortunately, my night had been determined a century ago, when Áine and I had struck our bargain. "I will be staying elsewhere."

Áine held out a hand, the ancient symbols on her skin glowing a faint gold. "Come with me. I have a surprise for you."

Couldn't the faerie see I was busy with the human? Once Keelynn was safely inside the tower house, I'd join her for whatever she wanted. She'd claimed me the moment I arrived so I didn't have to stay up all night letting the others use me as a feckin' scratching post. Ours was a relationship of convenience. I wanted sleep, and she wanted Rían.

"I'll join you in a moment." The wasp was my first priority.

A handful of other faeries in their human forms sank onto stones around the crackling bonfire.

Considering her lack of knowledge about the Danú, I doubted Keelynn knew much about the faeries beyond the lies written in her beloved fairy tales. "They can choose one day a season to walk the island as humans do."

A deep V formed between her brows. "Isn't that convenient."

I certainly thought it was. Communicating with them when they were this size was infinitely easier than when they were small. "As I was saying before, choose any room you want, but be sure to lock the door once you've gone in."

"Am I not allowed to stay out here?"

After hobbling around all day on sore feet, I assumed she'd want to head straight for bed. And with her hatred of my kin, I thought she wouldn't want to associate with "things" like us. "Do you *want* to stay out here?"

If she wanted to stay, there wasn't much I could do to stop her besides lock her in a room and create a tost so no one could hear her scream.

But I didn't have enough magic for that, and there were too many witnesses, *and* I still needed that ring.

Keelynn shrugged as if she didn't care either way.

"I'm not sure it would be safe," I said. "Things can get out of control, and there's no telling what you'd see." For someone like Keelynn, the way everyone here carried on would surely be too scandalous.

"I will be fine."

I told her she could stay but asked that she avoid the wine. The rotten taste was usually enough to keep people away, but this woman had proven particularly stubborn. Too much faerie wine led to terrible decisions.

I should know.

None of the food the faeries had laid out looked appealing except the blackberries. I grabbed the whole bowl and headed straight for the white-haired faerie waving from the far side of the fire. What'd Áine have in the basket hanging from her arm?

Cinnamon and vanilla swirled around me when I lifted the cloth on top. God love the woman, she'd gotten her hands on a spongy cake dusted with icing sugar—probably stolen from some human's kitchen.

I didn't ask because I didn't care. I ate slice after slice, feeling the sugar hit my system with a jolt, giving me more energy than I'd had in days.

"Tell us a story, Tadhg," Davine said, a wide smile on her lips. A few faeries I didn't recognize had draped themselves in her blue hair.

"I'd rather he take off his shirt," muttered Etain. She toyed with the hem of her dark green skirt that barely reached the tops of her dark thighs. When she caught me staring, she spread her legs and giggled.

Áine's grip on my arm tightened. I managed to tear my gaze away.

"Take off your shirt *and* tell us a story!" someone in the back shouted.

"Leave yer shirt on and take off yer breeches!"

It must've been a while since a male had passed through. If it weren't for Áine's possessiveness, there would be no hope of me getting any rest.

"Since I haven't the energy for much else," I said, setting the empty basket on the grass, "I suppose a story will have to satisfy you tonight."

A few faeries groaned, but most looked pleased.

This was how I'd spent much of my childhood: breathing in the smoky smell of a bonfire, listening to ancient stories passed down from generation to generation. My father had been an excellent storyteller, transforming himself into each character as he went along.

Before these curses, I had been able to change my face and form as well. Although I hadn't been as talented at mimicking others as my father—or Rían.

"It's been said that magic was born beneath the Airren hills," I began, wiping my hands on my knees, dusting them in white sugar. "If you sit in just the right spot when the sun is setting, you can still see a faint glow rising from the emerald grass. The faeries were first to arrive, soaring on iridescent wings from neighboring islands, settling in the trees of the lushest forests. Then came the others, ancient ones without names, searching for freedom. For centuries, our ancestors lived in relative harmony. Justice was swift and absolute. Peace reigned from coast to coast."

I had been born at the end of that peaceful century, when my father, a fae prince, had married the witch Bronagh. I spent my youth in blissful ignorance among the faeries and pooka and grogochs.

"Hundreds of years later, boats landed on our shores, carrying strange beings without magic flowing in their veins. Most were kind, learning to live and work alongside the Danú. When their king heard of our riches, he sent an army wielding iron weapons to claim them, along with our land."

I'd been six years old when I met my first human, my magic still untried and untested. He had been a captain in the king's army whose regiment had moved into a nearby town. Ruairi had convinced me to come with him to see their bright red uniforms and shiny swords. I had been intrigued by the way they spoke, their language strange and unfamiliar. So intrigued that I'd gotten too close to their encampment.

When the captain caught me, he dragged me to a platform in the center of the camp where two pooka and a leprechaun swung from ropes. I had been so terrified that I pissed myself. I tried to speak to him, to tell him I hadn't meant any harm. If he understood a word I said, it hadn't mattered. He had narrowed his cold blue eyes, called me a monster, and impaled me with his iron sword.

The blow hadn't killed me, but it had been close.

"One burst of power would've killed them all," I said, watching Keelynn as she listened. "But what of the innocents? The children? Those we had married? Those who had become part of our world instead of trying to steal it?

"The Danú and their leader refused, and it cost us our island."

I'd chosen this tale specifically for the human watching me from across the fire, flames reflected in her wide eyes. I don't know why it mattered so much for Keelynn to hear our side of this story. For her to understand what we'd been forced to endure. But it did.

"The Vellanian king slaughtered our leaders, those who were most powerful, ultimately taking control and *gifting* us a tiny patch of land in the northwest as a sign of goodwill." *Gifting*. As if the land had been his to give in the first place.

"They expected us to keep to that land or follow laws created to make us 'equal' to humans. Laws that made practicing magic illegal. Laws meant to keep us from fighting back. Laws that stole the lives of our mothers and fathers, sisters and brothers."

The faeries' heads bobbed. Murmurs of agreement lifted with sparks from the blazing fire.

In showing mercy, my father had condemned our people to the shadows. Unlike many of my fellow Danú, I didn't believe humans should be punished for what their ancestors had done. The ones who had themselves committed atrocities, sure. But hurting innocent people didn't fix anything.

All we wanted was true equality that didn't come at the expense of who we were.

I opened my mouth to say as much just as I heard hooves thundering from the forest at my back. My eyes found Keelynn's. With her weak human senses, she wouldn't know what approached.

But I did.

And I was dreading it already.

17

"WHY ARE YE WASTING THE NIGHT LISTENING TO THIS OLD bollocks drone on about the past?" Ruairi called from the trees. "I thought it was the fourth of the month."

Of all the feckin' days for him to show—

Áine shrieked, jolted to her feet, and ran for Ruairi and Cormac.

Keelynn's face paled.

Twin flashes lit up the night, leaving my mate and his friend in their human forms.

Ruairi's nose lifted and eyes glowed, golden orbs searching the gathered crowd. In a blink, he'd evanesced to Keelynn's side. "What do we have here? A pretty little human has decided to join our soiree?" he drawled. "Who invited you, pet?"

His hand reached out, but before his fingers connected with Keelynn's hair, I was at his side, blade in hand, pressing the tip to his thick neck. "Touch her and I'll send you to the underworld."

"Ah . . . she's one of yours then." Ruairi's hand dropped. "Pity." He should've moved on except the man had a death wish, so he sat next to her. Far too close. A shift in position and he'd get his disgusting scent all over her. "What's your name, human?"

I looked like a crazed eejit with my dagger, so I put it away. For now. "Lady Keelynn, this is Ruairi."

"A *lady*. How fancy." He sniffed her like the animal he was, getting too feckin' close but never touching. "She doesn't smell like a lady. But she doesn't smell like you either," he said with a smirk.

If Keelynn and I had been sleeping together, Ruairi would've been able to smell my scent mixed with hers. And he wouldn't have dared to get within ten feet of her. An arrangement himself, Rían, and I had made centuries ago. Speaking of my brother . . . "Is anyone else coming that I should know about?"

Ruairi shook his head. "I couldn't convince Rían to leave his hovel."

For some unknown reason, my brother had bought a cottage in shite up the coast near Hollowshade. Heaven only knew what plans he had for the dilapidated thing. Probably some sort of torture chamber. At least this new obsession was better than what he'd done the first few months after Aveen had died.

"Who is Rían?" Keelynn asked.

Ruairi answered before I could. "Rían is Tadhg's younger brother."

Technically, he was my bastard half-brother, a biproduct of my father's philandering ways. Not that I wanted to talk about either.

Keelynn gripped the edge of the stone with shaking hands. When I asked if she was all right, she glared and claimed to be fine.

"Are you sure?" I dropped to one knee. Her forehead felt cool, but her face held no color.

"I said I'm *fine*." She shoved me away and stalked toward a half-full bottle of wine someone had left on a stone.

I shifted the thing before she could do something she regretted. That shite was pure alcohol. "What did I tell you about the wine?"

Ruairi stole it from me and gave it back to the wasp. "If the *lady* wants a drink, then I say let her drink."

Keelynn's chin lifted as she took the wine and drank straight from the feckin' bottle, only to gag and spew drops of drink into the night air. Ruairi's laughter echoed around the forest while the rest of the gathering giggled.

"That's enough." Any more than that and she'd be flat on her arse in the next twenty minutes.

What'd the wasp do?

She took another feckin' drink.

And a third.

Defiant eyes met mine, glassy and glazed. *That's it. End of.* I wasn't spending my night worrying over this woman. I caught her arm, holding firm when she struggled. "You're going to bed if I have to lock you in the feckin' room myself."

"No, I'm not. I'm going to stay and have a chat with the handsome pooka."

Ruairi? *Handsome*?

The bastard's grating chuckle would be his last.

"Keelynn—"

"Let the human go." Cormac clapped a hand on my shoulder, squeezing until my neck hurt. "All it takes is one."

What had I been thinking, touching her like that? I knew what happened when I let my emotions get the better of me. If Keelynn reported me for manhandling her, there'd be hell to pay. And not just from the Airren authorities but from Rían as well.

Cormac helped her right herself, keeping his hands at her arms.

A possessive hand snaked down my chest. "She's not worth it," Áine insisted. "Besides, you and I have some business to attend to."

Not now, *dammit*. Couldn't she see I was busy? "You can wait until I'm finished here."

"I've waited long enough," Áine whined. "You promised, remember? I'm calling in our bargain."

That was the problem with bargains made under the influence of copious amounts of alcohol. They always seemed like a good idea at the time.

I gave Keelynn one final pleading glance before following Áine into the dark forest. Light from the moon broke through the trees, falling on an ancient altar.

"He's not going to be pleased to see you," I said, trying to drudge up the energy and magic for what needed done.

"Rían is always pleased to see me," she countered, brushing her white hair back from her slender shoulders.

That may have been true a few years ago, but now he had Aveen.

Dammit.

Why did he get a soulmate who loved him? How was that fair?

With a flash of white light, Áine was back to her tiny, vicious self. I tucked her into my waistcoat and evanesced to the castle. The wards wouldn't let her through unless she came with me. The moment we reached the parlor, Áine dislodged herself from my pocket. A fire blazed in the fireplace, flickering off Rían's boots sticking out from his favorite chair. This time, Áine's transformation was blinding.

Rían scrambled to his feet. With his collar undone and cravat hanging loosely around his neck, it was the most disheveled I'd seen him in months.

He jabbed an accusatory finger toward the faerie at my side. "What the hell is she doing here?"

Áine stepped forward, sending Rían stumbling back. "Is that how you speak to me?"

An empty bottle of faerie wine had been discarded on the coffee table next to a half-full one.

My brother looked more panicked than the last time I'd tried to choke him. "Go home, Áine."

"You don't want me to do that. Not really," she crooned, stalking Rían until she had him pinned against the floral curtains.

My brother made no move to push her away. His gaze dropped to her mouth, and she pressed her lips to his. The moment Rían lost his hands in her white hair, my feet unlocked from the stones, carrying me into the hallway.

Rían cursed.

Áine called his name.

Stomping footsteps grew louder and louder until my brother appeared.

"What the hell were you thinking?" Rían snarled, shoving me against the tapestry of the Queen, crushing my windpipe with his forearm.

"She asked to see you," I choked, reaching for the dagger at my waist. With his magic holding me hostage, I'd have to kill him the old-fashioned way.

Before I could grip the hilt, Rían dropped his arm and raked his hands through his hair, leaving the dark strands standing on end. "So you brought her here? To my home?"

"This is *my* home."

"Dammit, Tadhg. My fiancée is upstairs."

"Are you reminding me or yourself?"

His eyes flashed, and he cursed again. "Get rid of her."

When I returned to the parlor, I found Áine on the floor in front of the fire, her knees drawn to her chest. Sparkling silver tears streamed down her cheeks like liquid diamonds.

I sank next to her, weary to my marrow. "I told you not to come." This wasn't like the other times. Rían was engaged and, much to my surprise, he was actually trying to avoid sleeping with his usual harem.

Which only made me feel worse.

"Last time, h-he said he cared for me." She sniffled, clutching the material at her waist in her fists. "I . . . I thought . . ."

"Rían lies."

"All men lie." She turned, tears clinging to her thick lashes. "Except you."

"Yes. Well. That's not entirely accurate." I lied by omission. I twisted the truth.

"He doesn't find me attractive anymore," she sniffled.

The idea that Áine wasn't attractive was absurd. She, like all faeries, was stunning. "We both know that's not the case."

"Do you?" she whispered.

"Do I what?"

"Find me attractive."

My stomach tightened. "You know I do."

Her knees pressed against my thigh when she scooted closer. "Then why won't you look at me?"

Beauty was a faerie's curse, rarely reaching below the surface. Most of them were like ripe apples hollowed out by worms: rotten on the inside. Áine didn't care about my brother—or me, for that matter. Áine only cared about herself.

"We should go back."

Her hand slipped up my thigh. "And if I don't want to go back?"

I caught her fingers, fighting the tug between us with everything inside me. "This wasn't part of our bargain," I managed through clenched teeth.

"Then I think it's time for our bargain to change. Go on, Tadhg. Give in. You know you can't resist."

I had no desire to touch the woman and didn't want her touching me, but all I could do was shake my pounding head and grip the rug beneath me until my fingers ached. My eyes screwed shut, and I held my breath.

Her hand stopped right before she reached my groin. "Why won't you look at me?"

Because I wanted to pretend the hand next to my cock belonged to someone else. "Let's just get this over with."

"Is that any way to speak to me? I have helped you for almost a hundred feckin' years, and you want to 'get this over with'? *Look at me.*"

I shook my head.

"It's that hideous human, isn't it?" she seethed, nails digging into my thigh. "You'd rather be with her over me?"

Finally, a question I could answer honestly. "A thousand times over." Keelynn didn't know any better because I'd kept her in the dark. But Áine knew better. And yet, here she was, trying to take advantage of my weakness.

Her lips twisted into a mocking smile. "I'd love to see if your little pet enjoys the taste of hellsbane as much as she enjoys our wine."

Hellsbane was the worst of poisons and nearly impossible to cure, giving those who'd digested it a slow, agonizing death. "You forget yourself, Áine."

"Go on, Tadhg," she crooned, her hand resuming its trek north. "Give in."

She wanted me to give in, did she? "All right," I whispered.

Her lips lifted.

And I kissed them.

18

Keelynn had her hand on Ruairi. It was just his arm, but I could tell from the stillness in his stance and the way his lips twitched into a smile that he never wanted it to end, and if she didn't stop, I was going to kill my best mate.

When I'd returned to the forest and found her seat empty, I'd hoped she'd heeded my warning and gone to bed. Then I evanesced into the tower and found all the feckin' rooms empty as well. Blind panic had seized my chest when I returned to the bonfire to search the few remaining stragglers for signs of her.

Then I'd heard tell-tale splashes from the nearby river.

And damn it all if I didn't come alive inside the moment I saw Keelynn stumble up the bank in one of the faerie's dresses. She was too busy laughing with a blue-haired faerie to see me. Seren wouldn't be much older than Keelynn, I'd imagine. With the way they carried on, giggling arm-in-arm, they looked like fast friends.

Ruairi and Cormac waited on the shore. Ruairi sniffed the air and turned his head, his eyes meeting mine from the shadows. He nodded toward Keelynn, as if to say he'd kept her safe. I nodded back, not quite ready to speak with her.

Not when I could still taste Áine.

I shifted a bottle of puítin from our stores and took a deep drink, washing away the lingering taste of Áine's sour lips.

Keelynn stumbled, catching herself on a mossy log, laughing so hard she snorted.

I am a lady . . .

She may have been raised a lady, but in that dress, all that gloriously pale skin on display, dancing beneath the moon, she looked as Danú as the rest of the faeries.

Ruairi the feckin' gentleman helped her to her feet. Unlike Rían and I, he'd been raised with morals. That he hung around with us still astounded me. His mother would've been appalled were she still alive. The woman had never approved of either of us. And who could blame her? Leading her precious son down dark, wanton paths.

Keelynn danced around the fire, blissful in her own world. No sign of her rigid shoulders as she twirled and lifted those long arms above her head. The movement made the already short skirt ride nearly to her arse. Not that it was a problem for me, but if Ruairi didn't get his eyes back on her face, he'd have a blade in his gullet.

I couldn't watch her anymore without my chest aching and I didn't want to ruin her fun with my dark mood.

After all she'd lost, she deserved to laugh and dance.

I trudged into the forest with my bottle, propped myself against a tree, and drank.

One for my misery.

One for my sins.

One for the human who wore my ring.

One for—

Feck it. One for no reason at all other than to make it an even four.

By the time I made it back to the fire, Keelynn was lying face-down in the grass next to Ruairi.

"Dammit, Ruairi. What'd you do to her?" I hadn't been gone that long. Had I?

"Me?" He took a swig straight from the bottle of wine, using his shirt to wipe his mouth. "I didn't do a feckin' thing."

"Why isn't she in the tower?" He should've brought her inside the moment he realized she was tired.

"Because she insisted on waiting for ye."

Keelynn smiled when I pressed a cool hand to her flushed cheek. "How much did she drink?"

"Not as much as she wanted, but considerably more than she should've."

Brilliant. She'd be sick as a dog in the morning.

I hefted her into my arms, cradling her close. Feckin' woman with her feckin' notions. Didn't she have an ounce of self-preservation? Hadn't I told her to avoid the wine? Hadn't I told her to go to the tower? Had she listened? No. Of course not. That would've been too feckin' simple.

Something warm and wet grazed my neck.

I shifted Keelynn in my arms to find her pink tongue sliding over her lips. "Did you just *lick* me?"

"You taste good."

Not as good as you, I wanted to say. But that was a dangerous path to be avoided—one she would most assuredly regret come morning. "Feckin' hell, woman. You must've had a lot of wine."

Her shoulder rubbed against my chest when she shrugged. "What took you so long?"

I didn't want to talk about the body I'd left in the castle. I didn't want to talk about anything. "Shhh. Go back to sleep."

The first few doors I checked were locked. It wasn't until I reached the fifth door on the third floor that I found an unoccupied room. Keelynn groaned when I set her on her feet, swaying like a tree in a gale. "Can you stand on your own, or do I need to bring you to the bed?"

"It would've been the second one if you hadn't gone off with *Áine*," she muttered, colliding with the wall.

"Yes, well, I didn't have much of a choice." This was the drink talking. People said all sorts of foolish things when they were drunk. "You need to get some sleep. Don't forget to lock the door." I paused, letting the command sink in. "Did you hear what I said? Lock the—"

"I heard you. Lock the bloody door." She narrowed her bloodshot eyes toward the handle. "Why does it matter? It's not like a lock could keep one of you out."

"I've already told you that evanescing into a locked room breaks one of our most important laws. So, while a lock technically wouldn't keep us out, there'd be hell to pay if anyone came in."

Her eyes dropped to my mouth. "Who's going to come in here?" she breathed.

The huskiness in her voice sent all my blood rushing south.

I checked she hadn't lost the ring before glancing toward the delicate pink skin of her lips. "A terrible monster who wants to take advantage of your inebriated state." A war raged inside me, telling me to leave, to get the hell out of this room before she made an offer I couldn't refuse. The consequences of spending the night with Keelynn like this wouldn't end well for either of us.

My stubborn feet refused to budge as my magic slipped free, curling about her bare ankles like phantom fingers.

"Do you think the monster would like my dress?"

I slipped a finger down the scandalous neckline to the swell of her breast, teasing just beneath the shimmering material. "He would love your dress." *On the floor.*

"He wouldn't think it was too short?"

It was too short for anyone else to see, but not for me. Not for the two of us in this bedroom, bodies meeting in all the right places. "He'd think it was just right."

I knew I shouldn't kiss her. But then my hand skimmed beneath the hem of her dress, finding her hip bare beneath, and I couldn't resist. Just one kiss. Barely a kiss. A graze to torture us both.

"This can't happen again. You said that. We don't even like each other." That's what she'd said. She may not like me, but she certainly liked what I was doing with my hips.

"I lied," she moaned, hips rising to meet mine.

What if I inched her skirt up higher, undid my belt, and let her bare flesh writhe against me until we both saw stars? *No, no.* Keelynn was too drunk, and I wasn't exactly sober myself, and with lust clouding my mind, I wasn't thinking straight.

Time to go. Beyond time. "Next time I tell you not to drink the wine, I suggest you listen." I evanesced outside the room, my curse and my body screaming at me to go back. "Lock the damn door," I called. If she didn't, there was no telling what I'd do.

~

The only way to keep myself from returning to that chamber was to drown my darkness with more drink. If I couldn't see straight, I couldn't find her. If I couldn't feel my limbs, I wouldn't be able to move from this spot next to the dying bonfire. I drank every last rancid drop from the bottle, chucked the thing into the fire, and swiped at my cursed lips with my sleeve.

Get drunk. Pass out. Pretend there wasn't a woman I wanted more than air sleeping so close I could still smell her. Solid plan.

Leaning back against the stone, Ruairi scratched his chin. "Yer in right trouble over that one, aren't ye?"

I couldn't answer without my head throbbing.

"Traveling across the country with a beautiful woman fer how long without takin' her to bed," he went on, giving my boot a nudge with his. "Not like ye at all, lad."

The bonfire had burned to embers and a few glowing orange logs. Seren was curled on the ground beneath Ruairi's dark coat. Giggles echoed from the tower, where Cormac and two other faeries had disappeared not long after I'd returned.

"She told you that?" It must've been the drink. There was no other explanation for Keelynn trusting Ruairi.

He smirked. "Yer human told me lots of things."

I sat up too fast, scraping my back off the feckin' stone. "Tell me."

His black hair fluttered when the bastard shook his head. "And betray my *new friend's* confidence? Not a hope, lad."

"Please." I had enough drink in me to beg.

Ruairi gave me a pitiful sidelong glance. "She wasn't a bit impressed that ye went off with Áine, I'll tell ye that much."

Keelynn wouldn't be impressed with a lot of things I'd done this week.

Ruairi collected a fresh bottle of wine from the other side of the stone, working the cork free with his fangs and spitting it toward the glowing logs. "I noticed something on her finger," he muttered before taking a swig and handing the bottle to me.

I hid my grimace with the bottle.

"Care to tell me what's really happening?"

It took a good deal of concentration, but I managed a tost to keep prying ears from overhearing. "She wants to kill the Gancanagh with an enchanted dagger to bring her sister back from the dead."

Ruairi withdrew a stack of clothes and boots from the far side of the rock. "Wouldn't happen to be this dagger, would it?"

The emerald in the hilt glowed when he handed it to me.

That woman. Did she realize how valuable this thing was? And she'd left it behind as if it were a piece of cutlery. Drunk Keelynn was more irresponsible than I thought. What was I going to do with her?

"She's far too fine fer the likes of ye," Ruairi said, passing me the bottle.

"You think I don't know that?" Even at her most hateful, she was too good for someone like me.

"Here's a mad idea. How about ye tell her the truth?"

I stopped drinking long enough to wipe dripping wine from my chin. The fire and faeries grew hazy, like staring through a thick fog.

The moment I told Keelynn the truth, she was either going to hate me or stab me. I scowled down at the cursed dagger glowing on the grass. "I know how . . . to deal withwomen." Knew all about them. *Alllll* about them.

Ruairi took the bottle, pointing at me with its green neck. "Seducing a woman's not the same as loving one."

"Ha! I don't lo—" My head started pounding. *No no no.* "I don't lov—"

Chuckling, Ruairi cupped a hand around his ear and leaned toward me. "What's that now? I can't hear when ye stutter."

"*Shit.*" I ripped the bottle out of his hands, raising it to my lips and drinking until I couldn't fit any more in my gullet. I did not love that infuriating woman. I barely knew her. I barely *liked* her.

Pathetic.

That's what I was.

The first woman in centuries I spent time getting to know, and my useless heart jumped right out of my chest and into her feckin' pocket.

I'd be better off stabbing myself with that cursed dagger. I swiped for it. Ruairi, the bastard, was quicker. "Ah, ah, Princey. Yer not dyin' on my watch."

"That'sfiiiine. Keelynn can . . . killme tomorrow." She'd be so happy if she did. *Soooo* happy. She'd have her sister, and Rían would have his soulmate, and I would be free. Didn't sound so bad right about now.

Ruairi caught my hand, dragging me to my feet. With my arm braced across his hulking shoulders, we stumbled toward the tower. "If ye die and leave me on my own with Rían, I'll never forgive ye."

My legs were utterly useless. Couldn't even lift them. They just dragged along, one after the other, catching on stones and tree roots.

"Quit movin' about or I'll drop ye on yer drunk arse and let the faeries have their way with ye."

The bestpart . . . aboutbeing . . . drunk . . . was that my curse didn'tfeel . . . as . . .

What was the word? *Ahhhh* . . . Heavy. That was it.

Ruairi hauled me inside and up the stairs. Why were there so many? The building wasn't *that* tall. He reached for a knob, twisted. A waft of musty air assaulted my nostrils.

"In ye go, drunken sod." Ruairi shoved between my shoulder blades.

I caught myself on either side of the doorframe. The wood groaned under the pressure when Ruairi tried again to push me in. "Wrong room."

"Right room," he insisted, shoving me again.

The bed linens were more tatty than my overcoat, and the dank darkness felt cold and empty, and, "I don't want to sleep in here."

He crossed his arms over his broad chest, scowling down at me like the imposing fecker he was. "Where do ye think yer going to go?"

Which floor were we on? Keelynn was near the stairs. I think. "I need to find someone." I ducked around him, heading for the first door. I'd knock on every feckin' one if I had to. Keelynn would let me in. I would ask nicely. *Very* nicely. I'd get on my knees and beg.

A hand caught my collar, hauling me back toward the open room. "Yer going to say or do something ye will both regret. And she'd have every right to kill ye for it. Into bed with ye."

Why couldn't Keelynn be ordering me to bed instead? I fell face-first onto the mattress. It smelled like sweat and old socks. Turning my head, I gasped for fresh air. "She smells *sooo* good."

"I've noticed. Now, go to sleep."

When he made to leave, I tried to sit up. "And where might you be going? *Hmmm*?"

"To keep a certain human from being mauled by a drunken prince."

"I would never—"

"Tadhg? Get some rest. After what ye did, yer gonna need it."

After what I did? What had I—

Oh, right. I'd killed Áine.

19

RUAIRI HAD BEEN RIGHT TO TAKE THE DAGGER LAST NIGHT. Because if I'd had it that morning, I'd be on my way to the underworld. My head. Pounding wasn't a strong enough word for the way it rattled. My stomach revolted when I rolled onto my side. The gray walls tilted. The wooden ceiling spun. If I hadn't died so many times before, I'd be convinced this was the end.

"Up and out, sunshine."

The moment I heard his voice, the pounding got infinitely worse.

I peered through blurry lashes at my brother's scowl. Rían perched on the window ledge, arms folded across his chest, judging me. Definitely not the first thing I wanted to see in the morning.

"What're you doing here?" I croaked, reaching for the pint of water waiting beside my boots with a trembling hand.

"I just missed your cursed face. What the hell do you think?"

Closing my eyes, I pressed the cold glass to my thumping skull. Was all the shouting really necessary?

"I went into the parlor this morning and found a feckin' body."

Oh, right. That.

Each stomp of his boots when he crossed the floor was like a hammer to my temple. "You killed Áine. *Áine.*"

"I know what I did."

"And did you consider the consequences of your actions?"

I'd ignored the consequences of my actions for years. What did it matter anyway? What were they going to do? Kill me? I'd welcome the reprieve from the feckin' hangover.

"Wallace called bright and early asking *me* what I'd done with his daughter. So I asked myself"—Rían tapped his pointed chin—"why would he be calling to me if Áine had left the castle with you?" He balled up my shirt and threw it at my face. "Unless she didn't leave the feckin' castle."

"She—"

Rían held up a hand. If he didn't get the thing out of my face, I'd chop it clean off. "I don't give a shit that she's dead. But I refuse to clean up yet another one of your messes. Now, sober up quick, put on something that doesn't reek of drink, and get your arse back to the castle. You have a murder to explain."

"You killed my daughter!" The accusation echoed around the great hall, sending my head pounding anew.

With the amount of wine I'd drunk, I'd known today was going to be shite, but the reality was far worse. If the fat little white-haired man didn't stop pacing in front of the dais, the bile climbing the back of my throat would end up on his boots.

Rían's eyes bore into my skull from where he sat on the smaller throne. Rían and his judgment could go and shite. If he'd slept with Áine, none of this would've happened. I would've returned to the bonfire, stopped Keelynn from drinking herself into a stupor, and spent the night in her bed instead of guzzling half a bottle puitín and faerie wine.

"Your daughter made threats against a woman in my charge," I explained.

"A feckin' *human*," Wallace seethed, his slightly crooked teeth flashing.

"Be glad my brother handled it before I did," Rían drawled, his smile laced with quiet rage. As much as he hated me, he hated the faeries more. Our father had been a faerie before giving up his wings for my mother. She'd used spells and dark magic to allow him to maintain his power without them.

Rían had never forgiven Midir for abandoning him with his mother.

Wallace's face paled. "You will pay for what you've done. Stealin' a year of my little girl's life away as if it's nothing."

Rían's eyebrows lifted toward his mahogany hair. "That sounded like a threat. Wouldn't you say, Tadhg?"

I didn't want to see the man dead. He was understandably distraught over his daughter. Still, I couldn't have him coming in here, delivering threats for all to hear. "Let's ask Wallace. Were you threatening me just now? Or did you speak out of anger and wish to apologize?"

His face reddened. I wouldn't have been surprised to see smoke coming from his pointed ears. "I am sorry, my prince."

Rían inhaled, a small smile playing on his lips. "I don't think you are."

With me being a true immortal, there was nothing Wallace could do that would have any lasting impact. Unless he acquired the cursed dagger I'd left with Ruairi.

Still, I couldn't let him get away with speaking to me like that. "Perhaps a day in the dungeon will change your tune. Rían?"

My brother's eyes lit up, making him look like a child who just got a new puppy. With a flick of his wrist, he and the faerie disappeared.

Before I left Tearmann, there was one more order of business I had to deal with. Something I had been putting off for days. With a burst of magic and a focused mind, I evanesced to the Phantom Queen's cliffside castle. An onyx monstrosity surrounded by the Black Forest.

I hated this place almost as much as I hated the gallows.

It wasn't just the stench of rotting vegetation mixed with the perfume of death that made my stomach lurch. There was always this niggling feeling of eyes on you, even though no one was around. Then there were all the feckin' crows pecking at the blackened ground. If I lived in this place, I'd be deranged too.

With my pounding head screaming at me to evanesce the hell out of there, I withdrew my dagger from its sheath and slid the sharp blade across my palm. Blood welled from the wound. I squeezed my fist, letting the deep red drops drip into the lock on the high spiked gates.

The lock *clicked*, and the gate whined as it eased open of its own volition.

Two guards on either side of the mammoth door peered from behind black masks, their outfits making it nearly impossible to tell if they were men or women. Not that it mattered when they had their swords drawn and aimed at your chest.

"What business do you have with the Queen?" Ah. A woman then. And a young one by the sound of her voice. No one knew where the old crow recruited her army of shadow guards. And no one dared to ask.

"I've come to discuss passage through the Forest."

Behind the guard who had spoken, the massive door opened. The Queen emerged, her black feathered skirts fluttering on the rancid breeze. An onyx crown came to a point in the center of her pale, wrinkled forehead, matching the blackness pulsing through her veins. "Nephew, what a pleasant surprise."

Being cursed to tell the truth meant I couldn't return the false sentiment. "Hello, Auntie."

She stepped aside, gesturing toward the white hallway beyond. "Do come in."

I was about to say there was no need, that I wouldn't be staying, but had to remind myself that I needed something from the Queen and being rude wouldn't serve my purposes. So I followed her into her lair, through the white marble hallway to a small parlor with a lone candle shuddering between two matching wingbacks.

"How's Rían?" she asked, taking a seat, and spreading her skirts about her ankles with a weathered hand.

I forced myself into the identical chair on the other side of the barren fireplace. "His usual delightful self."

She smirked at that. "Any news from Tearmann?"

As if she didn't already know. The witch had spies everywhere. "Not a bit."

"And from Airren?"

"You know as well as I do the situation in that forsaken place." Dire. That's what it was.

Her nails clicked against the chair's arm as she stared down her straight nose at me. "What do you plan on doing about it?"

I wouldn't tell her even if I did have a plan. "I'm not here to discuss politics."

"Then why are you here?"

"I need—" No. I couldn't say I needed anything because then she'd know she had me bent over a barrel. "I would like to ensure safe passage for a human into and out of Tearmann."

Her nail stopped tapping. Black eyes narrowed at me. "This is most unusual." Her mahogany hair slipped over her slender shoulders when her head tilted. I offered no more information, holding my breath as I awaited her answer. Thankfully, she didn't keep me waiting long. "As much as I would love to help, I'm afraid allowing one human to pass through the Forest would set a dangerous precedent. Now is not the time for leniency."

Feck it anyway. I'd known she wouldn't help me. That's why I'd held onto my only bargaining chip. "I'll pay the tax."

Her eyes seemed to swallow the light from the lone candle "*You* will pay?"

"Only once for two crossings, on the day of my choosing." In case Keelynn decided to stay, this would ensure safe passage.

"Exchanging your life force for a human's . . . Interesting.

Very, very interesting." Her nails trilled against the chair, sending chills skittering down my spine.

"Well?"

The Queen held out a black-veined hand. "We have a bargain."

~

With the way my day had started, I never thought I'd be in such a good mood. That's what happened when you spent the afternoon with your soulmate.

I waited behind Keelynn as she stared into a shop window at a blue dress, watching her wide-eyed, wistful expression in the glass's reflection.

"If you like it so much, you should buy it," I suggested. I would've bought it for her, but Kinnock wasn't the friendliest of cities. A place like this, the moment I tried to walk in, they'd probably kick me right out.

Her shoulders fell. "With what money?"

I hid my hand behind my back and flicked my wrist before telling her to check her purse.

"I don't have a—" She opened her cloak to find a full purse hooked to the black sash at her waist. Her eyes met mine, glistening with unshed tears. "You got it back."

As much as I loathed my brother, Rían had his uses. He'd caught up to the villain who'd killed Padraig and sent him to the underworld with his . . . unique flourish.

"Did I?"

The smile she offered was small but genuine. A smile that made my head swim like I'd had one too many drinks. "Thank you, Tadhg. Sincerely."

There was a ruckus behind us. Soldiers in black leather uniforms led prisoners to a wooden platform at the base of a high stone wall. More executions. Rían was here somewhere, adding their names to the ever-growing list of our people killed in Airren.

I'd never understood why they insisted on staying instead of living in Tearmann and just *visiting* Airren. But after meeting Keelynn, their decisions made more sense. I never wanted to leave her side. I wanted to be her feckin' shadow, glued to her skirts. The thought of leaving her on her own made me physically ill.

And that felt like more than the whole soulmate shite.

Deeper. More final. More devastating.

And I wasn't sure how to cope.

Keelynn tugged on the back of my shirt. "What do you think they've done wrong?"

I didn't need to see the list of offenses to know they had done nothing wrong.

"Besides being born different, you mean?" There were ten of them. Ten lives being snuffed out because they weren't human. "Could be anything. That grogoch may have sneezed on a human. The pooka may have been caught shape-shifting. The abcan may have written a poem that painted the king in a less-than-favorable light." Words were the only weapons the tiny poets had at their disposal. "And I'd imagine the far darrig at the end didn't pay taxes on the magic he wields but isn't allowed to use. They're notoriously tight bastards." I was forever bargaining and negotiating with them over taxes and rates.

The executioner, a hulking brute in a black cloak, wielded a heavy black ax. Despite the hundreds of people gathered, I could smell the coppery tang of the blood staining the wooden platform.

"You really think they'd execute someone for a poem?" Keelynn asked.

"I've watched one of my friends executed because a human accused him of being rude."

Daithí hadn't yielded his spot on the footpath to a group of males. And he'd been hanged for it.

Her eyes widened with horror.

I understood her ignorance. She had been brought up in a safe world on the east coast, as far from the Danú and magic as one could get on this island. But she couldn't be ignorant any longer.

"It's not about the poem or the taxes or even the magic," I told her, hoping she would take my words to heart. This sort of injustice would never end if people like her, good people, didn't open their eyes to the state of our world. "It's about being born different in a world that sees no value in diversity. It's about living under a regime that desires ultimate power over its citizens, one that is willing to murder anyone they believe could be a threat." Realization crossed her upturned face, so beautiful in its seriousness. "It's about people with fear so ingrained that they won't even sit in a field at dusk to look up at the stars because they believe the darkness is reserved for monsters."

I wanted to sit in the darkness with this woman.

To see starlight reflected in her gray eyes.

To prove to her that the darkness had its uses. That there could be beauty beyond the fear.

The sound of the heavy axe slicing flesh cut through my fantasy. The sloppy wet *thud* of the grogoch's head landing on the wooden planks left my stomach twisting.

Humans surrounded us, watching, as though this was a performance at the theater. Men, women, and children, eating sweets and laughing in the sunshine.

"Most of the monsters I've met have lived in broad daylight," I confessed. The humans putting those innocents to death, *they* were monsters.

The pooka was next. He didn't struggle, just knelt on the dais.

Closed his eyes.

And lost his head.

"I'm so sorry, Tadhg."

"As am I." More sorry than I could ever say. These were my people, and instead of trying to save them, I was off gallivanting with Keelynn, trying to free myself from a punishment I actually deserved.

I needed to do better.

And that started with telling Keelynn the truth.

"Come, let's get you to the inn." I couldn't be here anymore, pretending I didn't feel every swing of the axe as if it were coming for my own neck. I had tortured and killed hundreds—perhaps even thousands—of people, yet I had been strong, smart, and attractive enough to receive a worthless title and a swathe of land to call my own.

I was born with the ability to come back from death. I could stand in the center of this bloodthirsty crowd without worrying for my own worthless life. The same could not be said for these poor souls.

Keelynn pulled free, demanding we do something. Insisting that what was happening was wrong.

"What do you suggest we do?"

Another pooka fell victim to the axe to the delight of the cheering crowd.

"I don't know," she cried. "But it's so wrong that they should be killed for no reason at all."

"Saving a handful of us won't change anything." The problem was bigger than those ten creatures. And saving them . . . Even with Rían's help, we couldn't be everywhere at once. "This is all part of a systematic extermination that's been going on for centuries, and it won't stop until magic is wiped off the island."

I heard a Danú prayer cut short by the axe—the abcan.

His head rolled across our path, stopping next to Keelynn's boot. Before I could get rid of it, she started screaming. Everyone turned toward us. I clamped a hand over her mouth and dragged her toward the inn. "Be quiet. You're drawing everyone's attention."

Dammit.

In our path were two soldiers beating the shite out of a grogoch.

Grogochs knew better than to come out on execution day, with tensions high and army presence even higher. Had this one honestly thought he could hide what he was beneath a feckin' cloak?

He collapsed onto the cobblestones. The two soldiers pummelled him with their iron-tipped boots.

"He didn't do anything, did he?" Keelynn whispered.

"Most likely not." I swore and scraped a hand over my face. I was exhausted and hungry and hungover and so far beyond angry. Of all the feckin' days. "Keelynn, listen to me. I need you to—"

"GET OFF HIM," she shrieked.

Before I could stop her, she sprinted for the soldiers in a useless attempt to stop the assault. One of the men knocked Keelyn to the ground, signing his death warrant.

Even fighting her hardest, she hadn't a hope of winning. I evanesced to her side. The man didn't see me coming before my fist slammed his temple. He slumped to the ground. The soldier on top of her muttered something, but I could only focus on knocking him away from Keelynn.

"Of all the feckin' days for you to want to commit treason." I lifted the beautiful, infuriating woman off the ground. Why couldn't she have let me handle it? "Get to the inn. *Now*."

I threw her my bag and drew my sleeves to my elbows. If I was going to fight, I didn't want to be weighed down.

Heavy boots stomped the cobblestones as more soldiers came to join the fun.

Keelynn's face paled. "Tadhg! Come with me!"

God, I loved hearing my name on her lips. "You need to run."

There was no time to make sure she did as I commanded before I bent to the grogoch. "Take this and go to my castle." I pressed Rían's cufflink into his hairy hand.

"Y-yes, my prince. I'm s-sorry. My son, he—"

The boots grew louder. They were almost here.

"Go now."

Seven soldiers formed a perimeter around me. I gave one of the bodies on the ground a kick. The man who had touched

Keelynn groaned. I crushed his windpipe beneath the heel of my boot, ensuring the satisfying gurgle would be his last.

Two soldiers lunged.

I could've evanesced.

But after the day I'd had, I really, really wanted to kill every last one of them.

Bones crunched beneath my fists. Blood sprayed. Not a moment later, they fell on top of their comrades. My shredded knuckles were already healing by the time I broke the next one's nose. They got smarter, three of them coming at once. The fist to my abdomen barely registered. The one that smashed my jaw stung a bit. Shackles closed around my wrists, searing and hissing. Feckin' iron burned like feckin' fire. They dragged me toward the dais. I found a pair of wide gray eyes watching from among the onlookers. I smiled so Keelynn wouldn't worry, letting her know before she turned away that everything would be all right.

My boots scuffed across the bloodstained wooden platform.

"Any last words?" the executioner asked, his breath reeking of garlic.

I glanced down at the gore in the basket, then over to the bodies piled on top of a massive wooden cart.

"Would you mind using a fresh basket for my head?" I nodded toward the empty one next to him. "I don't want to have to go searching for the damned thing later."

He laughed, then sobered. "Yer serious?" he choked, incredulous.

"As serious as that blade in your hand. And," I said, kneeling to take my place on the chopping block, "you might clean that disgusting thing before you use it on me."

The people at the front of the dais exchanged confused expressions. I found my brother's serious blue gaze set in a black-haired man's face. When I winked at him, he rolled his eyes.

The clean basket made a scraping sound when it slid beneath the block. The executioner lifted a pristine axe over my head.

And let it drop.

20

Every time I swallowed, it felt like someone had shoved a red-hot fire poker down my gullet. Peering through heavy lashes, I saw a bed with a thick green canopy looming against the far wall.

Rían had brought me back to the castle.

A pair of gleaming black boots stopped next to my head as I waited for the feeling in my extremities to return.

With a flick of his wrist, a tub appeared. A moment later, he filled it with steaming water. The stench wafting from my clothes made my eyes burn. Thankfully, he hadn't left me on the bed. No sense in making more of a mess than necessary.

Rían nudged me with his toe. "You need to wash yourself. You smell like a dead carcass."

My hands and arms came back first. I managed to push myself upright against the foot of the bed. "How many this week?" I asked.

Rían knelt, helping me out of my shirt and throwing it into the fire.

He flicked his wrist. A stack of three black ledgers appeared in his hand. The first ledger landed on the floor with a *thump*. "Forty-three." *Thump*. The second ledger fell on top of it. "I filled this one last month." *Thump.* Then the third. "And this one the month before."

"I didn't realize how bad it had gotten."

His eyes flashed. "You didn't care."

I hadn't cared. I had been distracted for so long that I'd forgotten that I still had a title. That I still had a voice when so many had lost theirs.

"I do now." After seeing the way Keelynn had gone after those guards, powerless as she was, how could I not do something? If someone so hateful and prejudiced could change her mind, put herself at risk to fight for one of us, what excuse did I have to remain silent?

It was high time we did something about this before our people were wiped out.

"Vellana are shipping over more soldiers left, right, and center. There's something big coming." Rían's lips pressed together as he glanced toward the sunny window. "As much as I hate the Queen ruling the Forest, she's our best defense. The humans won't go near the border."

"And the sea?"

"Muireann says her folk haven't seen hide nor hair of a Vellanian ship on the west coast. On the east coast, however . . ."

Were there any options that didn't lead to unnecessary bloodshed? I didn't want to kill humans, I just wanted them to stop killing *us*. "What can we do?"

Rían sank onto the edge of my bed, massaging his right hand. I could almost hear the gears turning in his mind. He always had a plan. Always. "We have no army and cannot fight," he murmured, more to himself than to me. "Outside these borders, the laws keep us powerless. Beyond a mass exodus—which no one will agree to as long as the Queen refuses humans entry—there's only one option." His expression darkened. "We renegotiate with the King."

We hadn't tried speaking to Vellana's King Marcellus since he took the throne. The ones before him had all said the same thing: we'd made our beds and were expected to lie in them.

Still, it couldn't hurt.

"Renegotiate for what, exactly?"

Rían shot to his feet, pacing to the tub and back. Now that I could feel my body, I managed to finish stripping and climb into the bath with a groan.

"Fair feckin' trials, for one," he said. "Ninety percent of the witnesses are lying. They almost never have proof. One human says one of us set a foot out of line, and we could have ten Danú claiming otherwise, and they still wouldn't believe us."

I reached for the bar of soap on the ledge. "Do you think the king will listen?"

Rían had gone to Vellana last year on a scouting mission, trying to take in the thoughts of the people and the mood in Vellana City regarding the Danú.

If he told me how it had gone, I couldn't recall.

Rían's footsteps quickened. "He would if he realized how many of us there really are in Airren. But asking those who've remained hidden for centuries to drop their glamours and step out into the light is a big feckin' gamble. The only way it would work is if we had some place for them to go if they lost their homes and livelihoods. But we simply don't have the space in Tearmann for everyone."

So many Danú had been executed, it was hard to believe there were that many of us still living outside Tearmann's borders. But if anyone knew the true state of things, it was Rían. "The king won't give us any more land." On an island as small as ours, land was too precious a commodity to just give away.

"And we wouldn't be able to protect it if he did. You need to ensure safety for your people in Airren."

"They're your people too."

Rían shook his head. "I have no people."

That wasn't true. He had me. And a reluctant Ruairi. And Eava. The old witch loved my brother for some reason.

I'd allowed this to go on for long enough. My people needed me. It was time to put aside the selfishness that had gotten me cursed in the first place. "As soon as I get the ring, we will set things right."

Rían nodded. "Get the dagger too. We may need it."

After I'd finished bathing and dressing, Eava sent up a tray of food. As delicious as it smelled, I knew better than to chance more than a few bites of buttery croissant until I was sure my throat had healed completely.

Back at the inn, patrons filled the tables in the small dining area. For all the drinking and carrying on, you'd think it was half eight at night instead of half eight in the morning. A scullery maid with more wrinkles than teeth stopped me on the way to the stairs, asking what I wanted. My stomach roiled as the tug between us grew stronger with each passing second. I told her I was fine and shot toward the stairs before she could ask anything else.

The room Keelynn had rented the day before waited at the end of the hallway. With a deep breath, I lifted my hand and knocked.

No one answered.

"Keelynn?"

No response.

Where else would she be at this hour? I hadn't seen her downstairs. What if something was wrong? What if she hadn't made it back to the inn? What if something had happened to her?

I tried the door.

Locked.

Feck it anyway. I evanesced inside. The twisted sheets smelled of lavender. An empty bottle of wine sat on top of the bedside table, my bag on the floor beside it.

I eased onto the bed to give my wobbly legs a break. Where the hell could she be? Shops wouldn't be open for another hour. Surely, she knew better than to go for a stroll alone in a new city. What was I thinking? The woman was as naïve as they came. I should've asked Rían to keep an eye on her before I lost my feckin' head.

But there was no telling what he would've said to her. Keelynn would learn the truth—but she would hear it from me.

My heart lurched as the door opened.

Keelynn was there. Face scrunched, breathing heavy, cheeks stained with tears.

"Hello, Maiden Death."

Her eyes snapped to mine. She took a halting step toward me. "You're alive."

"Disappointed?"

Her hair fell in a dark curtain when she shook her head. "Relieved."

That was something at least. That she didn't wish me dead at present. "Afraid I'd leave you to locate the Gancanagh on your—"

She launched forward, wrapping her arms around my neck.

There wasn't time to check for my ring before her lips claimed mine. I drank her in, wishing there could be some way to bottle her up. To carry her with me forevermore.

She tasted of life and youth and something else. Something I'd tasted long ago. Something I'd forgotten.

Freedom.

Trembling hands began to undress me, from my worn overcoat to my loose cravat.

"You don't want this." I spoke the words even as my cursed hands tore at her dress. She'd regret it the moment it was over. This wasn't real for her. An escape from the darkness lurking outside this room. Darkness lurking inside me.

"Yes, I do."

With my curse, I couldn't have turned her down even if I wanted to. But I didn't. I wanted this more than I'd ever wanted anything. More than I wanted that ring.

"Turn around." She whirled, and I caught the satin laces holding her in, letting them slip through my fingers.

"Magic would be quicker," she breathed.

If this was the only time I had with her, I was going to make it last. "I'm giving you time to change your mind."

"I'm not changing my mind." Sincerity shined in the gray depths of her eyes when she twisted to face me. "I want you."

Women always wanted me.

"Wanting me and being with me are two very different things." Her neck tasted like heaven. I'd live there if I could. Against her neck, breathing her in.

She dragged at my shirt. I sent it away.

I set my magic free, stealing inhibitions, heightening senses, drawing sighs and murmurs from lips I never wanted to stop kissing. Bed. I wanted her on the bed. Beneath me. Crying for me. The moment her spine met the mattress, her gloriously pale thighs fell open, calling me home.

I managed a semblance of control, building and rocking, her hips grinding against mine with sweet abandon.

Her eyes squeezed closed, chest heaving.

"Keelynn?"

Her lips lifted.

"Look at me." *See me.*

Glittering gray eyes fluttered open, hazy and unfocused.

"Are you sure?" *Are you sure about me?*

"Yes."

I refused to let this curse taint the memory of how it felt to sheath myself in her tight, wet heat. Right. Perfect. Everything I'd been searching for and never thought I'd find. This woman, nails raking down my shoulders, hips rising, drawing me deeper. Losing myself felt like being found.

Her eyes closed again. Was she somewhere else? With someone else? Her husband? The man she loved?

My hand slipped between our connected bodies, finding the spot I knew would drive her mad. Her back arched straight off the feckin' bed. Nails imbedded in my back. Hips meeting mine with reckless desperation. I began to lose myself, my body fighting to keep pace, when I noticed a change in the rise and fall of her chest. Holding her breath. She was holding her breath. Body clenching, legs trembling.

"Yes. *Yes . . . Tadhg.*"

My name. She'd called my name. Pulsing around me. Sighing with her release. I swallowed the whimper from her cursed lips with mine, fisting the sheets on either side of her head, chasing her delicious rapture to the soul-searching end. And when I found it, I knew life would never be the same.

21

"There's more than one?" Keelynn gasped.

Perfection. That's what she was.

Her choice of topics, however: not perfect.

I didn't want to discuss my trip to the underworld or my curses. I wanted to talk about her breasts peeking from beneath the sheet and the swell of her hip and the things I wanted to do to her.

"At this point, I'm more cursed than not," I said. How was her skin so soft? Like the brush of a sun-kissed flower petal. "And no. There is one other way."

"What is it?"

My hand fell to the bed. "You're the one who reads fairy tales. You tell me."

A wrinkle appeared between her delicately arched eyebrows. "True love's kiss."

"Now you have it."

The wrinkle deepened, then smoothed as the corner of her lips lifted. "That shouldn't be hard for you. You're not hideous."

"High praise, indeed, Maiden Death." Just what I wanted to hear from the woman who had slowly stolen my heart. "Every man wishes a woman would refer to him as 'not hideous.'"

"You know what I mean." She swatted my chest before curling into me as if content to stay in my arms forever. "You're handsome and you bloody well know it. Surely you could find a woman to fall in love with you to break your curses."

I didn't want just any woman. Keelynn had shown me her worst qualities from day one, and I'd found myself falling for her despite it all. I wanted this hateful wasp who smelled of lavender and made my heart swell and my body ache. "If only love was that simple."

Attraction wasn't love.

Women loved how I could make them feel. My title. My magic.

They loved the idea of me. Not the cursed truth.

The truth.

How could I claim to love her when all I did was lie?

I said, "There's something I need to tell you," at the same time she said, "We need to talk."

The heat from her laugh went straight to my heart. "You first."

Me first? Not a feckin' hope. I wanted to delay the inevitable for as long as possible. "*Ladies* first. I insist."

Her shoulders lifted and fell when she sighed. "All right." When she left my arms, I knew she'd never be back. "I've decided to return to Graystones."

This had been my plan all along. So why did it feel like someone was holding me underwater with my breath running out?

"But we're only a few days out from Tearmann." I couldn't say goodbye to her now. Not yet. I wasn't ready yet.

"I'm not going to Tearmann. Not anymore." She pulled the ring from her finger, offering it to me. "Take it. It's yours."

I told her no, but she insisted, giving me reason after reason for leaving me. Reasons I'd been planting since the moment we met. She put the ring in my hand, and I had exactly what I'd come for, and yet none of this felt right. It felt so feckin' wrong.

I tried to talk her out of it, but my words fell on deaf ears.

For centuries, all I'd pined for was freedom. Now the ring—my freedom—was in my feckin' hand and all I wanted was to shove it back at Keelynn and beg her not to leave me.

"I want you to take the ring and go home," she said.

Those words shattered the illusion I'd created in my mind.

She didn't want this. Didn't want me. Who in their right mind would?

Take the ring and go home.

She may as well have said, "Thanks for the ride. Here's a little something for your time."

I thought we'd connected on some higher level. I felt something for her that I'd never felt for anyone.

But it was only Fiadh's curse at work again. How could anyone care for what I was? What I did? She'd seen me go off with how many women? How did she know it wasn't because I wanted to?

I went to tell her, the words on the tip of my tongue, but I stopped.

I was a means to an end.

According to Keelynn, the end had arrived.

I closed my mouth and let the words die.

She tried to kiss me, but I jerked away in the nick of time. Without that ring on her finger, she'd be in the underworld the moment her lips touched mine.

I muttered an apology, slipping the emerald onto my smallest finger. A whisper of energy, like a blanket being thrown over you when you're almost asleep, warmed my skin. If only it could go deeper and clear the frost overtaking my heart. "Force of habit."

I brushed my lips against her cheek, a silent goodbye.

I should've dressed myself to conserve my magic, but I couldn't stay in this room for another second. I collected my coat and sent my bag away, not having it in me to carry the feckin' thing. And then I turned back to the only woman I'd ever truly cared about and said thank you and some shite about appreciating everything, even though all I wanted was to beg her to let me stay.

All she did was nod.

There was nothing left inside of me. I'd given it all to her. I turned on my heel and left through the door, praying for her to call me back. To give me some inclination that she could want me half as much as I wanted her.

I'd thought Keelynn was the one. I'd thought after all these years, I had done enough good to erase the terrible decisions of my past. If we'd had more time, I was sure I could make her love me.

"I was wondering which room ye were in," said a woman with a gravelly voice from behind me. I turned to find the maid from downstairs, her clothes reeking of bacon and stewed meat.

Desire rolled off her in invisible waves, drawing my curse to the surface like a bucket in a well. If only I could have evanesced but I couldn't move. Magic hummed in my veins. Just there. Just feckin' there. But I couldn't access it.

For centuries I had waited to get my ring back. To be free.

And it didn't feckin' work.

I swear I could hear Fiadh's grating cackle at the clever spell she must have wrought to negate its protective magic.

"I was just on my way out," I told the woman when she drew closer.

"Ye should stay," she said, opening a door to the right that led to a wide linen closet. "Would be such a shame fer ye to lose that pretty head again."

Shit.

She must've been at the executions yesterday.

With the offer made, there was nothing I could do to stop my feet from following her into the linen closet and reaching for the buckle on my belt. Well, that wasn't quite true. I could kiss her.

No no no.

I couldn't take another life. Refused to take the easy way out. No matter how many times this happened, I deserved it. How many women had I gone through like glasses of wine? How many women had I lied to? Used? Cast aside? There wasn't a book big enough for those names.

If I just closed my eyes, it'd all be over soon. If I just plugged my ears so I didn't have to hear the woman's low moans, I could pretend I was somewhere else. My body knew what to do, so I let my mind wander away.

Three coppers landed next to my boot. Three feckin' coppers.

The woman opened the door and disappeared back toward the staircase. I ripped the useless ring from my finger. I may as well tell Keelynn the truth and hope she killed me quickly.

She could have the ring.

She didn't deserve to be cursed.

She hadn't known any better when she'd bargained with Fiadh.

I rose on unsteady legs, tugged up my breeches, and fastened my belt. Back in the empty hallway, my heavy footsteps thudded against the worn planks.

When I knocked on Keelynn's door, she didn't answer. Had she left? I couldn't have been gone more than ten minutes, and there hadn't been any footsteps from the hallway while I was in the linen closet.

"Keelynn?" I knocked again, then tried the handle. The knob turned, the door opened, and the coppery stench of blood slammed into me.

Shit.

Keelynn's body was on the bed, still naked, still wrapped in sheets. Only instead of being white, they were stained red.

I said her name again and again, but there was no response. No flutter of her lashes. No words from her lips. Her face was too pale. What the hell had happened? I'd only been gone ten feckin' minutes.

I tugged the sheet down, and my chest swelled with dread when I found a deep black gouge in her stomach.

I knew what had happened.

I knew who was responsible.

I knew who would stab her in the perfect place to inflict maximum pain and let the curse from the dagger do the rest.

Fiadh.

What should I do? I couldn't let her die. *Dammit.* Even if I'd had all my magic, it wouldn't be enough to heal her. I had to stop the bleeding.

I sliced a clean section of sheet with my dagger to create a makeshift tourniquet. If only I hadn't taken the ring. It wouldn't have saved her from being stabbed, but it would've stopped the curse. I pushed the enchanted emerald onto her finger anyway. It could've been my imagination, but I thought her cheeks regained some color, and the blackness seemed to stop spreading.

Perhaps hope wasn't lost. Perhaps it wasn't too late.

What now? I didn't want to leave her, but what choice did I have? I needed help.

Summoning the dregs of my magic, I evanesced to the castle gates. Sea air wrapped me in its salty embrace as I stumbled forward. I needed food. I needed sleep. I needed to save Keelynn. My body shook. I had nothing left.

My knees slammed against the ground. I fell forward, unable to catch myself before my face met sharp gravel.

A crowd swelled. I knew their faces but couldn't remember their names.

"Rían," I croaked, my mouth so dry. "Get Rían."

My eyes fell closed until I heard footsteps crunching in the stones. When I opened them again, black boots waited by my nose.

"Why must you insist on making a scene at the feckin' gates?" Rían grumbled, bending down, catching me by the shoulder, and hauling me to my feet. "These people already pity you enough without the dramatics."

When he led me toward the entrance, I tried and failed to pull from his grasp. "We have to get to Kinnock."

"No feckin' way am I going to that bloodthirsty city again."

He had to come. He had to help. "Fiadh tried to kill her."

Rían went deathly still. "Where?"

"Bluefield Inn."

Cursing, he evanesced with me back to the inn's dark hallway.

"Which room?" he snarled.

"There." I gestured to the door at the very end of the hall. Inside, sunlight streamed through the windows. Keelynn hadn't moved.

She must be dead. Rían rushed to her side. I collapsed against the mattress, tears blurring my vision.

She was dead. I'd let her die.

"Her pulse is weak, but she's not gone." He lifted the sheet and peeked beneath the bandage. His eyes flew to mine. "*Dammit*, Tadhg. I can't heal her if she was stabbed by a cursed blade. There's nothing we can do."

"This is your fiancée's sister. Aveen will never forgive you if you let Keelynn die." And neither would I. "We need to bring her to Brigid." She was the best healer on the island. If anyone could save Keelynn, it was Brigid.

Rían raked his fingers through his hair. "What about Oona?"

The last time I'd seen Oona, she'd threatened to cut off my genitals. "Brigid hates me the least of them." Although that wasn't saying much.

"Fine," Rían groaned. "But I'll need to get more help since you're so feckin' useless." He shifted a silvery blue silk dress. "Put that on her."

"No." It was blue. Rían's women wore blue.

"Let the others see her naked. I don't care." In a blink, he vanished.

It wasn't worth wasting the energy on a new dress. I picked up the silk and tried to figure out how the hell I was supposed to get it on Keelynn without using magic. I'd dressed my fair share of dead bodies, but never by hand.

Her head lolled when I pulled the garment over her hair. Her arms were too floppy when I tried to pull them through the sleeves. Somehow, I managed to get the thing on and the skirt down to her ankles before my brother returned with Ruairi, Cormac, Ger, and Shay.

"Shit, Tadhg." Ruairi scrubbed a hand down his stubbled beard. "What happened?"

"Fiadh happened. We need to get her to Brigid."

Their expressions tightened, but all of them nodded. I wouldn't be any help, but I held Keelynn's hand as we evanesced to the forest outside Kinnock, then finally to Brigid's small cottage, tucked between thick pine trees on the banks of a burbling stream. Together, we lifted Keelynn's limp body onto a bench below the window box.

"You'll have to ask her," Rían whispered, dropping Keelynn's hand. "If she sees me, she definitely won't help you." He motioned toward the trees and slipped away with the others.

I recited the only proper prayer I knew on my way to Brigid's door. One my mother used to say.

Answer. Please answer. Please just—

The door opened a fraction. Next thing I knew, the redheaded witch on the other side had wrapped me in a vanilla-scented embrace. She'd obviously missed that my clothes were drenched in blood. "Tadhg!"

"Brigid. I . . . um . . . I need your help."

Her hands fell away. "I should've known this wasn't a social call. What is it now? What's wrong?"

I glanced toward where Keelynn laid. "My friend was stabbed by a cursed blade, and I need you to—"

Brigid followed my gaze. "Is that your friend there?" She took a step toward Keelynn, but I blocked her path. "Tell me you didn't bring a human to my home," she hissed. "And you expect me to help her?"

"For me. Please."

"I don't owe you anything. Isn't that what you said to me?"

In the wake of her husband's death, she'd used me to get through the worst of her grief. We'd been friends for centuries.

She knew my curse and had let it be my choice . . . at first. I'd wanted to help her the only way I knew how. But she'd wanted more.

"I was saving you from yourself. You were distraught, and I was the last person you needed to—"

She held up a hand, green eyes glowing. "Let me stop you right there. The only way I would even consider helping *that*"—she gestured toward Keelynn—"is if she was Danú. So, unless you can use that magic of yours to make her into something besides a feckin' human, you both can go straight to hell."

The door slammed in my face, rattling the single-pane windows. All hope slipped from my chest, leaving me cold and bitter and hollow. No amount of magic could turn Keelynn into one of us.

Ruairi and Rían emerged from the darkness.

This couldn't be happening.

I wasn't supposed to lose her.

"I know a way to change Keelynn," Rían said quietly.

"Please. I'll do anything. Anything."

His cerulean eyes gleamed. "You have to marry her."

22

I HAD MANAGED CENTURIES WITHOUT BEING DRAGGED TO AN ALTAR. I wasn't going to let Fiadh force me into doing something I didn't want to do. And I couldn't bind Keelynn to me that way. She'd never forgive me.

"I just need a minute to think."

Keelynn groaned.

"You don't have a feckin' minute," Rían growled. "Do you want to save her or not?"

Feck it all, I did want to save her, but not like this. Not by taking away her choices. Forcing her to be with me. "How will this change her?"

"You're going to have to trust me."

Trust my brother? I didn't trust him as far as I could throw him. The only reason I'd gone to him at all was because of his connection with Aveen. He never did anything that wasn't beneficial to him. Never. What other choice did I have? I couldn't fathom the alternative, and I couldn't even use the ring as an excuse anymore. This was purely a decision based on my unrequited feelings for a human.

"Do it quickly." Before I talked myself out of it.

Rían shifted a length of ribbon. I gripped Keelynn's icy fingers in mine, letting him bind our hands together. "To you, I pledge my body and soul . . ." he began.

I repeated the words through the thickness in my throat. The vows. The promises. Binding myself to this woman as a weight settled on my chest. I could hear the iron bars on an invisible cage slam closed and the lock click into place.

When it came time for Keelynn to say the vows, Rían used his magic to force them through her lips. It may have been her voice, but she wasn't the one saying them.

This wasn't real.

She didn't want this.

I was taking away her free will the same way Fiadh had taken mine. But what other choice did I have? I couldn't let her life end because of me and my selfishness. Surely, this was better. Women had wanted to marry me before.

It was only a handfasting.

It would be all right.

This could give me the time I needed to make her fall in love with me. She was attracted to me, that much I knew for sure. And she had to hold me in some regard. Marriages had been built on less.

I blinked and realized no one was speaking. Everyone was staring at me.

"What? What is it? Is it over?"

"Rían said to kiss the bride," Ruairi murmured with an unsteady smile.

Grimacing, I pressed a chaste kiss on Keelynn's cold cheek. A sigh escaped her lips.

There was no time to over-analyze what it could mean. It was a sigh. That was all. The ribbons binding us together vanished. I dropped her hand, slipped my arms beneath her, cradled my wife against my chest, and hurried back to Brigid's door. With my hands full, I gave the barrier two swift kicks.

Brigid yanked the door open. "I already told you—"

"She's one of us now," I said, showing her the black band

around my ring finger that matched the one on Keelynn's.

"She's as good as Danú in the eyes of the law," Rían announced, appearing by my side.

Keelynn's social standing would be stripped away, and she'd be cast aside by every human she knew. Everyone human she loved.

"You said you'd heal her," he finished with a sneer. "Now, do it."

Brigid stomped into her sitting room and motioned to the rolled-arm sofa. "I cannot believe you tied yourself to a feckin' human." The betrayal in her dark green eyes didn't touch me. If she had healed Keelynn as I'd asked, we wouldn't be in this situation.

I laid my unconscious wife on the sofa.

Wife.

I had a wife.

And my wife started to convulse—

"Do something," I begged, my voice cracking. "Please don't let her die. Please." Feck it all, if she died, I didn't know what I would do.

Brigid told me to move back. I couldn't leave Keelynn. Instead, I crouched where her dark hair fell across the cushions. She didn't flinch when Brigid shifted a dagger and slit the dress across her abdomen, or when the blood-soaked bandage was cut free. Worry furrowed Brigid's brow, and my stomach sank when I saw how far the curse had spread. Webs of black had reached her ribs. Soon it would be in her heart.

Swearing, Brigid shifted herbs and bottles to the space beside where she knelt. Using a mortar and pestle, she crushed them together in a frenzy, then lathered them onto the gash.

Keelynn cried out. I'd never heard a sweeter sound. She was hanging on. She was fighting.

"Once, I cut holes in the back of an old crier's cloak," I whispered, running a hand across Keelynn's fevered forehead, stroking her matted hair. "He ended up showing his arse to the entire market."

Her lips didn't so much as twitch. I'd give anything to see them smile. Or frown. Or tell me I was a monster.

I kept talking while Brigid worked, interlacing incantations and spells with pungent herbs, not wanting Keelynn to think she was alone. I told her about the time I'd hogtied Rían to a fence-post. When I'd goaded Ruairi into the north sea in the dead of winter. The time they had joined forces and I'd woken up in the courtyard fountain stark naked.

"Tadhg?" Brigid said quietly, carrying the bottles strewn across the floor to a sideboard beneath the window. "I've done all I can."

The wound was wrapped again with crisp, white bandages. It could've been my imagination, but the blackness seemed to have stopped at Keelynn's ribs.

"Only time will tell if she'll survive the curse," Brigid said quietly. "With that ring, there's a chance."

At least I'd done something right by giving back the ring. I tried to take some solace in that. "Thank you, Brigid. Sincerely. I owe you a great debt."

Brigid's dark eyebrows drew together as she stared down at Keelynn. My wife's breathing was steadier now, and she had stopped shaking, but her skin was still too pale, and I didn't like the look of the sweat beading on her brow.

"I've given her something to help her sleep. Would you join me for a cuppa in the kitchen?"

"I'd rather stay here."

"She's asleep, Tadhg. She won't know if you're here or in the next room." When I didn't budge, Brigid told me that I looked like death warmed up. "I can imagine you're hungry as well," she said, her skirts swaying as she made her way toward the hallway, "and I have fresh apple crumble."

My stomach gave a pitiful gurgle. Eating would help restore some of my energy, and I would need all of it once Keelynn woke.

If she woke.

"One slice," I agreed. I could bring my plate into the sitting room and eat it in here.

Brigid's kitchen was just as I remembered it, with potions and ingredients and herbs and animal parts in jars on shelves that reached to the exposed beam ceiling.

A crockery dish of fragrant apple crumble sat on the stone worktop. She cut and plated two civilized portions before collecting a bowl from beside a basket of green apples. "Fresh cream?"

"Please." When she added a generous portion, I thanked her. But when I tried to leave the room, the door snicked shut.

"Who is she to you?" Brigid asked in a tone as frosty as the ground in January.

"My wife."

"Before she was your wife," she pressed, setting her own dish down and moving to stand in front of me.

My relationship with Keelynn was none of her feckin' business. "An acquaintance."

"I can't imagine you saving a mere acquaintance, much less marrying one."

What she could or couldn't imagine had nothing to do with me.

Her hand dropped to my belt.

"What do you think you're doing?" I choked.

Brigid's face flushed. "I should think you'd know by now when a woman is hoping to share your bed, *Gancanagh*."

Feck it all. I owed her for helping Keelynn, but I didn't want to do this. I didn't want her to touch me. I didn't want *anyone* to touch me. "No."

Her hand stilled on the leather strap. "Did you just tell me no? How?"

I . . .

I didn't know how.

And I didn't care.

All that mattered was that I had turned her down.

"I appreciate what you did for my wife," I said, pushing her hand away. "But I'll not be sleeping with you tonight."

Her face flushed the same color as her hair. "I . . . um . . . I need to go."

And with that, she evanesced.

I sank onto the ground and ate the entire dish of apple crumble all by myself.

~

"What do you mean you told her no?" Rían asked for the second time, watching me through narrowed blue eyes from his perch on the chaise. Shelves of books flanked the fireplace at his back.

"Just what it sounds like. She wanted a ride, and I said no." Those two letters had never tasted as sweet.

The others had returned to their homes, leaving only Rían, Ruairi, and I in Brigid's sitting room, contemplating the strange turn of events.

"Shoulda told the witch I was outside," Ruairi said with a laugh. "I woulda given her a ride to remember."

"Brigid prefers princes over feral beasts," Rían said, stretching his legs out in front of him.

Ruairi's fangs gleamed in the firelight. "That's what ye think."

Keelynn's head thrashed on the pillow. Rían had fixed her dress, but the bloodstains remained. I needed her to realize this was necessary. That I wasn't lying when I told her I didn't have a choice.

The carpet did little to save my arse from the wooden boards beneath it. I took Keelynn's hand, still too damn cold, studying the black band staining her blood-drenched fingers.

Married. To a human. And I didn't feel like impaling myself on an iron sword. Who would've thought?

"Could it have to do with the marriage bond?" I asked no one in particular.

"It's the only thing that makes sense," Rían replied.

None of this made sense. Not one bit. I nudged my brother's boot. "She needs another blanket."

"Four is more than enough."

"Her face is too pale." And her lips held no color.

"She's probably too feckin' warm." Ruairi unbuttoned the collar on his shirt. "It's roastin' in here."

"One more blanket. Please."

Rían rolled his eyes but shifted another blanket. I tucked the heavy wool around Keelynn's still form, then settled back onto the hard floor to wait for some bit of color to return to her cheeks.

"Stop staring at the poor woman," Rían ordered. "It's unnerving."

"Do I tell you to stop staring at Aveen? No. Now leave me the hell alone." He spent far too much time in the room where he kept her. Sometimes I heard him talking like a loon, as if she could hear him from the other side of death.

Rían shot to his feet and stalked toward the door. Cursing, Ruairi swiped at his brow. "It's too feckin' hot in here, lad. I need some air."

I waved him away. I didn't want him in here when Keelynn woke anyway.

I was *married*. I should've been more upset. Instead, I felt . . . elated?

It wasn't fair. She'd wake up devastated, and here I was smiling like a lovesick eejit. First things first. Get off this floor and put some distance between us. The chaise below the window. Perfect. Now I needed to find something to occupy my hands so I didn't look nervous when she woke.

I dragged a book from Brigid's shelf. *History of Magic*. Brilliant.

The moment my arse hit the chaise, I heard the sweetest sigh. This would be all right. We would find our way through this. Keelynn would forgive me.

~

Why would you do this to me?

I am not your wife.

You should have let me die.

Cold night air kissed my cheeks, darkness closing in from all sides as Keelynn's words invaded my brain. Instead of keeping a level head like a grown male, I'd let my temper get the better of me. What right did I have to be upset about the awful things Keelynn had said to me? Everything had been true. I deserved the insults and the hate.

Keelynn stomped through the door of Brigid's cottage, avoiding my gaze where I waited next to a smirking Ruairi.

What had I honestly thought? That she would just accept being tied to me and be happy about it? It was only a year. Was a year with me so bad? Look at what had happened between us in a matter of weeks.

If I had an entire year . . .

A year of freedom.

A year of *her*.

How could I ask her to make such a sacrifice?

I could marry someone else. But I wouldn't. Not even to break these curses. How could I trust someone not to take advantage of me? Look what had happened with Áine and Brigid.

Ruairi shifted into his horse form, and I offered Keelynn assistance into the saddle, an olive branch. The woman looked at my hands as if they were made of serpents and mounted by herself.

I had two options. Have her behind me, arms wrapped around my waist, breasts pressed against my back. Or have her sitting between my thighs. Knowing it would probably be the last time I'd have her anywhere near me, I chose the latter.

I climbed behind her, and we started down the road. The infernal woman wouldn't sit still. She was obviously having trouble getting comfortable, but every time she adjusted herself, she would wiggle and remind me she was basically sitting on my lap, and she smelled so good that I thought I would go mad if I breathed at all.

"When we reach Gaul, we can stay with one of my friends in the city," I said once she'd settled and I managed to unclench my jaw. Lorcan and Dierdre would interrogate me later, but they wouldn't mind the company. "We should be safe there until I can find a magistrate willing to grant us an annulment." Unless I could convince her otherwise.

"Why can't I just stay at an inn?" she asked.

"The inns are the first places Fiadh will check."

Her spine stiffened. "Fiadh is coming back?"

It was a wonder the hateful witch hadn't come back already. "Fiadh never forgives or forgets. What do you think she'll do to you if she finds you again?" I could guarantee the witch wouldn't just stab her in the stomach.

"You can do what you want, but I'm not staying with your *friend*."

Obstinate feckin' woman. Didn't she realize what was coming for her? "Have you been listening to a word I've said?" I reached for her shoulder. The wasp shrugged me off. She didn't want me touching her. Fine. But she would listen. "The inns *aren't safe*."

"I have friends too, you know. And it just so happens one of them lives in Gaul."

"What's your friend's name?"

"Why does it matter?"

It mattered because I feckin' asked a question and I wanted a feckin' answer. "It doesn't."

Ruairi huffed a laugh. I dug my heel into the bastard's sides. He didn't even have the decency to shudder. Hours later, we reached the outskirts of Gaul. Ruairi asked where to go, and Keelynn gave him the address with a feckin' smile. Me? The cold feckin' shoulder. And after I'd saved her life. Heaven forbid she thank me.

We ended up on the high-street side of town amongst row after row of quaint townhouses. Her friend had money. No surprise there. Keelynn came from money, so it made sense her friend would as well.

Ruairi dropped us in an alley and shifted back into his human form. Although people would wonder what he was from his sheer size—and if they glimpsed his fangs there'd be no question—it was safer for him to move about the city by himself on two legs instead of four. Some pooka, the ones without as much power, didn't have that luxury.

Keelynn tried to get me to go with him, but there was no way in hell I was letting her wander around on her own. She didn't look thrilled, but I didn't care.

She fidgeted with her cloak the whole time, eyes straight ahead. When we reached the end of the street, she stopped so abruptly, I nearly ran her over.

"Take off that kohl," she clipped, giving me a disapproving once-over. "And tie this properly." She flicked the ends of my cravat where it dangled around my neck.

"You can choose one or the other," I told her with a smirk. "Not both."

I was who I was, and if her "friend" didn't like it, she could sod off.

Her black lips pursed. "Kohl."

So much for knowing whether or not her friend had magic. Although from Keelynn's ignorance, I'd say it was fairly safe to assume she didn't. I dragged my cravat from around my neck and scrubbed my eyes clean. Keelynn's pout remained, but her lips were back to being the most kissable shade of pink.

She stilled outside number thirty-six's low fence. "You should wait out here. I'd like a chance to explain our situation without an audience."

I only agreed to appear reasonable. Plus, I'd be able to hear every word she said as long as the street stayed quiet. "You have three minutes."

Nodding, she eased aside the gate, crossing to the steps to knock on the red door.

And a man answered.

I knew who he was from the way he collected her in his arms and kissed her hair. From the smile and the sigh on her lips.

Robert.

23

Robert put his hands all over Keelynn, and it took everything in me to keep from chopping them clean off. Who was he to deserve her attention? To hold her? To kiss her forehead and her hair and her cheeks? What the hell had he done to deserve a feckin' moment of her time?

My darling.

It's all right.

You're here now.

That's all that matters.

Enough of that sappy shite. I evanesced to the bottom stair and cleared my throat.

Hazel eyes slammed into mine. "Get inside. *Quickly*," Robert hissed, hiding my wife behind his back as if I couldn't send him flying head-first off the top step with a flick of my wrist. "Leave us alone, you filthy monster. We want nothing to do with you."

Feckin' brilliant. I didn't want anything to do with him either.

"He's not going to hurt us," Keelynn insisted.

I wouldn't hurt her. *Robert*, however. His life had been forfeit the moment he touched my wife.

"Robert, this is Tadhg," she explained as if he'd care. "He's helping me get Aveen back."

The bastard put his arm around my wife's shoulders. She didn't stop him. She pulled him closer. Bile scorched my throat. Heat blurred my vision.

"What do you mean get Aveen back?" Robert asked.

She gave him an adoring look, as if he'd told her he'd buy her the feckin' moon. "I have so much to tell you," she said. "Do you mind if we come inside?"

Robert opened the door. "Of course. We can speak in the parlor." Before I could follow, the bastard threw an arm across the threshold. "*You* will wait out here."

"I think that's for the best," I agreed. I needed to get ahold of myself before I did something else unforgiveable.

His red door slammed in my face. As if I wanted to go into his small, miserable house. Suited to a small, miserable man. A feckin' thimble. That's what it was. A thimble with godawful shutters. Pitiful excuse for a garden. Couldn't even swing a feckin' cat in there.

I listened to the two of them arguing inside, hope swelling in my chest when Keelynn insisted on defending me to her *love*.

What a feckin' joke. If she loved *Robert*, she wouldn't have gone off with me. She didn't tell him we were married. No surprise there. Who in their right mind would want to boast about being tied to me for a feckin' day, let alone a year?

"*My darling, my darling. What do you need from me? Just name it and it's yours*." The bastard's head would look good impaled on a fence post.

Keelynn asked if we could stay there. Both of us. At least that was something. That she wasn't trying to rid herself of me. Yet. He agreed, saying he would do anything for her. Didn't she see I would do the same? That I was here, sitting on this shite step in this shite neighborhood, risking life and limb to keep her safe. And all she wanted was feckin' *Robert*.

The door opened, and I could smell her perfume on the breeze.

"Well? What did he say?" I asked as if I hadn't heard every feckin' word.

"We can stay for as long as we need. Robert's organizing dinner for us inside," she added.

"I'm allowed in, am I?"

"Tadhg, you must understand—"

I understood perfectly well. Humans only cared for us as long as we were useful. And the moment Keelynn had decided to give up this pointless quest, I'd ceased to be of use to her. "Save the excuses for someone who cares. Go inside so you don't freeze. I'll join you shortly." As soon as I didn't feel like murdering anyone.

Robert feckin' Trench. All pomp and circumstance in his fancy clothes with his tiny tea set. And the tiny knife sitting on his lap. What did he plan on doing with it? Poke a hole in my shirt? And the wine. Revolting. Like drinking piss. The food tasted like chewing on an old boot. My wife didn't seem to notice as she fawned over her lover, giving him all her smiles and letting him put his filthy hands on her knee. He kept filling her drink like she wouldn't want to be with him if she were sober.

She'd been with me sober. Twice.

I barely listened to their conversation. What did I need to listen for? It wasn't as if they were including me.

"There's no need to thank me," *Robert* said in his bland voice with his bland smile and bland feckin' face. Then his bland eyes landed on me. "No lady should be forced to wear blood-soiled rags to dinner."

I would've shifted her another dress if she'd asked. But she hadn't. Far be it from me to take away another one of her choices. If she wanted to waltz around the city in a blood-soaked gown, then that was up to her.

"Any gentleman worth his salt would feel the same," *Robert* kept on. "I'm only sorry I don't have garments here for you to change into."

I stabbed a bunch of carrots, pretending they were *Robert's* fingers. "Don't forget, Keelynn, you and I have some business to attend to before we leave the city," I reminded her, forcing the woman to tear her attention from *Robert.*

Keelynn grimaced.

"What business is that?" *Robert* asked, giving my wife more wine.

Bottle tipping, glass filling. Drinking more and more. I'd seen her drunk. Lines blurred. Boundaries pushed. If Robert had seen her in that faerie's dress, would he have held back? Something in my gut told me no.

"It's nothing," Keelyn muttered, giving me a kick in the feckin' shin.

"*Shit.*" What'd the woman have on? Steel-toed boots? That feckin' hurt. I gave her a dig back to see how she liked it. "I think *Robert* deserves to know," I said with my most innocent smile.

Her gorgeous eyes flared to life. "It's only a tiny misunderstanding that hardly warrants any attention at all."

A misunderstanding. Is that what this was? If it was a feckin' misunderstanding, then why was she so put out with me over saving her *life*?

The wasp's glare turned into a sweet smile when she turned back to *Robert.* "It was so good of Robert to offer us rooms, wasn't it, Tadhg?"

Robert thought it'd be a good idea to touch my wife's hair. "My home is your home."

This was the type of place where Keelynn belonged. In this world, with a man like this. Pampered and pretty. Not traipsing across the countryside, living among the outcasts. I threw my fork onto the table. I needed something stronger than this shite wine. "It was very kind of your *friend* to make such a generous offer."

"It's better than being murdered in our sleep," she clipped.

I respectfully disagreed.

Keelynn shot to her feet, excusing herself and taking me along with her into the tiny hallway of the tiny house.

"What the hell was that?" she hissed, throwing a hand back toward the tiny dining room. "Robert has offered us a place to stay so we don't get *murdered*, and you're acting like a petulant child."

"Me? You think *I'm* the problem here? He's the one keeping his feckin' knife on his lap like he expects me to attack him. As if a knife would do anything to hold me off if I decided to break every bone in his worthless—"

"Tadhg!"

My mouth snapped shut. I could dip him in boiling oil. *No*! Cut off his feet and hands, then throw him into the sea. *No*! Evanesce to the top of the cathedral and accidentally drop him from the roof.

"I'm calling in our wager," Keelynn said, dragging me from my fantasies.

"Excuse me?"

She rolled her eyes toward the tiny chandelier. "You promised to act like a gentleman for two hours. I'm calling it in."

She expected me to act like a feckin' gentleman with Robert-the-bland glaring at me from across the table with his smarmy smile and tiny knife and . . . *Wait*. My lips lifted. "Are you sure?"

She bobbed her head. "Yes."

I shifted *darling Robert's* pocket watch straight from the prick's waistcoat to check the time. "Two hours, starting now. And you remember what I get if I win?" I slipped the watch into my waistcoat for safekeeping.

Her eyes widened, but it was too late.

Tonight, I would be unlacing my wife's stay.

"Do you remember this, Keelynn?"

"How about this?"

"*I have such a good memory.*"

"*Aren't you impressed by my tiny table?*"

Every word out of this prick's mouth sent me that much closer to the edge of my sanity. Did Keelynn remember that *darling Robert* had been engaged to her sister and hadn't done anything about it?

"So, Tadhg," *Robert* began, his nasally voice grating on my last nerve. "I'm still a little confused as to your role in all of this."

My role. He wanted to talk about my feckin' *role*, did he? Should I tell him about making her come with my tongue or leaving her crying my name with my cock?

"Didn't Keelynn tell you?" I said, nice and slow, allowing all sorts of delicious pauses to plant seeds of doubt in this little man's tiny mind. I kissed my wife's hand, hoping he heard the way her breathing hitched when my lips met her skin. She may not care for me, but she sure as hell liked the way I made her feel. "I've been hired to bring this stunning woman to the Gancanagh's castle."

Her tongue nipped out, leaving her lips wet. I felt the tug around my core tighten.

"Are you still confused, or would you like me to draw you a picture?"

Robert's face turned the same shade of red as the terrible wine he added to my wife's empty glass.

"You must excuse Tadhg," Keelynn breathed, her voice huskier than usual. "He doesn't understand how a *gentleman* should act at the dinner table."

The wager. Remember the wager.

It was precious the way Robert stared me down. As if I would fear someone like him. "Does he understand how a gentleman acts elsewhere?"

I smiled. "Ask Keelynn."

Robert's dull knife came out, aimed at my chest. "You bloody bastard! If you touched her, I'll kill you."

I checked the watch. Forty minutes left. "Now, now, Robert. Surely a gentleman shouldn't make such threats."

Keelynn tossed her serviette onto the table. "Stop it. Both of you." She levelled those beautiful, steely eyes at me. "I know what you're doing, and it ends now. You will be civil to one another."

I had been perfectly civil.

Robert grabbed his glass, slumping in his seat like the child he was. "You expect me to be civil to a monster who is clearly taking advantage of you? I've half a mind to call the guards and have him arrested."

I'd love to see the little prick try. I'd have his entrails spilled on the floor before he could set foot out of this room.

I sent the gravy boat toward his lap.

Keelynn saved him.

So I choked the bastard.

"Robert?" she cried, hurrying to help him. "Are you all right?" Bless her, she tried. But beating his back wasn't going to keep my magic from forcing all the air from his lungs and sending him to the underworld, where he belonged.

"Tadhg! Do something."

Feck it anyway. There went the wager. Strangling the host wasn't exactly gentlemanly of me.

"Please!"

The terror in her voice left me pulling back. The man breathed long enough to curse.

Keelynn's arms came around *his* shoulders.

She touched *his* face.

Kissed *his* cheek.

"What do you need, my love?"

My love.

He shrugged her off every time she tried to help him, and all I could do was sit there and hear those words fall from her lips over and over again.

She hadn't chosen me.

I'd been forced on her.

She'd chosen *Robert.*

24

I COULD HEAR KEELYNN AND ROBERT DOWNSTAIRS IN THE PARLOR. Their mumbled conversation. An occasional giggle.

The worst was the silence.

If they weren't speaking or laughing, they were doing something else. And I wasn't foolish enough to think that they were staring into each other's eyes. He carried her up the stairs like a groom on his wedding night. Only he wasn't the feckin' groom. I was.

They had been together.

Perhaps not *together* together.

But Robert sure as hell had put his filthy mouth against my wife's beautiful—now swollen—lips. Her hair fell free from its pins. The front of her shift wasn't tucked in as it should be. The sides of her skirts were folded in on themselves and—

Dammit. I should have killed him at dinner.

Should have let him choke and die, then I wouldn't have to see him try to weasel his way into my wife's bedroom, touch her with his fat, bumbling fingers and—

"I hope I'm not interrupting," I called, knowing damn well that I was.

Robert stepped away from my wife and told her goodnight.

When he turned, he flashed me a look of such unveiled hatred that I nearly respected him for it.

"Goodnight!" I shouted.

He walked with the stiff gait of a man who hadn't found release, and I had never been happier to see someone so uncomfortable.

The closer I drew to Keelynn, the stronger the scent of Robert's cologne on her skin became. My hands itched to climb up her arm, to force the memory of Robert's touch from her mind, to replace his scent with mine.

Instead, I hid my hands in my pockets and said, "You and I need to talk."

Keelynn closed the door in my face.

I evanesced into her room, making myself comfortable on the edge of the windowsill in case she asked me to stay. We were married, after all. "Slamming a door in a man's face when he's speaking is terribly rude."

"So is trying to kill our host," she snapped.

"Kill our host? Such a terrible accusation."

"You promised to be a gentleman."

I hadn't promised. I'd agreed to try. "Turns out seeing another man fondling my wife brings out the monster in me." Just thinking of that dinner made my blood boil anew.

She huffed a breath, turning to the armoire like she couldn't stand the sight of me any longer. "My relationship with Robert is none of your business."

"None of my business? Have you forgotten that you and I are married? And if I hadn't been at dinner tonight, you would've let your precious *Robert* bend you over the table and have his way with you right on top of the feckin' turkey."

Keelynn's hand connected with my cheek. Stinging pain exploded behind my eyes.

"How dare you speak to me like that."

She'd slapped me. Actually slapped me.

I'd taken things too far. Let my mouth get ahead of my brain.

"I am *nothing* to you," she spat.

Nothing to me? Couldn't she see that she was *everything*?

". . . and you are nothing to me. A means to an end. An escape from reality. A handsome distraction."

She didn't mean that. She couldn't. "Keelynn—" I reached for my wife, and you'd swear from the way she jumped away that I'd been the one to strike her.

"No. You don't get to talk to me. I want you out of this house. And don't think about coming back until you've organized a magistrate."

Shit. Shit. Shit.

Don't kick me out. Please, don't kick me out. "I'm sorry. I don't know what came over me." I raked my fingers through my hair, tamping down my rising panic. I couldn't leave her. Alone. With *him*. "I shouldn't have said that, and I shouldn't have acted so childish at dinner. I'm sorry."

The fire in her eyes went out, replaced by a shield of ice. "Save your worthless apologies for someone who cares and get the hell out of my room."

I'd screwed up. Royally screwed up. There was no talking to her in this state. Not knowing where else to go, I evanesced to the castle.

Rían was in his chair, reading yet another book on Tearmann law. The man was a walking library. He must've read each one at least three times. Why he insisted on doing so again was beyond me.

Rían glanced up from his book, surprise flickering across his features. "Where's your assassin?"

"With feckin' Robert."

"You jest."

"Does it look like I'm jesting?" I needed something . . . something to do with my hands. I needed a feckin' drink. I shifted a bottle of puítin, not bothering with a glass. Fire scalded my throat, burning all the way down to my churning stomach.

Rían hopped to his feet, the book vanishing. "This is feckin' brilliant."

"What part of my wife being with another man is brilliant?" I snarled, drowning my rising panic with three more swallows. Keelynn was staying the night alone with another man. A man she loved. Why hadn't I kept my cursed mouth shut?

Rían snorted, gesturing for the bottle. I took another drink before handing it over. "What were you going to do? Keep her? You were never part of the plan. Keelynn was always supposed to end up with Robert."

Rían and his feckin' plans.

"What can you offer her that Robert can't?" he went on, shoving the bottle at my chest. "You know she loves him. You know he can give her a good home, a safe, quiet existence. They can grow old together, have children, and do all the other things mortals do to be happy."

I wanted Keelynn to be happy. I really did.

I just wanted her to be happy with me.

A means to an end.

An escape from reality.

A handsome distraction.

"What can you offer her besides a lifetime of being hunted? A lifetime of heartbreak when you fall back on old habits? And when Fiadh finds out that you married her . . ." He left a lengthy pause. "What do you think she's going to do to your *wife*?"

Shit. He was right. All I'd been thinking of was what I wanted. Not what was best for Keelynn. And what was best for her wasn't me. Keelynn belonged in her world of daylight, not my world of danger, death, and darkness.

~

The gray light of morning danced on lapping waves as ships sailed into Gaul's main port beyond two stone arches overlooking the vast sea.

After only a few hours of fitful sleep, I'd rolled off of the sofa in our parlor and stumbled for the door, making my way through the empty courtyard toward the gates. Once Tearmann's ever-warm air had kissed my cheeks, I'd evanesced back to watch the city of Gaul awaken alongside the seagulls and fishermen.

The clock in the city square struck nine, its deep gongs echoing off the three and four-story buildings on either side of the cobbled street. Without consciously thinking of where I was headed, I found myself in front of the courthouse attached to the city jail. Inside, a line of humans waited to speak to a woman sitting at an imposing mahogany desk.

"Excuse me." I tapped the man's shoulder in front of me. When he turned, his smile faltered. "Is this where you go to speak with a magistrate?"

"Y-yes. It is," he stuttered, stepping away.

I smiled and thanked him. He threw a few suspicious glances over his shoulder as we waited but seemed to relax when I didn't attack him. The line moved slowly, but eventually I reached the front. "I would like an audience with the resident magistrate, please," I said with an encouraging smile.

The woman's eyes narrowed, even as the invisible thread gave a tug. "I'm afraid he only hears complaints from your sort on the third Tuesday of the month. You will have to wait until then."

My sort. That's the way we were going to play this, then?

"That doesn't work for me. I need to speak with him today."

Her eyes flashed to two guards standing on either side of the main double doors. "I'm afraid you will have to wait."

I wasn't in the mood for this shite. "Does this gentleman have to wait to speak with him?" I asked, pointing to the human behind me.

"No, he does not."

"And why is that?"

"As I have already said, Sir Martin only meets with your kind once a month. He is quite busy."

Boots clicked across the tiles, growing louder as the guards approached. With a flick of my wrist, their bodies slumped to the ground. Not dead, but they'd wake with a helluva headache. Humans gasped and started running for the exit, scurrying away like mice.

"It appears as though Sir Martin's day has just opened up," I said slowly, tapping my nail against the edge of her desk. "Where's his office?"

Stumbling from her chair, the woman pointed to a large wooden door at the end of the hallway.

The magistrate balked at first, but he thankfully ended up being more cooperative than his secretary. It helped that he was a greedy bastard and I had offered him more money than he made in a year. By the time I left his office, the annulment was little more than a formality. Turns out a handfasting wasn't as binding as I'd originally thought. With one signature, Keelynn could be rid of me forever.

By chance, I found Keelynn sipping tea at a quaint blue tea house by the water in a form-fitting black mourning gown. The sun broke through the clouds, and she lifted her face toward its rays, a serene smile playing on her lips. I wanted to remember her this way. Smiling and happy.

"I see someone's away with the faeries," I said, dropping into the only open chair at her table. Probably reserved for *Robert*. The half-eaten cherry tart waiting on the plate in front of her looked as delectable as she did. "Where's Prince Charming?"

Her feckin' hero. Saving her from monsters like me.

Offering me the rest of her dessert, she said *Robert* should be arriving shortly.

Brilliant. I couldn't feckin' wait.

"Then I suppose I'll make this brief." I didn't have it in me to deal with *Robert* today. "We have a meeting with a magistrate on Friday at four."

She sipped her tea thoughtfully, lips slightly pursed. "I cannot believe you actually organized it." The teacup clicked when she sat it on the saucer.

As good as the tart tasted, it left my mouth frightfully dry. I snagged her teacup and took a sip. The cold, bitter drink could do with more sugar. A lot more sugar. "Even *handsome distractions* such as myself have been known to keep the odd promise."

Keelynn's cheeks pinkened. "I'm sorry for saying such awful things to you last night. They were spoken out of anger."

"Save your worthless apologies for someone who cares," I said, mimicking her words. "You are nothing to me, and I am nothing to you."

"Tadhg . . ."

"No, no. It's all right. I like knowing where I stand with people. Makes life easier." Robert's head bobbed among the others walking toward us. I tossed a sugar cube into my mouth and forced a smile. "I'll meet you on Friday at half three in the Arches pub. Wear something nice."

Then I got up and walked straight to the pub to drown my sorrows in something stiffer than cold tea.

Ruairi was already sitting at the bar, hunched over a pint. The moment he saw me walk through the door, the smile fell from his lips. "Lorcan!" He gestured toward the black-haired barman. Lorcan took one look at me and nodded. Two minutes later, I found myself staring into a pint of amber cider, wishing it was Friday.

Every minute brought the world that bit closer to nightfall. That bit closer to bedtime.

Robert would try and sleep with Keelynn.

It felt like someone had stabbed me repeatedly with an iron sword and there wasn't a damn thing I could do to stop it.

Ruairi clapped me on the shoulder, nearly knocking me off the feckin' stool. "Yer proper miserable, aren't ye?"

There was no point denying it anymore. "You don't know what it's like to have the only person you want choose someone else."

"Do I not? My best mate and his brother are two fae feckin'

princes. Yer literally cursed to look like a woman's fantasy. The only reason a woman wants to be with me is to get to ye."

"That's not—"

He held up a hand. "It is. It's true. I've accepted it. Yer problem is that yer never this invested. Ye never cared enough. Havin' her choose him is shite. But there's nothing ye can do to change it."

Ruairi was right.

Dammit.

Why did he have to be right?

"I love that infuriating woman." This was my punishment. Not the churning guilt from the lives I'd taken. Not the bound magic or cursed kiss. My punishment was finally finding the one woman I was meant to be with only to have her love someone else. "How am I supposed to survive this?"

Ruairi gave my shoulder a squeeze. "The same way ye survived everything else, lad. She's not the only bird out there. That muck Rían spits about soulmates is pure and utter shite."

It wasn't though.

I knew Keelynn had been made for me.

Yet she wanted to be with feckin' *Robert.*

25

"It's a pretty name, isn't it? Keelynn. *Keeeelynnnnn.*" The pint I stared into had no comment.

My best mate sitting next to me, though, he nodded and said, "Tis a pretty name, lad."

A pretty name for a pretty woman.

Rolled off the tongue.

Speaking of tongues, mine felt swollen and sluggish. I stuck it out and tried to check but could only see the tip. I swung on the stool toward Ruairi. "Doesthislookstrangetoyou?"

"Get yer tongue back in yer head and speak properly."

"Never mind," I muttered, dropping my head onto the drink-splattered bar and running my tongue along the back of my teeth to get some feeling into it.

Ruairi's massive hand slammed into my back. "It's late, lad. I'm heading up."

Lorcan and his wife Deirdre, the owners of the Arches pub, lived upstairs. They'd gone to bed ages ago, after plying me with drink and prodding me with intrusive questions. Friends did that. Asked too many questions. Not for gossip but out of genuine concern. You know what came with concern? Pity.

I may have been in a pitiful state, but that didn't mean I wanted their pity or anyone else's.

"Are ye comin?" Ruairi asked with a poke.

I didn't want to spend the night in the apartment upstairs. I wanted to spend the night with Keelynn.

God, I loved that woman.

She didn't love me, though. No, she didn't. Not at all. She loved Robert.

Robert.

Stupid name, that. A stupid name for a stupid human.

I slid off the stool, catching myself on the edge of the bar. "I'm staying somewhere else."

Ruairi's golden eyes glowed in the dim light. "Where might that be?"

"None of your business, now is it?"

"Tadhg—"

Before he could give me a lecture, I evanesced straight to *darling Robert's* back garden.

Why did the lights in Keelynn's room have to be off? Why couldn't she be reading at the window by candlelight? Or staring into this shite garden, pining for me? Was she even in there? What if she'd gone to Robert's bed?

I should probably check.

No. Bad idea. *Baaaaad.*

A terrible, awful idea. But I just had to be sure. And then I would find her bed empty and know all hope was lost, and I could move on.

Ha. Move on. Who was I kidding? It'd taken me centuries to get here. I wouldn't be moving on any time in the next hundred years at least.

Biting my lip, I glared at that dark window. What if Fiadh showed up? She could, you know. And then Keelynn would be killed. But not if I was inside. Fiadh would stab me with that dagger instead.

And I'd let her.

Right, so.

I had a duty to go in. End of story. I was going to do it.

Magic hummed beneath my skin. I focused on the room above me, and with a burst of power, I found myself inside. My eyes adjusted quickly to the darkness. My heart leapt in my chest when I saw a still form with dark hair lying in the bed.

It shouldn't mean anything, except it meant everything.

If hope was for fools, then I was the most foolish of fools because seeing Keelynn asleep on her own left tears prickling the backs of my eyes.

I blamed it on the drink.

I stepped forward in the darkness and accidentally rammed into something hard.

Feckin' table. Who put that table there?

Probably *Robert.*

The vase on top rocked and fell, and I knew what was going to happen before it happened but couldn't get my feckin' feet to move so I could keep the blasted thing from shattering on the floor. Roses and broken glass ended up everywhere. Well, feck it anyway. So much for being stealthy. I would've left them except I didn't want my wife to cut her beautiful feet. So I shifted them into my brother's room just for fun.

"*Tadhg*?" Keelynn's voice sounded all bed-warmed and sleepy and sensual.

"Shhhh . . . Go back to sleep."

Like usual, the woman didn't listen.

She sat up, lifting her arms toward the ceiling in a slow stretch. "What are you doing?"

What did it look like I was doing? Trying to stand up straight and not knock into any of this tiny furniture set out like a feckin' death trap in the darkness.

My boot caught on something, sending me into the wall. *Hello, wall. Thank you for catching me.*

"Nothing. I'm not here." *Completely invisible.* Stealthy as a shadow.

"Yes, you are. I can see you."

"No, you can't." If she could see me, then she would be railing and screaming and calling for *Robert* to come and save her. She wasn't doing any of those things. She was getting out of bed and coming toward me in nothing but a white shift.

Long, shapely legs on full display.

"Are you drunk?"

"Yup."

"You're drunk and you came here?"

Drunk or sober, I didn't want to be anywhere else. "If Fiadh wants to kill my wife, she's going to have to"—a hiccup escaped, making me seem far less imposing—"go through me first."

"And you thought you could defeat her in this state?"

I couldn't even defeat a feckin' squirrel in this state. But that wasn't the point. "It's not about defeating her. It's about giving her a more enticing target." If I had an ink pen, I'd draw an "X" on my chest, so she didn't miss my heart.

"Tadhg—"

"I like the way you say my name." Always with a hint of exasperation. Liked her nose too. I tapped the upturned tip. She had a beautiful nose.

She didn't look impressed by my confession. "You like the way I say your name?"

"I like a lot of things about you."

Keelynn scooted closer. That was a good sign, right? Unless she was trying to get within arm's reach to slap me again. "Like what?"

"Don't think I should tell you. Don't want to get slapped again." That shite hurt my face and my useless pride.

"I promise not to slap you."

"Ah, but you can lie." Broken promises were the only ones I seemed to get these days.

She removed the ring, placing it on the floor between us. "There. I promise I won't slap you."

What did I have to lose? Not a damn thing. "All right. Why

not?" I eased forward, inhaling the fragrant strands of hair falling down her shoulders. *Heaven*. "I like the way you smell."

"That's it?"

Oh, my darling wife, I'm just getting started. "No. I like the dreadfully high collars you wear that conceal this lavender-scented patch of skin right here." I stroked her neck with my fingertip. "I like the way you taste." She drove me out of my mind. "But most of all," I whispered, feeling her heart hammering beneath my lips on her throat, "I like the way you hate me."

"I don't hate you."

Not now, maybe. But she did. She should. "Loathe? Or detest? Ohhh, *despise*." Funny word, that. *Despise*. "That's a good one. You *despise* me."

"And you think that's a good thing?" she breathed.

Having this woman despise me was the best thing that ever could have happened. "If you didn't hate me so much, I would've seduced you that very first night and never gotten the chance to know you."

Her lips tugged down into a frown. "You don't know me."

Didn't know her. Was she serious? I may not know everything, but I knew what mattered. "I know you love your sister and would do anything to get her back. I know you didn't care for your husband. I know you hate mourning dresses and like hydrangeas." That day at the market, she'd touched them differently. Her eyes had glazed over just a bit, and her smile had changed. I'd bet my castle they were her favorite. "I know you don't complain, even when you're in pain." Her heels had been hurting during our trek to the faeries, and not once did she whine or ask me to heal her. "I know you whimper when you find release." The sound. Just thinking about it made me hard. "And sigh just before you fall asleep." I'd heard her. The night we'd snuck into the inn. The day she'd fallen asleep on my shoulder. I'd felt it against my neck in the shifted cottage. "I know you are stubborn, but not too stubborn to admit when you are wrong. You fear the dark. You loved Padraig like a father. You are a wasp when you're hungry and can't handle your stout for shit."

I could go on and on. But I wouldn't because there was no feckin' point.

"Most importantly," I said, taking her hand in mine, allowing her warmth to seep beneath the surface, "I know that you are the type of woman others are willing to die for—myself included."

She stared at me as if I'd lost my mind.

I had. Hopefully, I'd find it in the morning.

"Right." Reluctantly, I let her go. "Wake me if the murderous witch shows up." If I was to die, I'd love a good night's sleep first.

I curled onto my side and closed my eyes. Who knew a floor could be so comfortable? Sure, it was cold and hard. But it was also close to *her*.

"Tadhg?"

"Hmmm?"

"Why did Fiadh curse you?"

I didn't want to tell her. But when you were saying goodbye, you told the truth. "I told women I loved them so they'd come to bed with me." Left them in the middle of the night or early the next morning to avoid the inevitable tears, never to see them again. "And one of them happened to be a hateful witch who doesn't know the meaning of forgiveness. She ripped away my magic, leaving only a pittance, and cursed me to be used by women the way I had used her. And then she took my lies and cursed my lips so that I could never escape.

"I deserved all of it." Every single curse. "I have done terrible things, things that would make you hate me more than you already do. But I am not the man I was." I'd changed in the last two hundred and fifty years. I was still far from good, but I wasn't the man I used to be. "I don't want to be a catalyst for death. I don't want to be used and cast aside like I am nothing. I have served my time, and now I want to be free." Unfortunately, what I wanted didn't factor into what I received.

"Here." She gave me the ring and told me I deserved to be free.

For the lives I'd stolen, I deserved to be right where I was. Still, I appreciated the gesture, even if it couldn't save me. "It doesn't work. I tried, but I couldn't lie. Or say no."

There was no sense keeping the thing when it was of no use, so I gave it back. "It was my mother's, you know. She enchanted it to keep me safe from curses." If only I had cared enough to keep it on my finger that day.

"Was your mother a witch?"

My mother wasn't just a witch, she was a feckin' saint. "She was called Bronah. She married my father Midir when they found out she was pregnant." They never should've wed. My father claimed to love my mother, and yet he was never faithful. He didn't deserve to breathe the same air as her and he feckin' knew it. "My father was never the same after she passed and didn't know what to do with me." I remembered him looking at me as if I was some sort of foreign being. Thank heavens for my governess and our cook Eava. Without them, there's no telling what would've happened to me. "He had more interest in women than raising a child. Luckily, I had this ring to keep me out of harm's way. Fiadh knew about the ring and must've tailored the curses to bypass the spell. She asked for it that day, said she wanted to see how it looked on her finger. I hadn't cared . . . about the ring. About Fiadh. About anyone but myself, really."

Keelynn stared down at the green stone. I liked that when I was gone, she would have a piece of me, of my history, with her. Although she probably wouldn't wear the thing after her curse wore off. Maybe one day she'd look at it and think of me and our time together with some semblance of fondness.

"I love you," she whispered, pressing kisses to my hair, my ears, my cheeks.

Although I knew she was only able to speak those words aloud because she wore my ring, my heart still constricted. "You don't have to say that."

“I want to.” Her lips grazed my cheek. “Let me help you.”

“I don’t—” The lie left my head feeling as if it would shatter. I couldn’t say I didn’t want to be with her because I did. More than life. “I’m too drunk to be of any use to you.” To be anything but a disappointment. At this stage, and with her looking like that, I wouldn’t last pissing time.

“I don’t want to use you.”

Then what did she want? I was good for nothing else, especially in this state.

“Come here.” She helped me to my feet and brought me to the bed. “Take off your shirt.”

Shirt off. I could do that.

Her breathing hitched, and that tug grew stronger. I liked the way she looked at me. The way her eyes raked down my bare skin like her nails had only a few days ago.

“Scoot over and lay down.”

I didn’t need to be told twice.

The mattress dipped when she climbed in beside me. “Head here,” she said, patting her left breast.

What did she want me to do with that? I knew what I wanted to do with it, but I was fairly certain I was missing the point. She patted her chest again.

I settled my head against her heart, letting myself be drawn into her embrace. If being inside her was heaven, then this was the next best thing. And when she started playing with my hair, I let my eyes fall closed, matching my breathing to hers. Her fingertip traced my ears, sending chills down my spine.

“That tickles.”

“Sorry.”

“You don’t have to stop. It’s nice.”

She went back to my ear. I may have liked it a little too much and had to have a serious chat with my lower half.

“What are you going to do about your curse?” she asked.

Ah, my curses. There was nothing I could do. Not really. “I can either wait for Fiadh . . . Or beg you to stay married to me.”

Imagine that. Staying married. A year's respite.

Keelynn spoke in hushed tones. I was too far gone to hear anything but the sweet husky notes of her voice. What if this was real? What if she cared for me the way I cared for her? What if she actually loved me? I let myself dream of that. Just for tonight.

If Keelynn loved me.

I love you.

"I love you too."

26

I LOVE YOU TOO.

No amount of cursing would get the confession out of my brain. But I gave it a good go anyway. What had I been thinking, showing up to that short, unimpressive human's house three sheets to the feckin' wind?

I was good at hiding away. Why hadn't I done that instead?

Drink. That's why. Made everything worse. *Everything.* But only if you sobered up. The black walls in the back room of the Arches suited my black mood. I'd woken with a start, my wife draped across me like a quilt. Her leg hitched over my hip. Shift bunched around her waist. My hand on her arse. And my cock hard as feckin' marble.

I had no plan on leaving, hoping Robert accidentally found us like that.

Then I remembered what my cursed mouth had said.

I love you too.

My hand shook as I reached for the fresh glass of puítin I'd gotten for myself from behind the bar. I would stay drunk until Friday. Give my wife what she wanted. And give in to the darkness.

A woman called my name from somewhere behind me. My

heart leapt until I realized the woman's accent wasn't right. No sense checking to see who she was. I didn't give a shite.

"Tadhg?"

She stood at my side now, watching me. A pretty thing with short, bouncy red curls framing a round face. I gave her what I thought was a smile. Mustn't have been since she didn't return it.

"Do you remember me?" she asked.

"Nope."

Her face fell as her eyes flicked to the empty tables. Lorcan hadn't been impressed when I made him open the pub at half five this morning. Told me I could drink in his apartments upstairs. But I hadn't wanted to drink in his happy feckin' apartment surrounded by himself and his happy wife and their pitying stares.

I wanted to drink alone.

The intruder fidgeted with her worn shawl, bunching the edge, letting it fall, and bunching it again. "We met once. Well, twice. But you didn't see me the first time, and . . . the second time we . . . ah . . . we had relations in a coat closet."

"You grossly underestimate how many times I've 'had relations' in coat closets." And stables. And privies. *Disgusting*, by the way. Bedrooms, bathing rooms, towers, dungeons, fields, rivers, the sea. The list of places I hadn't had sex was probably shorter. Like my own bed. Never had a woman there.

"My name's Marina."

The name brought something back.

A cottage on the coast.

"What can I do for you, Marina?" Wasn't sure why I asked. Humans only wanted me for two things.

Tears sprung from her bright blue eyes. "I want you to kiss me."

I finished my glass, slamming it on the table next to the other four. "No."

Her mouth opened and closed. "I thought you couldn't say no."

"I just did." I'd say "no" to everything while I still could.

"Please, Tadhg. Please. I can't do it anymore."

Her threadbare shawl slipped off her shoulder, revealing deep purple bruises on her arm. I was already drowning in misery. I didn't need to deal with hers as well. For some reason, my cursed mouth asked where she got the marks.

"My husband is . . ." The words trailed off when her gaze landed on the empty glass clenched in my hand. "Steven is fond of the drink," she finished in a whisper.

Fond of the drink.

The polite way of calling someone an alcoholic. Just like me. Except, even at my worst, I'd never hurt a woman.

Marina . . .

Marina.

Hold on. I *did* remember Marina. She'd done that thing with her tongue. My curse wasn't the only thing that stirred.

"What of your children?" I asked, adjusting myself in my breeches. I remembered her having at least one. Maybe two.

"He'd never lay a finger on the little ones."

A man who struck a woman was capable of anything. "I won't do it. You need to—"

Marina lunged, catching my shoulders. My reactions were too sluggish. Her lips had barely grazed mine, and yet it had been enough to tear a relieved cry from her throat as she collapsed at my feet.

Ruairi appeared, hair standing up at the back, shirt untucked over loose black trousers.

The moment he saw the body on the floor, he groaned. "Have ye lost yer mind? Lorcan will have yer head fer this."

He could take his judgement and go and shite. "And is Lorcan my ruler?"

Ruairi's eyes narrowed.

"That's what I thought."

My mate's meaty fists clenched. Maybe he would hit me. At least the pain would rid me of this numbness.

"Fer once in yer life, can ye think about someone else? How do ye think a dead human is going to affect his business? When the Airren authorities find out—"

"What are they going to do? Kill me?" I snorted, shifting a bottle of wine from behind the bar.

Ruairi dropped to the stool and took one of my empty glasses for himself.

"I don't want company."

"And I don't want a drunken eejit as my best mate, yet here we are."

He slammed the glass down in front of me. I filled it to the brim.

"The magistrate has kindly agreed to annul our handfasting. I'll sober up then." *Dammit.* Why couldn't she give me a year? It was a feckin' *year*. Less, since we were wed three days ago.

"Handfasting?" Ruairi's drink stilled halfway to his mouth. "Lad, yer not handfasted. Yer proper married."

"No. Rían did the thing with the things." I gestured toward my hand.

"Ribbons."

"Right. Ribbons."

"He could've wrapped ye both in ribbons and it wouldn't have made a blind bit of difference to the vows."

Vows? I'd been in such a panic I couldn't remember what I'd promised.

Snippets came flooding back and . . . *Shit.*

Dammit.

The process for annulling a proper marriage would take a lot longer and require more paperwork, if they agreed to do it at all.

"Have ye tried explaining to Keelynn about—"

Explaining? What good had that done? I'd explained my reasons for keeping secrets—which were pretty feckin' solid—and the woman moved in with another feckin' man.

I dragged my dagger from my belt and tossed it across the table. "Kill me now."

Ruairi sent it right back. "And give Rían cause to end me? Not a hope."

"I'll give you a royal pardon."

"Won't do me much good in the underworld."

Feck it anyway. I'd just have to find someone else. Then this cursed reminder tattooed on my finger would be gone, and Keelynn would be free and . . .

My gaze landed on Marina. It'd only be a matter of time before the authorities showed.

At least dead, I'd get a respite from all this shite.

Four hours—and one tongue lashing from Lorcan—later and I was still sitting at this feckin' table waiting for someone to murder me.

I heard the whispers. People knew Marina. Knew her situation. No one seemed to care beyond being the first to taste a juicy bit of gossip. Wouldn't be long now. Surely someone would take offense at the dead body curled around my boots.

I smelled Keelynn before I saw her: lavender and sunshine.

Ruairi, ever the gentleman, knocked the whore from his lap. Giselle's wings had been clipped by my brother for some grievous offense. I couldn't rightly remember what it was. The pooka clambered to his feet. "Lady Keelynn. What a pleasant surprise. We weren't expecting ye."

He could say that again.

What was she doing here? It wasn't Friday already, was it?

"I can see that." Disapproval oozed from those four words. Was it the body or the booze that bothered her?

"Who the hell is *she*?" Giselle whined.

"She's, um . . ." Ruairi looked at me. He could deal with this on his own. "She's no one."

If only I could tell my heart the same thing.

Keelynn's shoulders stiffened as she moved closer.

"Pardon me."

I glanced down to where she'd knocked Marina's dirty shoe. Dead bodies were so quiet. Easy to forget. No sense apologizing to them. "She can't hear you. She's dead."

"She's what?" Keelynn gasped, stumbling and ending up in a heap on the ground next to the dead woman. "Why'd you kiss her?"

Why'd you kiss Robert? "I didn't kiss her. She kissed me. I told her not to, but she didn't listen. And now she's dead, and her children will starve because her husband is a worthless drunk who spends more time drinking in the pub than working at the mill."

The extra information I'd gleaned from whispers. Marina's situation had been dire. But instead of leaving the man and taking her children somewhere safe, she'd abandoned them.

Cursing, Ruairi helped Keelynn to her feet. I would've done it but figured she didn't want my hands anywhere near her. "Ye must excuse Tadhg this morning," Ruairi growled. "He's in a foul humor."

Is that what we were calling this now? A foul humor?

"Oh, she's one of *his*."

Feckin' Giselle. Most whores I could take. But this one, she'd always rubbed me the wrong way. Even when she was rubbing me the right way. "Do us all a favor, Giselle, and slither back to the hole you crawled out of."

Her jaw gaped. She reached for Ruairi as if he was going to do a feckin' thing.

"It's time for you to go," he murmured.

She made a show of stomping toward the door, short skirt riding up her arse.

"You can't let her children starve," Keelynn said. "This is your fault. You have to fix it."

Giselle didn't have any children—

Keelynn wasn't looking at the faerie. She was staring at the dead human.

What was one more dead human to me? Why did Marina

deserve my help when she'd done this to herself? Why was I always the one expected to help everyone else?

When was someone going to help me?

"What would you have me do?"

"Give them money."

Money in an alcoholic's pocket was like drink in his glass. Gone in a few swallows. "So their father can use it to buy drink? Not a feckin' hope. There are too many of you humans on this island anyway. You procreate like feckin' rabbits."

Unlike the Danú, whose children were rare and to be protected at all costs.

Ruairi dug the toe of his boot into my shin.

"*Dammit,* Ruairi!" He'd dented my feckin' leg.

"Where do they live?" Keelynn pressed.

"In a cottage by the sea."

"Take me there."

This woman. Was she truly that ignorant to the way the world worked? I almost laughed. She'd agreed to let me into her life; Keelynn was as ignorant as they came. Still, going to that cottage wouldn't make a blind bit of difference. "No. Now, tell me why you're here or leave me alone."

I couldn't be around her without wanting to feel her skin on my fingertips. My need was slowly driving me insane. I didn't want to feel anything for a woman who cared so little for me. I didn't want to feel anything at all.

I took another eye-watering drink.

"You said something before you passed out last night, and I wanted clarification."

Shit.

Shit.

Shit.

"What did I say?" I asked, hoping she was referring to something other than the fact that I had confessed my love for her.

"You don't remember?"

I remembered plenty. Thus, the binge drinking.

"You said that you wanted to stay married to me."

Three of the other patrons in the bar must've found that fact interesting because they stopped their drinking and conversations to stare at us.

I flicked my wrist, creating a tost, a soundproof barrier between the two of us and the world. "Have you lost your damn mind? I don't need everyone in the feckin' pub knowing my business." To associate herself with me so blatantly would ruin her. It was a good thing her sort didn't frequent places like this. "I never said I *wanted* to stay married. This isn't a matter of *wanting* anything." Because if it was, there'd be no hope. I didn't get what I wanted. "It's a matter of accidentally discovering a loophole in my curse."

When I'd first been cursed, I'd tried to get around Fiadh's intricate spell by using the truth curse to my advantage. I'd promised Rían to never sleep with another woman.

That night, I'd fucked two.

Nothing worked.

Until Keelynn.

Her lovely, lovely lips pursed. My eyes reflexively checked to see if she still wore my ring. There it was, glinting on her left hand, hiding our black bond. "What loophole?" she asked.

"Have you listened to wedding vows?"

"Of course I have. I was married, remember?"

How could I forget? Married to someone else before me. I hated the man and I didn't even know him.

Keelynn looked at me as if she were still confused. I thought I'd made perfect sense.

I took her hands, dragging her until I could see myself reflected in her steely eyes. "To you, I pledge my body and soul. All that I am and all that I have is yours."

I'd said the words, promising this woman things I never thought I'd give to another.

"What are you doing?" she gasped, tugging on her hands.

I wasn't ready to let her go. Not yet. Not even when Ruairi

shoved from his chair, knocking it to the ground, and stalked forward. "I bind myself to you and you alone, forsaking all others."

"Stop talking," she whispered. "Let me go."

"In giving you my hands, I give you my life, to have and to cherish until death do us part."

Ruairi slammed his fist against the barrier. Looked like he'd changed his mind about killing me.

I loosened my grip, feeling her fingers slip through mine as she stumbled as far away as the barrier would allow. "What the hell has gotten into you? What is that?"

"*That's* what I promised when I saved your life. That ring cannot save me from this curse, but you can."

"How does being married help you lie?"

"I don't give a shit about lying." I'd lied just fine for the last two centuries. "And I no longer care that death lives on my lips. Anyone foolish enough to kiss me despite the consequences deserves to die. But I am done being used. I am the Crown Prince of Tearmann, and I cannot even turn down an ancient feckin' scullery maid looking for a ride. All a woman has to do is say she wants me, and my body, my magic, responds. I am powerless to stop it. Or at least I was powerless until I married you."

Searching eyes scoured my face for answers. "I still don't understand."

Dammit. How many times did I need to repeat myself before she understood? "I bind myself to you and you alone, forsaking *all others.*"

Her narrowed eyes widened as her mouth fell open in an O. Her little gasp reminded me of the noise she'd made when I'd first pushed inside her. Not what I needed to be thinking about at present. "Because you made that vow to me, you're free to make your own choices."

Free? I almost laughed. Couldn't she see that I was her feckin' slave? "I will never be free. But at least I don't have to go off with anyone else for as long as we are wed." I may not have been paying attention to the words, but my heart had been behind every promise.

"We're getting an annulment in two days."

"And this is where the begging comes in," I muttered, scraping my teeth across my cursed lips. "You know who I am. You know what I'm capable of. And yet you seem to hold me in some regard. Last night, you said you didn't hate me. But you used to. You hated me so much I could taste it. And if you can go from hating me to caring enough to give me that ring in only a matter of days, imagine what could happen in a month—in a year. All I'm asking for is a chance, for a respite from the burdens I've carried for so long."

"It doesn't have to be me. You could marry anyone."

I didn't trust anyone else. I didn't *love* anyone else.

Love was what had set me free.

Putting her needs above my own. Setting my own selfishness aside. Marrying anyone else would be for the most selfish reason of all. I'd done this for her. And in doing so, I'd found the reprieve I'd craved for so long.

"And give someone else power over me? Not a feckin' hope. There are very few people in this world I trust, and you are one of them."

Her head started shaking the way I knew it would. And then her mouth started saying the words I knew she would say. "Tadhg . . . I'm sorry, but I cannot stay married to you."

I'd known that would be her answer from the beginning. She was finally with the man she loved. How could I expect her to give up her life—her happiness—for me? She hadn't done anything wrong. This wasn't her problem.

It was mine.

I took out my dagger, studying my face in the gleaming blade. "Then I want you to kill me." For her to know she was the one cutting out my heart. To punish her for choosing someone else.

"Are you mad? I'm not killing you."

I gestured toward a fuming Ruairi. "I'd let him do it, but I think you'd enjoy it more."

She insisted that no one was killing me.

"*Until death do us part,* Keelynn. If you want out of this marriage, one of us needs to die. And unless you're immortal and haven't told me, I'm the only one who can come back from the underworld."

She took the dagger, but hesitated. "What about our annulment?"

"Apparently, my eejit brother doesn't know the difference between a handfasting and proper wedding vows. And as we were in a bit of a rush, I didn't take too much notice of the words at the time." I wouldn't put it past the bastard to have done this on purpose. Rían remembered everything. "Even if we went ahead with the annulment, it wouldn't break the promises I made to you or the ones you made to me. We would still be married."

The tattoos on our fingers would remain. That was one of the differences between humans and Danú: proper weddings involved magic, and magic didn't come unraveled when a magistrate signed a piece of feckin' paper.

"Won't it hurt?"

It already hurt.

Loving Keelynn was the greatest pain I'd ever endured.

"Does it matter?" I made her press the blade until I felt the familiar kiss of steel beneath my ribs. "Go on, Keelynn. This is what you wanted, isn't it? To kill the Gancanagh. Now's your chance."

Kill me.

Cut out my heart.

Take it.

It's yours.

After all I'd done, Keelynn should want me dead. Why wasn't she killing me? "What's wrong? Don't you want to screw Robert-the-bland with a clear conscience?" Once the words started, I couldn't stop. Vicious vitriol spewing from my cursed lips. "Don't you want to rid yourself of our marriage bond? Although, going back to a human after you've been with one of us will be disappointing. Just ask Marina. Oh, wait. You can't. She's dead."

"I know what you're doing. But it won't work. Hearing you spew hate doesn't make me hate you, Tadhg. It makes me *pity* you."

I let go of the tost, shame heating my neck and jaw. Ruairi-the-feckin-hero escorted my wife to the exit, fawning over her, throwing hateful glances over his shoulder.

I didn't give a shite what he thought.

He didn't know how I felt.

No one knew.

The moment the door swung shut, he stalked back to our table. I picked up one of my pawns from our forgotten game of draughts and moved it forward a space.

"You and I need to have a little chat," he ground through a clenched jaw.

"I have nothing to say to you."

"Too feckin' bad, Princey. Killing this human was one thing. But *that*"—he threw a hand at the door—"whatever the hell that was, was unacceptable. See these people?" He gestured to folks who needed to mind their own feckin' business. "They're all witnesses. And they saw ye hold a human against her will and manhandle her. Yer brother is going to have yer feckin' head."

Like I was scared of Rían. "Let him have it."

Ruairi cleared the whole table, the glasses, the draughts, all of it with one sweep of his arm. "No more drink. Yer comin' with me."

"That's not happen—"

The bastard threw me over his shoulder and carried me up the back steps into Lorcan's kitchen. I shifted a bottle of puítin. He stole it and dumped the entire thing down the sink.

So I shifted another.

That bottle shared the same fate.

"I can do this all feckin' day, Tadhg."

I couldn't. If I kept this up, I'd end up killing myself. I'd come back without the brand and *poof*. Problem solved.

My knees wobbled, and I sank to the floor.

Ruairi shoved a glass into my hand.

It didn't smell like anything. "I don't want water."

"That's all yer getting until ye sober the hell up."

I drank what I could, feeling sicker than a dog. "It's making me sick."

"Sure. Blame it on the water and not the vat of drink swimming in yer guts."

He was right. Of course he was right. I dropped my head into my hands, wishing there was some way out of this hell. "She said no."

"Can ye blame her?"

No. I couldn't.

"How many years has it been, lad?"

Too many. Far too many.

"Ye can't keep doin' the same shite expecting a different outcome. And ye cannot expect a woman to care fer what ye are. Ye need to do better. Be better."

"I don't know how."

"That's a load of bollocks, and we both know it."

Do better.

I knew I had problems, but knowing you had problems and doing something to fix said problems were two very different things. Marina had had a problem. And she'd done something about it. Speaking of Marina . . .

"We need to get rid of the body downstairs."

Ruairi nodded. "I'll get Rían. Ye need to sleep this off."

Guilt churned in my gut, not mixing well with the water.

You can't let her children starve.

This is your fault.

You have to fix it.

I called for Ruairi before he could evanesce. A plan formed in my drink-drenched mind, meaning it was probably a terrible idea. Still, I smiled and asked, "How do you feel about kidnapping?"

27

THE WAVES MEETING THE SHORE MADE IT DIFFICULT TO HEAR anything beyond the walls of the one-story cottage tucked at the base of a craggy hill littered with stones and briars.

"Can we get this over with already?" Rían whined, tucking his hands deeper into his overcoat pockets and scowling into the night. "I'm cold."

"Do you ever shut up?" Ruairi muttered, black hair flying loose in the sea breeze. The animal hadn't even bothered with a feckin' coat.

Rían's eyes ignited. "What did you just say to me, *dog*?"

I gave the two of them a shove, knocking them a few steps forward. "Both of you. Quiet." If they didn't shut their gobs, we'd wake the neighbors. The last thing we needed was witnesses.

It was a moonless night, perfect for stealing things that didn't belong to you.

Rían flicked his wrist. Something large and dark appeared in his hands.

"What's that?" I asked, giving his shoulder another nudge.

"Burlap sacks."

"We're collecting children, not vegetables."

His nose wrinkled. "Equally as dirty and disgusting, if you ask me."

My brother and dirt. I could still remember his face the first day I'd thrown him into the oubliette. Horrified, that's what he was. Of course, that was a long time ago. With my magic bound, I was the one who ended up in the pit more often than not.

"You're not putting them in a sack," I said, allowing no room for argument.

No smoke twisted from the cottage's moss-riddled chimney. I tried to remember if this was Marina's home or if it was one of the two next to it that looked almost exactly the same.

There was something about this one that felt familiar, with its shutters hanging off their hinges and door painted a faded blue. This had to be it. I was almost certain.

"How else am I supposed to get it to the house?" Rían grumbled, opening one of the sacks and giving it a shake. The wind caught it, blowing it open like a barrel.

"You'll figure it out." He was the man with the plans, after all. How hard could it be to convince a few children to leave this hovel and hide somewhere else until their Mammy came back from the dead?

With a quiet curse, the sacks disappeared.

First things first. We needed to make sure Marina's husband wasn't going to catch us. The lack of smoke was a fairly good sign, but if the state of her clothes was any indication, they may not be able to afford fuel for the fire. Best be sure, just in case.

I sneaked past the sheets still flapping on the laundry line to find the door unlocked. Tiny shoes waited by the threshold. There were two bedrooms. Both empty. A kitchen that stunk of vinegar, and a living room the size of our dining table. All empty as well.

The husband wasn't there.

But neither were the children.

"They're not in the house," I told the lads waiting in the shadows out front, closing the door behind me.

Ruairi sniffed the air, brow furrowing. Rían gagged, holding a hand over his nose. All I could smell was piss and pig shite.

Then I heard something.

Soft sniffles.

The others must've heard it too, because we all hurried for the back garden at the same time. Ruairi reached it first, raising his nose toward the sky.

To the right sat a pig sty with a few pigs huddled in the corner. To the left was a garden, wilted and dry.

And slap in the middle stood a shed.

A shed someone had bolted and locked closed.

Rían glared at the rusty lock dangling against the gray wood. "The door is locked."

Feck it anyway. With the door locked, there wasn't a hope of convincing Rían to help. I wouldn't have enough magic to get the children to the path toward town, let alone all the way back to the portal in Gaul.

Ruairi nudged the sagging corner with his shoulder. The wooden shack groaned. "A gust of wind could knock over the rotting thing."

The sobbing inside the shed grew louder, accompanied by hushed whispers.

We didn't have time for this. There were children locked inside of a feckin' shed. Ruairi reached for the lock. I stopped him with a hand on his elbow. Breaching a locked door was a capital crime. It didn't matter that we had a good reason. And Ruairi couldn't come back from death.

"What's that over there?" I pointed to the sea's cresting waves barely visible on the horizon.

Rían and Ruairi both turned to check.

I yanked the lock, breaking the fastenings. "Oh, would you look at that." I flicked the dangling metal. "It's not locked anymore."

Rían's jaw worked, but for once, he kept silent. If he had a problem, I had no doubt he'd kill me over it later.

I drew the door aside to find three pairs of tear-filled eyes staring at me from the darkness.

The tallest child had a round face with delicate features and shorn red hair. In her arms, she cradled a tiny baby. Couldn't be more than two or three months old. The little boy at her side clung to her grimy dress.

"You can come out now," I said quietly to keep from scaring them. "We won't hurt you."

The little boy whimpered, burying his face in his sister's skirts. To them we must have looked frightening, three giants draped in shadows, eyes glowing. I dropped to my knees to make myself appear less imposing. Cold mud seeped through my breeches.

"Da says we have ta stay in here till our Mammy gets home," the tallest one said in a mousy voice.

Their Da was lucky I hadn't found the bastard inside. Otherwise, he'd be the one covered in shite locked in a feckin' shed. "I saw your Mammy today," I told her.

Her eyes widened. "Ye did?"

The little boy peered up at me.

I nodded. "She had to go away for a little while, but she will be back. We're going to bring you someplace safe until she returns."

The baby began to wail. The boy took off, sprinting around me toward the sty.

"Cian! Get back here!" the girl roared.

I smacked Ruairi's knee. "Catch him before he gets away."

He took off after the little boy, probably scaring the life out of him. Nothing to be done about it now. Once they were safe and warm, they'd see we meant them no harm. Until then, we'd have to keep them quiet. Maybe I'd been too quick in dismissing the burlap sack.

I offered the girl a hand. A hand she ignored as she clutched the baby closer, standing on legs thinner than twigs and starting for the door.

Ruairi had the boy cornered, darting this way and that until the little lad's backside met the fence. "Easy there. *Eaaaasy.*"

"They're not animals," I reminded him. "They're children."

"I don't see ye making any headway," Ruairi growled.

"What's your name, sweetheart?" I asked.

The girl bounced and swayed, patting the crying baby's back. "Mila." It'd been a while since I'd been around children. She could've been nine, maybe ten. Far too young to be left alone with a baby.

"My name's Tadhg."

The baby began to quiet, nuzzling into the little girl's neck. "Da says we're not to be trustin' the ones with the pointy ears."

Out of the corner of my eye, I saw the little boy dart through Ruairi's legs and hurtle over the fence into the sty.

"Tell you what," I said, reaching out my hand a second time. "If you come with us, I give you my word as a prince that you will be well fed, warm, and safe. And if you aren't happy in your new home, I will bring you back here myself."

Her glare bounced between my hand and my ears. "Ye don't look like a prince."

"Do I not? What should a prince look like?" I'd never given too much thought to what my cursed glamour would look like to a female child.

The little girl pointed to a smirking Rían. "'Cept he needs a crown."

"Rían?"

With a roll of his eyes and flick of his wrist, a gold crown appeared on Rían's head.

"Do you want to know a secret about the prince?" When she nodded, I cupped my hands around my mouth to whisper, "He hates dirt." I picked up a clump and threw it at him. He cursed. "Do you want to try?"

She grinned and collected a handful. Rían evanesced before the dirt could connect.

"What's this little one's name?" I patted the babe's curly red hair.

"Mammy calls her Shona."

Shona, Mila, and Cian. I shifted a bag of sweets from Eava's personal stash, figuring she wouldn't mind. "Here." I held out the bag. "Take these while we get your brother. Will I have the prince hold Shona until you're finished?"

Nodding, she traded me the baby for the bag and scrubbed her dirty hands down her dirty skirts.

The little thing felt too small and breakable in my clumsy hands. "Here." I thrust the wriggling bundle toward Rían's chest. "Do something useful."

"Oh god," Rían choked, holding the baby out from his waistcoat. "This one smells." One of the burlap sacks reappeared.

"Don't even think about it," I clipped, giving his ankle a kick.

Ruairi lumbered toward us, the boy tucked beneath an arm, thrashing and squealing. "Ye have to bring Jordie," he cried. "Ye have to bring Jordie! Please! I can't leave her!"

"There's another one?" Rían groaned.

"She's my pet," Cian wailed.

Right. What was one more? "Where's Jordie?" I couldn't see a dog or cat anywhere. If we couldn't find it, then the thing stayed. I'd get the boy a new pet.

When he pointed toward the pigs, Rían choked. "Give me the girl." He gestured to Mila. "You get the swine."

The little boy thrashed and wailed, his cries muffled by the growing wind. Ruairi cursed, dropped the boy, and clutched his forearm to his chest. "The little fecker bit me!"

"Ye have to bring Jordie," Cian bellowed, sprinting for the sty. "Please. Please, don't leave her. She's the best pig we got."

I evanesced in front of him, stopping him in his tracks. When I asked which pig it was, he said she was the cutest one. As if any of the animals covered in shite could be considered cute. "That one?" I pointed to the smallest of the lot.

Nodding, the boy scrubbed his dirty, tear-stained cheeks with his grimy sleeve.

The fence was low enough to step over. My boots immediately sank into the muck. I'd never cared too much about dirt, but the way my footsteps *squelched* left me wincing. This wasn't just muck. It was a sloppy mix of mud and shite. I'd never get rid of the foul stench.

Jordie slept with the rest of her piggy family. Before I could pick her up, one eye opened, and she took off like a feckin' banshee, squealing and racing toward the gate.

I'd almost grabbed the little bastard when my feet slipped, landing me face-first in shite. I managed to get my feet back underneath me only to slip again.

By the time I left the feckin' sty, I was head-to-toe in the foulest smelling dirt I'd ever come across.

Rían took one look at me and said he'd take it from there. I didn't have it in me to protest, handing Cian his pet and making my way toward the beach to let the icy waves beat me clean.

Keelynn was the first person I wanted to talk to about what had happened. An hour later, I found myself back in Gaul, standing in Robert's small, shadowed garden.

As much as I wanted to, I wouldn't break into her room again. Still, I didn't need to go inside to be near her. I sank onto a bench next to some dead roses and stared at her night-darkened window.

"*Tadhg*."

The hair on the back of my neck stood on end. I could've sworn I heard my name. *Wishful thinking*.

"*Tadhg? Are you there?*"

Not wishful thinking. Keelynn had called for me.

What did she need? Was she in trouble? What if Fiadh showed up again? What if she changed her mind about staying married to me?

"Where are you, Tadhg?"

I evanesced into the room, and before I knew what was happening, Keelynn's arms were around me, and she was hugging me and pressing her face into my chest, and I was so happy I'd bathed and changed after my fall in the sty.

"What is it?" I choked past the lump swelling in my throat. "What's wrong?"

"It's awful," she cried. "I'm so sorry. So sorry."

"What's awful? Tell me what happened."

"Robert's friends showed up. I think they killed Ruairi," she sniffled. "I mean, I don't know if it was him, but I'm afraid it was. And if it wasn't, then they killed some other poor pooka, and I'm so sorry, Tadhg. I didn't know. I swear I didn't know."

Someone else had killed a pooka, and she was apologizing? "First, Ruairi is fine. There's no fear for him, all right? Second, there is no need to apologize because you did nothing wrong." I'd have to let Rían know when I got home later. He'd see if there was any truth to the matter and deal with things how he saw fit.

"I'm one of them. Isn't that wrong enough?"

"You're human, but you're *not* one of them." Not by a long shot. "I know better than to judge an entire population based on the actions of a few." That's what the humans had done to us. Doing it right back wouldn't make things better. It would make life worse. "This isn't a rare occurrence. My people have been persecuted for centuries. There is risk involved for those of us who choose to live outside of Tearmann. Everyone knows that, including the pooka they killed."

"You're sure it wasn't Ruairi?"

"Positive. Ruairi spent the evening with me. We had to get Marina's body to the castle." The confession made me feel weak and pathetic. I should've been able to clean up my own messes instead of relying on everyone else to do it for me. "I couldn't stop thinking about what you said about her children. So, we went to her cottage and . . . It was bad. So much worse than I'd imagined." What would've happened if we hadn't helped? I shuddered at the thought.

"Tell me."

"It'll upset you."

"Tell me anyway."

I told her what had happened at Marina's. The sorry state of her children. "We may have stolen them."

"You *stole* children?"

"Technically, Ruairi did." And Rían. "I just took a pig." My truth curse made me a liability. If we were ever caught and charged, I couldn't lie about my involvement like the others.

"A pig?"

I explained a bit more, about Cian and Jordie, and where we'd taken them. Even though we would be going our separate ways, I wanted to make her proud of at least one thing I'd done.

"Look, I am dreadfully sorry for the way I treated you earlier. You'd think at this stage I'd be used to not getting what I want, but for a moment, I saw a light at the end of this long, miserable tunnel and thought it was within my grasp. I never should have suggested we stay married. No one deserves that kind of punishment." Least of all her. "And I shouldn't have asked you to kill me when Rían will be more than happy to do it when I get home."

That's what waited for me back at the castle. Death as punishment for kidnapping a bunch of children and breaking a lock to do it. A punishment I deserved and would gladly pay. The only upshot was that I got to kill him too.

Keelynn's brow furrowed, then smoothed the moment our gazes locked. "I forgive you. For everything."

There must me something wrong with my ears. I could've sworn she said she'd forgiven me.

"You do?" How? *Why*?

Keelynn nodded.

"You *forgive* me." People didn't just forgive. "That's it? You have no requests or bargains? You don't desire reparations?"

"Padraig always said true forgiveness is freely given."

She forgave me. For lying. For marrying her without her consent. For treating her like shite today in the pub. For being a murderer. *She* forgave *me*.

"Padraig was a good man." I should've given my life to bring him back.

Her eyes glittered with unshed tears. "Yes, he was."

The coals in the fireplace burned a dull orange, reflecting off the marble hearth. I could sit here all night, enjoying the silence, so long as she was by my side. But Keelynn didn't belong to me.

She never had.

"I'm . . . um . . . I'm going to go." Otherwise, I was going to say or do something to muck this up. This was the sort of memory I wanted to leave her with. This was how I wanted her to remember me.

I drank in the sight of her. Hair long and loose about slim shoulders.

The bow of her lips.

The faint flush of her porcelain cheeks.

When Rían killed me, this would be over. She would be free.

"How did you know I needed you?" she asked, peering up at me through the thick curtain of her lashes.

"I may or may not have been sitting in the back garden." Like a lovestruck eejit.

She blinked once. Twice. "You were sitting in the garden?"

"I said may or may not."

A ghost of a smile played on her lips. "If you *happened* to be sitting in the garden, what would you have been doing there?"

I shrugged. "I would've been making sure a vengeful witch didn't murder my wife in her sleep." Not the first reason, but one of them.

She was full-on smiling, making my stomach flip. "Careful, now. I may start to believe you actually care about me."

Care about her? I did a helluva lot more than care about her. After centuries on this earth, the cursed Gancanagh had finally fallen in love.

"That would be disastrous," I said, laughing it off as if this were all some kind of joke. "Could you imagine the scandal? I have a terrible reputation to uphold."

"It would only be worse if I believed you loved me."

My legs nearly gave out, and my palms started to sweat. "You're right. That would be far worse."

My breathing hitched as she slowly approached. "Because you don't."

"Don't what?"

"Love me," she said.

Desperately. Irrevocably. "Don't be absurd. I've only known you for a few weeks."

"I want to hear you say it. Say you don't love me."

I opened my mouth to deny it, but nothing came out.

"Go on," she teased with a smirk. "It's easy. Four little words. *I don't love you.*"

Tell her the truth.

It's now or never.

It wouldn't make a feckin' difference.

"I—*Shit.*" My head pounded and eyes burned and—"I don't—*Dammit.*" What was I fighting for? Keelynn deserved the truth. She deserved to know that if there ever came a day this life wasn't for her, I'd be her escape.

My hands fell to my sides, open and empty, and I spoke the words I never thought I'd be able to say to another person for as long as my mouth was cursed to tell the truth.

"I do. I love you."

And then I evanesced down into the garden, bracing myself against the cold plaster. I was such a feckin' coward. But I couldn't face the pity in her eyes. Didn't want to hear her scramble for words to ease the sting of her truth.

That she could never care for someone like me.

28

I WOULD'VE GLADLY KILLED ROBERT TEN TIMES OVER. I'D BEEN this close. *This* feckin' close. Except my wife had stopped me. Then he'd kicked her out, expecting her to leave in her feckin' shift. I provided for her though. I would take care of her for as long as she let me.

I wasn't under any illusions that she had chosen me over him. I'd been a last resort. A backup. Still, that didn't change the fact that she was with me now, in this moment, on this dark street, walking toward the dim glow of the city.

I brought her straight to Lorcan's pub, knowing he'd answer at any hour. The lad barely slept. My friend opened the door on the second knock. Eyes glowing golden, still in his white shirt and braces from a day of work.

"I apologize for calling this late, Lorcan, but would it be possible for us to sleep here tonight?"

"Of course." Lorcan flashed Keelynn a grin. "Come in, come in. Hello again, pretty human. I see you found your Tadhg."

Your Tadhg.

If only.

She wouldn't even be here if Robert had been a half-decent man. Not that I was complaining.

Keelynn's cheeks flushed. "Please, call me Keelynn."

"Lovely to meet you *officially*, Princess Keelynn."

I caught her frown from the corner of my eye when she said, "I'm not a princess."

Ah, but she was. As long as she was married to me, she'd be a Princess of Tearmann. Not that it amounted to much. She'd never be a queen. There was only one of those, and none of us wanted to be associated with her.

"I thought the two of you were married," Lorcan pressed.

Would she admit it to my friends or try to keep me hidden the way she had with Robert? *Robert.* After she went to sleep, I would have to pay the bastard a visit—and bring my brother.

"Yes," she said. "We are."

My heart leapt.

She didn't sound disgusted or resigned, but matter-of-fact.

Even with Lorcan's eyes boring into the side of my head, I couldn't pull my gaze away from Keelynn's. Did she feel the same as she had the day we'd arrived in Gaul? Did she still want an annulment, or would she consider my suggestion to remain married?

Now wasn't the time for that conversation.

Soon, though. Tomorrow.

The living room upstairs consisted of two sofas and a pile of cushions on the floor. Surprisingly comfortable for sleeping. Then again, when I was drunk, I could pass out just about anywhere.

Ruairi perched on the arm of the farthest sofa. He'd changed out of the clothes he'd worn on our mission earlier tonight. "Hello, human."

Keelynn squealed his name, launching herself into his arms. Surprise flickered in his golden eyes when they met mine, leaving my heart in my throat. I understood her relief after believing the man dead, but did she have to be so feckin' enthusiastic?

"And ye thought I was messin' when I said she'd rather marry me," he said with a gruff chuckle.

Keelynn shoved away, blushing. "I'm sorry. I don't know what came over me."

"I have that effect on most women. Don't worry. I won't tell Tadhg ye secretly fancy me." The bastard winked at her.

Women only fancied Ruairi after they learned my brother and I had no genuine interest in them. The pooka was a better man than the two of us combined. We all knew it. That was the reason he'd never settled down. He refused to be someone's second—or third—choice.

I wasn't Keelynn's first choice. Probably not her second either.

Again, it didn't matter because tonight she was here with me.

I dropped to the floor and threw my boots by the fire. Deirdre would have my head if she saw them near her new cushions.

Speak of the devil! The woman blew into the room, a whirlwind of skirts and smiles. Deirdre may have been human, but she could hold her own with us. When she saw Keelynn, her eyes darted to me. "Is this who I think it is?"

I nodded.

Deirdre curtsied. At least I thought it was meant to be a curtsy. She'd been raised a farmer's daughter, about as far from Keelynn's "polite" society as one could get in the human world.

"It's such a pleasure to finally meet you, Princess Keelynn," Deirdre said. "Tadhg has told us such wonderful things."

Keelynn shot me a wide-eyed glance from over her shoulder. "Has he?"

That's what I got for pouring my heart out over one too many glasses of puítin like a lovesick eejit. "Don't listen to Deirdre. She lies." What I'd told them hadn't been wonderful. It'd been pathetic.

Deidre told Keelynn not to mind me. "He's been in a foul mood all day. Would you like some food, princess? Or a drink, perhaps?"

A foul mood. The polite way of saying I'd been drinking myself into a stupor, wishing for death.

"A bit to eat would be lovely, thank you. And please, just call me Keelynn."

No drink? Interesting. I'd assumed she'd want to drown her sorrows as well. Instead of taking the free sofa, Keelynn sat on the floor next to me. I knew better than to think anything of it. She was only being polite, leaving the sofa for Lorcan and Dierdre. And there wasn't room on the other sofa with the way Ruairi laid across it.

When she leaned closer to me, her lavender scent tickled my tongue. "Is Deirdre a witch?"

"She's human."

"Oh. Right." That wrinkle between her eyebrows appeared. "And she and Lorcan are . . . ?"

"Married." Two years this Yule. One of the only weddings I'd attended where I'd actually gotten to watch the vows. The black marriage bond on my finger caught my eye. Seeing it there made my heart swell.

"And Lorcan is a . . . ?"

"A thieving bastard who stole my feckin' woman," Ruairi muttered from the sofa.

He may have spotted Deirdre first, but she'd only ever had eyes for Lorcan.

"I was never *your* woman," Deirdre announced, shoving a cart of cakes and tea from the apartment's tiny kitchen. "And to answer your question, Keelynn, my husband is a pooka."

Ruairi snorted. "Like hell he is. He's a rutting half-breed who wishes he was one of us."

Pooka. I rolled my eyes. No one cared if one was full-blooded or half-blooded except another pooka. Lorcan's mam had been human, his father a purebred pooka. He'd inherited his father's magic and his mother's features, straddling the line between humans and Danú. That was the only reason he was able to own a successful business in the city. It wouldn't survive on the east coast where Keelynn was from, but it thrived here.

Humans came to the Arches for a taste of the wilds of Tearmann without having to brave the Forest. And Danú came because the drink was good, the food was cheap, and they weren't going to be thrown onto the street.

Lorcan brought two bottles of wine from the kitchen. "You're just jealous because I'm prettier than you."

"Ye are not."

"Am too. Ask Keelynn. She can't lie."

I was about to tell them to leave my wife out of their silly discussions, but then Keelynn smiled.

"Sorry, Ruairi. Lorcan is prettier because he doesn't have scary fangs."

Lorcan bowed in victory. "Thank you, milady."

Ruairi did not look impressed. "Ah, come on. These little things?" He showed off his elongated incisors. The size of a pooka's fangs was a sign of his virility. Or so I'd heard. Probably a load of shite spouted by a long-toothed beast who wouldn't get a female otherwise.

"They wouldn't hurt ye—unless yer into a bit of pain with yer pleasure," Ruairi added.

Keelynn's head tilted as she considered his words. The last thing I wanted was for her to start asking what *that* meant. Ruairi would be only too happy to show her, and then I'd have to kill him.

Thankfully, Deirdre distracted her with a tray of miniature desserts. "Has that line ever worked for you?" she threw over her shoulder at Ruairi.

"Ye'd be surprised what some humans like. Just last month, I met a woman who wanted me to—"

Not a hope was I letting Ruairi tell *that* story. I cleared my throat, shooting him a withered glare. I nodded my chin to my wife. What an eejit. We were in the presence of a *lady*.

Ruairi's mouth snapped shut. "Let's just say she didn't mind my fangs one bit."

I knew all too well the strange things some people were into behind closed doors. I had stories that'd horrify them all.

Deirdre offered me the tray. I selected a pear tart, glistening with sugar. One bite in, Deirdre started giving out about her cushions, throwing serviettes at me, asking if I was raised in a field.

Sometimes it felt like it. I'd grown up in a castle, but the fields, the seaside, the world had been my home.

I muttered, "Sorry," between bites, doing my best not to ruin her cushions.

Deirdre nodded, then turned back to my wife. Her features softened. "What would you like to drink, milady? We have faerie wine, witch's brew, puítin, and stout."

I'd told Lorcan time and again that if he named the drink "witch's brew," no one would dare touch the stuff. He'd vehemently disagreed. I had yet to see one person order it.

"I'll have tea, please," Keelynn said.

Deirdre asked me what I wanted, and I ordered the same. If my wife was to be sober, then I should probably be as well. Saying goodbye tomorrow would be hard enough without a hangover. If tonight was to be my last night with Keelynn, I wanted to remember it.

"Wine for me, Lorcan," Ruairi announced, even though no one had asked.

Deirdre made three cups of steaming hot tea. I didn't love tea, but it kept my hands warm, and if you added enough sugar, it didn't taste like bog water.

Keelynn told me I ate too much sugar.

She wasn't wrong. My diet drove Rían mad. He had to exercise and watch what he ate to keep in shape. I could eat nothing but sugar and still look like this. Fae blood, cursed glamours, and all that nonsense.

"Sickening, isn't it?" Deirdre muttered, sinking onto the free sofa. "These bastards could live on custard and cakes and not put on a feckin' pound. And if I so much as look at sweets, my stay feels too tight."

"I see nothing wrong with your stays, love," Lorcan said,

pouring himself and Ruairi some fae wine, then falling down next to his wife.

I'd always thought Deirdre lovely. She was with Lorcan by the time I met her, for which I was thankful. Every once in a while, I'd feel a slight tug from her, but only when she had drink on board, and it had always been easily ignored.

"That's because you get distracted by what they're holding in," Deirdre teased, giving her husband a nudge. Lorcan's cheeks pinkened.

"Someone stab me, please," Ruairi whined. "I refuse to watch the couples in the room make moon eyes at each other all feckin' night."

"You're just jealous," Deirdre shot back, throwing a cushion at the pooka.

"You mean relieved," Ruairi countered. "What's love ever done but make folks miserable? Take this human here." Ruairi nudged Keelynn's foot with his. "She's in love, and she looks proper miserable."

Keelynn's lips pursed as she studied her tea. "I'm not in love," she said quietly. "I'm not sure I ever was."

She still wore my ring. She could be lying. Or she could be telling the truth. I had to find something to do to keep from reaching for her. Just because she didn't love *him* didn't mean she cared for me.

"So you're not marrying your childhood sweetheart?" Deirdre asked, eyes on me. I focused on unfastening the buttons at my wrists, ignoring the heat swelling in my chest.

"I'd rather not marry a man who's been screwing the maid."

My heart sank. I'd screwed plenty of maids.

"Oh, you poor dear." Deirdre gave Keelynn's shoulder a pat. "Did you kill him? I would've stabbed the bastard straight in the heart. Isn't that right, Lorcan?"

"That's right, love."

Deirdre gave Keelynn a nudge. "I've him well warned."

"No, I didn't stab him. But I should have."

Yes. She should've. Or she could've let me handle him. Oh, the fun I could've had with *Robert.*

The conversation moved on quickly to our seaside venture. Ruairi took great pleasure in sharing all about it, including the fact that I'd been left chasing that feckin' piglet.

"Like you could've done any better." Ruairi was big, but he wasn't exactly agile in his human form. "You had the easy part."

"*Easy*?" Ruairi scoffed. "The little one *bit* me." He showed us his arm as if the little one's teeth would've actually left a mark.

Keelynn's giggling was like a balm to my soul. "I would've loved to have seen it."

"Tell you what," I said, fighting a smile. "Next time we decide to go kidnapping, I'll be sure to let you know."

She looked at me as if I'd lost my mind. Then her head dropped. It took me a moment to realize my hand was on her knee. My palm started tingling as if I'd touched her skin. As much as I wanted to hold on, I let go.

But then her hand came over mine, keeping me still.

Deirdre muttered something about the time, and I knew everyone was leaving, but all I could do was stare at Keelynn's hand on mine, relishing the burn.

Her wide gray eyes returned my steady gaze, her expression unreadable.

Her perfect lips parted, and I expected her to tell me to stop touching her, but she didn't say a word. The invisible cord around my core twisted.

"Sorry they kept you up so late," I managed, my fingers moving to trace the skin at her knuckles. My ring. "You must be wrecked."

"I should be," she breathed.

Time slowed as she leaned forward, her lips grazing mine. She tasted like cherries and fire. My new favorite flavor. Our tongues met, and the distance between us felt like too much. My hands knew what to do, finding her hips, pulling her on top of me.

"This is a terrible idea," I managed even as our hips met and rolled and met again.

Her head fell back as she moved, chest thrust forward, breaths coming in gasps. "It would seem your body disagrees."

"Yes, well, my body and I are rarely in agreement." Except when it came to her.

She stopped moving and I wanted to scream. "I'm sorry. I thought you wanted to—"

"I did. I do." More than I wanted anything else. "*Shit.* I really do . . . I just . . . I don't think . . ." *Dammit.* My head felt like it would split open. I couldn't say *I don't think it's a good idea* because right then, it was the best idea I've ever had. "After everything that's happened today, I'm not sure it's what either of us need."

She was only here because she'd been betrayed. Not because she cared for me. Not because she wanted to stay married. Keelynn was here because she had nowhere else to go. If she pushed it, I'd give her the best night of her feckin' life. But I'd already given her enough regret.

She rolled off of me, falling onto the cushion at my side. My body screamed so loud I was sure she could hear it. The moment she fell asleep, I'd have to take care of myself in the feckin' privy if I wanted any chance of sleeping tonight.

Keelynn's perfect mouth pulled into a frown. I knew how to take her mind off of all her troubles but needed to stay the course for as long as I could resist. My newly awakened heart couldn't handle more pain.

"You look troubled."

Her eyes glistened with unshed tears. "I don't know what to do."

"About what?"

"Anything."

She didn't have to decide tonight. Or tomorrow. Or even this week. I'd be here for her until she figured it out.

I thought back to the other night when she'd held me. How

good it had felt to be in another's arms without the expectation of more. Without agenda.

"I know what you need."

She blinked at me. "Do you, now? What's that?"

I adjusted myself on the cushion, trying to find a comfortable position before patting my chest. "Head here."

Her smile left my heart singing as she snuggled closer. Could she hear it beneath her ear? Keelynn's dark waves felt like silk between my fingers. She sniffled softly, and I could feel dampness soaking into my shirt, cleansing the darkness from my soul.

Tomorrow would bring more decisions and darkness.

But tonight, when my eyes fell closed, I let myself dream.

Of the woman in my arms, happy and smiling.

Of being free.

Of a future together that would never be.

29

I awoke to Keelynn trying to extricate herself from my arms, the loss of her heat like the splash of a winter wave. She refused to look at me as she adjusted her bodice and the hem of her skirts to cover her bare ankles.

"What's wrong?" I asked.

She glanced over her shoulder. "Nothing."

Nothing. Right. The pained wince told me differently. Although I'd wanted to stay awake and commit to memory each and every sleepy sigh that fell from her lips, I'd lost the battle with exhaustion as dawn peeped through the drawn curtains. My bones ached from the floor at my back and Keelynn using me as a mattress. Not that I was complaining.

"You don't have to come with me today," I told her, my heart breaking a little more. Last night, I had mentioned her joining me in Tearmann, never asking what she wanted. "I could bring you to Port Fear and back to Graystones." She could return to her old life of fine dresses and balls. Safety and security.

Each second she took to consider left my stomach sinking lower. Eventually, she put me out of my misery. "I don't want to go back there. I want to be with my sister."

Nothing to do with me. Still, knowing she would be near left my black heart singing. "Right so. We can grab something from the kitchen and be on our way."

Lorcan and Deirdre offered to make breakfast, but I wanted to get out of Gaul in case Keelynn changed her mind. Not that I wouldn't bring her wherever she asked. I just didn't want her to think too hard about where we were headed.

I met with the priest for the key to the portal in the basement of Gaul's cathedral. The portal had been there first, the gray limestone cathedral erected on top centuries later. Each priest took over as a keeper of the portal when the previous keeper passed on. An arrangement I'd made with the original priest long ago.

Keelynn remained silent, lost in her own thoughts.

When she met the children we'd kidnapped on the other side, she was clearly intrigued but kept her questions to a minimum.

We traipsed through fallen leaves, twigs snapping beneath our boots on our way through a forest of pines, until we reached the line of onyx stones marking the hard line between my world and hers.

The start of the Black Forest was always the worst part. The magic here was so toxic, breathing the air felt like swallowing poison. Keelynn must have felt the malice as she shifted nervously and stared into the blackness.

Having agreed to pay the Queen's death tax, I had permission to bring her safely across. But the moment the Queen killed me, our marriage would be over. That's where we were headed anyway, but perhaps Keelynn wouldn't mind staying married a little longer.

And the longer I had, the more I was convinced I could make her love me. Show her how I could be good. How I could lead my people.

Maybe she would find some happiness in Tearmann.

It was worth a shot. We'd have to be stealthy, stick to the enchanted path. Remain calm so our hearts didn't give us away.

"I want you to listen carefully," I said, locating my kohl in my bag, spreading the stinging goop across my eyes. Once it settled, the spells the Queen had cast to keep mortals out of her realm were as plain as the fear on my wife's face. To Keelynn, the forest would have looked as black as Ruairi's hair, but the Black Forest was actually the color of the many bones littering the ground.

"You need to follow in my footsteps," I told her, heading for the shifting black path cutting through the rolling ground, "and remain completely silent. All right?"

Off the path, the earth was like quicksand. A step or two wouldn't be fatal, but any more than that and the ground would swallow us and hold us prisoner until the Queen's minions brought her to us.

"I think I can handle that."

Behind me, I could hear Keelynn's breathing, harsh in the silence. When it began raining, the drops washed away my kohl, burning the shit out of my eyes. Wiping them with my sleeve only made it worse.

A sea of crows spread before us, pecking at the remains emerging from the depths.

"Why can't things go right for once in my cursed life?" If I had my way, we would have met them closer to my land.

I turned to find Keelynn staring wide-eyed at the birds. She needed to put on the kohl to see the path. But if she put on the kohl, she'd see me too.

What did it matter? With the crows, the Queen wouldn't be far behind, and I'd be her next meal as agreed.

I dragged out the tin. "You need to put this on in case we get separated." Staying on that path was the only way to avoid being eaten alive by this place.

Nodding, she reached for the tin. I couldn't bring myself to let it go.

"Do you want me to put it on or not?"

Feck it anyway. She might as well know the truth about me now. I let go of the tin, watching as she smeared blackness over her eyes. I knew the moment the enchantment took effect. Her eyes widened as she looked around. And then those wide eyes fell on me.

Her harsh intake of breath was all I needed to hear. I'd looked at myself once. Saw the death curse crawling on my lips. The shifting glamours. Never again.

"Don't look at me." I hated the way she stared. The horror on her face. What had I expected? That she'd see past the curses? How could any mortal see past death? "We cannot linger any longer. Do you think you can run along the path?" The sooner she crossed into Tearmann, the better. "My land borders the Queen's," I explained, indicating the green patch beyond the river. It was so feckin' far away. "If we can reach it in time, she wouldn't dare cross it."

"Is she near?" Keelynn whispered.

"She's always near." I wouldn't put it past the witch to be hiding somewhere among the crows.

"I can run," Keelynn said with a resolute nod.

Right. Time to go. The path cut straight through the crows. Keelynn managed to stay a few steps behind. When she yelped, I twisted in time to see her falling over an ancient skull. I caught her elbow and hauled her along behind me, closer and closer to that line of green where she would be safe.

Thump thump thump.

Shit.

They were coming for us. At least two horses. Maybe three.

Thump thump thump

"Going somewhere?" The Queen's clear voice rang through the barren forest, more deadly than the curses surrounding us.

I came to an abrupt halt, Keelynn careening into my back.

In front of me, the Queen wore her full regalia, feathered cape, and onyx crown. Two of her phantom guards sat astride their black steeds, the eye holes in their helmets trained on me.

"Hello, Auntie," I greeted, removing the rest of my kohl. Where I was going, I wouldn't need it.

"I take it you don't plan on staying for tea?" she drawled,

shifting on her white horse and adjusting the reins in her hands. Her black eyes narrowed.

"Must you always ask the most inane questions?" I shot back, knowing full well it would piss her rightly off.

The Queen clicked her tongue, and I could taste her bitter magic swelling with her irritation. "After all these years, I'm shocked you haven't found any manners."

Her gaze landed on Keelynn.

"If I had manners, I wouldn't waste them on you," I said, stepping in front of my wife. The queen could do anything she wanted to me, but if she so much as laid a finger on Keelynn . . .

"You and Rían missed my birthday last month." Her lips curled into a smile that made my heart constrict in my chest. "But I suppose the pretty present you brought me makes up for it. Come out here, girl. Let me get a look at you."

"I'll pay twice the next time," I said, figuring it was worth a shot.

"That's not the way this works, Tadhg." She urged her mount forward. "Such a pretty little thing you are," she said, addressing Keelynn. "My dear nephew knows better than to try and smuggle humans into Tearmann."

Always with the games and the talking. We had an agreement. The Queen may be an evil witch, but she was an evil witch who stuck by her word. This was her way of warning Keelynn not to try and cross again without permission.

"Do you know the penalty for being caught crossing the Black Forest without my permission, *girl*?"

Keelynn's hair rustled when she shook her head, her face as pale as the skulls behind her.

The Queen's silver dagger glinted when she pulled it from beneath her cloak. "One life."

The witch had the gall to point it at my wife. I evanesced in front of her and knocked the thing to the cursed ground.

"You arrogant little—"

"Oh, be quiet, you old crow." I turned to my wife to tell her goodbye. "It's been a pleasure being your husband." The greatest pleasure of my cursed life. Then I told the Queen to make it quick.

The Queen's black eyes narrowed with her twisted smile as she leaned forward. "You never told me she was your wife," she whispered before plunging her blade into my chest.

30

Coming back didn't hurt nearly as much as it usually did. My brother, for all his faults, had a jug of water and a thick slice of lemon cake by the bed, ready and waiting. He'd changed me into something clean and with all the buttons. I wasn't fond of the stiff shirt but didn't have the energy or inclination to change it.

The moment I regained feeling in my limbs, I rolled off the bed, drank the entire jug, and shoved the cake into my mouth, crumbs spilling onto the worn wooden floor. My chest felt like I'd been trampled by a herd of wild horses. From the sun peeking through my window, it looked to be about noon. Meaning the meeting with the Danú was already well underway. All I wanted was to check on Keelynn, but for once in my life, I needed to put duty first.

The thought of her seeing what I did in Tearmann left me giddy. For the first time in a long time, I didn't feel like drinking. I took the steps from my chambers to the entry two at a time, nodding and waving to the line of Danú curling from the great room into the hallway and out the door. There were so many of them. Were there always this many?

Rían slouched on my throne, pretending to be miserable. He loved being in charge, even though he claimed otherwise. Keelynn stood with a hand on the back of Rían's smaller, empty chair, watching my people with an expression of bewilderment and fascination. Seeing her in my castle made my innards warm and tight—things I had no right to feel.

"You're going to have to come closer than that," Rían muttered to three iridescent faeries at the bottom of the dais.

"Apologies for being late," I said, striding past at least thirty people. This was going to take forever, and all I wanted was to drag Keelynn into the study and ask if she was all right. "I was unfortunately detained for longer than expected."

As usual, Rían rolled his eyes. "Oh, thank heavens." He evanesced to his own throne, still looking bored out of his mind. I'd told him time and again that if he wanted people to like him, he should at least pretend to care about their plights. He insisted there was no point. That people had made up their mind about him long ago.

Keelynn's lips quirked into a smile. I wanted to kiss those lips until she was sick of me. But now was neither the time nor the place. So I gave her a wink and sat on my throne. "Now, let's get down to business, shall we?" I clasped my hands together and braced my elbows on my knees, bringing me closer to the fluttering faeries. "Muire, Lena, Sorcha, what seems to be the problem?"

I had to concentrate to hear their issue; it was always difficult when they were this size. Nearly impossible for my brother, since he was half deaf in his left ear. Not that he'd admit it to anyone. But I noticed the way he always tilted his head slightly to the right when he was actually listening.

Their tree had been cut down by humans. No surprise there. Having a faerie tree on one's land was considered bad luck in Airren. It didn't matter that the old Hawthorne had been there for at least a century. According to the treaty, the humans had every right to cut it down. Leaving thirteen faeries homeless.

I glanced at Rían; his eyes narrowed imperceptibly. For all the Danú's hatred of him, no one realized my brother *was* the "bad luck" that befell humans. He'd handle the farmer who took the tree in his own unique way. I never asked how he dealt the humans, and he never told me.

"Ladies, you can move your family to one of the trees outside of Mistlaline. Choose one closest to the portal there." According to myths, the territory was haunted by the Sluagh. And the land was shite for farming, so the woods should remain safe enough.

The three faeries bowed their heads and flew into the hallway.

Eoghan Blackie was back to bicker about Connor McManus's sheep grazing on his land. This had happened every winter since I could remember. I ordered Conor to pay his neighbor for use of the field, allowing for the rising cost of living, and that seemed to appease them. I didn't know why they insisted on coming to me when I said the same thing every year. Part of me thought it was simply an excuse to make a trip to the castle. An annual pilgrimage of sorts. The two would be drinking in the pub later tonight, laughing and slagging each other like the best of mates.

Eilis and Dillon came forward, hand-in-hand, asking for permission to marry. No sign of either of their fathers. I asked if they came of their own free will. They both blushed when they said they had. I glanced at my brother, and he nodded in confirmation.

I gave my blessing, shifted a purse of coins as was customary, and the happy couple skipped out the door.

A clurichaun paid his taxes in fish. My stomach roiled, but I managed a smile as I thanked him and sent the disgusting fare straight to the kitchen for Eava to deal with. She'd make something for Rían. And Keelynn as well if she wanted.

My wife—er, my former wife. My smile faltered when I saw my bare ring finger.

No matter. She was here for now. What more could I ask for?

The line of people kept coming. It was my fault for neglecting my duty these past few weeks. People were understandably wary of Rían, preferring to meet with me instead.

More small squabbles were brought to the dais, along with

requests to strengthen wards and invitations to yearly celebrations and the like. Then two men stomped forward, exchanging looks of unveiled hatred.

"Tis my fruit tree," the tallest said.

"No, it's not. Tis mine."

As if he knew I was thinking of him, Rían turned to Keelynn and whispered, "This is going to take ages. You're welcome to stay and watch the crowd fawn over my brother, or you can escape with me."

As if she would ever want to go anywhere with—

"I'll go with you," Keelynn said.

What? Why? Where were they going? What were they going to do?

Rían stood, and Keelynn followed.

Heaven only knew the lies he'd tell her. Would he show her the bodies in the room? I needed a chance to explain. *Dammit*, Rían. I shouldn't be angry with him. He'd all but ruled our country for the past few weeks and he deserved a break from all this, but why did he have to invite her?

I looked at the two glaring men, floundering for an answer. Fruit tree. Right. "Just split the yield fifty-fifty," I told them, anxious to move on.

Although they grumbled, they lumbered out the door, leaving me with ten more people. Ten more. That was all. Ten more and I'd be free.

The moment the last person walked out of the great hall, I launched from my throne and hurtled past Oscar out into the hall. The door where we kept my victims remained closed, and I couldn't hear anything down here except for Eava's soft humming in the kitchens. Meaning my brother had either taken Keelynn outside or upstairs.

Keelynn would be anxious to see Aveen, so I ran up the stairs.

"What're you doing? Let me go." *Rían.*

I took the stairs two at a time.

"I said, *look at me*," Keelynn demanded. She sounded upset. *Dammit.* If my brother had said anything to her, I'd kill him.

"*Edward*?"

I stopped dead in the doorway. *Edward.*

Keelynn's face was white as a sheet, a trembling hand covering her open mouth. My brother's eyes bulged as he twisted toward me.

"What do you mean, *Edward*?" Why was she looking at my brother and calling him by her husband's name?

Rían shook his head. "I don't know what she's on about. You know humans and their fanciful notions."

Liar. Liar. Liar.

He couldn't tell the truth to save his feckin' life. "Keelynn?" I stopped when I reached her. She didn't look at me. She just kept looking at *him*. "Why did you call my brother by your husband's name?"

"I recognize his eyes from the night we . . . from the ball."

I didn't need to hear the end of that sentence to understand. Padraig had told me all about what had happened between *Edward* and Keelynn.

I focused every bit of magic still in me, wrapping it around my brother's throat. He'd accosted her. Gotten caught. Been forced to *marry my feckin' soulmate.*

"It's not what you think," he insisted, his face turning the most satisfying shade of red. "I swear. We weren't supposed to get caught, but her dress ripped, and her father found us, and it all went to shit."

Feck it all. It was true. All of it. My brother had married Keelynn first. She couldn't be mine when she was *his* first.

"Is that true?" I managed, begging Keelynn to tell me something different. That Rían was lying again. That they hadn't gotten married.

Keelynn nodded. The panic in her eyes left my heart in ribbons.

"Shit, Tadhg. Don't. Don't feckin—"

My dagger sliced the bastard's gullet before he could finish his plea. Warm blood showered over me, but all I felt was ice when his lifeless body flopped onto the floor.

"What have you done?" Keelynn sobbed, clutching her chest with one hand and wiping the blood trickling down her pale face with the other.

"Till death do us part." If the bastard hadn't died since they'd exchanged their nuptials, they were still married. I cleaned my blade, returning it to its sheath. What I'd done didn't matter. Nothing mattered anymore.

Rían had claimed Aveen was his soulmate. What a load of feckin' bollocks. If he cared at all for Aveen, he never would've married her feckin' sister. He'd lied to my face about their relationship. He had every opportunity to tell me the truth about Keelynn, and he'd chosen to maintain his feckin' lies. Leaving me to look like a fool.

The truth always came out.

Always.

The thought of Keelynn and my brother . . . *together.*

My stomach revolted. I couldn't be near her right now. There was no telling what I'd do. What I'd say. I needed a feckin' drink to clear my head.

"I am sorry my brother deceived you," I managed through my swollen throat. "He's not known for his honesty." If I was the Prince of Seduction, Rían was the feckin' Prince of Deception.

"He told me he and Aveen were engaged," she whispered toward Aveen's golden coffin.

I took Keelynn's cold hand, towing her toward the door. "I wouldn't believe a word out of that lying bastard's mouth."

She didn't protest when I brought her to one of the spare bedrooms on the second floor Eava had aired and prepared. Right next to mine. Not that it mattered now. I would've put her somewhere else—somewhere far, far away—if one of the other rooms had been ready.

"Stay here until someone comes to get you for dinner," I told her, barely able to stand looking into her beautiful gray eyes. "There are a few matters I need to take care of, and I cannot leave you to wander about the castle on your own."

I left her there, returning to the room where my brother was keeping Aveen. When the bastard woke up, he would have a *lot* of explaining to do.

31

RÍAN AWOKE WITH A GASP TO FIND HIMSELF BOUND WITH STEEL-dipped iron chains. The dungeon may have been his realm, but I wasn't above using it on such an occasion.

His blue eyes flashed to where I leaned against the far wall, gritty stones digging into my shoulder blades.

"Tadhg—"

"You don't speak unless it is to answer one of my questions truthfully." And even then, I wouldn't know if it was the whole truth. He was the only one of us who could taste lies.

"Did you accost my—" I bit my lip to keep from saying "wife." Grinding my teeth together, I tried again, my dagger banging against my thigh. "Did you accost Keelynn?"

The bastard rolled his feckin' eyes. "Of course not."

"Why the hell were you with her?"

"Why the hell do you think?" he shot back. The chains holding him to the ceiling rattled with each labored breath. He winced when he swallowed, the scar across his throat already turning silver, matching the others he bore. "To keep her away from *you*."

I opened my mouth but couldn't find words to respond. He knew what I was—and so did Aveen. How could I blame either of them for wanting to keep Keelynn from becoming another name in my book of victims?

The heat of anger subsided, replaced by the cold fingers of despair.

"Were you . . ." The question died on my lips. I couldn't bring myself to ask if he'd been with her. The truth was, I didn't want to know. That had been before we met. Another lifetime.

I flicked my wrist, unlocking the shackles keeping my brother hanging against the wall. He collapsed with a curse and a choke, his breaths sawing in and out.

I sank onto the cold stones, letting my head fall back against the wall. All of this had started with Aveen falling in love with my brother. Foolish, foolish human.

"Aveen is going to kill you."

He dragged himself next to me, his shirt stained black from blood. "I know."

I flicked my wrist. The air grew heavy from the tost. It'd do no good to have anyone overhear our conversation.

"How did you convince her to fall in love with you?" I asked, feeling like an eejit. How could anyone in her right mind fall for my brother? Still, someone had. If Aveen could fall for him, then perhaps there was hope for me as well.

The corner of his mouth lifted. "She doesn't love me."

"She died to be with you."

He shook his head. "She died so she didn't have to be with *him*."

Him.

Robert.

"All the other shite I told you was total bollocks," he muttered, raking a hand through his hair. "If it weren't for her betrothal, she never would've sought me out. She cares for me about as much as you do."

"And when she wakes?"

"When she wakes and learns all I've done, she'll want nothing to do with me." Grimacing, Rían nudged a clump of hay with his boot. "It wasn't as if I had a feckin' hope anyway."

"You love her though." That part wasn't a lie. Rían never did anything out of the goodness of his heart. He *had* no feckin' heart. He never would've offered to help her if he hadn't cared deeply. And I'd seen him after she'd died. He'd been a mess. Of course, knowing he'd been forced to marry her sister wouldn't have helped.

"Aveen is . . ." A sigh. "She is everything."

I understood the sentiment to my marrow. In only a few weeks, Keelynn had consumed my world. Rían had known Aveen for months before she'd died. I'd believed his lies because they weren't complete lies. He loved her. Believed she was his soulmate.

Look at the two of us. Sitting in a feckin' dungeon, whingeing over our sorry situations. I never thought I'd have so much in common with my brother. "We are pathetic." No bones about it. Two pathetic males pining over women.

"I am pathetic," he agreed with a nod. "You are pathetic and weak."

With that, the bastard flicked his wrist, eliminating my tost, and evanesced out of the cell. I don't know how long I sat there, trying to figure out what to do.

Rían had married Keelynn out of duty.

Keelynn had married Rían out of necessity.

Maybe we could find a way past this together. We'd been through worse betrayals, right? Maybe this wasn't as hopeless as it had seemed.

Keelynn was wearing blue.

My wife entered the dining room on my brother's arm, wearing his color, and I couldn't even hear the words Shona and her companions were saying because all I could see was my wife in my brother's color.

Our father used to have all our toys painted green or blue to keep us from fighting over them. AND MY WIFE WAS WEARING BLUE.

I should've known better than to believe that feckin' sob story from my feckin' brother. *She is everything*. He didn't care about anyone but himself.

"If you'll excuse me for just a moment," I muttered to Shona, continuing to where my brother had claimed my wife.

The bastard had the gall to smile at me when I took Keelynn's hand from his arm and brought her to the corner near the garden doors. I was going to kill him. I was. And then he'd have the right to kill me twice. And I didn't even feckin' care.

My hand tingled from her touch. Instead of making me feel warm, it left my stomach twisting. I told myself to calm down. This could've been a coincidence. "Where did you get that dress?"

Keelynn glanced down at the blue silk that hugged every blessed inch of her. The skirt *swished* quietly when she gave it a slight shake. "Rían gave it to me."

The bastard grinned from across the dining room.

"You are free to do as you please, of course. But I would appreciate it if you did not flaunt your relationship with my brother so blatantly in my face." All I'd gone through to get her here, and he was the one who benefitted.

Her brows drew together. "I wasn't—I didn't mean—"

I refused to listen to her excuses. She couldn't help the way she felt. Rían had saved her from ruination. Of course she would feel some sort of gratitude toward him. Perhaps she had even learned to love him at one point in those months they'd spent married. I'd been grateful for her forgiving nature before. As I walked away, I cursed it.

Rían didn't deserve her forgiveness. He didn't deserve to breathe the same air as my wife—and if he didn't stop smirking, I was going to make sure he stopped breathing altogether.

I took my seat at the head of the table, giving Shona a tight smile before shifting dinner for the rest of us. I could barely stomach the food, but if I didn't eat, I'd only make myself weaker than I already was. I reached for my wine but couldn't bring myself to drink any. It wouldn't help. Nothing would. And waking up with a hangover would only extend my misery into tomorrow.

Shona chatted about the children she and her wife had adopted. Four in total. I feigned a smile and nodded, only half listening.

Daithi and Daragh had come to discuss the possibilities of shipping goods from the fae in Iodale. Keelynn remained quiet in her seat next to my brother. When she finished, he escorted her into the hall and up the stairs.

The wine was there. Full and within reach. Begging me to take a drink.

Just one.

No.

No.

One would lead to two, and two would lead to an entire feckin' bottle. And with a bottle of wine onboard, there was no telling what I'd end up doing or where I'd end up going or whose bed I'd end up waking in.

My head started pounding. I couldn't do this anymore. Between dying and coming back and dealing with the Danú and my brother's betrayal, it was all too much.

"I'm sorry," I said to Shona, "but I need to get some air."

The selkie smiled, her dark eyes reflecting the flickering candlelight. "Not a bother. I'm exhausted anyway. Will I take my usual room?"

"That would be fine. Daithi and Daragh, you're more than welcome to whatever drink is in the parlor. My brother will be down shortly to join you." After he finished with my *wife*.

I escaped outside, raking my hands through my hair. The wards made the air thick, too hard to breathe. At least the sound of the sea made me feel a bit better.

Dammit.

I finally had the chance to make things right between us. Our journey had finally come to an end, and Rían—

Someone called my name. It sounded like . . .

Keelynn?

I evanesced to where my former wife stood at the entrance of the maze, hair unbound. My fingers itched to comb through her glossy waves, to drag her against me, to lose myself in her. "What is it?" Scanning the darkness, I found only hedges and shadows. "Is something wrong?"

"Yes, something is terribly wrong." She caught the ends of my waistcoat, drawing me closer.

"Tell me. Was it Rían? I swear, if he did *anything* to harm you, I'll run him through and lock his corpse in an iron casket for all of eternity." He'd deserve every bit of it. For harming her. For marrying her. For stealing her away.

"I haven't seen Rían since dinner. In all honesty, I'd be happy never seeing him again."

Hold on . . . Was she . . . Was she being truthful?

"Nothing *happened*, Tadhg. Between your brother and me, I mean. Yes, I kissed him to make Robert jealous, but we didn't have a *real* marriage. He was barely around, and when he *was* around, we didn't see each other. And he insisted on sleeping in his own chambers."

"The two of you didn't . . ." I couldn't bring myself to say it aloud, even as my heart swelled.

"No. Absolutely not."

Oh, thank god.

"You may not care for him, but that doesn't mean you care for me." I'd fulfilled my end of our bargain. She was only here because of her sister. Because she didn't want to go home.

"That's just it. I *do* care for you. When the Queen killed you, I couldn't stop crying. It was like she'd stabbed me in the heart as well."

"You *cried*? Over *me*?" That's what she'd said, wasn't it? That she'd shed tears over my death. "But you knew I'd be back."

She laced our fingers together, touching where the marriage bond once lived. "But you wouldn't be my husband."

I needed to see her eyes when she said those words. Needed to know they were true. "Are you saying you *wanted* to stay married?" I held my breath, afraid to hope.

"Yes."

The ring. She was wearing my ring. "I know you're lying." There was no other explanation. "You saw the curse and now you pity me. That's what this is, right?" I let her hand drop, my magic coiling inside my chest, my feet itching to bring me away. "You think I'm some sort of charity case? Well, I'm not, you know. I may want to be free, but I'll not accept your life as payment for my sins. It was wrong to have asked you to keep our vows in the first place."

She pulled the ring from her finger, letting it fall to the gravel by my boot.

And then she said words I never thought I'd hear falling from her lips. "I want to be bound to you."

32

I WANT TO BE BOUND TO YOU.

This woman. This beautiful, fierce, naïve, loyal, forgiving woman wanted to be bound to me. *ME.*

"Why?" I whispered, needing the truth to keep me from drowning in hope.

"What do you mean, 'why'?"

"Why would someone like you want to be with something like me? Is it all of this?" My castle? My magic? "Is this what you're after? Because it sure as hell isn't my winning personality or impeccable style or flawless manners."

She must be mad. There was no other explanation. I loved a stark raving madwoman.

Her brow furrowed, and she bit her lip, and I hated that my words had struck home. Why had I opened my foolish mouth? I should have kept quiet, basked in her light before it was too late. Before she tore it away and left me with darkness.

Eventually, Keelynn said, "I want to be with you because you make me laugh."

"I make you *laugh*?" What the hell kind of reason was that? Lots of people made me laugh. You didn't see me wanting to marry them.

"Yes. Even when I know I shouldn't," she said, moving closer to where I stood. "You left food for Padraig and gave an apple to the boy in the market. And you saved that grogoch in Kinnock. You stole a pig and kidnapped those children." With each reason, she took a step, erasing the distance between us. "You have taken care of me and kept me safe even when I was rude and condescending and horrible."

Her hands met my chest, warm and steady as they slid toward my shoulders. "Today, you died for me." Her cursed lips met my black heart.

I couldn't keep still any longer, my hands finding her waist, bringing her into my embrace. Bringing her home.

"So the real question isn't why someone like me would want to be with someone like you." The confession may've tickled my jaw, but I felt it deeper, in my very marrow. "It's whether or not someone like you would want to be with someone like me."

Didn't she know? Hadn't I made my feelings for her painfully obvious? "There will never be a time or place when I won't want to be with you." In this world or the next, forevermore, this woman would have my whole heart.

She eased forward, our lips almost meeting.

Something flashed green on the ground. *The ring*. I evanesced, collecting it from the gravel. The way starlight played in her hair, the heat of the night, and the sparkle in her eyes culminated in a vision I would hold close for the rest of my days.

"Since I'm already down here, I may as well ask you to marry me."

When Keelynn's eyes widened in panic, I stumbled to my feet. "Don't feel like you have to say yes," I blurted. "It's just that it'll be impossible to make you fall madly in love with me if I'm forced to go off with every woman who invites me to her bed."

She blinked away the stars in her eyes, her brow furrowing. "Is that the best you can do? 'I may as well ask you to marry me.'"

Was that the best I could—"No. I can do better." I pulled her toward the heart of the garden, between laurel hedges, blocking our view of the castle—of the world—until it was just the two of us. "Wait here."

I spun around the garden, calling on far too much magic to give my soulmate the proposal she deserved. Faerie lights for the hedges. A bouquet of her favorite flowers from where they grew at the far corner of the property. Shifting ribbons to hold them together and leaving it on the edge of the stone fountain.

Part of me was convinced this was all a dream, that when I rounded the hedge, she wouldn't be there. But she was. Keelynn was there. Waiting for *me*.

I took her hand in mine and drew her into the garden. She turned in a slow circle, her mouth forming a silent O. With a flick of my wrist, the bouquet I'd made appeared in her hand.

"Lady Keelynn Bannon," I said, kneeling and keeping my face from showing any sign of discomfort as gravel ground into my kneecap. "I'd given up hope of ever finding someone I loved. And then you waltzed into a pub and threatened to kill me. I am wrecked by you, completely undone. I would trade my soul for a smile. My kingdom for a kiss. My world to call you my wife. Will you give me the honor of a second chance to be your husband?"

I shifted the same ribbon Rían had used to bind us the first time, holding my breath while I awaited her answer.

"You want to get married *now*?"

"What's wrong with now?"

Laughing, she shook her head, dark waves curling over her shoulders. "Nothing is wrong with now. Now is perfect."

She placed her hand in mine, of her own free will. I wrapped the lace around us, binding my heart, my life, my world to hers. The vows I'd said in a panicked haze only a few days ago came back with crystal clarity. I pledged myself to this woman, knowing life could only get better. That this momentous occasion would live in my heart and head for eternity. When I finished, I slipped my ring onto her finger where it belonged.

Before I could prompt her, Keelynn began reciting the vows back to me.

"To you I pledge my body and soul," she said, her husky tones curling straight for my chest. "All that I am and all that I have is yours. I bind myself to you and you alone, forsaking all others. In giving you my hands, I give you my life, to have and to cherish until death do us part—"

I caught her glorious hair with my unbound hand and kissed the mouth that had made each promise, swallowing them, letting each syllable settle in my heart.

Something fell next to my boot. Keelynn's bouquet. The cool fingers of her free hand slid around my neck, her chest molding to mine. My wife.

Mine. Mine. Mine.

I wanted her more than my next breath. Needed her right here. Right now.

The scraps of lace tying us together fell away, allowing me to shift my bed to the middle of the garden. Keelynn gasped when I lifted her in my arms and carried her to the silk sheets.

She may not have been the only woman I had ever been with, but she was the first to lie in my bed.

My desperate lips fell to hers, tasting her sighs. "What would you say to a wedding night, Maiden Death?"

The wasp bit my lip.

"I'm taking that as a yes," I growled, scaling her glorious body, prepared to stake my claim. Slowly, I rocked my hips against her center, finding a rhythm, making intimate music. Her gasp told me when I hit the right spot. Her clumsy fingers told me she was ready.

"*Hurry.*"

She wanted me to hurry, did she? In this, I'd be happy to disappoint. "My dear mortal wife, if you think I'm going to rush this, you must be mad. Although, you did marry me of your own free will, so perhaps you are."

A sound of pure indignance left her throat. She tried to catch my belt buckle. I knocked her hand away.

"Don't make me stab you," she ground out, eyes flashing.

Hearing the need vibrating in her voice only made me want to build on it until she came out of her feckin' skin. I held up a finger, keeping my gaze locked on her blown-out pupils as I dragged that finger from the delicate arch of her foot, over her heel, along the swell of her calf, the underside of her knee, to hook in the top of her stocking.

And pulled it down, baring creamy skin kissed by starlight streaming through the open curtains. My body hummed with cursed magic, slipping free to dance along our bodies as I removed the second stocking the exact same torturous way.

The silky hem of her skirts felt liquid against my fingertips.

My wife began shaking her head. I stilled, a moment of panic clearing the lust from my thoughts. She shouldn't be saying no. She should be crying yes.

Her lips lifted in a seductive smile. "My turn."

Feckin' right it is.

She raised to her knees, pushing me onto the mattress. I held my breath, watching her climb on top of me, straddling my hips, skirts bunched up to her waist. When she rocked her hips, my cock ached. Then she did it again.

"*Shit.*" This woman would be the death of me.

One by one, she unfastened the buttons of my shirt, killing me slowly, grinding her center against my swollen flesh. And then the siren raised to her knees, taking my sanity with her.

"My dear immortal husband," she rasped, chest heaving as she gasped, "if you think I'm going to rush this—"

Enough teasing. Enough torture.

I had my wife flat on her back before she could throw the rest of my words at me.

My magic surged and swelled, finally breaking free, sending what remained of our clothes away. I breathed it in, hearing Keelynn do the same. Allowing the heady euphoria, the tingling high to consume us both.

"Wicked, wicked woman." Could she see what she did to me? How she ignited my body, leaving me overcome by flames? My mouth found hers, desperate for more than a taste. I wanted everything. Every gasp. Every sigh. Every curse. Every word of hate and lie of love to wash over me like a summer rain.

I nudged her thighs apart, ignoring the way she reached for me when I drew away. Keelynn had more skin to explore, more secrets to uncover. The hardened peaks of her high breasts. The line of her ribs. The dip of her naval. The curve of her hipbones. The valley between.

The taste of her left my cock heavy and aching. The sound she made when my cursed tongue found her center drove me to the edge.

She cried.

She begged.

She pleaded.

Keep going. Don't stop. Yes. Yes. Yes.

She came with a breathless whimper, legs trembling against my ears. I sank home in one earth-shattering thrust, catching the final pulses of her orgasm. Her tight, wet heat clenched when I began to move.

As good as it had been the first time, nothing compared to this. No unspoken questions stretched between us. No barriers. This woman was mine, and I was hers. I'd fucked for centuries. But this . . . This was the first time I'd made love.

"Lie to me," I begged.

"I love you."

I love you. I love you. I love you.

I slammed into her bucking hips with wild abandon, all rhythm and pace slipping away. "Again."

Keelynn's short nails pierced my back. "*I love you.*"

The sweetest lie sent me over the cliff, freefalling into the arms of the woman I loved more than life itself.

This.

This was what I had spent centuries searching for.

This.

33

THE SCENT OF FRESH BASIL PERMEATED THE WARM AIR DOWN IN the castle kitchens, accompanied by our kitchen witch's hums and the occasional metallic *clap* of lids meeting pots. The gray-haired woman slid a finger down the thick recipe book open on the high counter next to the hob.

As if she sensed my presence—or could hear my growling stomach—she gave me a harried wave. "Morning, Tadhg."

"Good morning, Eava."

She whipped around, the wooden spoon in her other hand clattering to the ground. "What's got my boy smilin' like a cat with all the cream?"

All I had to do was show her my left hand to send the old witch into a fit of shrieking and bone-shattering hugs. "I knew I liked her," she gushed, squeezing tighter. "Knew it all along."

"You haven't even met her," I managed with what air remained in my lungs. After breakfast, I'd remedy that. Eava had been like a mother to me for centuries. Keelynn was going to love her.

"Any girl who convinces the likes of ye to marry her twice must be worth her weight in gold." She lifted onto her toes, peering over my shoulder, as if she expected Keelynn to magically appear.

"My wife is still abed."

The old witch laughed, giving my cheek a pat with her calloused hand. "There's a good lad. She'll be needing brekkie when she wakes. What does yer darling wife like?"

What did Keelynn like to eat for breakfast? I'd never asked, just shifted whatever was available. "I don't know." I obviously would've asked but hated the thought of waking her when she slept so soundly, her soft snores like a morning bird's call.

Eava gave a brusque nod, dragged out one of the stools at the high butcher block table in the center of the kitchen, and gave the top a pat. The herbs she'd dried from hooks on the ceiling's dark beam now lived in jars displayed an arm's length away.

In no time at all, Eava handed me a tray of toast and eggs, savory bacon, and fresh apple slices, shifting a silver lid for the lot to keep it warm.

Before I could thank her, she shoved me toward the door. "Take care of yer wife."

"Don't worry," I smirked. "I plan to." At least twice before my meeting at noon to discuss next month's shipment from the continent.

I brought the tray through the hallway and out into the bright courtyard. A small, niggling part of me worried the light of day would bring regret, but I squashed that down as far as it would go. Keelynn may not love me yet, but I was fairly certain I loved her enough for the both of us. And if I could make her happy . . . Well, happiness was its own kind of love, wasn't it?

A few early risers milled about the courtyard. I returned their nods and waves with a smile. Birds flew overhead, unaffected by the magical wards. Distant waves crashed. Had the laurels always been this green? Had the flowers growing in the center of the maze always been this vibrant? It felt as if my life until now had been muted, my vision cloudy and gray. Keelynn had stripped all of that away, bringing color and light into the world.

I set the tray on the edge of the fountain and shifted one of the small tables from the castle, along with two chairs. With my heart singing, I approached my bed, took hold of the emerald-green curtains, and drew them aside.

The bed was empty save a tangle of sheets and pillows and the note I'd left for Keelynn. She'd probably gone into the castle.

At least that's what I told my racing heart.

I called on my magic, prepared to evanesce, when I heard a familiar gasp. Not in the direction of the castle but at the gates. I found my wife outside the wards, hands braced on her knees, breaths sawing in and out as the breeze ruffled her loose hair.

"Keelynn?" I touched her shoulder, and she jerked away.

"Why did you kill them?" she choked, accusation in her wide eyes.

Kill them? Kill whom?

"You have an entire room full of dead bodies!" she cried, tears gathering along her dark lashes.

Dammit.

Had she found them, or had someone told her? That was the sort of thing Rían would do. If he couldn't be happy, no one could. Not that it mattered now. "You know who I am. You know what I've done. I've already told you—"

She threw a hand toward the castle. "Did all of those women force you to kiss them?"

"No. They didn't." Some, but not all. Not that it mattered. All of their deaths were on my hands. "Clara McNulty was a whore. Her life was shit, and she still had three years left in her contract." In that line of work, three years may as well have been thirty. "I kissed her so that she could be free. Orla Crowley was a fool and fancied herself in love with me. You see how that turned out." The glamoured barmaid from the Green Serpent and I had been friends forever. She'd mistaken her lust for love. Something that happened far more often than anyone would expect. "The barmaid from the Black Rabbit thought it'd be worth it. It wasn't

The innkeeper from Newtown refused to let me leave the room. And you already know about Marina."

"What about Áine?"

Right. Áine. I explained to Keelynn about our arrangement, and what the wicked faerie had threatened. And then I took a deep breath and told her the truth of my depravity.

"In two hundred and fifty years, there have been seven hundred and eight-eight bodies in those coffins." Seven hundred and eighty-eight women. All cursed because of me. Most of them humans who didn't have years to waste. "I've tasted their last breaths. Held them in my arms as their souls left their bodies. Watched the light of life vanish from their eyes. And I remember every single one."

"Do you remember me?" The high voice sent chills down my spine. Dread stabbed my chest. Although I hadn't heard that voice in two hundred and fifty years, I knew who she was.

The witch who had cursed me stood behind my wife, a twisted smile on her bloodred lips. The green in her eyes had been replaced by the black of a bottomless pit, filled with hate and directed at me. "It's been too long, my love."

Hearing the familiar endearment flayed my heart where it clambered in my chest.

"*Shit.*" I grabbed Keelynn's hand, dragging her behind me. She wouldn't make it beneath the wards even if she sprinted. And I couldn't evanesce through them with her.

We were trapped.

Fiadh's head jerked like some invisible force had broken her neck. Black hair caught with leaves and twigs dragged along the ground. The witch in front of me looked like a shadow of the strong, vivacious woman I once knew.

"I see you met my human friend. She's a dote, isn't she? So young. So *naïve*." The cursed dagger appeared in Fiadh's hand, emerald glowing. *Impossible*. She'd shifted the dagger. How the hell had she shifted it? Enchanted objects couldn't be shifted. What sort of unholy power must she possess to do the impossible?

"I'd thought her dead," Fiadh cackled, "but this is far more delicious."

I dared a glance toward the gates. The Danú inside had begun to gather, remaining behind the safety of the wards. Where the hell was Rían? He was the only one strong enough to defeat her.

"Your fight is with me, not with her," I reminded Fiadh.

The witch's head jerked to the other side. "Look who finally found someone he loves more than himself. If only our young friend's weak human heart could love a murderous monster."

"Evanesce," Keelynn whispered, tugging on the back of my shirt.

Did she honestly think I would abandon her to face this vindictive witch? Not a hope would I leave her behind. I stepped forward, prepared to face my fate. "I am sorry for what happened all those years ago. I was young and foolish and too in love with myself to care about those I hurt. But this has gone on long enough." She'd taken enough from me. This ended today.

"You're *sorry*?" She cackled, her hand tightening on the glowing dagger. "You think an apology can absolve you of all your sins? You took my life from me. *You* made me what I am. This is all *your* fault."

She was right. This was my fault.

And I'd borne my punishment.

Her black eyes swung to Keelynn. "I'm calling in our bargain, *girl.*"

Keelynn had never mentioned a feckin' bargain beyond the truth curse. *Dammit.* What else had she promised?

Keelynn came around me, sweat beading on her pale skin. "Evanesce, Tadhg. Please. I'm begging you. Go."

I wouldn't leave her here. I wouldn't.

A soft glimmer danced along the ground as Fiadh's magic drew her forward. "You said you'd kill the Gancanagh." Fiadh's smile shot ice through my heart. "Now, *do it.*"

Kill the Gancanagh.

Shit shit shit.

The only way to release Keelynn from Fiadh's unearthly hold was to fulfil the bargain. She had to kill me.

Keelynn turned, dagger in hand and tears spilling down her cheeks.

"It's all right, Keelynn." I opened my empty hands to the air. That's what I had been before her. Empty.

She shook her head, her hair tangling with the breeze. "You don't understand. I can't stop myself."

I did understand. I understood better than anyone the consequences of a foolish decision.

Her pleas fell in a jumble, shattering my heart into a million pieces. None of it mattered. Not the reasoning behind the bargain or how foolish she had been to make it in the first place.

"This isn't your fault. It's mine." All of it, from start to finish. Yes, Rían had been the one to ask for my help with Aveen, but if I hadn't treated Fiadh and countless other women the way I had, I wouldn't have been cursed in the first place.

I darted a glance at the small crowd to find Rían pushing his way to the front. His eyes met mine, brows drawn together. I shook my head. Fiadh could shift an enchanted object. There was no telling what else she could do.

If he didn't succeed in defeating the witch, the Danú would be left with the Queen. Someone had to stay behind and protect our people.

"This will be a mercy," I assured my wife. "You'll be ending a cursed life with a cursed blade."

Something flickered in Keelynn's glistening eyes.

"Thank you for giving me hope. Thank you for letting me love you." Having her choose me was more than I could've hoped for. More than I deserved.

She took my hand, pressing something cold and hard against my palm. My ring. A ring to neutralize curses. The dagger was *cursed*. My beautiful, brilliant wife had just given me the key to surviving this. I was about to slip it on my finger . . .

Until I realized what would happen.

Fiadh never forgives. Fiadh never forgets.

The hateful witch would never let Keelynn or I survive this. The moment she learned we had thwarted her plans, she'd hunt us down. How could I expect the woman I loved to remain hidden in a castle with me for the rest of her life? What sort of life would that be for her? For me?

The tip of the dagger kissed my chest.

I couldn't do it.

I let my forehead fall against my wife's, looking into her beautiful gray eyes one final time, and said, "Thank you for setting me free."

Then I held my breath as the woman I loved thrust the blade into my chest.

34

Out of darkness shines a light.
Bringing day to darkest night.
Find your soul's one true mate.
For she will save you from your fate.

35

My eyes flashed open to find a gray sky looming above. Pain lanced through my very marrow; lightning flew through my veins. My heart beat so hard and strong it rattled my ribcage.

"Kiss her. *Quickly*," a voice called from the distance.

A voice I knew.

Rían.

That's when I saw Keelynn lying on the grass, her arm outstretched toward me. Rían shoved my shoulder. My body sprang into action, rolling her over, panic seizing my chest when I met sightless eyes. With the world tilting, my lips claimed hers tasting blood and magic, quivering as she gasped her last breath.

A woman shouted for Keelynn from the other side of the path.

Aveen.

How the hell was she here?

Fiadh's body lay prone in front of the gates, black hair spread across blood-drenched grass. It didn't take long to figure out what had happened.

Keelynn must've killed Fiadh.

The cursed dagger in Rían's hand disappeared into a sheath at his side.

He'd brought me back.

The bastard had brought me back and let Keelynn die.

I picked up my wife's body, cradling her against my chest. Sightless eyes reflected the clouds while her black mouth gaped at the crows soaring past. She felt like a doll, lifeless and limp.

"It wasn't supposed to be her." Rían should've known, and yet he'd resurrected me anyway. "It was never supposed to be her. I was the one meant to die. Why didn't you save her?" He could've used Fiadh's life force to bring her back and he'd wasted it on me.

She was gone. Not forever. I knew that. I did. But in that moment, it didn't matter.

"As weak and pathetic as you are, you serve a purpose," Rían snarled, pushing away from the ground, turning to face Aveen as she stumbled toward us.

"Let her go!" Aveen roared, voice hoarse and dry like the morning after a night on the drink. Her knees cracked off the ground. She took Keelynn from me, touching her hair, her face, her throat. Crying and pleading to ears that couldn't hear because she was dead.

Dead.

Dead.

Dead.

Magic leaked from my pores, not as strong as I remembered but stronger than it had been for centuries. Darkness lurking, a coiled snake prepared to strike.

I caught Aveen's hand. "Give me back my wife."

Aveen's mouth opened and closed. Panicked blue eyes darted to a grimacing Rían. Let him deal with his own feckin' woman. Mine was dead.

I took Keelynn from her sister, carrying her through the crowd of Danú hiding behind the wards. Cowards, the lot of them. Not one had come to our aid. *Not a feckin' one.* I'd ruled them for centuries. *Centuries.* And they couldn't even take a feckin' step beyond the wards to aid us. They'd come to me week after week, expecting me to help them. And they hadn't even tried.

The moment I breached the wards, I evanesced into the castle, unable to stand being near them a second longer.

My wife's corpse felt like a leaden weight in my arms. I started down the hall where the other bodies were kept, then stopped.

She didn't belong down here. I needed to keep her somewhere safe. Somewhere far away from these people who had left us to die.

With a flick of my wrist, I shifted Aveen's coffin back to the room where Rían had kept her for the last six months. At the top of the highest tower, overlooking the sea, I laid my wife to rest beneath the sun-drenched window.

If Keelynn had never met me, she'd be alive.

If she had never met me, she'd be happy.

If she had never met me, she wouldn't be dead.

But she had met me. And I'd have to live three hundred and sixty-six days without her smile. Her laugh. Her warmth. A year of her too-short human life wasted. A year we could've spent making memories.

I could think of only one way to get through this. One way to survive.

I sank onto the ground and shifted a bottle.

EPILOGUE

(Three-ish Weeks Later)

"Get out of bed, you sad sack of shite." Rían's voice cut through me like a jagged piece of glass.

I didn't know what day it was. Didn't care. He'd probably end up telling me at some point in one of his rants that had become frequent as of late.

"Go away," I groaned, rolling over, pulling one of the extra pillows over my face. "And close the feckin' curtains." My eyes were on fire.

"I said, get up." He grumbled something else and stomped to the door.

"Close the feckin'—"

The pillow disappeared. Icy water hit me in the face.

I shoved dripping hair out of my eyes, summoning magic to end my brother. "You have a death wish?"

My desire to kill him faltered when I saw the dark bruises beneath his eyes. The awful state of his usually pristine clothes.

He kicked one of the many empty bottles of puítin strewn

about my room with boots that no longer gleamed. "I'd rather see you murderous than wallowing. You've had three weeks. That's long enough."

I fumbled for the full bottle I'd left on the bedside table. "Is it?" The warm liquor made my eyes water.

Rían snagged the bottle and chucked it against the wall. It exploded in a satisfying spray of glass. "The world is going to hell out there, and poor Tadhg is too busy feeling sorry for himself to give a shite."

"And you think pointing out the obvious is going to get me out of bed?" The world had been going to hell since the humans took over, and nothing I had done had made a blind bit of difference.

I fell back onto my soaked mattress, prepared to wallow some more.

Rían dragged his dagger from its sheath, aiming the curved blade at me with an unsteady hand. Like death was some sort of threat instead of a retreat from this miserable world where Keelynn no longer existed.

"Go ahead." I tore open my soaked shirt, sending buttons scattering across the floor. "Kill me. I won't stop you."

Cursing, he returned his dagger to its sheath. "I need your help."

"Nothing you say could make me help you."

His eyes darkened, and there was a wobble in his voice when he said, "Aveen is in prison for murder."

ACKNOWLEDGMENTS

I usually acknowledge my readers first, but for this book, I'm changing it up a bit. First and foremost, I'd like to thank Tadhg for taking root in my brain and begging for your own story to be told. You beautiful, broken man. You will always and forever be one of my favourites.

Now for the rest of you. The readers who loved this tale so much that you wanted more more more. To those who were brave enough to purchase print copies to proudly display for all to see despite the suggestive title. I hope that you love Tadhg as much as I do because otherwise you probably hated this book.

To my own dark-haired, banter-filled Irishman, the love of my life, thanks for being so supportive of this journey and my maniacal giggling while I write steamy scenes.

To my beautiful, amazing, ever supportive betas Miriam and Krysten, thank you for being "Team Tadhg" and for helping me get this story where it needed to be.

My talented cover designer Fran, you have worked such magic on these books. I honestly don't know what I would've done if I hadn't found you. I owe so much of my success to your brilliance. I want you to make all the pretty things for me forever and ever.

Meg. My brilliant editor. I lived for your comments on this one. I count myself lucky that you let me take up so much of your time. As I say in every book: don't ever leave me.

Elle and the rest of the Midnight Tide Publishing team, thank you for giving my stories a place to flourish and for being the most supportive community an author could hope for.

ABOUT THE AUTHOR

Jenny is the founder of the PANdom and a lover of books with happily-ever-afters. A native of Oakland, Maryland, she currently resides in County Tipperary, Ireland with her husband and two children. As much as she loves writing stories, she hates writing biographies. So consider this the "filler" portion where she adds words to make the paragraph look longer.

ALSO BY JENNY

The Myths of Airren

(NA Fantasy Romance)

A Cursed Kiss

A Cursed Heart

A Cursed Love (TBA)

Prince of Seduction

Prince of Deception (2023)

YA Fantasy Romance

Married by Fate (Sept 2022)

The PAN Trilogy

(YA Sci-Fi Romance with a Peter Pan Twist)

The PAN

The HOOK

The CROC

Omnibus Editions

The Complete PAN Trilogy YA Omnibus

The PAN Trilogy (Special Edition Omnibus)

MORE BOOKS YOU'LL LOVE

If you enjoyed this story, please consider leaving a review. Then check out more books from Midnight Tide Publishing.

A CURSED HEART

BY JENNY HICKMAN

Living on an island plagued by magic and mythical monsters isn't a fairy tale . . . it's a nightmare.

Aveen is the perfect lady, placid and well-mannered, concealing her discontentment beneath false smiles and gentle nods. As the eldest, her duty has always been to her family legacy and her sister's happiness. But when she finds herself forced into betrothal to a man she loathes, she swears she'll do anything to escape. Even if it means bargaining with a wicked fae prince.

Rían is a devious half-fae with a dark secret, concealing his true nature beneath glamours and lies. When a fascinating human accidentally catches his eye, it's clear he'll do anything to take her for himself. Including making promises he can't—or won't—keep.

Confronting hidden dangers and haunting pasts, the two reluctantly come to rely on each other to survive a world where nothing is what it seems and darkness encroaches from all sides.

Will their tangled web of lies bring freedom they crave . . . or will it unravel them both?

THE CASTLE OF THORNS

BY ELLE BEAUMONT

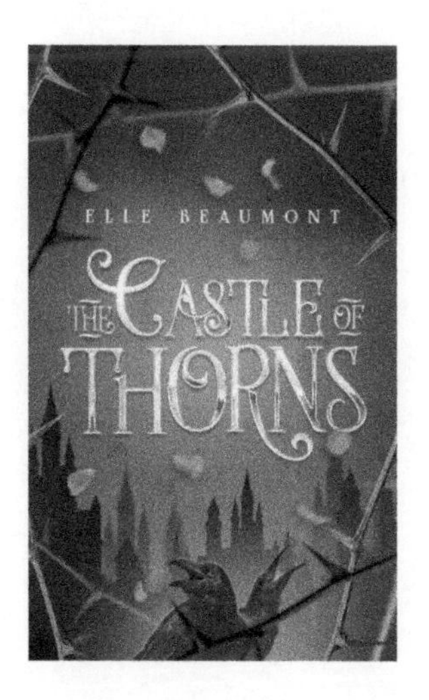

To end the murders, she must live with the beast of the forest.

After surviving years with a debilitating illness that leaves her weak, Princess Gisela must prove that she is more than her ailment. She discovers her father, King Werner, has been growing desperate for the herbs that have been her survival. So much so, that he's willing to cross paths with a deadly legend of Todesfall Forest to retrieve her remedy.

Knorren is the demon of the forest, one who slaughters anyone who trespasses into his land. When King Werner steps into his territory, desperately pleading for the herbs that control his beloved daughter's illness, Knorren toys with the idea. However, not without a cost. King Werner must deliver his beloved Gisela to Knorren or suffer dire consequences.

With unrest spreading through the kingdom, and its people growing tired of a king who won't put an end to the demon of

Todesfall Forest, Gisela must make a choice. To become Knorren's prisoner forever, or risk the lives of her beloved people.

For fans of Sarah J. Maas, Jennifer Armentrout, A.G. Howard, Casey L. Bond, and Naomi Novik.

Genre: New Adult, Dark Fantasy, Retelling

Buy link: https://books2read.com/u/4ERzel

Lightning Source UK Ltd.
Milton Keynes UK
UKHW040653061022
410034UK00004B/387